TREASURES

A Mallory O'Shaughnessy Novel

by Paula Wallace

Order this book online at www.trafford.com
or email orders@trafford.com

Most Trafford titles are also available at major online book retailers.

Cover map courtesy of Arkansas State Highway and Transportation Department

Printed in Victoria, BC, Canada.

ISBN: 978-1-4269-2800-0 (sc)

Our mission is to efficiently provide the world's finest, most comprehensive book publishing service, enabling every author to experience success. To find out how to publish your book, your way, and have it available worldwide, visit us online at www.trafford.com

Trafford rev. 3/17/2010

Trafford PUBLISHING® www.trafford.com

North America & international
toll-free: 1 888 232 4444 (USA & Canada)
phone: 250 383 6864 ♦ fax: 812 355 4082

Proverbs 21:20

There is treasure to be desired and oil in the dwelling of the wise; but a foolish man spendeth it up.

Other Titles by the Same Author

DWELLING BY THE WELL (A Daily Devotional Guide)
Genesis 26:12 Then Isaac sowed in that land, and received in the same year an hundredfold, and the LORD blessed him.

DAZZLING(A Mallory O'Shaughnessy Novel) Volume 1
Proverbs 4:18 But the path of the just is as the shining light that shineth more and more unto the perfect day.

TREASURES(A Mallory O'Shaughnessy Novel)Volume 2
Proverbs 21:20 There is treasure to be desired and oil in the dwelling of the wise; but the foolish man spendeth it up.

Contents

Preface

THIS NOVEL IS fiction. Any similarity to actual people and events is coincidental.

Everyone knows that America is not without her problems. As these characters from this novel meet Jesus as their Savior for the first time, or as seasoned Christians, strive to please Him and put Him first in their lives, they are making a difference in staying God's hand of judgment, and they receive His blessings for obedience.

Although everyone who seeks God's aid, may not find out their property is a wealth of diamonds, they do discover that He is everything they need.

In His infinite wisdom, foreknowledge, and planning, every need that presents itself, has been prepared and provided for since the beginning of the world!

With Mallory we can quote:

Psalm 104:24 & 25

O LORD, how manifold are thy works! In wisdom hast thou made them all: the earth is full of they riches.

So is this great and wide sea, wherein are things creeping innumerable; both small and great beasts.

Chapter 1

TRANSITIONS

KERRY LARSON HAD been in his law office since early morning. His large, Thompson study Bible lay open on his desk, but his gaze was far off, even farther than the views afforded by the expansive plate glass windows. His penthouse office, expensively appointed, and masculine surrounded him physically, but his mind was in a little Arkansas town. He tapped his steepled fingers together thoughtfully. He had left his heart there, too! Tears escaped down his cheeks again; he didn't stop them. His attorney's brain, usually sharp and lucid, had turned into a thick soup of muddled images. He had fled the little town more than two days sooner than what the plan had been. He thought if he could get his Porsche on the road, with his gospel music playing, get back to Dallas; he could sort things out! He swished his ice in his empty tea glass.

The receptionist's voice interrupted his reverie. "Daniel Faulkner on line one, Sir."

Kerry sighed; he was surprised his friend and business associate had waited this long to call. He didn't want to talk to him; he didn't want to talk to anyone. Reluctantly, he picked up the receiver.

"Daniel, what can I do for you?" he asked.

"You can start by telling me what's going on! Thought you were sticking with us until yesterday when we got her into the house. It actually didn't go too bad."

"Hey, this isn't a good time; can I get back to you later?"

Kerry could tell Daniel wasn't wanting to be put off, but he didn't want to talk to him until he could figure out something intelligent to say. He had been dwelling on it for more than three days, but he hadn't been able to get his mind wrapped around things yet. He cradled the receiver as his friend tried to protest. His cell on the desk vibrated. It was Faulkner; the guy didn't give up easily; one of the reasons he was successful.

Kerry refilled his tea glass and flung himself back down into the comfortable leather chair. He had a text, from Faulkner, and he accessed the message:

"She's too young for you!"

"How did he even know?" Larson asked himself. Barely admitting his feelings to himself, he sure hadn't said anything to anyone else! There was a lump in his throat where the sobs were struggling to free themselves.

The cell was vibrating again; he turned the background music lower and answered the call.

"I told you, I'm busy." He tried to sound natural, but he could hardly force the words out. "I'm glad you got Mallory settled in; Did Delia and Shay stay overnight?"

Kerry really did care about everything that was going on, so he listened to Faulkner talk. His conscience seemed nearly as guilty as Kerry's was. It had been kind of a tough deal!

"Delia and Shay hadn't stayed; no one had stuck to the plan!" That was sort of the accusation that Kerry picked up on.

Evidently feeling like he had addressed his topic and made some small talk, Daniel demanded outright what the deal was about Tammi Anderson.

Larson felt defensive. How much did he owe the guy? If he didn't want to talk about it, should his friend try to force his confidence?

"You may think this is none of my business." Faulkner went on, since the attorney hesitated in answering him. "Maybe it isn't, but I thought we had an agreement. If you want to change things, you could let someone know. I figured you'd be there running the rapids; that's usually the crazy stuff you like! So, you talked to John Anderson Friday afternoon; then you left? Did he tell you to leave and never come back?"

"No! He didn't!" Kerry bristled at that. "Far as I know, I'm still in good graces with everyone. Guess the little town and all the murderers got on my nerves! Sorry I stampeded."

"Kerry, tell me what happened."

"Nothing happened. I just saw a girl who is the most beautiful person I've ever met, and I've been trying to sort things out ever since. I think I would have felt the same, anyplace, under any circumstances. But I keep thinking about the fact that Adams nearly murdered her, and how traumatized she still was! I cry every time I think about it. Until this week, I don't remember the last time I cried."

"Kerry, she's fifteen!" Daniel replied, as though hearing him say it, would bring his friend to his senses any faster. "You need to start coming up here for weekends; we'll introduce you to some career women in our Sunday School class." As he was saying it, he knew it was useless. "I'm sorry, Kerry," he apologized. "That was pretty insensitive."

"It was, but apology accepted. Look, I did go to church, and I've been reading my Bible this morning. I know it's crazy! I've been talking to myself nonstop, ever since she barged into my heart. I've never been in love; I've wanted to be. High school, college, law school; people falling around me to the love bug. Never did get bit! Until now!"

"Should have rubbed down with one of those insect repellent towelettes, Buddy," Daniel had responded gloomily. "I can't see any of this helping the outcome of any of our joint ventures. You sure Anderson didn't tell you to hit the road?"

"He didn't, but then, I didn't tell him, 'hope you don't mind that I'm in love with your little girl'. Thought I should keep it to myself."

"Wisest course, I'm sure. So, you didn't tell Tammi your feelings?" Faulkner felt like he had to know.

"I didn't say anything to her; it just hit us both like a bolt of lightning, at the same time. It's like the first time our eyes met~"

"I have an incoming call," Faulkner interrupted. "I'll get back to you."

Mallory Erin O'Shaughnessy finished her devotions and was nearly presentable when someone in a Doggie Coddling uniform arrived for Dinky. They arrived in a mobile salon, saying they had received a call about Mallory's dog. He was slated to be bathed, dipped, and taken to a veterinarian appointment. The lady seemed nice, and Dinky followed her peaceably.

He really did need all that done, Mallory agreed. She certainly didn't want a flea infestation in her beautiful new home.

After applying the finishing touches to her hair and make-up, she added jewelry. Going downstairs to retrieve her Daddy's ring from the safe, she slid it onto her slender finger.

She grabbed the keys to the Jaguar, a bottle of water from the refrigerator, and one of the big apples from the polished granite kitchen bar.

She backed the sporty car from the garage, lowered the garage door, then studied the dash curiously. She wanted the top down, if she could figure it out. Not being able to tell immediately, she left it up and headed down the drive. The gates opened away from her as she approached. The console contained ten of her favorite CD's, and she wondered if her dad had chosen them for her.

Tears filled her eyes again. He had known he was dying, and had been working desperately to move everything into place for her! She still wished she had known that he was sick. Suddenly, for the first time in over three months, she realized how incredibly merciful the Lord had been to her, in not letting her know! Once again, she was forced to acknowledge that, "He hath done all things well!"

Turning up the music, she pulled out onto the road. No specific destination in mind! Just surveying her new neighborhood! Everything was incredible! Crepe Myrtles blossomed everywhere, and all the trees were totally leaved out. Mallory could catch glimpses of other mansions tucked behind high walls and extravagant landscaping. The sky was a lovely cloudless blue, and the sunshine felt soft and warm.

When she came to an intersection with a traffic light, she turned toward a shopping and restaurant area. She was looking for a nail salon, because she had always thought having her nails done would be the height of elegance and luxury! She had adored Diana Faulkner since she had first seen her enter the lodge near Murfreesboro, Arkansas. Barely more than a week earlier, but a lot had happened to cause Mallory to admire her more than ever!

Now, as she parked in front of the salon, she breathed a prayer, not just to imitate her outwardly, but to emulate her spiritually, with the same joy in the Lord!

She grabbed the car manual from the glove box and entered the salon. Telling the tech at the first station she wanted a new set of nails and a pedicure, she chose a polish color and sat where she was directed.

An hour and a half later, she emerged with beautiful finger and toe nails, polished in a springy, pinkish-coral, which resembled Diana's "sunrise" color.

She had discovered the secret of the convertible top, and it slid down smoothly. As she returned the manual to its place, she checked the car registration and insurance: Mallory Erin O'Shaughnessy!

Catching sight of a jewelry store across the busy boulevard, she navigated her way around carefully so she could cross at a signal. Metroplex traffic was kind of beyond her skill level.

The jewelry saleswoman surveyed everything about the teen before she made it through the large, arched doorway! Auburn hair, luxurious and shiny, fell around her shoulders in cute, swingy layers. She wore a soft, yellow sweater with a flatteringly curvy denim skirt. Her shiny new pedicure was evident through sandals which matched the sunny color of the sweater. Hazel eyes, huge and expressive, framed by long, sweeping eyelashes, took in the jewelry display cases. Porcelain skin with a faint hint of color, and flatteringly stained lips; she was at once elegant and wholesome. A fresh new set of fingernails matched her pedicure in a bright, happy color. Everything about her was gorgeous, but the ring she wore caused the jeweler to gasp in awe!

Mallory chose an exquisite "Canary" diamond, encircled with white ones, set into an intriguingly-designed pendant of eighteen karat white gold. Also choosing white gold and diamond "Love-knot" earrings, she charged the purchases to one of the credit cards. Skipping the gift boxing, she wore them from the store. On the back of the receipt, she scrawled, "For promoting the diamond industry as CEO of DiaMo Corporation. And, in the service of the King!"

It was noon. She opened the bottle of water and bit into the apple. She was becoming perplexed as to why she hadn't seen any security around her. Shrugging, she decided they must just be keeping their distance!

Her call rang; it was her friend Tammi Anderson. Hesitating only momentarily, she answered.

"Hi, Tammi! How's everything going there?"

"I've been better." Tammi was crying.

"Hey, what's wrong?" Mallory was immediately sympathetic.

"Just all by myself at lunch! Are you sure you can't move back?"

"I don't think so, Tammi. You should see the house my dad has for me! Why don't you see if you can come here this week end? We can swim, and play pool, and tennis. What's so wrong there?"

"Well, yesterday, David was here, and we ate lunch together and talked about the camp. That was fun. But, today, they sent him and my mom to Nashville to look for recording studio equipment. So, I'm alone at school today! And I have to help my dad with my little brother and sisters. Have you seen Kerry Larson a lot?" she finished timidly.

Mallie had stopped behind a long string of traffic. "How could I see him a lot? I've only been here one day! I haven't seen him at all! I'm eating one of those big apples from his dad's orchard. How long do you have to help with the kids?"

"I think they're coming back Friday. They went in a private jet. When David gets back, I won't be quite so lonely without you."

"What was David doing, eating lunch at school?" she queried curiously.

Mallory didn't know if the Faulkners would know or care that she was talking about David Anderson! They had just told her not to talk <u>to</u> him!

Tammi was caught! Her older brother had dropped out of school the previous fall term. Everyone had been mad at him, including Mallory! In January, he had started back, not only catching up to the rest of the junior class, but was now about ready to graduate by the end of May. He had kept Mallory from knowing, doing much of the work on-line with the principal's help. David was still trying to surprise her. Now, Tammi was unsure what to say!

"He just came by to eat lunch with me, because he knew I'd be lonely with you gone. He brought the Bible Camp site plait! Mallory, we can't believe what all your dad was doing for our family!"

"M-m-m-h-m-m" Mallie agreed vacantly. Driving in heavy traffic, talking on the cell, and trying to determine what was the truth, all at the same time, had her pretty challenged. "My dad was the greatest all right," she agreed. Tammi wasn't good at changing the subject to avoid answering a direct question, and she had lied!

Tom Haynes, the school principal, hardly allowed any lunch-time visitors onto his closed campus! Mallie was pretty sure he wouldn't make an exception, for David of all people!

Someone honked at her.

"Tammi, I can't talk and drive in this traffic. I'll call you later." She disconnected.

She was still puzzled about her security detail. Now, she was wondering if she would be in trouble with the Faulkners. One of the few rules, was that she wasn't to ditch her team. Her brow furrowed in concentration. She had no intentions of doing anything like that. She was planning to adhere to their rules, because their rules reflected her daddy's wishes for her.

Continuing to angle northeast through the suburbs and into rural Texas, the little car sped along two-lane highways. In Paris, Texas, she stopped at Sonic. She laughed at herself. In Murfreesboro, they always grumbled about wishing for more fast-food choices. Now, she had passed nearly every other chain, to pull into Sonic for a corn dog and tater tots. When the food arrived, she presented the credit card, tipping and giving the car-hop a Gospel tract. She scribbled the expense memo on the receipt, "therapy and the Service of the King!"

The elegant lady driving the sleek car drew quite a bit of attention from the local clientele. Many of them recognized her from the news stories of the previous week. She thanked the Lord for her food, then carefully squirted ketchup packets into the cardboard next to the corn dog. These were her first "tater tots" since she had lost her father. When they used to play with walkie-talkies, his handle had been Irish Spud, and Mallie had been Tater Tot ! Also, they had spent a lot of time at Sonic on father-daughter dates, talking about everything imaginable! She ate the corn dog, but the potatoes didn't really taste good to her, even drowned in ketchup!

While she sat there, she made up her mind! Leaving Paris, she headed north into Oklahoma. At Hugo, she took highway 70 east into the Ouachita State Forest, toward Arkansas, and her hometown!

The smooth car responded obediently to her acceleration. She didn't have a whole lot of experience driving, but she knew this level of performance was exceptional.

As she neared Murfreesboro, she suddenly grew nervous! She wasn't really sure why! She guessed she was afraid the Faulkners would be mad at her for straying so far the first day! They trusted her, and she didn't want to violate that trust! She couldn't figure out where her hired protection was. If they were behind, they were too far back! Mallory had barely escaped death here in the past several days. Of course, she told herself, she shouldn't be nervous about those guys! Adams was dead; they were pretty sure her uncle, Ryland O'Shaughnessy was dead, too. Her cousin, Shannon, was in Federal custody in Boston. And Oscar Melville and Martin Thomas were in Federal custody in Little Rock!

She couldn't shake off the uneasy feeling. She decided just to check out the DiaMo Corporation Diamond Mine before heading straight down to Hope! She would invite her mom and Erik to join her for a steak at McKenna's before she headed back to Dallas. Maybe Erik would call Daniel and Diana for her, to make sure she didn't get into trouble.

As she approached the property where her home had stood, she was amazed to see that the fence that had been well underway the previous morning looked as though it were coming back down! Her "No Trespassing" sign had disappeared, as well as the "Beware of the Dog" one. From the road, she couldn't see anyone around. No sign, whatsoever of the round-the clock security that was supposed to be safeguarding the diamonds! There were no vehicles in sight!

Her shyness around Daniel Faulkner forgotten, she had him on his cell phone.

He answered quickly, immediately concerned for her safety!

"Hello, Mallory, he answered. "What's up? Are you okay? Where are you?"

"I'm fine," she responded. "I'm in Murfreesboro. The mine site looks deserted; the signs are down! There's less fence now than there was yesterday morning! I don't see a soul, or any cars!"

Faulkner heard her words; he was having a hard time grasping it! How had she gotten to Arkansas without any of her security people letting him know? Why would the fence be coming back down at the mine? Why wouldn't the mine personnel all be working in the middle of the afternoon on a Tuesday?

"Let me make a couple of calls," he instructed her. "I'll let you know what's going on, when I find out!"

Mallory pulled in to the property. It was less muddy than the previous morning, and she pulled up close to the shed. As she opened her car door, she picked up a rock. Holding it at her side, she cautiously moved toward the dark entrance of the building.

"Hello, Tad," her voice was loud enough to carry, but no one responded. "Hey, Tad, it's Mallory! I was just on the phone to Mr. Faulkner!"

Trying to peer into the cavernous darkness, she hesitantly took a few steps forward. Sensing a movement beside her in the semi-darkness, she whirled toward whatever it was!

"Well! If it isn't Miss Mallory O'Shaughnessy!"

Mallory gasped in horror, stunned to see him! She started to call him "Sheriff", out of habit; then remembered he had resigned from that post in disgrace! She didn't know he had gotten out of jail!

"Hello, Mr. Melville," she managed to stammer. "Have you seen Tad Crenshaw, or any of the guys?"

He advanced toward her, leering!

"Don't think there's anyone here but you and me! Maybe now I can thank you properly for all the trouble you've caused me!"

Mallory eased backward a couple of steps, out of the shed, and into the afternoon sunlight.

"I haven't caused you any trouble, Mr. Melville. You made your own mistakes! Why don't you go over to the church? There's a big mirror in the back. You can look your real troublemaker in the eye!"

Stung with fury, the man lunged at her, grabbing her by the throat, hard! With both hands! They felt like iron! He jerked her roughly back into the darkness! She felt like she was dying! Fast!

Still clutching the rock, she swung her fist up, striking him a glancing blow! Surprised, he released his hold on her throat!

She staggered back, dazed. Then, he was coming at her again! The first blow had mostly hurt her hand! Readjusting her hold on the rock, she smacked him again, this time without her fingers cushioning the blow! He went down! She grabbed a board and hit him again. Sobbing, she made the safety of her car and roared away!

Once out of the small town, she dialed 911. When the Sheriff's Department answered; she gave her name, then told them Melville was hurt and where he was. She continued toward Hope. Her lovely outing had turned disastrous! Mr. Faulkner hadn't called her back. She called her mom.

Daniel Faulkner couldn't get anyone to answer his calls! Not Tad Crenshaw, the mine foreman; not Darrell Hopkins, Mallory's security head: and then Mallory herself wouldn't answer back! Dread flooded over him! He was at home, in his spacious office that opened through high, dark, polished wooden doors to the pool. He had promised his three children he would come swim with them; that was before this latest problem! Usually a decisive and able problem solver, he suddenly felt overwhelmed!

"Lord, I don't know what to do," he confessed. "Please help us!"

He caught a glimpse of Diana's car as she approached the garage. Their plan was for a quiet night at home, just the five of them. Now, he was trying to figure out how to tell her the latest! She was such a trooper, she deserved a break!

"Honey!" She had entered and was running up the stairs "Erik called! He thinks we need to get back to Hope right away! Your mom and dad are on the way to pick up the kids!"

She changed her shoes into a more comfortable pair.

"What did Erik day?" he was asking her, but the kids had seen their mom and were coming in from the pool.

He knew she wouldn't answer in front of them. She was helping them get their overnight bags packed for their grandparent's house. They were excited! They never got to do sleepovers with their grandparents. Their dad's mom and dad were mad at all of them for being saved, and Diana's family all lived in Africa!

The senior Faulkners arrived for the children in both cars since neither of their back seats could hold all three children. They were being trailed by their own security. Diana was a genius! This would be the safest solution for the kids until Daniel could figure out what was going on. They both hugged and kissed all three of their children. Diana was thanking her mother-in-law; Daniel was telling all three kids the dire things that would happen to them if they misbehaved at their grandparents'.

Then Daniel and Diana raced away in a corporate Suburban to a small private airfield near their Tulsa mansion. Their personal security with them, they boarded the luxurious GeoHy helicopter and headed southeast toward Hope, Arkansas.

"What did Erik say, Honey?" Daniel questioned again.

"He said that Mallory showed up to meet them at McKenna's for a steak, saying she thought she killed Oscar Melville. Erik called the hospital, and he's in pretty bad shape, alright. He's afraid Mallory will be in a lot of trouble if Melville dies. He wants us to pray for him to live."

They joined hands and prayed.

Diana had just returned from a medical appointment, where her doctor had assured her that everything seemed perfect.

"Well, that's good," Daniel told her, "I thought things were going to get calmer for you once yesterday was over. Do you know why Mallory went back to Murfreesboro today? What do you mean, she almost killed Melville? Isn't he in jail? Did she just walk in and shoot him? I can't believe any of this is happening! If I'm having a nightmare, will you please pinch me, and wake me up?!"

They couldn't decide whether to call any of the other corporate members, so they decided to wait until they learned more details. Diana suggested calling Kerry to give him a head's up about his client. He was her corporate attorney, but he would know someone if she needed a criminal lawyer. They decided to wait.

Chapter 2

TRAUMA

MALLORY MET HER mom and her mom's new husband, Erik, at McKenna's Steak House. Erik Bransom, an FBI agent who headed the agency's division for western Arkansas had called the Faulkners. He had been trying to get more specifics from Mallie about what had transpired with the former Pike County sheriff. She just sat across from them, shaking her head dazedly and crying. On the phone, she had told them she was afraid she had killed the man. Then she had hung up. Since they had met, she hadn't spoken a word. She hadn't taken a bite of food, either. All of them had been worried about her not eating during the turmoil of the previous week.

Daniel and Diana raced to the restaurant as Erik had requested them to do. As they joined the threesome, Daniel pumped Erik's hand, and Erik rose in deference to Diana.

Diana took one glance at Mallie. "She doesn't have an airway! She can't breathe! Honey, call an ambulance! Get her on the floor before she falls! Get ice!" Diana was barking orders while they all stared at her uncomprehendingly.

Finally, Bransom found his phone and summoned emergency response. Another diner had jumped to his feet to help them ease the girl onto the floor. Diana was already emptying drinks into plates, trapping the ice, wrapping it in a linen napkin to apply to her throat.

As she applied the ice, she saw what she had already known! Mallory's assailant had grabbed her by the throat! Bruises were beginning to show; her entire neck would be black and blue, if she lived! At the moment, that was very much in question. The nurse could see and hear every tortured breath as Mallory's throat continued to swell from the injuries inflicted by Oscar Melville. Diana knew there was a real possibility that Mallory's neck was broken, too; in addition to the soft tissue trauma. Tears were streaming down her face! She couldn't imagine how their carefully screened security personnel had blown it so badly the first day!

"Mallory, can you hear me? Mallory, they're almost here. We'll get you some oxygen."

Mallie kept trying to open her eyes in response to the soft repetition of her name. Her throat hurt, and she couldn't answer.

"Don't try to talk right now, Mallory," Diana was soothing. "Your voice won't work until the swelling subsides. Just relax! Don't cry; that uses too much oxygen! You're gonna be ok."

She wasn't sure about that. Finally, she heard sirens. When the EMT's rushed in, Diana filled them in. Nodding agreement, they immobilized Mallory's neck. The swelling was already severe! Even after oxygen was applied, her system was receiving far too little! Diana packed as much more ice as she could around the girl's neck, which continued to swell visibly.

Shocked by the sudden emergency, the gravity of the situation hadn't really sunk in with Daniel Faulkner, until he realized the emergency personnel seemed to think the lovely teen-aged girl wouldn't survive the ambulance ride to the nearby hospital. By then, he couldn't decide whether to go ahead and let Diana ride in the ambulance, or if he should insist it be Suzanne.

Erik helped him decide. Suzanne, sitting helplessly, had watched detachedly as Diana administered first response care to her daughter. Bransom knew Suzanne wouldn't be able to deal with the ambulance ride, so he asked Diana to accompany Mallory. Then, realizing Daniel didn't have ground transportation, the three of them sped after the ambulance in the big FBI sedan. Bransom had called his FBI office to order a crime-scene response team to the O'Shaughnessy property.

In the ambulance, Mallory continued to moan and cry. The nurse in Diana knew the girl's every cell was screaming for oxygen. She took her hand, trying to soothe her; that was the first time she noticed the bruised fingers. She rubbed the scrapes lightly. She had stopped praying for Melville to live; her only prayers were for the girl lying prone on the stretcher beside her. She eased off the elegant jewelry: the ring from Patrick, the ring from DiaMo Corporation, the beautiful Canary diamond pendant, and the little post earrings, and secured the valuables carefully in her handbag. They were at the ER doors, and Mallory had survived the ride. It would be a long night!

They all watched, dazed, as the gurney rolled into a trauma room.

"I guess we should notify everyone," Diana suggested, her voice shocked and soft.

"Maybe we can call Kerry and make him do all the rest of the calling,"

"I'll do it," Erik volunteered. As a Federal agent, breaking bad news had been part of his job training! That was always tough enough. When it was people you loved so much, it was pretty unbearable. He went outside: the air was cool and fragrant, the early evening beautiful. A bird was singing. Erik was praying. His first call was to David Anderson.

David was on his way through heavy traffic to Nashville International Airport when he saw that he had an incoming call from Bransom.

"Is she dead?" he demanded immediately. He was crying.

"No, she's still hanging on," Bransom had responded in amazement. He wasn't sure how the kid knew she was in trouble. "Where are you?" the agent asked him.

David explained that his dad had called him and his mom about Mallory, and they had thrown everything into their suitcases. They were trying to work out travel arrangements, but the best they could arrange was a flight arriving in Dallas at eleven thirty. Then they would have to drive back to Hope. There were no more flights into Little Rock until early in the morning.

Bransom told David he would see what he could find out about private flights and call him back.

When he went back inside, Diana was on her cell; he couldn't see Daniel anywhere. He didn't have to look far before he found him on his face in the small hospital chapel, crying so hard that Bransom thought surely Mallie must not have made it.

"Hey, Faulkner!" his voice was strident. "Pull yourself together! David Anderson and his mom are trying to get here commercially; nothing's comin' together for 'em. You got one of those private planes you can line up for them faster than three in the morning?"

Daniel rose to his feet.

"It's not your fault, Faulkner!" the agent slapped the other man on the shoulder as he strode out past him.

Daniel Faulkner didn't feel comforted: he sure felt like it was all his fault!

Pastor John Anderson arrived, bringing four of his children with him. All of them were crying. He was a chaplain to the Hope police force, fire department, and hospital. He had received a call when the ambulance was dispatched. When he made the realization that the victim was Mallory, he was shocked! He still didn't know exactly what had happened, but he had been able to tell the prognosis wasn't hopeful. He hadn't known how to break the news to his son. He wasn't sure if he should tell his wife, Lana, and let her tell David. But when David answered the phone, John told him what he knew.

Suzanne O'Shaughnessy was the first one to notice her pastor enter the ER waiting room. She thanked him for coming and asked him if anyone had called David. She had called her mother and father, and Delia and Shay O'Shaughnessy. Shay was still in Denver, but everyone was coming as quickly as possible. Suzanne was numb! One minute, Mallory had been sitting across the table from them; the next, Diana was saying she wasn't getting any air! Suzanne couldn't figure out how she had never had a clue her own daughter was in such distress!

The trauma doctor performed a tracheotomy on Mallory, as Diana had assumed they would. It still wasn't a guarantee. When they were allowed to see her again, two visitors at a time, she still looked awful. They reassembled to pray again.

Delia, Mallory's paternal grandmother, had managed to charter a jet in Boston to fly to Texarkana. Daniel Faulkner arranged for David Anderson, and his mother Lana, to arrive from Nashville, Tennessee. By coincidence their two flight were expected to arrive within half an hour of each other. No one wanted to leave Mallory's side to make the trip to Texarkana, but Ivan Summers, a friend from the Arkansas Bureau of Investigation had offered to make the airport passenger pickup.

Mallie continued to struggle. Her mother and Diana kept constant vigil beside her. Diana was still concerned about the possibility of fractures. Mallie was fighting the neck brace, the trach, and the I.V.!

Diana continued a steady stream of soft, soothing instructions, stroking her hair, patting her hands. "Take it easy, Mallory. Don't fight. Save your strength. You need more oxygen when you struggle."

As Suzanne watched Diana, she felt more inept as a mother than she ever had. She just really didn't know what to do. Finally, she asked Diana, in a quavering voice, if she should go find more ice.

"Yes, please," Diana answered.

At first, it seemed that the ice wasn't making that much difference to the swelling; now Diana realized whatever slight difference it was making, could be a critical difference.

It remained touch and go. Bransom notified Diana that both flights had landed, and Summers was on his way with the passengers.

Except for fastening into his seat for take-off and landing, David Anderson had made the entire flight, prostrate in prayer, in the aisle of the luxurious little jet. Finally, prior to landing, he accepted a cup of coffee. He had stayed informed that Mallory was still alive.

Lana loved Mallory, of course; she had watched her grow up in their church. The toughest part for her, though, was watching her son suffer so. Her attempts to comfort him or try to encourage his faith, were feeble, at best.

He dashed down the steps and toward the waiting ABI car. They had to wait for Delia's flight to land, and it couldn't land until the jet they had arrived in, could be moved. The small airport wasn't really equipped for so much extra activity.

David paced while he waited, talking to his dad on the phone. During the flight, he had been able to find out a little bit about what had transpired. He knew it had something to do with Oscar Melville. What he hadn't figured out was why Mallory had been in Murfreesboro, rather than in the big gorgeous North Dallas mansion he had heard so much about. He couldn't figure out if she had already been really unhappy, and was running away from the Faulkners and her court agreement. He felt like she must have come to find him, and he had failed her by not being there.

John patiently tried to explain what he had pieced together, but he wasn't sure how much his distraught son was listening. He was trying to prepare him for the shock it was going to be to see her, if they could even keep her breathing until he arrived!

At last, Delia's flight cleared to land, and Summers got everyone and their hastily assembled baggage loaded. He placed a light on the roof of his agency car, turned on the siren, and put the "pedal to the metal". They raced up Interstate thirty toward Hope.

No one said much, everyone gripped by terror, laced with the unreality of it all.

The application of more ice gradually helped reduce the swelling, and Diana immediately perceived the almost imperceptible improvement in her condition. It was her first hint that Mallory might possibly survive. She was about to tiptoe out to make a positive report to the rest of the group when Daniel came in to whisper the report that Summers was nearly there with David.

Mallory was still so terrified of her new guardian that all she wanted to do was put distance between them! "Whatever you want, I'll do it; just don't come any closer," was what her plan was going to be for dealing with him for the next five years!

Now, when he entered the cubicle and said something to Diana about David, it caused Mallie to panic. She once again began to gasp desperately for air, and her blood pressure shot up!

"Honey, go out!" Diana ordered. "You're giving her a panic attack! She's still too scared of you!" She was trying to push him physically past the curtain.

He was resisting, "Di, she's gonna have to get used to me!"

"M-m h-m, but not tonight!" She shifted into a funny little Chinese accent, "I said, 'You leave, now'!"

Laughing at her, he obediently retreated.

Mallory hadn't calmed down again before David was looming over her. All she could think of was that she wasn't to be allowed to see him for six months. She couldn't figure out why he was there! He was going to get her in trouble! Her only response to him, was to stare at him in terror as tears flowed. Then sobs were choking off her breath.

Diana was trying to get him out, too, telling him he could visit again when she was more stable.

David really liked Diana, but he pulled his arm free and turned back down toward Mallory, gently releasing the neck brace.

"It isn't tight," Diana assured him, explaining her concern that the attack might have broken some vertebra in Mallie's neck. Still, her breathing did improve slightly when he released the brace.

He wanted to see her throat, where the man had grabbed her. Tears filled his eyes at the sight of the ugly bruising, the viciousness of the attack.

Mallory's little purse was beside the chair where Suzanne had been keeping vigil. David rummaged through it for the new camera, and took shot after shot of the marks from every angle.

"Mallory," he questioned anxiously, "Did he hurt you anywhere else?"

She met his steady gaze and mouthed the word, "No!"

Tom Haynes, the Murfreesboro High School principal arrived with his wife Joyce and son, Tommy, Jr. They had been crying and praying during their hour ride. Then Brent and Connie Watson arrived, and Connie explained they had barely caught the story on the ten o'clock news. She had called her mom and dad, Roger and Beth Sanders, who had gone to Washington state to convince their daughter, Catrina, to finish out her college semester. They were returning as quickly as possible.

David felt like the room was starting to spin, so he half-collapsed into a chair in the waiting room. His dad dropped down across from him.

"She's scared, Dad!" David whispered to him.

"You mean of Faulkner?"

"Yeah, Dad, she's so scared she can't even breathe. She shouldn't have to live in fear."

John Anderson eyed his son suspiciously. "Maybe she isn't scared enough of him; do you know why she came back here today?"

Mallory was improving; at least it seemed like it. Actually, with the injuries she had sustained, there was a possibility that the swelling could worsen for three or four days. They didn't want to get too optimistic, but even a glimmer of hope was something.

Daniel had returned to the chapel to thank the Lord for the improvement. He returned to the group in the waiting room. His overwhelming load of fear lightened, he took stock of the group. Kerry Larson wasn't there. He called him on his cell. He wondered if they had even called him, in the midst of the confusion.

"Daniel, how is she?" Larson asked, answering on the first ring.

Suddenly, Daniel began weeping. "Actually, she's doing better," he finally managed to get out. He had moved farther from the group so he could speak privately and hear better.

Kerry had seen the story of Mallory's attack on the news and couldn't believe it. He figured no one called him because they were mad at him about Tammi. Daniel realized he never had called him back from the morning conversation. Even as he conversed with the attorney, he became aware that Tammi Anderson was watching him intently. "Like she has radar," he thought, with kind of a detached amusement.

"Should I come there?" Kerry was asking him. Tammi was nodding "yes" at him, although he was sure she couldn't hear.

"No, don't come. For one thing, she is a little better. For another thing, I need you to check out things there for what went wrong. Don't go solo. Call the police. Get your security. Hire a private investigator if you have to. See what you can find out about what happened to all the staff at that house, from security head to dishwasher! Find out what happened to her dog!"

"What actually happened there?" Kerry finally questioned.

Faulkner told him what little they knew. As usual, there were more questions than answers. He told Kerry about Mallory's call to him that the mine was moving backwards rather than ahead. Before he could find out what was happening, she had already tangled with Melville on the mine property. No one had heard a report about Melville's condition since the early evening. He looked at his watch; it was two a.m. He couldn't answer Kerry's question as to why Mallory had decided to return to Murfreesboro. That was one of the things he and Bransom both wanted to know. Diana wasn't allowing them to ask her.

Kerry promised to call as soon as he had any new information.

When Daniel ended his conversation with Larson, he found Bransom and asked if anyone had gotten any updates on Melville's condition.

Bransom showed him the photos David had taken of Mallie's bruised throat.

"Doesn't matter to me what happens to him now." Bransom's voice was a fierce growl. "Looks like Mallory was strictly acting in self-defense!"

"Agreed! But here's the thing! Diana won't let me close to Mallory to ask her anything. But, if Melville's conscious, and you have that badge, we can go choke an answer or two out of him!"

A sadistic grin crossed Erik Bransom's face. "I knew there was something I liked about you besides your pretty face!" He gave him a smack on the back!

Brent Watson had returned: no one knew he had left. He was trying to juggle his way in with cups of steaming coffee and bags of breakfast sandwiches from an all-night fast food place.

Joyce Haynes went in to sit by Mallie so Diana and Suzanne could come out for some nourishment. Erik sagged wearily next to Suzanne, and Daniel pulled a chair closer for Diana so she could prop up her feet.

"She still doing better?" he questioned.

"I guess. I can't get her to rest! She acts so fretful. She's keeping herself worn out and still really oxygen-starved."

Diana hadn't eaten anything all day except for a light breakfast before her medical appointment. She hadn't realized she was so hungry. She devoured a couple of the sandwiches and leaned back to savor her coffee. Daniel grabbed it to keep it from spilling. Exhaustion had overtaken her.

Leaving her napping, Daniel joined David and Tammi. They didn't act overjoyed about it. He was pretty tired, himself, so he really didn't care.

"You told Kerry not to come, didn't you?" It was a hostile question and an accusation from Tammi.

Daniel was amazed, to say the least, that she used that tone with him. He didn't know for sure how he kept from losing his cool, but he responded in an even tone that, " Mr. Larson was looking into the situation from the Dallas angle."

David had been shocked at his sister. He didn't like Mr. Faulkner too much, either, but he was curious what he meant by "the situation and the Dallas angle".

"Do either one of you know anything?" Daniel asked them suddenly. "Do you know why she was back in Murfreesboro? Did either one of you talk to her today?"

David was trying to keep from being sarcastic with the guy. "Why wouldn't she want to come back to where her life had been?" He refrained.

Tammi was starting to move away haughtily.

"Tammi!" her brother's voice arrested her motion. "The man asked you a question. I want to know, too. Did you talk to Mallory today?"

She glared at him defiantly. He grabbed her cell from its clip on her bag and began accessing her call log; she was desperately trying to get it back from him! John Anderson crossed the room in a couple of bounds!

"Would you two grow up? David, don't tease your sister!" He returned to his conversation with the Haynes.

David handed her phone back; her eyes weren't meeting his.

"She made a couple of calls to Mallory around noon." David answered Daniel Faulkner's question.

"Tell us about it, Tammi!" David ordered his sister.

"I don't remember all of it. I was in the cafeteria and I didn't have any friends to eat lunch with, so I called her to see if she can move back. She said her house was great; asked me to come visit this week end."

"That's all?" Daniel and David posed the question in unison!

"Did she say she was on her way here?" Daniel asked.

"No. She said she was driving in Dallas traffic. She liked her car; maybe she decided to get it on the road. Can I go now?" She was moving away again.

"Did she talk to you at all about David?"

"None of your business!" she hissed. She whirled away, leaving Daniel Faulkner to deduce that they had discussed David. His eyes had followed Tammi briefly as she stomped away, then his gaze returned to David.

"Guess girls talk about us guys," he laughed as he rose to stretch his tense muscles.

Chapter 3

TRUCE

DANIEL FAULKNER CHECKED on his wife. She was still sound asleep. Suzanne was talking quietly with John and Lana Anderson, and Tom and Joyce Haynes.

Taking advantage of the situation, Daniel slipped noiselessly to the curtained cubicle where Mallory lay. Connie was sitting by her, but when Daniel motioned to her that he had been sent to relieve her, she smiled acknowledgement and left.

He sank into the chair Connie had just vacated and watched the girl lying there, still struggling and moaning restlessly. Her right arm was immobilized with the I.V. For the first time, he noticed the scrapes and bruises on her hand.

Bransom and Summers were on their way up to visit Melville in the small Murfreesboro community hospital. He wasn't sure they would find out anything. Daniel felt tired; his contacts had been in for a long time! He never used rewetting drops, but now he wished he had some! He closed his eyes~ just to rest them for a second!

Mallory's eyes drifted open, and her gaze wandered around the small area. It was four o'clock, according to a big clock that was noisily ticking seconds. She didn't know if it was morning or afternoon. Her throat hurt, and her mouth felt dry; she was still having to work hard for every breath. She tried to feel again for her new necklace. There was so much stuff around her neck that she couldn't be certain; but she was pretty sure it was gone! She was pretty sure David had been talking to her, too! She didn't know where her new car was! She should have stayed in Dallas! She just knew she was in really, really, big trouble with Mr. Faulkner! Tears flowed into her hair and onto the sheet that covered the hard mattress. She tried to move a little bit to get more comfortable. She sobbed noiselessly, but her thrashing startled Daniel awake.

"S-s-h-h. What's the matter, Mallie?" he questioned softly.

She turned her head to look at him; she was afraid of him, but relieved he was there. Now, she could just confess everything, and have a clear conscience again. However he might punish her, at least she could quit being so worried.

She tried to talk, but her throat hurt, and no sounds were coming out.

He stood up next to her bed and bent over her. He didn't know how to cover the trach tube so she could speak. He figured his wife was going to kill him when she found out about this.

"S-s-h-h. Don't try to talk. You have a trach tube in. Can I ask some 'yes' and 'no' questions. You can shake your head." (Not a good idea if she had broken bones in her neck, but, then, he wasn't a nurse.)

She was waiting, but he suddenly didn't know where to start. "Mallie, you aren't in any trouble. We're just trying to piece together what happened. Melville is going to pull through, but he'll be back in jail as soon as possible, and he won't bond out again. Diana told me you seem to be worried; please don't be afraid. I'm sorry I let you down so bad with the security. We're addressing everything again, we will get it right from now on! I promise you. You haven't done anything wrong."

He pushed her hair back again, like Diana had been doing. His touch was gentle, and her fear drained away. She felt the same relief she had felt when she was seven years old and asked Jesus into her heart. He had covered her transgressions, leaving her blameless!

She finally fell into a restful sleep.

Diana tapped Daniel on the shoulder, and he followed her out of the cubicle.

"You made peace with her?" she questioned in amazement. Her blue eyes were beautiful.

He shook his head negatively. "I'm not sure that can happen as long as I stand between her and David." His voice sounded sad. "Let's just say, maybe we established a truce."

"You're way too nice of a guy to play the heavy," she agreed. Even in their family, Diana was the firm one.

Chapter 4

TRAIL

DIANA WENT OUT into the waiting room to announce continuing improvement. She told every one they could disseminate to find rooms and get some rest. Brent and Connie had already gone home, asking to be kept aware of the situation. Tom and Joyce were opting to stay a little longer. Delia had flown from Boston as soon as she had gotten the news, but once she arrived, she didn't go in to see her granddaughter. She still felt guilty for the way she had treated Mallory, and she was afraid her presence might be upsetting. She was waiting for Shay.

David had gone to find his sister. The hospital was relatively small, but she had disappeared. He called her cell! No answer! She was making him mad; and, he was worried. He sent a text. "Where r u?"

He continued his search. He shoved open a door into a stairway and pounded his way up a floor. There she sat, crying.

"Leave me alone," she snarled.

"Un-uh, I don't think so. I have too many questions for you, and it took me too long to find you."

"I don't plan to answer any of your questions!" She was attempting to walk away, but he was blocking her.

His eyes blazed into hers. "Come on, Tam, what gives? Just tell me what you know about Mallie. Is she in some kind of trouble?"

"Yea, I think she is; she can't breathe!" Tammi replied, stating the obvious! She was trying to bluff her way past him, but it wasn't working. Her smart-alecky answer had just made him mad! He grabbed her arm in a vise-like grip! It hurt!

"Ow, you big ox! Turn me loose!"

"You better tell me what I asked you, or I'm gonna have Dad take a look at your call log!" His voice was low, but intense. He had pushed her button. The defiance melted away. A scared expression crossed her face before the hard mask reappeared. "What?" she questioned huffily. "What do you think I'm holding out on you about?"

"Evidently, lots of stuff," he responded. He was genuinely perplexed and suddenly pretty curious about what his little sister had going on.

"Tell me everything you and Mallie talked about yesterday. You called her, and~?"

"Well, the first time was after third hour. She didn't answer. Then, I tried again at the beginning of lunch. I had fun having lunch with you Monday, but then you went to Nashville, so I called Mallie. She didn't answer my first call, because her 'nails were wet'. She had been to some salon. I asked her if she could move back. She started bragging about her new house and told me I could come visit and swim and play tennis and pool. I bet she doesn't really have any of that stuff!"

"Did you tell her I was in Nashville?" he interrupted her catty comments. He was losing patience with her getting to the relevant stuff.

"I guess so," was her response. She didn't want to tell him that she had practically told Mallory about his graduation surprise.

"So, she decided to come home, because she knew I was gone?"

"I dunno! She didn't say she was coming home. She said she was having a crazy time driving in Dallas traffic; she said she'd call back, but she didn't!"

"That's it? She didn't tell you she was having any kind of problems to need a lawyer?"

"No, what do you mean? She has her own lawyer, anyway!"

"Then why does your phone have so many calls to Kerry Larson?"

On the drive from Hope to Murfreesboro, Summers warned Bransom that he would really need to control himself with Oscar Melville. He hadn't been sure the visit was a good idea. He thought Bransom should have sent one of his agents to conduct the interview who didn't have such a lit fire about it. Not only had Bransom watched Mallory fight for every breath, but he had been trying to console Suzanne through it, too.

Bransom had some questions he was wanting some pretty quick answers to!

When they arrived at the hospital, the officer who supposedly had Melville under guard was gabbing with the medical staff at the nurse's station. He couldn't see Melville's room or the elevator from where he stood. Summer's couldn't believe that even small community law enforcement was so sloppy. Like Bransom had been on the rampage about the previous week; there was stupidity, and there was duplicity. Sometimes, it was really hard to tell the difference.

They entered Oscar's room, and his guard had no clue they had.

"Hey, Oscar! Wake up!" Erik Bransom was right down in the man's face. "I have some questions for you."

The man gaped at them foggily through the narcotics.

"Who sprung for your bail? How'd you make it back to Murfreesboro? What were you doing trespassing on the DiaMo Corporation property? What kind of assault were you attempting with Mallory O'Shaughnessy?"

"She called me, asked me to meet with her out there. Then she attacked me with a rock! That crazy girl killed her father; she knows I'm still trying to prove it!" He had difficulty talking, but he had evidently prepared a story

"Summers, call a judge. Get a warrant to search Oscar, here's remaining few possessions." Bransom was instructing the Arkansas agent.

"Melville, you should have quit when you got a chance!. We'll get your phone and Miss O'Shaughnessy's phone and see if she's been calling you up!"

Summers moved to the door to work on the warrant. The warrant was necessary, but he figured the federal agent planned to use his absence to make more headway with the suspect. Summers was grinning.

Diana had called her in-laws. Her mother-in-law, Patricia, told her they were all having a fantastic time. Relieved, Diana didn't talk long. Daniel was heading toward her, drinking a cup of coffee. She reached for it, but he pulled it away.

"The RV's back, Honey. Tom and Joyce are going to take you to it on their way home. I want you to get some rest. You saved Mallory, now take care of yourself, too. Security's back up, I hope! Were you just checking on the kids?"

She was exhausted, even though she had napped for thirty or forty minutes. "Your mom just said they're all having a great time. Praise the Lord. Can I look in on Mallory one more time before I go?"

He walked with her. Now that Mallory was more stable, the attending physician had ordered neck X-rays. She was to be moved into a room soon.

She was sound asleep, and David was keeping the bedside vigil. He started to rise so Mrs. Faulkner could take over, but Daniel motioned for him to stay put. The lights were dim, but Diana turned them bright. She had to see how Mallie's color looked before she could leave for several hours. The ice was totally melted, and the water had nearly reached room temperature. The bruising was deeper and uglier, and she had dark circles beneath her eyes. Daniel raced from the room for more ice. The bright lights had roused Mallory slightly, and Diana was speaking her name.

"Mallory, I'm leaving for a little while. David's here. If you need anything, tell him. Your mom's here, too. She sits for awhile, then goes and walks around, but she plans to stay." She kissed her lightly on the forehead. At the curtain, she turned back. "I have all your jewelry. I took it off of you in the ambulance."

She left the lights bright, instructing David to keep a close eye on changes in her coloring.

David sat there. Mr. Faulkner had returned with the ice. He had wanted his wife to go get some rest, but David was pretty sure he had wanted her to fix Mallie's ice pack back up first! The two of them managed to do it without killing her.

Then Mr. Faulkner told David he had some calls to make, and left him alone with her.

When Mallory was certain her guardian was out of hearing, she brought her left hand to her throat. Her right one, with the I.V. was maddeningly immobilized. It was her first attempt to speak since the tracheotomy.

"What's up with you being at the high school?" she demanded!

David laughed. "You're such a faker; you sound fine to me! Why shouldn't I be at the high school? I'm a student there! I thought you acted mad! You worried about me being valedictorian now, instead of you? What difference does it make? You're not even in Murfreesboro any more! Guess that leaves me the undisputed leader! I'm actually about to graduate!"

He hadn't intended to surprise her about it quite this way. But she had always been so much fun to tease!

"You are mad, aren't you? Ha, beat ya again!"

Her finger still covering the trach tube, she responded. "Well, I thought you dropped out!"

"I did! But I dropped back in again!"

"Well, it isn't fair. My daddy died, and I've had people trying to kill me, and I haven't had anyone to help me with my Geometry!" She was trying not to cry.

"I know," he responded. "That almost takes the fun out of it for me!"

She couldn't help laughing at him. She couldn't stay mad. Trying to laugh made her winded again!

Daniel went outside to make his calls. The air was pretty frigid, and he shivered. It still felt good, though, after the stifling hospital atmosphere. He looked around for Tammi. She wasn't around, so he placed a call to Kerry Larson. The sun was rising, and God's paintbrush was applying dazzling combinations of color and light. He smiled to think Diana was snapping it every fifteen or twenty seconds, in spite of her exhaustion. The color and beauty would rejuvenate her spirit more than several hours of sleep would.

Larson answered. "Is the sunrise gorgeous there?" was Faulkner's first question.

There was silence, then the attorney burst out laughing. "Guys don't ask guys about sunrises! And no, it's cold and rainy and miserable. I'm at Mallory's. The police have been here. The place wasn't messed up too bad. The safe was sawed to pieces. Was there anything in it? One of the maids thought Mallory had sent Dinky to get prettied up. It could take more than a month to get that dog rebuilt from the ground up!"

Faulkner roared with laughter!. He was pacing in the cold, and as he turned, he caught sight of Tammi Anderson! She was really starting to make him annoyed! He strode out into the parking lot, and frowned his sternest frown at her. She still didn't go in out of the cold!

"I haven't been able to get any response from Darrell Hopkins, or any of the rest of Mallory's security detail. What could have happened to them all? I can't figure out if they were all traitors, or if they're victims of something."

"The police want to know what was in the safe," Kerry reminded him again. He told Daniel it was too early to figure out what had happened to all of the personnel. He didn't seem to think the dog-grooming story was out of the ordinary.

Daniel told him about the cigar box with five or six thousand dollars in hundred bills, and the fair-sized uncut gem that were in the safe. He thought he had noticed Mallie was wearing her two diamond rings when he and Diana had first arrived at the steak house.

He glanced around him again, then changed the subject. "About what we were discussing yesterday morning~"

Shay finally arrived from Denver! The snowy cold-front that had hindered his travel had made its way into Dallas as a cold, drizzly rain. It would continue east into Arkansas by midday. His face showed some ravages from sleeplessness and concern. He was young and handsome. His grandmother, who had felt somewhat at a loss without him, had come to life at his presence. She had nearly stopped worrying about Mallory so she could worry about him. He couldn't believe she hadn't been in to his cousin yet. Shay was trying to keep from having a panic attack, himself. He hadn't been into a hospital since his mother had been in a fatal car accident the previous autumn. The décor, the sounds, the smells, all so universal to hospitals; had practically overwhelmed him!

He and his grandmother, with equally shaky knees, paused at the ER area where the curtain was drawn all the way around.

When David saw their feet, he rose to meet them. "Mallie, it's Shay and your grandmother," he announced softly.

Delia and Shay approached her, and Delia stretched over her to kiss her on the cheek. Shay turned and bolted toward an exit!

"Do I look that awful?" Mallory mumbled as she fumbled to cover the tube with her finger.

"You look the most atrocious I've ever seen you look," David answered quickly. "But your waterproof mascara's still on. For fifty dollars, it should be."

"David, behave," Delia swatted at him with one of her little diamond spangled hands, and he ducked mockingly.

Delia stood by Mallory's bed for half an hour, and Shay finally reappeared. His face was pallid, and his green eyes were startling in contrast. David couldn't believe how much alike Mallie and her cousin looked.

"Has anyone taken pictures of those bruises?" Shay demanded. That was what had caused his empty stomach to churn. He thought he only got queasy at the sight of blood, but now he realized he was just wimpy! He plunked heavily into the chair he should have offered to his grandmother!

David pulled Mallory's camera out to snap more pictures. The bruises had darkened and spread since the earlier photos. He pulled out her iPod, too. He started it playing and tucked the ear bud into her ear. She smiled appreciatively. Diana had told them not to let her talk, and David realized guiltily that he hadn't followed her orders.

Kerry Larson had commandeered one of the corporate helicopters and had been combing over north central Texas looking for anything suspicious. He had felt impressed to continue searching for clues as to where the O'Shaughnessy security team had vanished. The weather was bad, making visibility poor. Added to that was the fact that the attorney didn't know what he was actually looking for. The area was mostly suburbs, small towns, and fields. He could see traffic on Interstate Thirty-five moving northward into Oklahoma. There weren't areas of forest like Arkansas, but there were stands of trees along creeks and around most of the homes and ranch buildings. Wherever people might be hidden, trees still pretty well blocked his view from the air. The wind was picking up, and the rain intensifying! The pilot was circling back to the south to call off the search until conditions improved.

Kerry lowered his binoculars and nodded agreement. He pinched at his tired eyes before returning his gaze to the landscape stretching below. A pitiful huddle of buildings caught his attention. As they had come from the north, the trees on the north of the little shacks had obliterated the area from view. Now, as the chopper had swung around, the squalid area had been revealed. A big red dog, trapped in a chicken wire enclosure, barked furiously.

Kerry's heart paused, then jumped into double-time! He tapped the pilot, indicating the site below. He had seen it at approximately the same moment. Neither of them were police officers, so they were suddenly uncertain what to do. Larson was pretty sure that if anyone were still alive, time would be evaporating for them.

The pilot called Faulkner to give him the coordinates. Faulkner phoned Bransom, who could have agents dispatched, and who could figure out the exact position for summoning local law enforcement.

Faulkner got back on with the chopper pilot, asking to speak with the attorney. The chopper had dropped lower. Kerry had taken pictures of the buildings and the dog, and had forwarded them!

Bransom came on and told them they should retreat. With the helicopter overhead, the kidnappers might panic. He didn't want hostages killed, if there were any. He didn't even want any harm to come to Mallory's dog. He had forwarded the pictures to his office in Little Rock. They could enhance the small image which had been shot through fog and rain. Bransom grinned. The ugly mutt looked like Dinky!

Chapter 5

TRAVESTY

ERIK BRANSOM COORDINATED with the Dallas office to get agents to the scene Larson had discovered, in north Texas. The FBI agents and the Cooke County Sheriff, with several deputies, had converged, moving forward, as low to the ground as possible. They were all coated with mud! The warm spring days had fled before an Arctic cold front. The dog grew more agitated as he detected the law enforcement officers' approach.

Jack Mercer, the head of the team, had led them as they crawled to an area where they could view the derelict buildings. No vehicles were around, but through his binoculars, Mercer could see deep ruts around, indicating that traffic had come and gone since the current storm system had dissolved the yard into a quagmire. The dog was going crazy. They could tranquilize him, but that would probably reveal their presence more than the barking. They held their position, watching. After thirty minutes, with no sign of movement within any of the buildings, Mercer motioned a command. Moving forward, they flanked the huddled buildings. Most looked to afford no protection from the biting elements. The most solid structure seemed to be an early 1960-era camping trailer set on blocks.

At last, on his signal, they stormed the door. They reeled backwards! Seventeen people were tightly bound and gagged, stripped to the barest minimum, trapped in their own waste, drugged and dehydrated.

Mercer's agents were quickly documenting the crime scene with photographs, and ambulances were arriving. There was an abundance of evidence; boot prints in the mud, tire tracks, other boot prints on the filthy linoleum flooring of the trailer. There were ash trays and Styrofoam cups that should yield DNA of the kidnappers. Trash and tree branches pulled up around the aging camper gave Mercer the impression that the plan had probably been to torch the place. Evidently, the rain had dampened that plan! The Sheriff's Department Animal Control came and picked up the dog.

Mercer called his superior on the status of the raid, who relayed info to Bransom, anxiously awaiting word. Some of the missing employees weren't with the captives held at this property. That meant that there could still be another hostage location; or those people had made more trouble and been eliminated; or they were the traitors, the "inside" people, who had so far, gotten away.

A large agency vehicle entered the property. Coffee, water, and snacks were distributed to the law officers. The hostages would receive medical evaluation before being given anything by mouth.

Daniel Faulkner had been in touch with Kerry throughout the entire operation. It was a miracle the way the Lord caused him to implement his own aerial search. The DiaMo Corporation employees hadn't been found a second too soon!

In the middle of the investigation, Erik Bransom received orders from someone far higher up within his organization to abandon the investigation, turn it over to the locals, and be at Bureau headquarters in D.C. at nine the following morning. In all of his years with the Bureau, he had never experienced anything like it. The Feds always investigated kidnappings, which this clearly was. There were two crime scenes, so far: the one at Mallory's mansion in Frisco, and the one in Cooke county. Bransom doubted those two agencies would cooperate very well without Federal oversight.

There were no instructions to keep the directive confidential, so he showed it to Faulkner. Faulkner just assured him that if the outcome were negative, the corporation would gladly snap him up for security and training. He was already receiving a sizable new stream of income from the varied interests that he was involved with. He wasn't over a financial barrel, at least-for the first time in his life!

Bransom was watching the news from Mallory's hospital room, when the little huddle of buildings suddenly erupted in flames. He already knew what the story would be! "That the evidence, which they gathered before the flames, had also somehow gotten lost!"

He knew justice in America was somehow being made a mockery of, once more. He felt like he already knew what they were going to say to him in his upcoming meeting; and he already had decided what his response must be.

Suzanne was sitting beside Mallie's bed. Diana had returned from her worried rest time at the RV, and she sent Erik and Suzanne out to the lobby to meet with Daniel. On the way out, Suzanne had asked Diana if she thought Mallie's color looked better.

Diana just gave her a hug. She thought the flush on her patient's cheeks, though lovely-looking, was due to fever. She listened closely to Mallory's breathing; the last thing the patient needed was pneumonia. She went out to the nurse's station. No one on the hospital staff had seemed to mind Diana and her skill. She was beautiful, and she had such a sweet way of wading in with both questions and demands. She wanted to know what the neck X-rays had revealed, and check about the fever and if they had gotten chest X-rays. She was beginning to feel that they should transport Mallory to Baylor, Dallas. It was an exceptional facility. She reminded herself that their trust must remain in the Lord, even more than in the type of facility. Ultimately, life and death were in His hands! She had seen God spare Daniel in the primitive conditions of rural-village Africa: not once, but twice! She smiled to herself. She was glad He had!

"Hello, Mallory," she spoke softly as she reentered the room. She gave a light squeeze to the un-bruised hand. The ice had been off for twenty minutes, and it was time to reapply it. Mallory's slim, elegant neck was still basically atrocious-looking; black and blue, and swollen.

"The radiologist read your X-rays. He didn't see any major fractures. I'm sending the films to a Dallas doctor for another opinion before we move you around too much. So far, the news is pretty good; I just want to be extra-careful." She elevated the head of the bed some more. One of the nurses had come in to start antibiotics into the I.V. Then, Diana gave her patient a sponge bath, promising her that if she kept getting better, and the second opinion confirmed no fractures, she would be able to shower by the following day.

Daniel wanted Suzanne to be able to accompany Erik to D.C., so he had made plans for the newly-weds to be able to attend church in Murfreesboro that evening, then fly by private jet, arriving around midnight. There would be a car and security for them, as they were shuttled to a large, elegant down-town hotel. In the morning, Suzanne would be escorted to view the Smithsonian while Erik met with the Justice Department big-wigs. They would lunch together, before returning to Arkansas Thursday afternoon.

The corporation had provided clothing for the couple's appointment. Suzanne received a beautiful taupe dress that was luxuriously soft; topped with a sweater jacket of equal softness, worked in a taupe and black pattern that was native to Ecuador. The ensemble was the elegant Alpaca fiber that Shay spoke so passionately about. Suzanne and Diana could see why. She was given a pair of quilted-pattern black patent pumps and matching handbag. The shoes featured low enough heels for touring the amazing museum. The cold front had continued barreling toward the east, so a mink coat had been provided. Dark, male Natural Ranch, Suzanne had gasped with amazement. The coat was further embellished with an impressive yellow gold and diamond brooch! The rest of her jewelry included a heavy, twisted gold choker and matching bracelet. Large diamond stud earrings completed the put-together look.

Bransom had let out a long whistle of amazement. These people should write a book about how to win while losing! They knew how to run a major psych game. He shook his head.

His clothes, to his relief, were slightly lower-key. There was a nice pair of black dress slacks, a white oxford shirt, and an Alpaca crew neck sweater, in the natural tones, worked into an argyle pattern. A supple, black leather bomber jacket with a sheared-beaver lining would supply another warm layer, if necessary. Black socks, without any holes, then a pair of new, tasseled, black loafers, and an aluminum attache case had also been provided. There was a fourteen karat gold box chain and a gold ID bracelet with his name engraved on it, if he wanted to add the bling. He had never even considered anything like that. He never had money for it, for one thing. At one time, his opinion would have been "No way!" Now, he had decided the "jury was still out".

They were both amazed. Just a week before, Suzanne had been sitting in the local jail for trying to pawn Mallory's jewelry. She had begged God to turn her hopeless situation around for her. She hadn't had very much faith to think He would. Since that time, things had been truly miraculous!. Of course, right now, the biggest thing on her mind was Mallie. She surveyed all of the elegant new possessions spread across a row of chairs in the hospital lobby. She knew none of this would matter at all if she lost her daughter. She knelt right there, to thank the Lord for Mallie's improvement and for Erik, and all her blessings. Erik knelt beside her; both of their hearts overwhelmed.

Kerry also saw the Cooke County crime scene go up in flame! At least, so far, the hostages they had rescued were doing fairly well. They didn't seem to know enough about who had nabbed them, to give out any information. Probably best for them that they didn't. All three agencies involved just dropped the case. The young attorney was amazed, but he didn't plan to advance beyond their figurative no trespassing signs. He was curious, but he reminded himself that "curiosity killed the cat." Smiling, he wondered where that expression had come from. He had lots to do. He called David Anderson.

"Find anything in Nashville before you had to rush back?" he questioned as soon as David answered. David gave him a quick report, that they actually had, but that they were going to do some comparison shopping.

"Well, time's money. Don't waste a ton of time to save a few hundred bucks. Patrick wanted this to progress right along. Probably should just find out who makes top of the line and get an order placed."

"Whatever you think," David responded. With his background of squeezing every penny, the attorney's attitude was almost shocking to his sensibilities. Still, things could really get bogged down in lengthy decision making processes. He decided to make the call. He would never be able to get his mom to understand such a different mind set.

He promised it would be done before close of business. Kerry moved on to business concerning the Bible camp.

Mallory's little house had been moved into place on the camp property and had been leveled up, as much as possible. Not surprisingly, it sustained some damage in the move. Brad Walters didn't think it would be too hard to repair the damage. The little place didn't look the best to begin with. A diesel generator had been moved into place, and Walters had called a sub in to get some electricity going. Fencing was going up, as were "No Trespassing" signs. Walter's brother-in-law bred and trained German Shepherds, and he promised to supply some good dogs. The Corporation didn't want to bring building equipment and supplies to the remote tract without first addressing security.

The next corporate meeting to be held in Tulsa was being moved forward. Originally scheduled for three weeks away, the new plan was to have the meeting beginning the coming Monday, April twenty-third. Faulkner had really been beating himself up about his security failure. At first, no one realized what a highly skilled team of criminals they were dealing with. Now that they were aware of it, they were anything but comforted by it. The entire thrust of the meeting was going to deal with security. Kerry told David everyone was going to be issued licensed hand guns and given training on the shooting range.

David completed the conversation in a daze. It was like the Lord was making all of his dreams come true! And things he had never allowed himself to dream about because they seemed so totally impossible! He had always assumed he would never be able to deal with the financial struggle of getting a degree! He loved being outdoors! He had wanted a gun and shooting range membership. Kerry also told him the corporation would pay for him to learn to fly, both helicopters and fixed wing craft. Whatever he was willing to be, they were eager to help him become!

Tammi had been watching him with her big ears flapping, so he went and found sanctuary in the little chapel.

"Lord, I haven't known how to grow up into the kind of man You want me to be. I mean, my dad's a good man, but I've always felt like he pounds round pegs into square holes, and vice versa. Like my mom had to learn to play the piano, and she still isn't that good. And I always had to help with little kids. I mean, maybe that wasn't such a bad thing. I guess I'm just amazed that since I relinquished control of my life last week, You have given it back to me a hundred times over, just like You promised! Of course, Lord, You know how much I love Mallory! And I've really been mad at everyone about the "Five Year Plan". I guess they're right, but Lord the next five years look really exciting and fun now. Like Your word says in Proverbs 4: 18 But the path of the just is as the shining light, that shineth more and more unto the perfect day. It isn't a matter of treading water and killing five years. I'm not just supposed to be five years older at the end of the time! You want me to be five years better! Mature, wise, accomplished, confident; like all these guys. I really want to be the kind of man she'll need." He dried his eyes.

No one had heard anything about the mine foreman, Tad Crenshaw, or any of those who had been on the property the previous afternoon. Everyone was still praying for them to be found unharmed. Regardless of that situation, Larson knew the operation had to advance. Brad Watson had a crew of workers on site there, too, rebuilding the fence and putting signs up at intervals along the property. Brad had actually installed a security camera!. It was hardly an unassailable system, but if someone just casually picked up a diamond or two, it might catch them in the act. Then he mounted a few dummy cameras around. His brother-in-law was in high gear, trying to get with other Shepherd breeders he knew to supply as many good dogs as they could find.

Larson left his office to go grab some dinner before church. His cell rang; it was Tammi. He wanted to talk to her, but once again, he ignored the call. He called John Anderson to tell him to check out the church's new web page. Then he explained to the pastor how to access the site from his iPhone.

John responded, "Thanks, Kerry! Haven't seen you in a while! You okay?" He listened to the attorney's response, then accessed the web site when the call was complete.

Tammi closed in on her dad, asking sweetly what he was looking at. The site was beautifully done, showing video of the Easter Sunday services. There was a way to access the entire Sunday evening concert with the Faulkner family's singing and Daniel's sermon. John Anderson could hardly believe the way the supportive group was pushing him and his ministry forward. Everything was beautiful in God's time!

Speaking of time, he needed to get his family gathered up and headed for home to get ready for the evening service. They all went back in to see Mallie, who continued to improve. Diana stepped out, and they allowed David to see her alone for a minute.

"Hey Erin," he flung himself into the chair next to her. "They're having a big meeting next week in Tulsa. I'm not sure if I'll see you there, or if we're about to start a six months separation from today. Just don't do anything this crazy again so you can get to see me, okay? I know how crazy you are about me~ I mean, it's almost humbling to me!"

Mallory tried to laugh, but it made her cough, then choke. "Wow, if I nearly humbled you, that's something!" she finally managed.

The Anderson family headed out into the parking lot to load into their decrepit old van, then reentered in a few short minutes, looking perplexed. Daniel and Diana had left Shay and Delia in charge of Mallory, while they accompanied the pastor and his family back outside.

"Now, what did you say was the matter" Diana questioned innocently. The afternoon weather was cold again, and drizzly fog hung in the air. She hoped Daniel didn't play this game too long. He was fun, though. She shivered.

Faulkner opened the passenger door to a shiny, new, red pick up, and was studying the vehicle registration. "This one says David Anderson." He was addressing his wife, but, of course, David heard him. John and Lana did too, and they stopped their panicky glances around the parking lot. Still addressing Diana, Faulkner asked, "Honey, do you have any idea where the keys to this truck might be?"

She pulled a bag of keys from her handbag. "I don't know where all these keys came from, or what they're to," she played along.

Daniel took the mix of keys from her. "Okay, these look like the ones to this Dodge Ram truck. Give it a try there, David," he encouraged. It fired right up! David couldn't believe what was happening. Of course, he would be hauling all kinds of loads in the building of the camp buildings. It was another prayer answered, before it had even been prayed! A maroon Ford Expedition awaited the pastor, and a beige Buick Enclave was next to it for Lana. Their well-used children's seats had been replaced with new ones. Both of the larger vehicles featured DVD players.

"Tammi, don't you just hate being fifteen?" Faulkner teased. "Fifteen-year-olds don't get anything!"

He knew she was taking drivers' ed, and she would be sixteen within a few weeks.

"You don't get anything," he mocked. Then he gave her dad another set of keys! To a new, bright yellow Mustang!

"You and Lana can work out with her when she might actually get to drive it! How good her grades need to be by the end of the school year, and everything."

"You guys better get going," Daniel encouraged. "I'll be there by church time. Diana might stay here with our girl."

Daniel and Diana, with locked arms, waved good-bye to the Andersons as they left in the three new vehicles. Tammy's had already been delivered to Murfreesboro.

Suzanne kissed Mallory good-bye, and she and Erik went to their apartment to get ready for departure immediately after church. They had been at the hospital since the previous evening, so by the time they cleaned up and drove to Murfreesboro, it was nearly church time.

Shay and Delia had hurried to the lodge in his rent car. They had adjacent rooms. Delia dressed in a charcoal wool skirt with the "stormy, lightning sky" silk sweater that Diana had given her. She topped it off with a charcoal gray Alpaca cardigan, hand-knit with big cables. She frosted it off with her usual array of diamonds.

Shay met her in less than an hour. Dressed in charcoal gray wool slacks, with a gray button-down collar shirt, and a soft yellow Alpaca crew neck, he looked extraordinarily handsome!. Delia hoped no one would mind that he was without a necktie.

They hurried up 278 toward Murfreesboro like a couple of guilty kids. They were planning on devouring a couple of foot-long chili cheese conies at Sonic before the service.

Diana settled in comfortably next to Mallory. The girl still had some fever, but over all, she was much better! A miracle compared to twenty-four hours before! They were both napping a little when Roger and Beth Sanders arrived. The Sanders had run into a few weather-related difficulties returning from Washington State. They had been able to stay apprised of Mallie's improving condition, and they were relieved to finally be able to see her for themselves. They were still shocked!

Faith Baptist Church still didn't have a new piano, so Pastor Anderson asked Daniel if he could bring his keyboard, and provide the instrumental music again. He was kind of surprised; he had surmised from Mallory's comments, that Lana Anderson was pretty possessive about the music. He prayed that no one would have hurt feelings; it didn't matter that much to him. He missed Diana! He was proud of her and loved having her with him. He was glad she was there for Mallory. He thanked the Lord again for intervening in her behalf.

He opened the prelude with "Oh What a Savior". People were gathering, though once again, the weather wasn't the most pleasant. He nodded at Erik and Suzanne. Then Delia and Shay entered, taking seats near the front. To his amazement, Ivan Summers, the Arkansas Bureau of Investigation agent came in. He had a cute girl with him, and Daniel did a double-take! It was Janice Collins, Summers' superior at ABI! She looked cuter in the soft dress with her dark hair falling into soft curls around her face, than she had the previous Friday when Patrick O'Shaughnessy's will had been made public.

Faulkner was trying to hold back the tears. Here was a couple that he was pretty sure was unsaved. He transitioned into "Jesus Loves Me". He had invited Ivan Summers to come to Tulsa and be in his and Diana's Sunday School class, and the guy had acted half-way interested. Faulkner knew, though, that the distance was too great! The perfect thing would be for them to get saved tonight and "plug in" right here. As a fundamental Baptist, Faulkner was aware that two Wednesday nights in a row with unsaved people in the crowd, was special. He was praying for the service and the two agents. David showed up, and joined them; the three were visiting animatedly.

Several members took their places. A group of little girls on the front row were excitedly whispering secrets. They made him homesick for his kids. Then, he thought he saw Alexandra, and he reminded himself that she was in Tulsa with his mom and dad. They would be missing church because Daniel, Sr. and Patricia, who weren't saved and only attended their liberal denomination services four or five times a year, certainly wouldn't get out in the cold to have them in church! He was just grateful that his parents agreed to keep them.

He played "What a Friend We Have In Jesus", wanting the songs to be extremely familiar so that Summers and his girlfriend might even know some of the lyrics. It was almost seven and time for the service to begin.

It was Alexandra! Arguing with Jeremiah about something! Faulkner couldn't believe it! Well, he could believe they were arguing; he just couldn't figure out how they had gotten there! Amazement was written all over his face as he made eye contact with his mother, and then his father. He hoped the kids hadn't been really awful. They sure were cons! He forgot to pray any more for the Arkansas agents. His mom and dad were finally sitting where they would hear the gospel!

When the service ended, John Anderson stayed on the platform while Erik Bransom dealt with the two ABI agents and Daniel showed his parents the simple plan of the Gospel. All four of the first-time guests confessed that they were sinners and asked Jesus to come into their hearts. Daniel couldn't believe that his dad wasn't arguing the same arguments he always had! Finally, he had raised the white flag of surrender!

When the service closed, everyone wanted to be the one to tell Diana the wonderful news! David suggested they should all make the drive to Hope and surprise her. The excited group moved toward their cars to form a convoy.

David pulled Faulkner aside. He was on his way to the camp property, so he asked Faulkner to tell Mallory he was still praying for her. Faulkner told him to be careful, and revealed where a handgun was holstered, right beneath the driver's seat of the new truck. He told him to keep it with him and use it if he needed to. There was a special provision license for it, since David was only seventeen.

Erik and Suzanne were going to stop by the hospital and check on Mallory again prior to their private flight to DC.

Diana was just getting ready to go see what was in the vending machine, when the happy, excited group swarmed in with sandwiches and milk shakes from McDonalds. When she first saw Daniel's mom and dad in the group, she was afraid that they had decided they had their fill of their atrocious-acting grandchildren, and were dumping them back off. She was almost afraid to find out. To her overjoyed amazement, the grandparents and all of their friends had been blown away by such happy, obedient, well-adjusted kids! The three had really impressed their grandparents by all of their prayer meetings for Mallory. The elder Faulkners had originally questioned their son's wisdom in agreeing to become a teen age girl's guardian for the next five years. They had been amazed how much Alexandra, Jeremiah, and Cassandra were bonded with the girl.

Diana was overjoyed at the answered prayers for her in-laws' salvation, and further amazed by the news about Ivan and Janice!

Mallory thought it was pretty cool, too. She was disappointed that David wasn't among all the joyous revelers. Then, when her mom told her good-bye until the next afternoon, Mallie burst into tears.

Shay stepped in. He was sure his cousin really wanted her mom to be able to take the important trip at her new husband's side. He could understand her becoming so emotional. He had lost his mother just six months before; he was pretty sure his father had been behind the "accident". Now, his father was probably dead, too. (No one was planning to search the Charles River very soon to be certain.) He sat down by his cousin's bedside and began reading to her from the Psalms.

The rest of the crowd went out to eat in the waiting room. When they were gone, Shay turned on his lap top. He showed Mallie the new church web site. She was delighted with it. Since the congregation of the church wasn't very large, there was quite a bit of footage of everyone who was there on Easter Sunday. Her Easter dress looked pretty cute; the color was good, after all. And there were lots of glimpses of David! Shay was pretty cool!

She couldn't believe that was just three days ago.

Suzanne had looked like elegance, personified, when Erik had kissed her good-bye in the spacious hotel lobby. Her security detail was hustling her toward a limousine to whisk her to the museums.

Erik slid into the backseat of the Defense Department car. He had decided to wear the gold jewelry. It was pretty handsome-looking stuff. He surveyed himself critically. He didn't want to show up in a bunch of girlie-looking stuff.

He had been awake early to read his Bible and pray. He had been doing the new routine for the week since he had given his life to the Lord. He had prayed for wisdom for the upcoming meeting.

Striding confidently into the room where the meeting was scheduled, he helped himself to some of the orange juice, coffee, Danishes, and bagels, which were arranged attractively. As he poured a cup of black coffee, he thought about Mallory and her weak, sugary brew. He was praying for her silently. They had gotten a report that she had had a restful night, and she was excited she was finally going to be allowed to shower. She was starting on a liquid diet, too.

The agent was a little surprised. He had figured this was going to be a short, sweet meeting in a cubby-hole office, where he would be told to do it " my way or the highway". He hadn't figured on the big fancy room with a breakfast and a lot of people. Most people were in suits. He was glad for the impressive business causal he was wearing. The Under-Secretary of Defense had arrived. He was shaking hands and greeting people. Politics-type schmoozer. Bransom was surprised at himself that that didn't irritate him so much any more. He guessed someone had to do it. Bransom was actually doing some politicking, himself. Well, actually, he was only being pleasant, but he had always equated them as being the same thing. He found a larger Styrofoam cup over by the milk and helped himself to a bigger cup of coffee. He staked himself an area on the back row of the seating area, carefully situating the large coffee on one side of him and the attache on the other. He pulled out the heavy leather binder and the Mont Blanc.

His immediate superior, Jed Dawson, had appeared, and Erik had risen to exchange pleasantries. Dawson had been amazed, to say the least. Usually, Bransom was far more brusque. Dawson had figured the agent might try to refuse to attend this meeting, or, he'd have a huge chip on his shoulder. Here the guy was, all smiles. "Maybe marriage was good for the guy," he had acknowledged.

Another guy that had known Erik for awhile asked him if he had been to a plastic surgeon.

Suddenly, Bransom realized they had him on the spot. This was when he told them about the miraculous change in his life, or he denied the Lord, crediting his new radiance to his new romance. The guy whose scowl had usually driven people away had suddenly drawn a teasing crowd.

He held up his hands in defeat. "All right, all right! You guys win! You all want to know all of my new beauty secrets! Hey, I don't blame you. If I was as ugly as all of you, I'd be yammerin' too."

The room had grown silent and everyone was watching the agent.

"I do have a beautiful new wife, and she is something to be happy about; but here's the real thing. A week ago yesterday, I went to a little Baptist church in Murfreesboro, Arkansas. I was investigating the sheriff's department there. While I was on that case, it led to the other case of the four brutally murdered young women that connected to the State Park. I just felt so overwhelmed about the immensity of the crime problem in the U.S. I didn't think I could keep going on. It just seemed like, no matter how hard I tried, the tide of evil was still winning. I went to see the pastor, and he started praying for me to have more strength and courage to do my job. One of the deacons came by, and he had the pastor help me pray a prayer, and I asked Jesus to come into my heart and save me.

Since that time, the Lord's given me a new outlook, a new wife, and some really amazing new friends. I know some of you in this room think Christians are cells of anti-American crazies, but they aren't. They are really the great and wonderful kind of people who built our nation. Well, that's what happened to me, and I recommend it."

He sat down, and the rest of the meeting was rather an anti-climax. The gist of the agenda was that government agencies weren't to be manipulated by rich people to help guard their stuff. Bransom guessed they meant the situation in Arkansas and the diamonds, specifically. But the O'Shaughnessy property had been a crime scene, overrun with real criminals.

Then, if rich people were trying to protect their own stuff, what were their limits? Bransom was thinking about Delia and the sniper's nest. Was everyone supposed to have their own military? Their own little fief-dom's? And if someone kidnapped a security force, did the government have no responsibility? Let everyone fight their own little wars?

It was almost, too, like a government agenda against rich people. Bransom had to admit that he had held similar opinions until Daniel Faulkner had pointed out to him how Socialistic the thinking was.

When the double-talk had ended, it boiled down to the fact that no one was to pursue the investigation into what had happened at Mallory's Texas Mansion on Tuesday morning, or what had happened to the DiaMo employees working at the mine the same day.

Bransom was given the choice of resigning or agreeing to let the investigation go. Everyone had bet on his resigning. To their surprise, he apologized for his reputation as being a hard-to-control maverick, and agreed to abide by the restrictions. He said there were still plenty of other bad guys for him to work on, and that he still felt like it was a great honor to be a Federal Agent.

His heart was a little bit heavy, but he turned it over to the Lord. The Lord, The Righteous Judge, was still on the throne!

Chapter 6

TRANSACTION

KERRY LARSON HAD returned to his office by one-thirty Thursday afternoon to find a large sealed envelope: a copy had been sent to him; the original document had already gone to Mallory O'Shaughnessy, CEO, DiaMo Corporation, in her room in the Medical Park Hospital in Hope.

The attorney had surveyed the document quickly. This company hadn't wasted any time between the investigation's being quashed in DC, and their offer to purchase the DiaMo diamond mine. He read it again; the offer didn't seem too bad. He figured it would necessitate an emergency shareholders' meeting. He wondered if Mallie felt up to it. Curious about what she was thinking of the offer, he placed a call to her cell phone.

Daniel Faulkner answered it since Mallory's throat was still damaged and tender. The trach continued to make communication tiring for her.

Daniel had stepped from the room. "Is that obvious, or what?" he stormed at the attorney. "Diana thought it was something like this! She grew up in Africa, you know. I told her Americans were different."

"Well, why did you tell her that? Human nature is human nature anywhere you go. The only things that make people act better are good, consistent training; or the regeneration power of the Holy Spirit. Not sure Americans are making the offer. This is probably a hodge-podge of Europeans, South-Africans, Israelis, Americans. Did Mallory say anything?"

"She thinks we should sell. She's cute; she's been lying here worrying that everything we all have is going to evaporate into thin air. She thought we've gotten everything by speculation about what the diamond mine might bring. You didn't do a very good job explaining to her what all Patrick had been up to."

"I did a good job. It's just hard for a seventeen year old girl to grasp so much all at once," Kerry defended himself. "When she gets home, I'll go over all of her portfolio with her again. You think she can tolerate an emergency meeting this afternoon? Can everyone make it? Maybe we can link to David and Brad ; they're pretty involved with materials for the camp this afternoon. Erik and Suzanne should be back by four."

"I'll get it together by then," Daniel confirmed. He reentered the hospital room. All three of his kids were on top of Mallory. He kept telling them to give her space, but she had become a real magnet for all three of them. They all three vaulted from her bed before he could verbalize it again. He gave them a good natured warning, shaking his finger at them.

Kerry scheduled one of the choppers to get him from Dallas to Hope in time to meet briefly with Mallory before the scheduled meeting.

Faulkner arranged for Tammi Anderson and her younger brother and sisters to ride the school bus home, so that her parents could be in the meeting. He knew the girl would be furious to learn that Kerry had come to Arkansas, and she wasn't going to get to see him. Faulkner double checked the security detail around the Anderson's home, and also at the Haynes home, where his own children and Tommy Haynes were being overseen by a security detail and a widow from the church. Diana had reminded him to make sure that Alexandra and Tommy weren't allowed to become too friendly. Daniel liked Tommy Haynes well enough, but Al was only eleven. His thoughts were crowded, and the defeating mind-set was attempting to encroach.

He opened his Bible in the quiet of the little chapel. He had already had his devotion time in the stillness of the morning. He gave a silent, mocking laugh, at the term, "stillness". The past ten days had been extremely hectic. He had turned again to the daily chapter in Proverbs. He had underlined a verse before, and he concentrated on it now,

Proverbs 19:11 The discretion of a man deferreth his anger; and it is his glory to pass over a transgression.

They had all been transgressed against. Their relatively small diamond mining company, being strong-armed by criminal activities, then the government stating it only owed protection to American citizens as long as they didn't accumulate enough to be targeted by criminal enterprises. The brazenness of the offer to buy the O'Shaughnessy property were all reasons to be angry. Great injustices were being done, crimes committed; and law enforcement had been instructed to leave the whole mess alone. The man sat there, anger and hostility etched in every feature of his handsome face.

The Holy Spirit ministered to his soul that was struggling with the immensity of the problem. "Lord," he breathed softly. "We aren't wrestling against flesh and blood, but against spiritual wickedness in high places. Help me to control my spirit so You can work Your will mightily, in all of our lives. Thank you Mallory is better. Please still help us find everyone else alive and well. Please protect us and our families. Please make America strong and great once more."

The meeting opened with a prayer. Mallory seemed in good spirits, and Kerry Larson read the offer that had been made for the purchase of the land and the mining stakes that DiaMo owned. The offer was reasonable and would mean the acquiring of solid cash to all involved. The minutes were being recorded by Suzanne Bransom, but it was also being recorded on videotape. Mallory, enveloped in a monogrammed white linen robe, was sitting up in a wheel chair. She was still on oxygen and IV's. although, she had managed a small amount of liquid sustenance. Diana had helped her apply a little make-up.

David, watching the video intently, thought she looked like a little ghost. She was still beautiful, though. She looked totally "ethereal and ephemeral." He was impressed with his own vocabulary. He was amazed. Who would have imagined Patrick O'Shaughnessy had been achieving such a vast estate, and that seventeen year old Mallory would be a CEO, sitting there, talking about sales, and acquisitions, and mergers. She knew the difference between projected growth on speculation and the reality of the value of the property.

David wasn't sure Brad was following the discussion. He was a really bright guy, but this business acumen was pretty new to him.

Mallory made the motion to sell the fifteen acres in question, as the offer set forth. She wanted to retain the DiaMo Corporation name, and continue to pursue gemstone mining interests throughout the remainder of Pike County, and along the Little Missouri River, into the Ouachita, then into the state of Louisiana to the Red River, then the Mississippi, the delta, and the gulf. After some discussion, the motion was seconded, then carried by a unanimous vote.

The sale would put cash into the coffers that wouldn't be forthcoming for years, if the group decided to stubbornly hold their claim. They knew they would continue to face criminal activity, and that they would be opposed by every environmental group ever imagined. TheDiaMo Corp. knew, after hearing from their president, why commercial diamond mining in Arkansas had never been really feasible. If the cartel, or whoever the purchasing group were composed of, ever mined this property, it would be after a battle.

Patrick had watched the programs about the "Ice Road Truckers" taking supplies to the hostile environment of northeastern Canada. Why would they struggle through those difficulties to mine up there, if Arkansas offered anything as good that could be recovered more simply? The facts were, Canadian diamonds had kept the players occupied, but they didn't want to lose control of another possible lucrative area. The industry had kept its eyes on Arkansas diamonds since the initial find. Many of the Arkansas diamonds were fabulous. The cut gem on display at the Crater of Diamond State Park Museum was one of the most perfect and beautiful ever found! Most jewelers never had opportunity to see such a colorless, flawless gem! Mallory only guessed that the Arkansas kimberlite simply didn't have as high a concentration of gemstones as other sites around the world. When the more lucrative and easily mined veins were depleted, she was certain that they would return their attention to Arkansas. Even with their clout, the legal struggles to have an open-pit mine in Arkansas were pretty formidable. The "big guns" had a better chance against environmental concerns, in America's courts than the small, unknown, DiaMo Corporation had.

The facts were, what everyone who had any dealings in the diamond industry knew, that the Cartel was a good friend and a formidable adversary. They did the marketing; they held control of the stones, thereby maintaining a high price for them. Their position could make them merciless, but if their power-base should dissolve, the industry would suffer far worse. The offer was to buy the property fairly, but a refusal to accept their generous offer could, possibly, bring repercussions.

Bransom had been trying to be his newer, gentler, Christian self; but the implied threat still troubled his sense of right and wrong. He was having a hard time with the kidnapping of the two sets of DiaMo Corporation employees, and the fact that someone had obviously been trying to capture or harm Mallory.

"I know what you mean, Erik," Mallory had concurred, her voice still distorted by the trach tube. "The truth is, the investigation was canceled before we knew for sure who was behind it. We only know it was somebody pretty big with some resources behind them, and some group with a big lobby, or political clout. It could be the powers that be in the diamond industry. It could also be members of any number of environmental groups. If we sell, maybe both sides will fight one another and leave us alone."

The vote was registered, and the group agreed to meet with the attorneys representing the purchasers in the DiaMo Corporate offices in Dallas at eleven the following morning.

The narrow time frame had been part of the offer, which was rather strange, too. Larson was impressed that his client could be decisive when she needed to be.

When the meeting adjourned, Diana helped Mallie back into bed, and asked for Tylenol for her discomfort. Diana had been trying to let the pain have its natural course to force Mallory to rest. Now, after her talking at length during the meeting, she was tired, and her throat hurt. She drank a little warm broth before she fell sound asleep.

Diana joined the group in the lobby as soon as Mallie was asleep. She wanted to make sure everyone knew the company policy of looking his best. She had seen footage of Erik and Suzanne in the hotel lobby in DC.

She had liked everything; but their watches looked bad. She considered that a serious chink in the armor. Details! Details! Details!

Since Kerry was on his way to Dallas, he was given the errand to visit a high end jewelry store and select timepieces that would speak more than the hours, minutes, and seconds. Diana took inventory. Suzanne, Erik, Mallory, John, Lana, David, and Tammi. Tammi would get a watch, but she would have to stay home and attend school. The Haynes and Walters wouldn't be required for the closing on the mine sale. Faulkner doubled security following Kerry, since he would have possession overnight of seven high end watches.

Once he was on his way, Diana was forced to admit she didn't know what she was going to wear, or Mallory, or any of the rest of them, either. Shay's having brought the wool and Alpaca items with him from Colorado had helped to save the day for Thursday.

Delia's eyes were sparkling. "Well, if it won't bother you too much not to be in silk, I might have some things to help out. Shay and I are going to go eat at Hal's, and then we'll be back later."

When Delia returned, she had an elegant outfit for every lady who would be at the closing. Each outfit was a linen hand-knit dress. The yarns were beautiful, raw linen, with slubs, and varying thicknesses, creating a lovely visual texture and a firm hand.

When Diana and Delia had their good-natured arguments about silk versus linen, Diana always faulted linen's ability to absorb dyestuffs for saturated color. Delia's dresses proved that that characteristic could be more enhancing than detrimental.

Diana's dress was two pieced, with a maternity panel in the skirt, and a slight flair to the tunic top. Hand crocheted lace iced the sleeves and the hemline. The color was a deep, inky bluish-purple, the lingering shades of dusk over Cape Cod. Delia was telling Diana that now she understood that the cameras didn't capture the colors precisely enough, and then getting the color reproduced in dyes was im-possible! Diana was glad that someone else finally understood. The unevenness of the dye saturation in the linen yarn was one of the lovely elements about the garment. Diana held it up, surveying her reflection carefully. She usually chose lighter blues and aquas. This shade made her blue eyes look stormy and deep. She liked it.

Suzanne's was a soft lilac two piece. The top was short sleeved with a softly draping cowl neckline; the matching skirt flared slightly to mid-calf. Again the color variegation just made the garment look expensive.

Mallory's was a soft, sea green dress with a yoke and puffed short sleeves. The color, cooler than the greens she usually adopted, made her eyes look more blue-green.

Lana Anderson's ran the gamut from a few areas of intense hot pink to the palest tints of the color. She was delighted by it. It was fitted, with short sleeves, and a jewel neckline, and had a little matching jacket. She gave Delia a special squeeze.

Their church had prayed for Delia to accept the Lord for more than ten years. Lana had admitted her faith had been weak. Now, Delia had become a special treasure!

Delia showed them her own garment, similar to Suzanne's in the styling. The yarn varied from deep, smoky charcoal to the palest pearly gray. She planned to wear her large black Tahitian pearls and her usual array of diamonds and white gold.

They all discussed the jewelry they should wear, as well as shoes and other accessory items.

Beth and Roger lived right in Hope, and with her husband's owning his own company, they felt like she would have something appropriate. The truth of the matter was, that she had become rather casual about her appearance. They were from a small community, and she always felt like people resented her if she dressed differently than they did. With Roger's encouragement, they went to the mall and found her some very beautiful new things.

By nine thirty the following morning, everyone had assembled in the spacious suite of offices of DiaMo Corporation. Mallory was resting in a deep leather sofa, in what had been her father's office. It was now hers. She was still on oxygen, but the dosage had been lowered. To her relief, the IV's were finished, as long as she kept fluids and soft foods' going down. The trach tube was still in place.

The entire group of people looked sensational, both corporately and individually. The men were all wearing dark power suits with brand new brilliant white, monogrammed, French Cuff shirts. They were banking on the advantage they would have over the other corporation's representatives, who would probably show up in Friday business casual. GeoHy and DiaMo didn't allow business casual. Some of the geologists, of course, got pretty grubby working in the field, and had grumbled, at first, about dressing for business when they were in the offices. But then, they enjoyed the perks that the company offered, compared to the relatively minor thing of being expected to look their best. Finally, it would dawn on people, "Why wouldn't I want to try to look as good as possible?"

Light brunch items graced buffet tables dressed up with immaculate linens and bright floral china. Mallory sipped a delicious smoothie, blended from some of the fresh fruit.

Both sets of attorneys had all of the paperwork in place. The spokesperson for the other corporation made a couple of comments that no one had actually harmed Mallory, which she thought was an odd thing for anyone to say. She refused to take the bait! Most of her employees were still missing! The ones who had been rescued had suffered deprivation and indignity. Only because the Lord had led her to leave her house, had she escaped the same fate! The papers signed, she had risen and said coolly, "Good day, Ladies and Gentlemen."

A week after becoming the CEO of DiaMo, she had sold much of the valued holdings. She watched as the enemy made a disorderly retreat.

When security reported that they had pulled out onto the toll way, she asked to have the doors closed. Then, she asked Kerry Larson if he was aware of anyplace else her father might have stashed more diamonds. The treasury department had spent a week going through his computers, the house and shed, the PO boxes and safety deposit boxes that they were aware of. That was one of the things the government had been miffed about. They were so sure that Patrick O'Shaughnessy and Pastor John Anderson were guilty of some kind of fraud, that they had fired up a huge investigation. The only purpose they had really served was that they had made an audit that was very useful to the corporation.

Kerry was pretty sure his client was wrong about more diamonds being stashed.

Mallory was pretty sure there were many more, somewhere, large and valuable!

Chapter 7

TROUBLEMAKER

IVAN SUMMERS AND Janice Collins of the ABI were continuing their investigation. Since the DiaMo mine site was linked to Melville, who was linked to Martin Thomas, who had, allegedly, murdered four women that were thought to have found diamonds at the Crater of Diamond State Park, the governor had insisted that his crime units not drop the case. He was thrilled the Feds were off, and his people were in.

By now Oscar Melville had been discharged from the hospital and been moved into confinement in Little Rock, once more. The two Arkansas agents were quite certain that Melville hadn't been behind the abduction of the mine employees. They thought he might have seen something of interest, which had led him to be on the site illegally. He was uncooperative. His attack on Mallory had been vicious; his story that she had called him there to meet with her had been an absolute fabrication. He had no friends; his bail had been posted by one of the deputies because Melville had threatened to tell of some indiscretions he was aware of. The deputy had bailed him out and given him a ride back to Murfreesboro. The former sheriff had evidently walked to the O'Shaughnessy place from his apartment. He wouldn't tell if he had been looking for diamonds, or for Mallory, or if he had just been puzzled that the valuable property had seemed abandoned by the new crew.

The Feds hadn't turned Martin Thomas over to any of the four states where he had left murder victims. The death penalty was being sought in his pending cases.

Collins and Summers had asked the Faulkner's for permission to interview Mallie about what had actually happened between her and Melville on Tuesday afternoon.

After the closing on the mine deal on Friday morning, the board members had taken the physically and emotionally drained girl back to her home. Erik had spent the afternoon trying to get the Cooke County Animal Shelter to release Dinky to him. Evidently the dog's disposition to the male employees had earned him a death sentence. Bransom finally told them he was going to call one of the major TV news channels. The shelter people always acted so compassionate about putting animals down, when they were in the public's eye. The threat worked, and he had been able to reunite Mallory with her dog.

Daniel and Diana gave the agents permission to come talk to Mallory, but she was nervous about reliving it and talking about it.

Janice was leading the investigation, asking the questions the Faulkners wanted to know the answers to. The incident at Mallory's Dallas mansion really wasn't part of the Arkansas case, but the agents asked her about it because they thought it would shed light on what happened later on in the day.

Mallory recounted the day from the beginning. She had fallen asleep on the chaise lounge on Monday night. When she awakened, she took her Bible and camera out onto the terrace and had her devotions and took some pictures while she ate breakfast. She was really excited about the upcoming travel to Turkey.

She bathed and dressed and was eager to go drive around in one of the cars and check out what was nearby. She had credit cards and money; and her new guardian that she had been so worried about, had told her to go have fun.

She was just about ready to leave~

Janice interrupted her. "Were your security people still in evidence during the entire morning?"

Mallory hadn't seen any of them, but she had been in her private area until she had gone to the library to remove her ring from the safe. She didn't remember seeing any of them around. Since it was her first day in her own home, and she had never been used to having personal security, she hadn't noticed their absence.

She was about ready to leave when the Doggie Coddling lady had come for Dinky. She paused and looked at Diana. "Did you call and set up those appointments?" she asked. She had figured it must have been Diana, and as much as she liked her, she had still kind of resented it.

Diana was amazed. "No, I didn't call anyone like that, Mallory. Why would I?"

Janice asked her over and over again what the woman looked like, what the mobile salon looked like. Did it have Texas plates? Did the lady have an accent? Was she alone? Did Mallie get a glimpse inside the salon? Did the paint job on the salon look sharp or tacky? Would it have been large enough to abduct eight or ten people? Were there any other vehicles? Any other strangers?

Mallory had begun to feel frustrated that she hadn't sensed anything amiss. The agents moved on.

"Were you planning on taking your dog with you?" Summers had interjected.

She said she was, and that she was disappointed that the grooming treatment had been arranged. She acknowledged that she was sure he needed all that. She had been stroking him gently. "He probably really needs all that now," she was growing tired of talking with the trach tube. "He probably really picked up fleas and ticks out in that awful place they took him to."

Collins and Summers felt like they were just arriving at the crucial point of the plot. They were pretty sure the entire operation had been orchestrated for the primary purpose of either kidnapping Mallory, or murdering her. Somehow, as her security team was being nabbed, and her watch dog led away, the girl had grabbed an apple and a set of car keys, avoiding capture without ever being aware of the close call.

Daniel and Diana's eyes had met in wonder. This was sort of what they had surmised. It was an absolute miracle!

"Where did you go first?" Janice was pursuing. "I know we're wearing you out, but it's all really important or we wouldn't be bothering you."

Mallory held up her hands to show her nails. Then she told of purchasing the expensive jewelry. That was the first that she had really wondered why she wasn't seeing her security detail. Then, her friend Tammi had called to tell her she was lonely at school because David was in Nashville, Tennessee. When she had heard that David was gone, she had decided she could go to her hometown without getting in trouble about him.

"I'm not sure why I wanted to go back. It was just a pretty day, and I liked the car and my music. I was going to call my mom and Erik to meet me for a steak and then go back home. I was going to ask Erik to call you and make sure I wasn't in trouble," she had turned toward Daniel with an agonized expression.

"Then, just before I reached the city limits of Murfreesboro, I started getting nervous, and I was really wondering why I didn't have any security. But I was thinking I'd be fine because all the scary guys were either dead or in jail. I didn't know Mr. Melville was out on bail, or I'm pretty sure I would have stayed in Dallas."

Tears had started to brim, and she had reached for a tissue. Dinky whined sympathetically and woofed warningly at Summers.

"As I passed by the property, I could tell from the road that nothing looked right. Early Monday morning, the entire fence was nearly in place, and the area was buzzing. When I went by Tuesday afternoon, the place looked abandoned." She had turned back toward Daniel Faulkner. "That's when I called you."

"Yeah," he acknowledged. "Wish I had thought to tell you not to check things out by yourself. I was so amazed that you were all the way home, and no one had even let me know you had left Dallas! I couldn't figure out what was going on. Then Tad didn't answer any calls and you wouldn't answer again either."

"Go ahead, Mallie," Collins had brought the conversation back to the girl. "The mine property looked abandoned. Did you enter the property?"

"Yes, ma'am. The mud had dried up a little. I didn't want to get the car stuck. I pulled up pretty close to the shed. I still wasn't seeing cars or people or anything. I don't know what Mr. Melville had driven there in. I thought no one was there at all, but I grabbed a big rock as I got out of the car. I was calling for Mr. Crenshaw, but no one was answering. I stepped inside the shed a step or two. That was when Mr. Melville moved and scared me."

"Okay, Mallie, you're doing great. Mr. Melville was inside the shed, where?"

"I-I-I'm not sure," she stammered. "It was dark, moving from the sunlight into the shed. I took a step or two and he just came from my right."

"So, I asked him if he had seen Mr. Crenshaw or any of the mine employees." She had begun to cry. Diana had moved protectively nearer, and so did her dog. Daniel told the agents they could pursue the rest of the story another time.

"No," Mallory shook her head sadly, the tears still streaming. "I'm ready to finish." Her throat was really sore, and the sobs tearing through it weren't helping.

"He kept coming closer to me, and he just looked sickening. He had the most awful grin on his face. He said there was no one there to help me, and, "he wanted to thank-me- properly-for-causing-him-trouble!"

Daniel felt sick at his stomach, and he didn't want to hear any more. "Slime Wad! Blaming her for his situation!" He wanted to go find the guy and beat his face in!

"Then what happened?" Collins continued to probe.

"I decided to try to bluff my way around him, so I told him I didn't cause him trouble. I told him to go look his troublemaker in the eye, in the big mirror in the back of the church! I shouldn't have said that; it made him madder than ever, and that's when he grabbed me. I had backed out of the shed, but when he grabbed my throat, he yanked me back in where it was dark. He had hold of me hard, and I couldn't focus. I swung my fist up with the rock in it, and it broke his hold on me. When he tried to grab me again, I hit him again with the rock, and then with a board; and I got in the car and took off."

"Did you try to get help for him?" Janice asked.

"No, I don't thinks so," the responded.

"Yes, you did, Mallory," Diana corrected her. You must have really been shocky on that entire drive down to Hope. Do you remember being at McKenna's?"

Her eyes looked stricken. "Yes, ma'am, she whispered, "I remember that part."

Chapter 8

TRUSTWORTHINESS

SATURDAY MORNING WHEN Mallory once more awakened in her elegant bed surrounded by billowing linen curtains, she felt amazed. Diana, ever watchful, had fallen asleep on the chaise lounge, but was awake immediately when Mallie moved around, causing a monitor on her oxygen to beep.

Diana, still in her clothes from the previous day, went out to see who else was awake. Daniel was in the back watching their three children try to play tennis. They couldn't hit the ball, but they were, hopefully, burning energy chasing it. He had his laptop connected and his cell phone beside him. He smiled at his sleepy, disheveled wife. He had a cup of coffee, and he rose to pour one for her. He gave her a kiss and a quick hug.

"Have you guys eaten breakfast?" she questioned.

"No, we've just been up, ourselves, for about forty minutes. None of us have cleaned up. Did you and Mallie get any sleep?"

"We really did. Why don't you get some breakfast brought out here? I'll go get Mallory. We can all have breakfast while we make plans. Looks like you've been busy working already." She was heading back inside to get Mallie as she finished speaking.

The staff was appearing with orange juice, and milk, and more coffee. Mallory was wrapped again in the monogrammed linen robe, pulling her oxygen canister. She had hastily cleansed her face and brushed her hair. After a second opinion on the neck X-rays, Diana had finally released her from the neck brace. The Dallas radiologist had echoed Diana's amazement that the injury hadn't created any fractures.

The three Faulkner children had paused in their efforts to play tennis, in favor of being with their mother and "new big sister". They all joined hands beneath the colorful umbrella to thank the Lord for the food and His blessings. There was an assortment of fresh fruits and berries, followed by ham and eggs with hash browns. Mallory was happy to be sitting in the gentle wash of sunlight drinking liquids. The back expanse of manicured grass and lush landscaping were a visual feast, and her gaze swept around appreciatively. The pool was beautiful, including a play area with a slide, all decoratively tiled.

Kerry Larson appeared. He liked the Faulkner kids, and after visiting for a few minutes, he challenged Jeremiah to a game of tennis. He taught him how to serve and some basic moves of the game. Then he let him win. The match was pretty entertaining to watch.

Daniel had accessed some web sites about traveling to Turkey. Shay had delayed his trip to South America. He was going to be accompanying Mallory to Houston early the following week to walk her through obtaining an expedited passport. The visa requirements for Turkey were pretty easy. Just have cash on arrival in the country; not even as much as many countries required. Daniel had never particularly considered Turkey as a travel destination. Everything looked really intriguing, though, ancient and captivating.

"Honey, you should check this out!" His tone was awed.

She glanced at it quickly, but Kerry and Jeremiah were being purposely funny.

Mallie's eyes were getting their sparkle back. The travel site intrigued her and the Faulkners were really fun. What a perfect morning after the events of the past few days! They all lingered around the table lazily, enjoying the opportunity for some calm.

Finally, Daniel had offered to oversee the kids' getting ready.

The Jacuzzi tub had been run for Mallie in her suite, and she luxuriated in the swirling, warm, bubbles. A courier had arrived, and Diana spread an adorable new outfit out on Mallie's bed. The outfit was made of soft denim, featuring a hooded, zippered-front jacket and matching skirt in the same soft yellow tint as the sweater that had been ruined by Melville's blood-spatter. Diana loved the color on the girl, and she still had the cute sandals. There was a coordinating, short-sleeved, silk, crew neck, knit top, which featured a picture of Dinky. He was so ugly he was funny. His dusty red color was cute against the pale yellow. Mallory was amazed. "I'm not sure how you do this," she laughed, in spite of the difficulty of the trach. "I still think you have a magic wand stashed someplace! Thank you! Did my dad really tell you all you were letting yourselves in for?"

"He tried to describe what a delight you are, if that's what you mean," Diana responded. "You are a true treasure to us. We feel you are a gift from God; we talked about adopting you. We didn't want to hurt your mom's feelings."

"You know, I really loved my dad, and I miss him. But in fairness to my mother, we did cut her out of our lives some of the time." Mallory was confiding, even though talking was still uncomfortable.

" I'm not sure why we did. I always felt bad, and I always liked things better when it was all three of us. I knew sometimes we were hurting her feelings, and I would feel bad, but I wanted to please my dad, too. Now, I feel like he isolated me from her so it would be just him and me; and then he died! I feel kind of mad at him, sometimes. I do want my mom back. I like Erik, although I tried not to. That's nice that you talked about adopting me."

Diana left Mallie to finish her make up and went to the guest suite to check on Daniel and her kids. They were showered and dressed cute. She showered and dressed in a pink dress made of the same soft denim. It had little pinch pleats from the yoke, to allow for some expansion. The matching cardigan was embellished on the back with a vase of pink roses she had photographed the previous Valentines' Day. The color was radiant-looking on her. She blew her hair dry and styled it expertly, but quickly. Then she styled Cassandra's. Alexandra had done a good job with her own hair. Diana applied artful cosmetics and instinctively grabbed her pearls. Pink sandals and bag completed the outfit. She was amazing looking; so was her family.

Daniel was amazed that the expensive Valentine bouquet, though gone, was not forgotten. His wife's eye for beauty always made him more appreciative of loveliness in his life. She always reminded him of Proverbs

31:10-31. She was diligent; she took care of business! And did she ever!

They took Mallory to an appointment with a pulmonary specialist: a woman in her mid-forties, her eyes danced merrily, and she had a delightful accent. After checking Mallie's oxygen absorption, she wasn't entirely pleased. But viewing the bruised expanse of her throat, she wasn't surprised. The attack could have been lethal. She wasn't in favor of removing the tube or of discontinuing the oxygen. Then, she listened carefully for the pneumonia, checking the records from the Arkansas hospital. Her recommendation was that Mallory should be readmitted to the hospital for intravenous antibiotics and more fluids Mallory had checked out prematurely in order to close on the mine sale.

Diana sat and nodded, not at all surprised. She had already confided to Daniel pretty much the same opinion. They called the hospital in Hope to see if a room was available. Mallory was trying not to cry.

"It won't be so bad, Mallory," Diana was comforting. "We are all going to go eat a very special dinner. Then, we'll get you to the hospital where you get your IV back; I know how much you've missed it. You'll receive the antibiotics. We should be able to get you out for the day tomorrow, and we can all go to Murfreesboro for church. You may need to go back in tomorrow night, again. You're getting better; we don't want to take any chances with you."

Mallie was trying not to get her hopes up that she would see David at church, or at training in Tulsa on Monday. In spite of trying not to get her hopes up, she was still hoping.

From the doctor's office, they drove to the Hyatt Regency in downtown Dallas. The hotel was very elegant, with uniformed parking attendants and bell men. Mallory was awe-struck. She watched as Daniel shoved some money into the valet's hand, who then hopped into the driver's seat to take the Suburban to a parking space.

Diana snapped pictures. They moved quickly through a spacious lobby and down an escalator. Mallie was aware that their group was drawing admiring glances. She remembered how dazzled she had felt by the Faulkners just two weeks previously. They had really stood out in little Murfreesboro; but they still made quite a statement in grown up Dallas! She had been so nervous and worried about them; now she couldn't remember why. Well, she was still pretty nervous when it was just Daniel. Now that she thought about it, she was pretty sure she wouldn't be seeing David on either Sunday or Monday!

They arrived at another little lobby, and someone did a brief security check of the ladies' handbags. Daniel had to show them his gun and his license. Then Erik and Suzanne met them, and they joined a crowd stepping into a large elevator. Their group, among the first to step in, moved to the back. The doors closed, and the car shot upward! They were against a glass wall, and at first, all they could see was the mirrored windows of the hotel across from them. Then, they shot above the hotel, and they could see the lights of Dallas stretching down and all around them, and they could see the night sky. The entire experience was unbelievable. Mallory wondered dazedly if the Rapture, itself, could be any more thrilling. But she knew it would be.

She had seen pictures of the beautiful, mirrored hotel, with the slim tower beside it, topped with a lighted ball. It was one of the familiar features of the Dallas skyline. Rumors had abounded that there was a restaurant in the ball, but Mallie had dismissed that as impossible!

The elevator door opened, and the diners filed out to be led by a hostess, to various tables. Plate glass windows from table level to the ceiling circled the huge restaurant. Beyond the windows, the main traffic arteries, bumper to bumper with car lights, snaked in all directions. The Metroplex stretched brightly and endlessly. It looked like they were in the center of their own starry little galaxy. She felt like she was sitting on top of the world!

Conversation wafted softly around Mallory, but since her throat kind of hurt, and talking was difficult, she tuned it out. She was caught up in the mystery of the revolving restaurant. She couldn't imagine how someone had even imagined a revolving restaurant. And then, getting from the concept to the actualization. She watched, fascinated, as the outer ring moved, almost imperceptibly.

Diana had snuffed the candle that was on their table. Mallory's oxygen dose was low, and the tanks and masks much improved for safety. The nurse in her still didn't want to take any chances, especially in a building where evacuation would be so problematic. With the candle out, and the restaurant lighting low for ambiance, everyone was having a hard time reading the menu. They all began with the bread. It looked good;

Mallory was hungry. Erik and Suzanne were having a hard time choosing, and Suzanne had asked, "What are you having, Mallie?"

Placing her finger over the tube, she croaked, "Soup".

Diana elbowed Daniel in the rib. They were trying to do something so special for Mallory because she was being hospitalized again. Even Diana, the nurse, had forgotten her patient wasn't ready for a steak, yet.

One of the soup selections was something called Lobster Bisque, and she ordered it.

It was thick and delicious, and everyone insisted she have another bowl. Everyone's food was presented in a way that Mallory, Suzanne and Erik had never seen before. The whole evening seemed like more of an event than Cinderella's going to the ball! Even the prospect of returning to the hospital in Hope, didn't break the spell of the enchanted evening.

A dessert tray was presented, and one of the selections was a chocolaty replica of the famous hotel landmark. It was cute, and the three kids split one of those; Mallory enjoyed a hot-fudge sundae and a latte.

When they were all on their way back through the main lobby, Daniel pulled Mallory aside to apologize to her for their thoughtlessness of her. She stared at him in amazement. She knew he meant about her not really being able to eat the meal. She wished it were easier to talk. She was feeling that if she could ever just speak normally again, she wouldn't take it so much for granted. She wished she could express her gratitude toward tham for everything. That would have been hard, even if she could talk!

Mallory decided to return to Hope with Erik and her mom. The Faulkners were spending the night at Mallory's elegant home. Diana hadn't been sure about relinquishing her patient, but Mallie was much better, and she did need some time with her mother.

Alexandra, Jeremiah, and Cassandra had all clung to Mallory as if they were never going to see her again. They had all won a special place in her heart, too. Then she insisted on their bringing Dinky with them when they came in the morning. They were mystified as to her reasoning, since they had her security team back in place.

Mallory explained that she wanted to go to the mine property with Dinky to see if he could pick up any clues about the missing employees. They tried to explain that Ivan Summers and Janice Collins, agents with the ABI, were continuing to work on the case.

Mallory knew they hadn't been able to do much. For some reason, they seemed to think that the Arkansas employees had been taken to the same vicinity as the group from Mallory's North Dallas home. She had been thinking about it, and it really didn't make sense to her. The north Texas hostages had been moved someplace fairly convenient for the hostage-takers. It only made sense that the group of workers from the mine wouldn't have been moved far.

Now, Daniel was telling her that Dinky wasn't really a tracking dog, and that the workers had probably been loaded into a vehicle and driven away, so they wouldn't have left a scent.

Diana phoned Mallory just before she went to bed. Mallie, with the IV in one hand, was having a hard time covering the trach tube and holding the phone to her ear with the other. Diana wasn't pleased that Suzanne hadn't stayed. She figured Mallory had insisted on her mother's going home. But that didn't mean she had to do it!

Mallory assured her that she was still drinking fluids, the IV was in, and the antibiotics were started. She said she felt okay, but she was tired. "Just sleep; don't worry about me. There are doctors and nurses here." she tried to joke. "Why did you really call me?" she questioned, suddenly perceptive. "To tell me you guys sent David somewhere else?"

There was a silence. "I just didn't want you to be disappointed."

Mallory readjusted her position so she could communicate better.

"You know, Diana, I don't really mind this. You can tell Daniel, too. At first I was kind of mad about everything. But now I see Tammi being so nuts about Mr. Larson and Alexandra liking Tommy. And I worry about them. I can see danger lurking for them that I was pretty blind about in my own life."

"What do you know about Alexandra?" Diana sounded worried.

"Nothing! Except she's eleven, and Tommy's fifteen; and they're both really young. They like each other, and as immature as they are, they act like they have a real handle on things, and nobody should have a problem with them. I'm not trying to make you worry about them, I'm just saying my dad could see the same thing with me. I'm sure I'll have my moments over the next five years, but I really want to do what I need to do. Do you know what I'm supposed to do about starting back in school?"

"Well, we need to get your passport. I think Daniel and Tom Haynes are working your curriculum out so you can finish everything on line and march with your class in Murfreesboro next spring. You can be working on some college courses, though, at the same time. We'll get everything squared away."

"Diana," Mallory had started to say something, then was unsure how to proceed.

"You aren't in trouble, Mallie," Diana had apparently read her mind. "It's a miracle you took off when you did, and a miracle you kept going. Evidently someone waited around quite a while for you to come back. Your meeting with Oscar Melville was horrible, but I guess things might have been even worse if you had stayed home."

"Will you guys trust me again?" she started crying, and crying made her throat ache more. "I didn't call Tammi; she called me. She told me David was in Nashville, but I didn't ask her about him. I went because I knew I wouldn't see him."

"I know." Her soft statement amazed Mallory.

"What do you know? What do you mean, 'I know'?"

"I know you went back because you knew the property wasn't secure from a diamond-mining perspective. I tried to tell Daniel he didn't know the first thing about diamond- mining and the special problems it creates. It wouldn't move fast for your father, either. I was glad you were ready to sell! It's just like you said, you need all the really sophisticated theft detections systems, but why bring in all that, if the environmental stuff keeps us from mining?"

"So, does Daniel know that's why I was back?" Mallory was trying to figure out his take. He was the one who could take the car keys. He had given her the keys and the credit cards, and she felt that she had blown it.

"M-m-m, let's just say, he knows you weren't trying to sneak around and see David. That's the main thing." She laughed. "He was pretty shocked you were all the way in Arkansas before he knew you had left the house."

Chapter 9

TRACES

TRENT MORRISON WAS sitting in the spacious Washington DC hotel lobby where Erik and Suzanne had stayed a couple of days earlier. He was under the Department of Agriculture as an agent of the US Forest Service. He knew about the FBI meeting where Erik Bransom had been ordered to stop digging into a mystery about some diamond mine employees disappearing in Arkansas. DC was still buzzing about it. DC was always buzzing about something. Usually only really scandalous stories lasted, but this had raised some eyebrows. Morrison knew Bransom, slightly. Their paths had crossed in some different training courses they had been required to take.

Morrison was studying a Forest Service map of the Ouachita National Forest. The Forest Service had the oversight of one hundred ninety-three million acres of forests and grasslands across the US and some of its territories. That was a lot of remote territory for bad people to do bad things, or to dump bodies, or evidence. Trent was meeting with Robert Porter, who oversaw the US Forest Service LEI for the Southern Division.

Porter arrived, and Trent rose to shake his hand. They moved toward the in-house restaurant for a brunch meeting. Saturday morning, the hotel restaurant was emptier than it was during the work week. Trent hoped they could have a quiet corner without too much eavesdropping. He sometimes thought every booth in DC must be bugged.

Both men ordered coffee and orange juice, and exchanged pleasantries about their families. The server brought their beverages and a plate of biscuits. They ordered, and Trent bowed his head for a silent prayer before he grabbed one of the steaming biscuits. He buttered it generously, then spread it with strawberry jam. Before he took a bite, he set it down, to meet the gaze of the agent sitting across from him.

"What have you heard about that Martin kid and the corrupt sheriff and all of those diamond mine employees?" he questioned.

"Why ya askin'?" Porter countered. "Since the FBI got pulled off, did someone ask you about it? Who's tryin' to involve us?"

Morrison bit into the biscuit, then took a sip of coffee. He was a patient kind of guy.

Bob Porter, a fisherman, himself, knew he was being hooked, played, strung along, by his superior. He decided he should be a little cagey himself. No use in his just jumpin' into the boat for the guy. He was trying to diet, but the biscuit temptation was winning.

Morrison continued to sip his coffee, watching Porter's responses, his body language. He liked setting the hook; he was good at what he did.

"So, you didn't answer me. What have you heard, seriously, about all that stuff? No harm you telling me what you've heard, is there?"

"Guess not," Porter replied, uneasily. "I've mostly heard what the news stories have covered. Probably not as much as you've heard. You been looking into it on your own?"

Trent was contemplating his cup of coffee, watching the steam rise. He was going to get answers if he had to sit here all afternoon.

"I heard about the four murders that Martin Thomas kid committed, and that he left one of the bodies in the National Forest," Porter finally responded. "That's the only thing out of all of it that involves us, right?

Morrison shrugged. He took another bite of the biscuit, and Porter couldn't resist any longer. He began smearing butter and jam.

"What do you make of Oscar Melville?"

"Dishonest lawman, I guess. He's going to jail, though, isn't he?"

"Pretty sure he is. You think he had anything to do with the people disappearing from the mine?"

Porter replaced the biscuit on his plate. "They don't seem to think so, do they? The way I make it out, he was just there, hanging out. Maybe the lawman in him, had him check it out because it didn't look right."

"Didn't he walk there on purpose, though? It's not like he was just driving past, and the situation looked wrong. Do you know if he ever visited the National Forest much?"

Bob Porter took a bite of the biscuit, before responding. "If he did, it's not a crime."

The breakfasts arrived. The men ate in relative silence for a few minutes. A baseball game was showing on a TV at the bar. Porter was a Braves fan, and he had gotten absorbed in the contest. It was trying Morrison's patience now.

"Why don't you just tell me what's on your mind; I'll say, 'No', and I can be home for dinner with my family?" Porter finally rejoined the conversation.

Trent Morrison's gaze met Porter's. "Here's what's on my mind! Eleven men have been kidnapped for sure, maybe murdered. The Justice Department told law enforcement to 'forget about it.'! I can't, for the life of me, figure out why! The men who disappeared are all law abiding American citizens, most with families, trying to work a job to support their families. If it were a mine collapse, the media would all be there, and rescue agencies would be in full gear. If they were hostages in Columbia, Delta Force would be on it. I mean, American citizens always matter! Who has the clout to get this particular incident buried?"

"Yeah, I guess that's about the same thing I heard. You have any reason to think the kidnappers used the National Park?" Porter was beginning to catch on.

"I don't have any proof they didn't!" Morrison was smiling.

By late Saturday afternoon, Morrison and Porter were pulling into a remote U.S. Forest Service Campground in the Ouachita National Forest in Arkansas. Named Bard Springs, it accommodated RV's and tents without hookups. The RV was far more sophisticated within than it appeared from without. They had been poring over various aerial photos, Forest Service maps, and even satellite imagery. Everything was spread across all the surfaces inside the RV; beds, sofa, countertops, table.

After Robert Porter had finished eyeballing one set of photos with a high powered magnifying glass, he straightened up with a groan. "Maybe you should tell me what it is we're looking for," he had good-naturedly suggested again.

"I told you, anything!" Trent responded. "We have over three million acres of forest just here in Arkansas. Has to be a lot going on here that shouldn't be. Just keep your eyes peeled for any anomaly."

They continued combing through the data. Porter had moved onto the satellite photos. He did some bends and stretches in an attempt to unkink his back.

"Whoever said, 'You can't see the forest for the trees', should have tried to figure it out from space," he observed in a mournful tone.

Trent Morrison had just taken a big gulp of coffee, and he blew it all over the photos in front of him. "Don't make me laugh!" he ordered.

When they outfitted, they had forgotten paper towels. He finally grabbed some toilet paper from the little bathroom to mop at the pictures. As he dabbed at a droplet, a tiny image caught his eye.

"What does that look like to you?" he asked the other agent in amazement.

"Is this a psych test?" Porter responded. "We can't afford ink blots, so you're spitting coffee?. It looks like some socially challenged guy blew coffee on a bunch of pictures!"

Morrison just shook his head. He placed the photo in the copy machine to enlarge it, then held the magnifying lens above it again. It looked like more than anything had, so far. He scanned the image into the computer, enhancing it section by section. What he was looking at, was some sort of RV similar to the one with the Doggie Coddling paint job, except this one seemed to be painted camouflage. He couldn't make a plate from it, and he couldn't see any tire tracks in the photo. Still, maybe it was a small piece of the puzzle.

Having noticed nothing unusual at that campground, they drove to the Albert Pike a few miles to the east. The weather was nice, so the campground actually had quite a bit of activity. Morrison and Porter gathered up their fishing gear to trout-fish along the Little Missouri. As they moved beyond the campground to the trail, they were taking note of the vehicles and tire tracks. A recently vacated campsite had disgusting litter left all over the place, and the Forestry Service agents were annoyed-at first!

"Let's just clean up for these pig!." Trent spoke loudly. Picking up one of the plastic grocery-store bags from the trash in the space, he began shoving the rest of the trash into it. A set of ruts weren't deep, but they looked like a possible match to photos from the crime scenes! Their bag of "trash" might yield valuable evidence.

They continued along the trail, disappearing into the woods. An hour and a half later, they reemerged with a nice catch. Darkness had fallen, and the night was chilly and clear. They headed to their RV for a fish fry.

Sunday morning dawned beautifully. Mallory was awake early in her hospital room. She drank the milk and juice that had come on her tray; she tried to swallow some lumpy Cream-of-Wheat, but it wanted to go the wrong direction. When the aide came in, Mallory asked about showering. The aide wanted her to take it easy, but Mallory was insisting she had to get ready to go to church.

"God doesn't even give you a break when you're sick?" she had said, half-seriously, half-mocking.

Mallory smiled in response. "God gave me a break when He sent Jesus to die for my sins. I like going to my church. Do you have time to help me? I think my friends will be here soon."

The woman checked the orders, and an RN came in to remove the IV, and help get her checked out for the day.

Mallie showered, then fixed her hair and make-up. She was getting ready to put her outfit on from the previous day when the Faulkners arrived. They looked incredible all of the time, and then came Sundays!

Diana was wearing a powder blue linen damask dress. The damask pattern formed a border print along the hems of the skirt and the tunic top. It was complimented with white gold and diamond jewelry. Silver sandals and bag completed the outfit.

Alexandra's was snowy white, cut in a sleeveless A-line. It had a short matching jacket. She had white sandals and pearls. She looked extra-cute. Mallie thought it might be because she would see Tommy at church.

Cassandra's dress was soft pink linen damask with puffed short sleeves, and it tied in the back with a sash. She wore pink ruffled socks and white Mary-janes. She was adorable.

"We brought Dinky," Diana announced.

Mallory laughed, or tried to; there was no sound. "Did he like the helicopter?" she closed the tube with her finger so she could speak. She figured he had been a pain and made a big ordeal out of bringing him

"He did all right. He's waiting for you outside."

She unzipped a garment bag, and Mallory squealed with delight. Then, tears filled her eyes. Her dress was pale yellow Damask with scalloped hem and neckline. Fitted gently, the waistline in the front was accentuated with a large self-fabric bow. Diana produced Mallory's jewelry, and except for the trach tube and the band-aid in the crook of her arm, she looked perfect.

The aide had looked them over critically. "Why do you have to dress up like that for church?"

"Oh, we don't have to. We just like to." Diana responded brightly. "Thank you so much for your help. Do you live here in Hope? I see you're married, do you have any children?"

The woman, who had been a little surly, responded to Diana's genuine interest in her. When she answered, Diana told her about the church in town that the Sanders were involved in, explaining about some of the children's ministries. Diana had moved seamlessly into the plan of salvation, pulling a little New Testament from a pocket of her bag. At first the woman's face had hardened, and she had taken a step backward. Her name was Nell, and as Diana had continued to say her name, kindly and persuasively, tears had welled in her eyes, and she had leaned in to follow the verses Diana was reading.

Mallory was sitting on the edge of the bed, awed. She was praying, but the RN had entered to make sure they were set to leave. The moment interrupted, Diana gave Nell a gospel tract to read to help explain everything again.

They hurried out to the vehicles and tried to make good time to Murfreesboro, but the narrow highways were crammed with boats and campers, heading to the mountains and lakes. Too bad people gave their spiritual needs such low priority.

By the time they reached the site of the DiaMo mine, it was nearly time for Sunday School.

"This isn't our property now, since Friday," Daniel had worried. Mallory just stroked her dog, saying nothing.

They all pulled onto the acreage together. Mallory, the Faulkners, Dinky, and the security people. Erik and Suzanne saw their convoy and followed them.

"What are you guys up to?" Bransom questioned uneasily.

Mallory released Dinky. He began to tear around, acting glad to be free of restraint. Then he headed into the shed. Faulkner pulled the SUV up closer to the building.

"I'll follow him," Bransom, driving Suzanne's Jaguar, pulled it up, too, and got out. The dog was barking at the concrete floor.

"Don't make me sorry I rescued you," the agent threatened him.

Mallory entered the shed and knelt next to her dog.

"Come on, let's go to church. Don't get your pretty dress dirty," Erik was coaxing.

"What is it Dinky?" her voice barely whispered.

He whined and looked at her pleadingly. He was running along one section of concrete, and then back.

Her eyes searched the floor of the shed. Surely, none of the sections of floor could raise, could they? She glanced pleadingly at Bransom.

"I've been ordered off, Mallory. And I promised. I can call Collins and Summers, though. They're still on every lead, big time. You really think there might be something underneath, here?"

Janice Collins had seen the group growing at her crime scene, and she ordered them off. She had already called Summers. He was in his Sunday School class, but he was on his way back.

Janice watched Dinky intently, pretty sure he was onto something. If not, the concrete floor would be torn up for nothing. She was already ordering jackhammers and other equipment. She wanted those men found! Alive!

Mallory and the Faulkners were a few minutes late for Sunday School. Mallory went to her small high school class. David wasn't there, but

Tammi was, and Tommy Haynes. A few other kids assembled. There were a few kids there that Mallory knew from school, but they had never been to Sunday School before. The quarterback told her he came because he promised God he would, if Mallory didn't die. She hadn't known what to say to that, and since speaking was so hard, she didn't say anything. The group tried to sing a couple of songs, but everyone was too shy to sing out. Diana had ordered Mallie to be really careful of her voice.

In the few minutes between Sunday School and the morning service, people had been grabbing Mallory, to hug her and tell her they had prayed for her. She was really feeling overwhelmed. She guessed she didn't realize what a close call she had.

Lana Anderson had managed to find a beautiful new baby grand piano during the previous week. Delivery was scheduled for the following Thursday, so the Faulkners once again provided their keyboard. Diana tried to insist that Lana play, but she had refused. Laughing, she told the guest musician she might not be so generous once the new piano arrived.

Diana had laughed in response. "I hope we're in our home church next Sunday, anyway. We've missed so much, they'll think we're visitors." Her hands were skillfully moving across the keys. "Sound the Battle Cry" was lively and inspiring. Then she went into "Onward Christian Soldiers." She laughed at herself, thinking she must be in a militant mood. She refrained from including "The Fight Is On", and intro'd into "At Calvary".

The congregation was gathering, creating a happy bustle of activity. Daniel's parents had come; she could hardly believe it. They had returned home at the end of the week, but now had traveled back. Amazing things were taking place, even in the midst of difficulties.

She glanced at Mallory. She looked good, amazingly. If the disaster hadn't happened with Melville, Diana wouldn't have sent her kids to their grandparents, and the grandparents wouldn't have gotten saved. "All things really do work together for good," she had acknowledged, quoting part of a verse from Romans chapter eight to herself.

A couple of guys she didn't know had entered. One carried a Bible, looking at ease. The guy with him looked miserable and nervous. Diana began to pray more for the service, for the new guy, and for Nell, whom she had witnessed to earlier.

Erik Bransom saw the two men and went over to shake their hands. Trent Morrison introduced Bob. The three men spoke briefly, but the pastor and song leader had mounted the platform. Jack Fielder had asked the congregation to stand and sing "What a Friend We Have in Jesus". The congregation had joined in enthusiastically, if not melodically. After the song service and the announcements, Mallory played the offertory. "By and by, when I look on His face, I'll wish I had given Him more." The song was beautiful, and she did a superb job.

Pastor Anderson stood and opened his Bible. His text verses were Isaiah 59:14 and Matthew 27:32

And judgment is turned away backward, and justice standeth afar off: for truth is fallen in the street, and equity cannot enter.
And as they came out, they found a man of Cyrene, Simon by name: him they compelled to bear his cross.

After reading both passages, he prayed and asked the Lord for power and blessing.

He leaned across the pulpit, intent on communicating the message.

"Ladies and gentlemen," he began earnestly. "The first verse I read was written by the Prophet Isaiah somewhere around B.C. 698. During his days, Israel was corrupt and idolatrous. Justice was habitually miscarried. People had departed from God's laws. God's just servant was condemning the carelessness of his day, and mourning the pitiful spiritual condition of the people. Truth, had indeed, fallen in the street.

Today, in America, our spiritual and moral fiber seem to mirror ancient Israel's decline. God wants us to be a great nation whose trust is still in Him and His righteousness. When Isaiah penned the verse, he was lamenting his day. But it was also a prophetic announcement of an event that was to take place seven hundred and thirty years into the future. The day around A.D. 33 when my Jesus was crucified; my Jesus, Who is Truth, personified; fell in the street of Jerusalem. All the laws of justice and fairness had been suspended at His mock trial. He was guilty of nothing. No one, not His disciples, nor those who had experienced His healing touch, had stepped forward to say a word in His behalf. And Truth fell in the street that day, beneath the weight of my sin and yours, beneath the weight of the cross He carried for me!" Tears were pouring down his face as he continued. "We shouldn't be surprised when justice is miscarried in our nation, but we should beg God to bring us back to Him, back to equity, back to judgment and justice."

He spoke for about thirty minutes, giving specifics of problems with justice in America. He saw the economic downturn of the nation presenting new dangers of increased crime as unemployment worsened. He saw fewer law enforcement officers fighting the tide, due to budget cuts; even fewer civil servants prosecuting crimes, again because of budget cuts in DA offices all over the nation. There would be more and more early release of prisoners as prisons continued to overcrowd.

"Our social concerns are grave," he was concluding. "But Jesus is still the answer. Let's covenant together to pray this week about the missing mine workers from our community. Let's pray for God to bless and help those in authority over us. Let's pray for God to enable and empower the people in law enforcement who labor to make our lives safe and peaceable. If you have never asked Jesus into your heart, please pray, right where you are: 'Dear Lord, I admit I'm a sinner. I ask You to come into my life and save me, so I can go to Heaven some day. In Jesus Name, amen.'."

Diana had moved noiselessly to the keyboard, beginning to play softly. "Just as I am, without one plea, but that Thy blood, was shed for me." She played through the invitation hymn again. No one came forward. The pastor closed the invitation and the church service. In his closing remarks, he had asked Daniel if his family would be willing to present another concert, and if Daniel would preach again. The guests agreed, and with that announcement, people were dismissed.

Bransom caught up with Porter and Morrison out in the yard to introduce Suzanne, then offered to buy their lunch at the lodge in Daisy. They agreed, and the two men headed north in the RV while the Bransoms followed in Suzanne's Jaguar. Erik had called both ABI agents, Collins and Summers, trying to find out if there was really anything beneath the floor of the shed at the former DiaMo property. Neither had answered his calls. He accessed internet news headlines on his phone. He let out an amazed whistle. Chalk one up to Mallory and her dog. The mine employees hadn't been found, but there were the beginnings of a mine pit beneath the floor. And-the mine employees had evidently been held there for some time, before being removed to another location. He called the Faulkners to tell them and Mallory the latest. There were lots of traces of the missing men, but no blood and no bodies. That was very good news.

At the lodge, all four of the diners ordered chicken fried steak with mashed potatoes, a salad, and iced tea. The conversation among the three men revolved around the evidence they assumed was being destroyed by the Arkansas agents. The Forest Service guys had no inroads into the case, unless it tied directly to Federal lands. Morrison was still convinced they would tie together. He was asking Bransom, who lived in Hope, if he ever spent much time hunting or fishing in the Ouachitas. He really didn't. Then they asked him if he had any idea how much Oscar Melville might be familiar with the forest.

At first, Erik hadn't followed their line of reasoning. Then a smile had spread across his face. Melville wasn't part of his "hands off" agreement with his superiors at Justice. He was mildly surprised that the two forestry agents thought Melville might be party to more than he was. Bransom had surmised that he was a lone goof-ball. But, what if he wasn't? Erik would like to nail him on more than he had. Maybe he had conspired, to at least show the out-of-town henchmen a hiding place, or two. Bransom had ordered one of the agents in the Little Rock FBI office to put together a more complete file on the corrupt little ex-sheriff. Bransom had never followed up on it. He sent an e-mail to the agent to forward the file to him asap.

Suzanne had been gazing at the lovely lake oil-painting spreading panoramically beyond the window. The colors vibrated, dancing in the play of shade and sunlight. Hummingbirds darted around a feeder, and a wind chime jangled softly. Flower beds and wildflowers created a riot of color, making her miss her garden.

She had surveyed it woefully, once more, when she had been on the property before Sunday School. Now, she was staring at a corner of a flower bed outside the window where several plants had been run over and crushed.

"Somebody sure doesn't mind running over flowers," she interrupted the masculine conversation suddenly. "The tire tracks look the same, too," she added.

The three men paused, gazing out the window at the area. Their gazes had met then, in astonishment.

Erik Bransom raced outside to corner a landscaper who was edging. Pointing to the crushed flowers, he asked the guy if he had seen who ran over the area; if he noticed the vehicle. The worker's English wasn't the best, but he told the agent that it was an army truck. He was mad because he had just planted there. Bransom nodded sympathetic agreement.

"That was useless," he had acknowledged glumly as he rejoined the group at the table. "He said it was the U.S. Army."

"Camouflage!" Morrison and Porter exclaimed in unison!

Chapter 10

TRAINING

I CHRONICLES *22:14&15 Now, behold in my trouble I have prepared for the house of the LORD an hundred thousand talents of gold, and a thousand thousand talents of silver, and brass without weight; for it is in abundance: timber also and stone have I prepared; and thou mayest add thereto.*

> *Moreover there are workmen with thee in abundance, hewers and workers of stone and timber, and all manner of cunning men for every manner of work.*

There was an excited buzz at the GeoHy Corporation Headquarters in Tulsa on Monday morning. An elegant catered breakfast had been spread across elegant, linen Damask-covered tables. Diana had watched, fascinated, while Delia O'Shaughnessy's nimble, diamond-sparkled fingers had pinched and folded the lovely fabric into pleated skirts for the tables, and created rich folds over the tops of the surface. The caterer had been taking note, too. Before the morning had ended, she had purchased a nice order of the elegant linen for her business. The package included a training video on the various methods of table dressing and napkin folding. Delia had moved to another table, forming swags, rather than pleats. Much of the conversational buzz had to do with the Faith Baptist

Church services the previous day, as well as the discovery of the pit beneath the shed's floor on the diamond property. Agents from the ABI, and the Forestry Service LEI were combing west central Arkansas for the missing employees.

The Faulkners had stayed in touch with the families of the eleven missing men from the Arkansas location, and the four who were still unaccounted for from Mallory's north Dallas home. Family members had been brought in for the meeting, and everyone was trying to comfort and console one another.

Diana, carrying a delicate china cup and saucer, was mingling with the staff that had assembled. She always looked beautiful, and always had something kind and helpful to say to everyone. She had placed her hand gently on the shoulder of one of the eight-year old boys, whose dad had just started at the mine. The employee was new, and Diana hadn't met the family before the abductions took place. She told the boy that his dad mattered, and that, according to what had been found, there didn't seem to be any injuries to anyone. Daniel had been speaking to people, too. The company had hired private investigators. Of course, they had to tread softly around the official investigation. Even so, they were gaining information of their own.

Delia settled in at one of the tables with an appetizing plate of food. She missed Shay, but the she had given herself a pep talk. She had always been able to mingle socially before she had become so dependent upon him. Widowed for twelve years, she had taken her business forward, being forced to overcome her natural reticence. Now, Shay was a treasure to her, the Lord had worked in their lives in a marvelous way. She was laughing at herself now, though, for trying to grasp onto him too ferociously. Her trust had to stay in the Lord.

Daniel sank momentarily into a vacant chair across from her.

"You look elegant this morning, Delia Sure glad you could stay. Thanks for your touch with the tables; I never realized what a difference some of these details can make. Glad to see the caterer placed an order."

Delia nodded agreement. She was dazed at the direction her life had taken, just within the last couple of weeks. Well, first with Shay coming to live with her and be so interested in the family linen business. Then they had both heard the Gospel story and had prayed that simple prayer. They had become reacquainted with Mallory, another special treasure!

Then they had met the Faulkners and all of the new friends to really branch out in the growing business empire.

"I keep humming that song Mallory played yesterday morning," she confided to him. "I liked all of your concert, too, and your sermon. But, does that song Mallory played have words to it? It was just pretty, and it's still playing in my mind. I'm sure I'm just a proud grandmother, but I really like to hear her play."

Daniel laughed. "You have good reason to be proud of her; she's an exceptional musician. She's an exceptional young lady! I miss Patrick; he was a great man. Can I get you another cup of tea?"

He was snatching her cup as he rose. He filled it with hot water, and returned with cream and a fresh tea bag. "Mallory's offertory was "I'll Wish I Had Given Him More".

It's a beautiful song; maybe we can sing it this morning. Thank you for asking about it."

He moved on to visit with some of the others.

Kerry Larson had arrived from Dallas. David, who had been Larson's houseguest since Saturday evening, was with him. Faulkner encouraged David to help himself to some of the lavish breakfast. Then, he closed the office door for a private conversation with the attorney.

"How'd everything go?" Daniel began.

Larson laughed. "Okay, I guess. I mean, he's not stupid, so I guess it seemed like a pretty contrived way to keep him from being around Mallory yesterday. He was pleasant and polite the whole time. The girls at my church acted pretty giggly around him. He didn't act interested in any of them, at all. A lady got saved, and we're starting our Missions Conference. I think he liked the church fairly well. I think he thinks Patrick was trying to set me up with Mallory."

Faulkner's eyebrows shot up in surprise. "You think he was?"

Kerry laughed again. "Pretty sure not. I bet it never entered his mind. He never gave me his Proverbs Nine talk."

"Which he probably would have if he had had any idea you'd fall for Tammi. I know you're hungry, but we still need to talk about that soon. Did you tell David you have a thing for his sister?"

The attorney, blushing, was suddenly studying his Italian leather shoes. "Uh, I might have mentioned it," he admitted. "I told him not to tell anyone. I thought it would help him relax about Mallory."

"We don't want him to relax about her. What, exactly did you say to him about his sister; what did he say? I mean, it must have shocked him."

I told him I love her, but, since she's so young for me, I'm keeping my distance for now. His response was typical brother, 'To know her is to hate her. If I want to get over her, all I need to do is be around her'."

Daniel laughed, in spite of himself. It was kind of his opinion, too! And he wasn't her brother! Maybe they could still all get Kerry's attention diverted to someone else. He wasn't counting on it, though.

He allowed the breakfast time to be extended, not wanting to waste time and money, but wanting people to be able to get acquainted, too. The relaxed atmosphere was pleasant, and the food was plentiful, attractive, and delicious.

He had asked the AV staff to display the Faith Baptist web site on a couple of screens. It was showing the Easter morning crowd, then the two Sunday night services that had featured his family. Most of the employees seemed to like it; some seemed a bit nervous. A few had already been startled when Pastor Anderson prayed before the meal.

The Faulkner children, on site, with a tutor, had been summoned. Then he found Diana, and the five of them began a quick-study on the hymn Delia had asked about. It sounded beautiful. He sent the lyrics to a tech to project onto the wall.

The employees were given an eight minute warning for restroom breaks and refilling plates and beverages. Then, the staff reassembled, turning their chairs to face the platform at the front of the large room.

The pastor prayed again, then the Faulkner family sang the hymn.

> *"By and by, when I look on His face,*
> *I'll wish I had given Him more…"*

Then attractively designed printed material was handed out to every person. At the top, were two verses from the book of I Chronicles, in the Bible. Mr. Faulkner read the two verses, then began some opening remarks. The training session was being recorded, and Suzanne took notes in shorthand.

"As usual, my wife is the one who noticed these verses and called them to my attention." He stopped and smiled at her. "The words were spoken by king David, near the end of his life. Some of you here, know the story better than I do; some of you may not know it at all. King David had wanted to build a magnificent temple to the God of Israel. Because David had been such a warrior king and had shed blood, God said that Solomon, David's son, should be the one to build the temple. I like what David did. He got busy anyway." Faulkner laughed. "I mean, God said he couldn't build it, but he didn't say David couldn't do anything.

So, David spent much of his remaining time, moving everything into place so his young and tender son could complete a daunting task. These verses move so quickly that it's easy to miss what they say. David stockpiled a hundred thousand talents of gold. Does anyone here have any idea how much gold is being spoken of here?"

No one responded; they were looking bored and sleepy. "Well," the CEO picked up again. "A talent in the Bible is a unit of weight, about ninety-six pounds. The book of Revelation mentions hail-stones that will weigh in at a talent each. Wow, a ninety-six pound hail-stone; but that's a different story. David accumulated a hundred thousand talents of gold for building the temple. Diana figured it out for me. A hundred thousand talents equals nine million, six hundred pounds of gold. Of course, we buy gold by the ounce, not by the pound. Nine million, six hundred pounds of gold equals one hundred fifty-three million, six hundred thousand ounces. This morning, I think gold was quoted around nine hundred dollars per ounce. At that rate, David's gold would have been worth nearly fourteen billion dollars. The silver would have been approximately one hundred sixty million dollars in value on today's market. Besides that, he had prepared hewn stones and timber and brass. David didn't pout about what God said he couldn't do! He did what he could. Okay! Don't y'all give up on me; I'm just about to get to the point of what my wife recently showed me.

"In verse fifteen, David tells his son there are workmen in abundance. Here's where y'all come in. I get all blown away by the 'gold and valuable stuff'. But, none of it's worth much until the workmen go to work to turn it into something beautiful. Sometimes, it's easy to miss the importance people play. Even with everything (all the material) on site for the building, Solomon couldn't have built the temple by himself in his lifetime. It took seven years, as it was. We need you here. We want you here. We want our people back that somebody took. We need your intelligence, your designs, your hands, your muscles, your resourcefulness. We're dealing first and foremost with security in this meeting, because people are important. After our people assets, we're concerned with security of our properties and products. We can't build the corporation on the abilities and efforts of a few of us. We need the synergy of workmen in abundance."

He took a drink of apple juice. It was made from some special apples Kerry Larson's family grew on their orchards in the Northwest. While he paused, a few secretaries were passing out application forms for obtaining handgun licenses. A few people glanced at what it was and pushed it aside.

"If you have a felony, you can't get licensed. I would like everyone to fill this out tonight and get it to me first thing in the morning. Everyone should apply, including you ladies. If you're a real anti-gun conscientious objector, I'll hear your case. The sad truth is that you ladies are more at risk for violent crimes than we men are." The photo came up of Mallory's bruised throat.

"We have a special treat in store for us. Erik Bransom is an FBI agent who is acting as a security consultant for us. He'll be teaching us a good deal about personal vigilance and safety. Then, when we all fill out our applications and receive our weapons, he'll be training us all about our weapons, also.

Bransom stepped up onto the platform and took the microphone. "Ladies and gentlemen, I want to tell ya, I'm a pretty new Christian. I have a new wife, too. Most of y'all have met her. Most of you know that was Mallory's picture with the bruises. Our first order of business this afternoon is security around children. Mr. Faulkner already mentioned that women are preyed upon more than men, but sadly, in our country, it's even worse for children and teen-agers. I'm going to show you an FBI DVD. You'll all receive a copy of it to watch with your children. It's graphic, but they need to see it."

The film began with pictures of beautiful missing children, all ages and nationalities. Some gave brief stories of how they had been abducted. There were horrible crime scene pictures of mutilated children, children who had suffered terrible indignities, before dying in some of the worst ways imaginable. Diana began sobbing, early on. It sounded like the entire darkened room was weeping. One of the employees felt so sick that he ran from the room.

Bransom paused it. "However awful the film looks, it's a hundred times worse being there in person. The smells, everything, it's just indescribable. I'm showing it to you, because this is the reality of wickedness in America. It's getting worse every year."

He pushed "play" and the video resumed. An agent was talking about the statistics, about pornography's effect on society. About how many sites there were for the filth, compared to religious sites and decent products. He continued about the technological sophistication the enemy had for propagating itself, and for protecting the identities of those involved. Cyber space was a formidable adversary for the crime fighting agencies who were stretched to capacity. The future of American children seemed even grimmer than the bloody present.

The second half of the video was a little more palatable, showing different police departments and agencies training children in school assemblies and Scout groups, different maneuvers for avoiding being taken and for fighting back. It taught children to fight loudly and make a scene, if someone were trying to force them into a car. Even if the kidnapper were threatening to kill them if they didn't be quiet, they should NEVER, NEVER just go quietly. Fight and make a scene! Scream, "FIRE!" It was practical. At first, Diana had thought she would never let her children see it. Tears were falling in her heart, that her children had to lose their innocence and trust so they could be warned of a danger that was so real. In the video, the children were practicing doing a twisting, ducking maneuver to escape the grasp of an adult who might try to grab them. It showed how to kick out tail lights of a car if they should be placed in the trunk. All really desperate things kids shouldn't even have to know about!

Bransom had their attention about the importance of security!

There was a film about evasive driving and some extreme things. Bransom warned about endangering the general public. That was a real concern. Running over a child while fleeing from a chase car; getting the wrong people in the line of fire. He mentioned the sniper's nest that the ABI had spotted the previous week at Lake Daisy. He had kind of glanced toward Delia as he mentioned it, but she didn't flinch.

He laughingly mentioned that, only in movies, could people dodge rounds of automatic weapon fire. Addressing everyone from the seasoned security personnel to the newest secretary, he communicated his point.

He hit briefly on the problems that could come with such a close-knit group, who were friendly and conversant with their personal security. His eyes met Diana's and then Daniel Faulkner's gaze. "I can see you two stepping in to save your security. That's all noble, and unselfish, and good; except then, what's the point of even trying to have personal security? The people you have are good. They know they risk their lives. They don't want to risk their lives unnecessarily. That's why you do what they say, and don't try to second guess 'em."

He had Brad Walter's brother-in-law enter with one of the newly acquired German Shepherds. "Same thing with the dogs, folks. PETA won't like it, but these dogs are not pets. Their job is to protect us; not ours to protect them. The kids will have a hard time about this. Maybe you need to buy 'em pets and teach 'em th' difference. I don't know."

There was a break for lunch, after which everyone was to be loaded onto motor coaches for transportation to the shooting range.

Bransom vaulted from the platform for a word with Delia. "Level with me, Mrs. O'Shaughnessy, don't you think a sniper was a little over the top?"

"Sounds like it; why are you asking me?" She hadn't conversed much with the stocky agent. She had thought he could have waited longer after Patrick's demise before he married Suzanne. She still hadn't spoken to her!

"You saying you didn't set the security perimeter around your cabins at the Daisy Lodge?" he was amazed.

She gave him a perplexed frown, not sure what to say.

"Shay arranged that?" he questioned incredulously. The thought hadn't occurred to him before. Shay's father had been a pretty notorious criminal; Shay was a lot different. Still, his background would have made him aware of pushing the limits for personal security.

"No, it was me." Delia decided to change her story, not wanting Shay to get in any trouble. She hadn't known the lengths he had gone to in order to protect them from the threats presented by his brother and father.

Mallory, accompanied by her cousin and a couple of security people, had finished the passport application process in Houston. Mallory had pled desperately to have the tube removed before leaving the hospital, but the doctor hadn't gone for it. It showed up in the passport photo.

"You'll have something to remember it by," Shay had commented.

Passport in hand, they headed for the Galleria, where they ate a late lunch, then decided to ice skate. Shay's growing up in Boston, had helped him become a good skater, but Mallie had never tried it. She couldn't believe how hard it was, but it was fun. Then they split up so they could both shop. Mallory found quite a few cute things. Spring finally seemed to have decided to stay, and she was choosing items with the upcoming trip to Turkey in mind. Her phone rang. It was Diana, who had traveled to Houston to join them as soon as the group had left for the gun range. She was waiting at Starbucks. The two teens joined her, and she enthusiastically checked out their purchases. She already adored them both. They visited animatedly as they finished the drinks, then made the return trip to Tulsa.

Chapter 11

TRENDSETTERS

THE HOUSEHOLD STAFF at the Faulkners had fixed a guest suite for Mallie, and the plan was for everyone to turn in. The problem was that Alexandra, Jeremiah, and Cassandra hadn't yet viewed the DVD. Diana's trip to Houston had been planned before Erik had sprung the film on everyone. Daniel had waited, so the kids were already up too late, and Diana had been trying to put the film out of her mind. She was pretty sure her three wouldn't be able to sleep after viewing it. She wondered if they would ever sleep without nightmares again. She released a loud sigh, of annoyance mingled with sorrow.

"Why couldn't children be allowed to be children?" She thought of her happy days growing up on the mission station in Africa. Surrounded by her parents and lots of little siblings, the greatest dangers were from the various animals. But they had learned the necessary precautions, and her life had been pretty great.

Daniel microwaved popcorn, and Diana burst into tears. "They'll probably just throw it up! This isn't just a family movie night." She figured he meant well. She had tried to send Mallory to bed, but Daniel was insisting she view it, too. Diana tried to insist that her patient was too worn out after the full day's outing. Daniel had already summoned her back. The house had a movie theater which seated about twenty people, but Diana wanted to watch the gruesome images on one of the smaller TVs.

Daniel and Diana rarely disagreed, so the kids were already pretty upset by the time the video finally began rolling. Then, with their eyes riveted to the screen, they didn't speak a word until the film ended.

When it had turned off, Daniel began apologizing. "Sorry you had to see that, kids. Mr. Bransom insisted everyone make their kids watch it."

The images had scared Mallory half to death. She had been feeling sorry for herself about the trach tube and hospitalization. She couldn't remember what had prompted her to pick up the rock that had helped save her from Melville. Seeing the children and teens who hadn't survived their attacks, made her feel very grateful.

The three Faulkner children didn't say much, except now they could understand their mom and dad's extreme preoccupation for their safety. They had all snuggled a little closer.

They were all ready for a bedtime snack, in spite of the video images. The children prepared for bed.

Suddenly energized, Diana ordered the snacks served in her design studio. They all joined in a bedtime prayer, asking for safety through the night, and for America to be safer again. They prayed not to have bad dreams. Alexandra and Jeremiah, in their sleeping bags, had sacked out on the two leather sofas in the studio. Cassandra was curled up in an oversize recliner.

Diana was showing Mallory some really amazing and cute designs she was working on. She was an unbelievable sketch artist, so any creative thought that went through her mind, exited through her hand.

"You're amazing that you're scientific enough to be a nurse and so artistic, too," Mallory noted. She was rifling through a portfolio, and the picture Diana had taken of the sparrows captured her attention. There were a number of different coordinate possibilities. One featured a brilliant sky-blue silk sweater, showing the power line stretched from the shoulder on the left, to the waist on the right. In the middle, were the four sparrows. The one with the "cutest" face was right in the center. The rest of the outfit featured a brown leather, slim skirt with matching three-quarter jacket. The sleeves were trimmed in fur in one illustration, and plain in another. A leather "hobo" handbag matched the sky- blue of the blouse. Brown boots were featured, or alternately, dark chocolate brown shoes with the slightest touches of blue trim.

"Is it going to have diamonds on it, anyplace?" Mallory asked her. "I love the one you wore with diamonds on the 'Evening Star' and on 'The Milky Way'."

Diana frowned at her drawings. "Hadn't thought about diamonds. Where would you put them?" she asked.

"I don't know; you're the designer," Mallory was suddenly timid.

"But you're the diamond person," Diana responded. "Tell me what you were thinking."

"Well, maybe a black or brown diamond for the eye of the cute little guy in the middle. You think it might work?"

"I think it might," Diana grew more enthusiastic than ever.

Another set of drawings showed a sky-blue, fine-gauge, v-neck sweater with a matching blue wool jacket, and a chocolate and blue plaid skirt. The outfit featured the "sparrows" on a matching silk scarf. Mallory suggested creating a "Sparrow" brooch, crafted in yellow gold, set with black and brown diamonds. Maybe the piece of jewelry could interchange to be worn as a slide on an Omega necklace, or as a pin. "He could perch on a little gold branch. How can we work in the '… of more value than many sparrows' motif?" she had wondered aloud.

Diana had spread out the sketches of the coordinating design ideas, and was surveying everything critically.

"Wish Daniel hadn't jumped the gun with the 'Sparrow' picture and his sermon. The fashion industry has to be so secretive. When he showed the picture and preached in that little church, he never thought about the entire thing being so accessed on the web site"

She laughed with amazement. "I mean, it's pretty neat! People are still emailing us or the church about getting saved, or being blessed because of it. There are already orders being placed for your pastor's books and pamphlets. But everyone who is familiar with my designs may jump on this before I can get the line out. Wish I could think of something else, too. Usually, I have inspiration to burn, but I'm stuck."

Mallory laughed. "I don't believe it; you're probably just tired. I know my deal has really placed demands on you. I'm really excited to have a passport. I always thought that would be something really cool to have. Are you sure we should do the trip so soon?"

"Absolutely! Mallory, the place looks captivating from east to west! I can't wait. If we don't go this spring, while I'm in my second trimester, I'm sure my doctor won't let me go until after the baby's born. Come on, help me think of something amazing for another fall line.

"Well, I've been thinking of some jewelry design ideas. Maybe they would look good with entire ensembles in the same theme."

"Don't hold out on me with ideas!" Diana laughed, and Cassandra sat up sleepily to glare at her.

"Okay, but if you don't like it, be sure to say so." Mallie was pretty sure she wouldn't have that much to contribute. "You have that awesome Chess set in the family room. I was thinking it would be a great idea for a set of jewelry. A charm bracelet with a few Chessmen in white gold and yellow gold, to represent the opposing sides. There could be, like a pawn, a rook, a knight, a bishop, and a king and queen in both tones. The kings and queens could sparkle with diamond settings, or maybe rubies, or emeralds. It could make a cute outfit, too, though, don't you think? The skirt could be black and white wool checkerboard plaid. The blouse or sweater could have Chess pieces represented on it, again with diamonds set into the kings and queens. Then the jacket could be solid black or white. There could be other coordinating pieces of jewelry, too. I think charms are cute on handbags. Why don't you ever call them 'purses'?"

"People in the industry always use the term 'handbags'," Diana responded. "Mallory, that is a gorgeous idea!"

Diana's hand was flying. She sketched the skirt with the checkerboard plaid, representing various size squares for the best proportion. She drew a blouse and a fine gauge silk sweater, experimenting with different background colors, and various configurations of Chessmen spilling across. It was looking amazing, and Mallory's eyes danced with excitement, as her vision took form on the drawing board. Diana drew the proposed bracelet, then she went to work to create an exquisite necklace. The kids were all sound asleep, and Mallory was watching, fascinated, as beautiful pictures emerged on the sketch paper.

Daniel had been finishing up some business in his office, and an e-mail had come through, late. Surprised, he printed it.

"You girls planning to turn in any time soon?" he was asking from the studio doorway. "Where do you want me to relocate the kids to?"

"Put them on the sofas in our suite, Honey. They may still get scared. We're about to give it up, too. Did you get much done?"

He was gone, walking Alexandra up to the master suite. He carried Jeremiah, then Cassandra, kissing each head as he laid each child, sleeping bag and all, on the sofas and chaise lounge.

He had come back down, and was looking at his wife's designs. He had been watching the 'Sparrow' designs emerge; now, he noticed the beautiful 'Chessmen' motif. "That's amazing-looking, Honey," he complimented.

"Yeah, I like it! Mallory's idea! It's turning out great!"

"I promise not to put it out in a sermon," he laughed. "Looks like my sermon about the sparrows made its way to Africa. You're not going to believe the e-mail we just got!"

"Africa!" Diana had repeated blankly. "What do you mean?"

He presented the printout with a flourish. Diana read it, uncomprehendingly, then looked at her husband blankly.

He laughed. "That's what I thought when I first read it. I couldn't believe it, either!"

Diana's eyes filled with tears, and Mallory was instantly concerned that it was bad news; but then Daniel's response had seemed more amazed than sorrowful.

"It's from my dad," Diana was trying to explain through her tears. "He's been really mad at me, but he sent this e-mail to tell us we're doing a good job."

Mallory couldn't imagine how anyone could be mad at Diana. Surely, any father in the world would be proud of her. She could tell the message meant a lot to both of them, so she was happy it had come. She wanted to know the whole story, but it was late. They were so fascinating!

Mallory fell asleep quickly, and was amazed to awaken with the beautifully decorated room drenched in sunlight. She showered quickly and dressed in an outfit she had purchased at the Galleria in Houston the previous day. After applying her cosmetics, she ventured from her suite. She hadn't had her devotions yet, but she wanted to make sure her sleeping late hadn't interfered with any plans the Faulkners had.

She tiptoed silently through an amazing array of rooms. There was a beautiful music room, housing a baby grand piano, among other instruments. French doors opened from it, into an indoor pool enclosure.

She could tell her host family was enjoying breakfast beside the pool. Suddenly shy, she had hastened back to the guest suite. She was finishing reading her Bible chapters when Diana came looking for her.

"There you are, Mallory," she announced. "Do you want to come eat some breakfast?"

Daniel had left to oversee the continuing staff security training, and the three children had begun their school day with their tutor. Diana joined Mallory at the poolside breakfast table. Mallie was trying a plate of scrambled eggs, and Diana was enjoying another cup of coffee.

"You look cute this morning," Diana complimented. "Clothes off the rack fit you like they're made for you. The plan today is to get you back to Dallas. I'm fairly certain the doctor plans to remove the tube today. Then, you can go home. Security is back in place, with a team of people that Erik has known over the years. Will you be okay being there by yourself?"

"The plan sounds great to me," Mallie acknowledged. It had only been a week since she had taken off for the nail salon. She was relieved to be going home; it had been a long week.

Late Tuesday afternoon, Mallory arrived home to be greeted by her dog. Tears flowed down her face as she walked through her elegant home once more. She was finally beginning to realize that it was hers. It was so beautiful that she had felt like it must be Daniel and Diana's. Now, with her trip to their home in Tulsa, the reality was dawning on her. This was her house! Bought for her by her daddy! It was as surely in her name, as the car registration had been! She checked the garage; the car was back in its place, almost as if she had never left in it.

Sitting down at the beautiful new baby grand piano in her own music room, she began to play hymn after hymn. It felt good. The doctor had removed the annoying tube from her throat, but her attempts at singing were not the best. She was still supposed to take it easy with her voice. She played the piano for another fifteen minutes. Then, she got her Bible and took it out beside the swimming pool. The late afternoon air felt soft and warm. She loved the mingled fragrances of the cut grass, the flowers, and the faint Chlorine from the pool. Dinky lay beside her, and she scratched his head affectionately. Her Bible lay open, but her gaze was on the aqua shimmers of the pool, and the antics of a couple of birds. She felt happy just to be alive, just to sit here in silence, absorbing the beauty. Her thoughts returned to David Anderson. He was hard for her not to think about. She laughed aloud at his farewell to her; not to have any more medical crises, just so she could see him sooner.

The air had begun to cool, and the sky had deepened into twilight. She rose and made her way inside. She turned on the plasma television in the game room, just in time to watch a Red Sox game. She texted her cousin to ask if he were watching, and he texted back almost immediately. They texted back and forth after each score, or error, and when Boston won!

Almost before she realized she was hungry, a sausage pizza and diet Coke had been wheeled in on a sports-motif serving cart. Dinky had come to life when the tantalizing aroma filled the room. Laughing, she shared it with him.

"You know, Dinky, we could become very spoiled," she warned, wagging her index finger at him.

Chapter 12

TRACT

A BRIGHT GOLDEN SUN was pushing its way up the eastern horizon when Mallory wakened on Wednesday morning. She felt alive and renewed. Stretching luxuriously, she sat up to survey the elegant appointments in her bedroom suite. She felt like she was home. Her daddy's picture smiled at her from a bedside table, and his last letter to her was matted and framed. She had it memorized. She thought about how agonizingly worried she had been about everything. Now, she realized how silly it had all been. God always blessed obedience. This surpassed anything she had ever imagined.

She called for coffee, juice, and toast, and opened her Bible. She read Proverbs 25 first, and then turned to the book of Acts in the New Testament. She was paying particular attention to references to New Testament locales that were now located in Turkey. She was excited about the upcoming trip, but she had a lot to accomplish before the departure date. She ate the toast while she finished reading and praying through her journal. She showered and dressed quickly in the navy suit with the white blouse. She grabbed the metallic copper heels and handbag and headed toward the garage. She had been relieved to see security staff stationed around the house and grounds, and her dog was at her side. She felt guilty about not making her own bed; then laughed to herself that she could get over it.

She set the guidance to direct her to her office, and prayed for help driving in traffic. Pulling into her reserved space in the parking garage, she hurried to the elevator with her special security key in hand. The elevator whisked her to the DiaMo Corporation penthouse offices, and she was humming as she stepped into the suite. She spoke a cheery "Good morning," to the staff who seemed less than pleased to see her, and even less pleased to see Dinky, and moved swiftly to the large corner office. Settling into the huge chair behind the polished desk, she buzzed the intercom for coffee. She frowned thoughtfully at the Styrofoam cup that appeared. "Find me some China patterns to choose from, let's get some real cups." It was an order, pleasantly presented.

"Well then, there'll be dishes to wash," the woman protested. Mallory nodded, "by early afternoon, so I can decide before I leave. We can get the order placed today."

She was trying to get into the pass-worded computer, and neither "Irish Spud" nor "Tater Tot" had worked. "What was my dad's pass-word? Do you know?" she had questioned the woman who hadn't yet moved to go look for China.

She said she didn't know; she didn't think anyone did. Patrick was always secretive. She wasn't telling the girl anything she didn't already know. "Call someone to get a new computer set up, who can get my dad's files installed in it." Her voice was pleasant, but authoritative.

"Well, what do you want me to do? Get China or a computer?"

Mallory was a little amazed, but she laughed. "Why don't you do both? It's called multi-tasking. It's a new buzz word. If you get right on it, I'm sure you'll manage."

She swung the chair around to let the woman know she was dismissed. She had noticed the polished wooden "In" and "Out" boxes on the credenza on her first two visits to the office. The "In" box was overflowing, so she placed the stack on the desk in front of her and began reading through all the items of business. One contract for one of her father's inventions from a sporting goods company, had directions that it needed her signature by Wednesday, April 25. She signed it and called Kerry Larson's law office to ask where it needed to go. She was amazed that the law firm was in the same building, on the opposite corner. Kerry's assistant had told her to send anyone over with it. She dispatched one of the other receptionists, and was involved with another set of documents when the receptionist told her Kerry Larson was on line one.

"This is Mallory," she answered as she picked up.

"Mallory, wow in the office! Good thing! I had no idea this contract was just sitting over there. How long are you going to be in?"

"I don't know. There's a mountain of paper here; and I'm not sure what to make of any of it."

"I have a deposition at one, but if you can meet me for lunch early, I'll look over some of the other stuff you have. Will eleven work?"

"I-I guess," she hesitated. She didn't want David or Tammi mad at her, but she didn't know the first thing about most of the paperwork. "Where?"

"There's a café down in the Mezzanine. The food's not the best or the worst, but it's convenient. They have good soup, salad, and sandwiches."

"Eleven," Mallory confirmed crisply and cradled the receiver. Puzzled, she returned her attention to the computer and tried "Suziecue". It worked. She probably still wanted a new computer with her dad's files installed, but now she could comb through his files. She thought she might find records of where he still had diamonds hidden, but nothing was obvious to a casual observer. It suddenly occurred to her that she should ask Mr. Faulkner who he trusted to have access to valuable files. She buzzed the receptionist to change her orders slightly. She instructed the receptionist to call Mr. Faulkner at GeoHy in Tulsa for information about the best system and technicians for the set up.

Mallory could tell she was meeting with resistance from her office staff, so she scheduled a meeting with everybody for one o'clock.

Within thirty minutes the receptionist was announcing that Mr. Faulkner was on line one to talk to her about the system and the techs.

"Mallory," she answered as she picked up.

"Morning, Mallory." Faulkner greeted. "Kerry said you were in the office. He said that contract was about to expire, and he didn't know if he would have been able to revive the deal, had it lapsed. Good eye. I can send a guy down tomorrow to get your system updated and customized for you. The good news is, I'll have your school curriculum ready, too!"

"Oh! Yea!" Mallory laughed good naturedly. "Tell me there's no geometry, please!"

"Well, there is! You're nearly done with it! Another month! Call Di if you get stuck! She's the genius! Turkey trip is looking good. We secured another tract of land for the ministry to expand for the Andersons." He was catching her up, and it was all exciting.

"Where will that be?" she asked. The original plan had been for the ministry buildings to be adjacent to the pastor's new home. With the expanded plans for the home, the one piece of property would have been tight. The group had also questioned how the Anderson family's privacy would be affected with the home and headquarters being adjacent. So, there had been a search on for an additional tract of land. She figured it should be south of Murfreesboro, toward Hope.

"Right next door to the church, that field to the west. The creek cuts through it, but it runs along the back, so there are about seven acres to build on in front. You know where I mean?"

"I do; I'm not sure it's a good location. Is the deal closed? Who's buying it? The Anderson's corporation or DiaMo?"

Faulkner was perplexed that she had an opinion. If John Anderson thought it was a good site, and he thought so, who was she to disagree? One morning in the office was turning her into a dragon lady?

"I can't say what's wrong with it, here in the office, over the phone. I'm meeting Mr. Larson for lunch at eleven. I'll tell him why it's a bad location, and he can tell you in better confidence. What else is new, that I should know about? Anything about the missing people or Mr. Melville?"

"Not that I've heard. Can you give me a hint why that piece of property isn't the best choice?"

"Not unless you care to join us for lunch!"

"Wish I could; guess I have no choice but to wait and hear from Kerry.! Your school work will be set up so you can work on it from home or the office. Your helipad should be operational by the end of next week. Then, you won't have to fight traffic to and from the office, unless the wind is too strong for the choppers. Diana just said for me to tell you not to get too tired."

Mallory laughed. "Oops; I've probably already talked too much today, and I still have a couple of meetings scheduled."

She spent the remaining time before the lunch meeting sorting out which "In-box" items seemed the most pressing. There was an attache case by her knees under the desk. She pulled it out, thinking it would be ideal for transporting the paper work to the lunch meeting. It contained several files, and she glanced at them quickly, then deposited the other papers in next to them.

She left the DiaMo suite to catch a public elevator to the mezzanine. Larson had gotten a table, and had already drained a glass of iced tea when she entered. Most people were going through a line, but someone came to the table to take their orders. She ordered hot tea and Minestrone soup, not really having a clue what it was. Luckily, it tasted delicious, and the warmth felt good to her throat.

She thought the cafe seemed a little expensive, but cute. She could hardly believe she worked in an office building; a CEO. While she was casing the joint, people were surveying her with a great deal of interest, too.

Larson was enjoying being part of the center of attention. A few of the guys he knew from the building were teasing him. "Hey, Larson, why don't you introduce me to your friend?"

When the food was served, and the staff had withdrawn, Kerry had leaned in towards her to ask what was wrong with the property. Mallory was slightly annoyed; she had been trying to get Daniel Faulkner to drop the subject until she could talk to someone without arousing the curiosity of the whole world!

Her eyes flashed a warning to the attorney sitting across the table. "Who's buying it?"

"Why does it matter?" he was really perplexed. He wasn't sure whether he was glad she was stepping in, or not.

"Well, if DiaMo is buying it for diamond mining purposes, it's a good thing. But, if-did the Andersons come up with a name for their non-profit corporation yet?-if the ministry is buying it to build their headquarters, it's a bad site for that. There are diamonds there." She was whispering as softly as she could, but she still felt like every table in the little café had fallen silent.

"How do you know?" Kerry questioned in amazement.

"I used to find them there all the time. My dad always told me they weren't really diamonds, but when I took some home from that property, he made me take them back. No one lived there, so I just threw them back in the stream."

Kerry Larson was speechless.

So, if our diamond company buys it, there are nice stones there," she continued. "If the ministry builds there, and there ever really is a bona fide diamond rush in Arkansas, people will just tear everything down that gets in the way."

Larson was amazed. It was DiaMo that was funding all the money into the non-profit corporation, so he had thought it was semantics when she had been asking who was actually purchasing the property. As an attorney, he realized she was right.

"Do we need another shareholders' meeting to decide what to do?" she asked. "Is the land already bought? Or has earnest money been put down? There has been a tract with about twenty acres for sale on 27 south of town, toward Hope. Maybe Pastor Anderson could look at it if it's still on the market."

"Sit tight, I need to go call Daniel on my land line. I'll be right back, and we can take a look at some of the rest of this stuff."

Faulkner was still in his office; Larson didn't want to risk the conversation on cell phones.

"What's the deal?" he asked immediately when he answered his private line. Larson explained it quickly. "How can she be so sure?" Daniel had demanded of the attorney.

"I don't know! Patrick said she could always find 'em," Kerry replied.

"I'll set up a shareholders' meeting at Hal's lodge!" Faulkner ended the conversation and gave his administrative assistant the job of contacting Hal and the shareholders.

Larson returned to the lunch, then ended up taking some of the paper work with him; some of it, he instructed her to have shredded. The rest, he gave instructions for the receptionists to file. Mallory was relieved.

Back in her office at one, she had assembled the office staff to basically inform them that she would be around, and she would have the oversight of everything her dad had worked for. She gave a brief overview of her expectations. Honesty, timeliness, pleasantness, and diligence. She asked to view the personnel files and a copy of the benefit package overview. Loading that information into the attache, she was ready to leave for the day. At the front reception area, she paused to look over the different patterns for China. She asked for input from the others, and they agreed on an attractive pattern that complimented the décor of the office suite.

Marge was already placing an on-line order by the time Mallory stepped into the private elevator to descend to her car.

As she battled her way onto the toll way, she was realizing her guardian had a good point about spending pointless time in traffic. She had planned to go home before heading back out for church. Realizing that would leave her no time, she headed south instead of north. Two or three exits up, and she was at the Galleria.

She waited in the car in the Macy's garage until a maroon Suburban pulled into a space a couple of spaces away. She left Dinky in the car and entered the gleaming department store with her security detail a discreet distance behind her.

It was four o'clock, and she wandered around the expansive store for awhile. She had selected a few items that looked nice. She decided to purchase them and try them on at home. As she sauntered out into the mall, her cell phone rang. It was Tammi.

She answered it, hoping Tammi hadn't already heard about her lunch meeting. No such luck! Her friend was livid. Mallory couldn't get her to listen to reason. She finally hung up. She texted, "I don't want to hear about it from you, every time I have to talk to him."

Tammi texted that she would tell David.

Mallory didn't care; David was a lot more mature than his sister, she hoped.

Having ordered a coffee beverage, she had sunk down at a little table to sip at it. She was watching people ice skate on the rink three tiers below. She texted Shay, and he called her. They yacked for a few minutes; she was telling him about the office staff and their resistance. He thought it sounded like she handled it pretty well. He already knew about the shareholders' meeting in Arkansas for Friday night, but he knew not to be too specific on the cell. It was an hour later in Boston, and he and Delia were getting ready to leave for church. Delia had grabbed the phone to tell her granddaughter, hello.

Mallory was planning to go to the church that Kerry attended, since she wasn't sure what to do about church. She had been a member at Faith Baptist in Murfreesboro since she was seven. She was actually dreading visiting a different church. She hurried to Nordstrom's and bought three really cute new pair of shoes. Then she hurried back to the parking garage and entered the church address into the car's guidance system.

She called Tammi back. "Can we talk?" she asked when her friend answered.

"I guess; what do you want to talk about? I told David you had a lunch date. He was not at all pleased."

"Tammi, you can be so annoying," Mallory sometimes wondered why she tried to be friends. "I went to my dad's office, and all this stuff had been piling up since before Christmas. Some of it was actually at critical timing. He's my attorney; my dad hired him. He knows stuff I don't. I'm going to his church tonight because I don't know any churches here. He's nice. I like him, but I'm not interested in him. I've told you that before." She didn't know why, but suddenly she knew David was right there, next to his sister. "Talk to you later," she ended the conversation hurriedly.

Diana Faulkner couldn't believe that DiaMo was purchasing another diamond mine in Murfreesboro. They still hadn't found the missing employees yet, from the previous fiasco. Still, she was amazed that Patrick had been right about Mallory's ability to spot the precious gems. She laughed at the story of Patrick's making his daughter throw back the stones she had found on the vacant property. It sounded like him.

She was working on her designs, adding to the choices that would be available for each line. She had designed a "Checkerboard" sleeveless dress with an ivory jacket printed with the elegant "Chessmen" motif. She was bringing out more detail, too, in the jewelry sketches. She still needed more ideas for additional groupings.

She studied her photos. Dinky was definitely cute, but he seemed to fit more into a children's line. She had never entered the children's apparel arena. She didn't know if she should attempt it. She decided it would be a decision to pray about.

She sketched an autumn outfit for Mallory. The girl was fun to design for. Tall and beautiful, she would look good in rags. The ensemble took form on paper. A sweeping trumpet skirt of supple leather with matching short jacket. The designer liked the lines and proportions. The color was rich, deep cinnamon. Mallory had a cute turtleneck sweater and shoes in the color already. Diana was smiling, thinking about the Wednesday night church service when Mallory had played the piano. She had such a natural talent for the instrument; but even with talent, it took discipline and commitment to excel. Diana's hand was skimming lightly across her drawing. She illustrated the costume with the chunky turtleneck, then alternately with an ivory finer gauge silk sweater with Dinky on the front. She had to manipulate the dog's color a little bit to match the suit, but he still looked like Dinky! Then, she took the "Sparrow" photo and manipulated the background sky to pale gray, rather than the vivid sky blue. The pale gray was lovely against the cinnamon. She played with the idea of adding a set of detachable silver fox collar and cuffs. It had a definite glamour-girl look. Thinking of their new emphasis on diamonds and jewelry, she began to capture those ideas on paper. She designed a convertible pin/pendant of the dog's face. She made him in gold with chocolate diamond eyes, and a sparkling diamond collar. Then, she fixed him in sterling silver, for a cute look on a more modest budget.

She put everything away and called her children from the playroom. It was time to eat and get ready for church. She was excited about being back in her home church. She listened to their AWANA verses, and they all loaded into one of the corporate Suburbans.

Faith Baptist was coming to life as the pastor's wife began playing the prelude. She was excited that a beautiful, new piano was scheduled to arrive the following day. The Bransoms had driven up from Hope, Ivan Summers and Janice Collins were there, and the two Forestry Service guys were all talking in the vestibule. Evidently a law enforcement pow-wow. Actually, Janice had stopped to check her hair in the big mirror, so then Summers was telling the others what Mallory had told Oscar Melville. That he had created his own problems, and he should come to church and look himself in the eye, in the big mirror.

Trent Morrison was the more mature Christian of the group, and he explained how Mallory had also been referencing the book of James, and checking yourself out by the Perfection of the Law.

They were also comparing notes about the abductions. Their evidence was coming together, but so slowly that it was agonizing. The bag of trash they had collected at the Pike campground was matching up. The criss-cross pattern tire-tread that had run across the flower bed at the Daisy Lodge matched the faint tread found at the Pike campground and, the mine acreage, and Mallory's driveway. The agents couldn't tell if the people they sought were using two similar vehicles, or if they had accomplished a fast paint job. They thought there were two vehicles, but they couldn't really prove it yet.

David and Tammi Anderson had evidently finished a sibling argument, and David had flopped down, annoyed, in a pew toward the back.

"These places saved, Cowboy?" Bransom questioned mischievously, as he sat down next to him.

"No, sir," the teen responded, polite from years of parental training, although Bransom could tell the kid was seething inwardly.

"You heard about another meeting scheduled for Friday night already?. These people call more meetings than the FBI does," Erik opened good-naturedly.

David laughed wryly, in spite of himself. "Yeah, guess there are some more items to 'revisit'." David's impersonation sounded exactly like Daniel Faulkner and some of his corporate buzzwords.

It was Erik's turn to laugh. "What were you and your sister fighting about?" he asked curiously.

"Nothing. She's just a crazy person."

"Yeah; that's how she struck me, too."

David knew the agent was baiting him, but he still liked the humorous agreement with his assessment. So he went on. "Okay, you know the rules that Mallie and I aren't supposed to talk, right?"

"Yeah," the agent admitted, somewhat noncommittally.

"Okay, so I'm trying to go along with everything. Tammi has lost what little mind she ever had, over Kerry Larson!"

That did amaze the agent, but he said nothing, so David continued.

"Well, she's always been insanely jealous of everything about Mallie. Now, she won't let it rest that she thinks the two of them are going to end up together. Today, Mallie met with him, I guess really about business. Tammi really gets on my nerves, anyway. Well, she's been extra-crazy all afternoon. Now, she's saying Mallie wants DiaMo to buy the property next door so she can have all the diamonds. Like, Mallory's trying to undercut our family out of something. No one's even supposed to know any thing about the property or diamonds, anyway, but she won't shut her mouth!"

Pastor Anderson was starting the service, so the agent had some time to mull the problem over. It really was a problem. He decided to pray about it. He didn't concentrate too much on the Bible Study. Keeping things quiet was really an important part of everything that was going on. He wondered if he could put some kind of bluff on the girl. He was surprised, too, because he had thought Tammi and Mallory were pretty close friends. Another instance of things not always being what they seem.

Mallory insisted on going to the teen age department for the Wednesday night service, even though her attorney had encouraged her to stick beside him and join the college/career group. She felt pretty shy, and she felt homesick for her church and friends, but all the kids were pretty nice to her. Some of them acted mad to be there, and some had excellent spirits about things. Mallie had asked if she could sit beside a quiet-acting girl sitting alone. Her name was Callie Cline. She was new, too. Mallory felt drawn to her. They had visited a few minutes before a guy named Mac had stood up to make some announcements. He was the youth group president, and he was real cute and funny. He seemed to be a cut above the rest; loving the Lord and life! His enthusiasm was contagious. A couple of kids moaned to a couple of guitars. When the song ended he thanked them for trying. Mallie thought he was so funny that she had dissolved into uncontrollable giggles. Her new friend had begun to shake, trying not to laugh. Eventually, the entire group fell apart, and Mac was insisting there was no such thing as a "Laughing Revival". Finally, everyone regained their composure and the Youth Pastor gave a really interesting Bible Study. There was pizza and pop, and Mallie realized she was delighted to linger. By the time she returned to the foyer, nearly everyone had dispersed. She and Callie walked to the parking lot together. They had already exchanged phone numbers. Callie had noticed the men watching them from the dark SUV, but Mallie assured her they were her security, and they were safe.

She turned the music up on the car stereo, and headed back toward the toll way. She liked the church and the people. But she missed her daddy and David. Tears were once more trying to escape.

Chapter 13

TRIANGLE

On the drive from Murfreesboro back to Hope, Erik Bransom drove in silence.

"What were you and David saying before church started?" Suzanne finally attempted to break the silence.

He looked over at her, winked, and gave her knee an affectionate pat. "He was fighting with his sister."

"Oh, those two," Suzanne sighed. "What now?"

"You ever around them much?" Erik questioned curiously.

"What, David and Tammi? I never could get rid of them. Lana always sent them both over to play. She kept having kids, so she always had whining and fighting to listen to. I just had Mallie, but I still had to listen to her two fight and whine at my house."

Bransom wasn't sure why he thought it was all so interesting. "What did they always fight about?"

"I don't remember. What didn't they fight about? Well, the main thing was over Mallie. They always fought about which of them she liked best. You know the old saying, 'Two's company; three's a crowd'? That was always the basis of the problem. Mallory and David were friends from the day the Andersons moved here. They would play for hours on end, with never a cross word. I never minded having David over. They always played nice together. David was always real polite.

Patrick liked him, too. Then here would come Tammi! Nobody to play with! So she'd come start trying to boss them both around and make them play what she wanted. Then she'd cry and pout and get David and Mallory both in trouble with her dad. Then she would whine to me about whatever Mallory was doing. I'd just tell her to go home. She still annoys me."

Bransom's laugh boomed in the car's small interior. He could imagine Suzanne really could tell a kid to get lost. He had noticed how blind the pastor seemed to be about his oldest daughter. Evidently, that wasn't a recent development.

"What was the fight about tonight?" Suzanne questioned, suddenly curious. Bransom hadn't told her yet, about the shareholders' meeting on Friday night or about the fact that Mallory had told them there were diamonds on the tract of land which had been proposed for the ministry's expansion. When he filled her in about that, he finished by telling her Tammi thought Mallory just wanted all the diamonds in Pike County for herself. Not the wisest thing to say to a mother!

Suzanne went ballistic!

Erik didn't blame his wife for being mad; and she was so cute! He listened to more about the history that had contributed to the present circumstances.

Finally, she had paused for breath, and he asked her if he could ask about something he had been wondering about.

She was surprised, and suddenly nervous about what it might be. "Well, yeah, sure, go ahead," she acquiesced.

"Well, you said what good friends David and Mallory always were and how well they got along."

"Yeah," she agreed.

"Well, have you agreed with trying to keep them apart?" the question had burst forth, and he wasn't sure he had a right to ask it.

Tears welled up in her beautiful blue eyes. "I suggested once, that they could probably really be happy if they married right after their senior year. That's why Patrick devised this whole elaborate scheme, I guess. Well, it's out of my hands now. I was shocked, too, when David did his rebellious thing. I'm glad he's doing better now. I think Tammi's every bit as rebellious as David was, but she's sneakier. I always thought David and Mallory were right for each other. If it's the Lord's will for them to be together, the separation times might strengthen their love. I like the Faulkners and everybody. I feel a little jealous of Diana's mothering Mallie so much; she has three kids of her own dying for her touch."

They fell silent once more.

Chapter 14

TRIALS

MALLORY PULLED INTO the garage and lowered the garage door before she sprang out of the car. With Dinky at her side, she entered the cavernous kitchen and moved toward the French doors of the formal living room. She let the dog out, and stepped out into the cool night, herself. A brisk breeze ruffled her hair and stirred the fragrance of the flowers. Enchanted, she sank down at one of the patio tables. The bright umbrellas were folded closed and secured. Soft night sounds enfolded her. She didn't like crickets, per se, but she was enjoying the symphony of nature. It reminded her of picnics with her dad. The sun would go down, and they would make S'mores over dying embers. The twilight music would be at full volume by the time they would load into the car to head for home. Finally, she broke the spell and stepped back inside.

Going down into the game room, she picked up a cue stick and took a jab at the balls arranged on the billiard table. She mostly missed, and the balls barely moved. She laughed at herself and returned the stick to its place.

She opened the attache case and glanced hastily over the personnel files. The employees seemed to have pretty good benefits. She thought she might check with Kerry about the fairness of the pay scale. Then, remembering Tammi's ire, and her telling David, she decided that was a bad idea. Maybe she could just mention it to either Daniel or Diana at the meeting on Friday. Besides, if people wanted raises, they could work better with happier attitudes.

She drank a bottle of apple juice and headed to bed. She was placing her toothbrush in its holder when her cell rang. It was her mom. They talked for just a few minutes, but Mallory was really happy she had called. Her mom could be hard for her to read. Her mom told her a few funny stories about David and Tammi and her when they were little. A couple of them, Mallie had heard before, but a couple of them were cute and funny about incidents she didn't remember. Laughing, she was thinking the three of them hadn't really changed, except to grow bigger.

She knelt beside her bed and thanked the Lord for the day, and that she liked the new church and had met some new friends. After asking for safety and protection for the night, she melted into her heavenly mattress and fell fast asleep.

She had only slept for a couple of hours when she was gripped by a nightmare. She was on an oppressively steamy school bus beside Martin Thomas! She was trying to fight free, but a toothless Pops was laughing maniacally. Every time she would get Martin's hands off of her, the school bus would lurch and throw her back into his arms. She finally fought her way back to reality from the shadowy dream world. Her entire body was soaked with perspiration, and tears were streaming down her face. She could smell Martin's disgusting breath and had been unable to take her gaze from his homely mouth. He was grinning at her sickeningly, and saying. "Filthy rich and sittin purty; marry me!" over and over again.

She launched herself from the snowy linen bed, as if the apparition still lingered there. Still shaking, she made her way to one of the sofas in the day area. She glanced around for her Bible. The dream had been so real, that now she thought she might get sick. She sat and gasped for air. She couldn't remember where her Bible was. She was afraid it was still at the church. She tried to think of some verses to quote to herself, to dispel the palpable evil. She turned on all the lights; then suddenly was terrified that he was outside and could see in. Turning off the lights, she was deriding herself for being silly. It suddenly occurred to her to wonder where Dinky was.

"Dinky!" her whisper was soft and urgent. "Dinky! Come here, boy!"

Her cell phone rang and vibrated on the night stand. The number was Erik Bransom's. She answered. The phone had finally wakened her snoozing dog, and he had slunk guiltily off the chaise lounge. Mallie was still torn between whether to call her mother's new husband, "Mr. Bransom or Erik." Not using either, she had answered with, "Hey, whazzup?"

"Just making sure you're okay." His raspy voice sounded reassuring. "Your security team noticed all your lights go on and then off again. They called me to ask what to do. If everything is okay, turn one lamp on and then off again. If your windows just stay dark, they'll know you're under duress."

Mallie reached for the lamp and gave the signal. "I'm not under duress. I just had an awful nightmare. I didn't mean to send out an alarm."

"It's okay, Mallie, just being sure. We do need to work out a system of signals and code words. You think you can sleep now?"

"I'm not sure about that. I dreamed about the school bus ride with Martin Thomas that last Monday morning before he got arrested. He's still in jail; isn't he? He really creeps me out."

"He is. I forgot you were on the bus with him that morning. David said the guy was whispering stuff in your ear. I should have asked you before this, what he was saying."

The girl hesitated momentarily before answering. "That's why I'm kind of glad someone woke you up in the middle of the night. We have thought that Melville didn't know anything about diamonds being on the property, but he knew something. He wasn't really just trying to buy a little retirement house and garden, cheap."

Bransom's assessment from early in the case had been that Melville really only wanted the little derelict piece of property. "What did Martin say to you that morning?" he asked again.

"He told me, and I quote, 'I hear yer daddy left you filthy rich and sittin' purty. Will you marry me?' I don't know how Martin would have known that. I didn't know it yet. Melville must have found some stuff out and told him. They both know more than they have admitted to."

Bransom was surprised by the new information. He instructed Mallory to try to get some more sleep, although he was now wide awake. Telling her to be sure to call if she needed anything, he disconnected.

Getting up, he assembled a number of files. Oscar Melville, Martin Thomas, Merrill Adams, Ryland and Shannon O'Shaughnessy, Lawrence Freeman, the pawn shop owner, and the guy who had been arrested after he had attempted to rob Mallory's stunning diamond ring from Suzanne. He also had a stack of people that he had been able to determine were behind the sudden offer on the O'Shaughnessy property. He hoped he wasn't violating his promise to his superiors by staring at pieces of paper.

He brewed a pot of coffee and prayed for wisdom to fit pieces of the puzzle together. He rubbed his hands up and down his face and read all the way through Melville's file once again He had ordered the file to have its blanks filled in, but to his amazement, it was still sketchy, at best. Maybe Melville wasn't who he was claiming to be! He simply lacked a cohesive background! Bransom's first order of business for the upcoming day was going to be visits with the former Pike County Sheriff and his cohort, Martin Thomas. He was suddenly sure their connection went deeper than he had thought.

He wrote down Mallory's quote of his repulsive suspect's words to her on the school bus.

"I hear yer daddy left you filthy rich and sittin' purty! Will you marry me?"

It made him want to go punch the crazy freak in his big, fat, hollering mouth. "Who would the social misfit be hearing gossip like that from?" Bransom wondered aloud. He had to admit Mallory must be right.

Patrick O'Shaughnessy had used Melville and his law office contacts to keep himself in the loop about what his gangster brother, Ryland, was up to. Evidently, the sheriff knew more about the secretive little Irishman's business than anyone had been aware of. So, Melville had brought accusations that Mallie had murdered her dad; why? Of course, he had only harangued her mercilessly; he didn't have evidence that there was anything but "natural causes" for the man's death.

The agent had a couple of questions nagging at his mind. He wished he had thought of them earlier before he had disconnected with the girl. It was two o'clock, but he called her cell anyway. He needed to know if the Martin kid had ever seemed to be in love with her. He also wanted to know more about what Melville had said specifically when he had accused Mallory of having something to do with Patrick's death.

Mallory had turned the TV on and pulled Dinky close. She wasn't even surprised when the agent called her back.

"Sorry your sleep got this interrupted," she answered apologizing.

Bransom told her about the gaps in information about Melville and asked if she was aware of anything particular in the man's background

Her laughter had rippled. "Just that he had to be called 'Sheriff Melville'. He hated being called Oscar. If it was an alias, why wouldn't he make up a name he liked better? I would."

"Um, I don't know. Maybe he's more clever than we've been giving him credit for. When he kept talking about your father's being murdered, did he say why he thought it could be a murder?" Bransom knew this was a very tender spot with the bereft girl.

When she hesitated; he hoped he wasn't making her cry again.

"No, I don't know. It was all such a nightmare. He told me there are chemicals I could have given my dad to make his death look like his heart gave out. With his documented heart trouble, I would be able to get away with it. Then my dad wouldn't be able to keep me apart from David. I guess that's about the gist of what he was saying. He told me I would have learned something about Potassium or something in Chemistry, but I haven't taken Chemistry yet."

"If you can think of anything else about Melville, let me know. Your mom told me he kept offering to buy your property. We can't find that he had any money, even for that. Do you know if he was a fisherman or hunter? Did he camp out, or anything that you know of? Was Martin Thomas in love with you? We found a wall in his room with lots of pictures of you. We don't know if he was obsessed with you, or if someone was trying to make it look like he was. Tell me what you know about him."

"I don't think he liked me at all. We used to invite him to church and VBS and stuff, but he never wanted to come. Of course, we didn't really like him, so I'm pretty sure we were glad he didn't come. He didn't like Christians. He was a bully, so sometimes I'd tell him to pick on someone his size. He never liked that much. I'm pretty sure someone told him my dad had an inheritance for me and told him to propose. But nothing really makes sense to me. I don't think the sheriff did too much outdoors stuff. He seemed kind of wimpy, don't you think? I guess he just rode around all the time. My dad once said that he'd like to see his mileage records. You know, how much was legitimate for the county and how much was just cruising 'cause he didn't have a life. And he was always real snoopy, not just about criminal stuff, but what everyone was doing."

Bransom was amazed. "Whoa, hold up a second. Did your dad just kind of confide that to you, or do you think the sheriff knew your dad was talking about asking for an audit of some of the county stuff?"

"You know, sometimes daddy was pretty vocal; especially at church. I think when David finally sent the e-mail to the FBI, it was based on a lot of the stuff my dad said that didn't add up about Mr. Melville."

Bransom had pulled out the O'Shaughnessy autopsy report. It was pretty mundane looking. The ME had ruled "natural death", but no tox screen had been performed. Now, the agent was seriously considering the possibility of foul play in the man's death. If Melville was abusing his office, and wasting county dollars, Patrick O'Shaughnessy would have definitely been a threat. Obviously, Melville had found out about the diamonds, too. More than enough motive for murder--- especially in view of the fact that, these days, people seemed to require less and less of a good reason for killing one another.

"Okay, Mallory, this is a real eye-opener."

She laughed. "Yeah, it is! Too bad it's the middle of the night."

Bransom laughed, too. "I hope you still get some sleep. This probably won't help you sleep, but you need to know about it. I'm ordering a new autopsy with a tox screen. It sounds like Melville was trying to get you ready to take a murder rap, just in case a tox screen showed up an anomaly."

He could tell his revelation had stunned her. "I may call you back," he informed her.

He placed a call to the detention center in Little Rock, to check on the status of Martin Thomas. He was informed that the kid had become violently ill and been transferred, still heavily guarded, to the hospital.

The information shocked the seasoned agent. It sounded like Martin was being transferred directly to where Melville was still recovering from his head trauma injuries. He called the Little Rock FBI office and alerted everyone to the situation. They had pretty much discounted Melville as a small town, slightly dishonest ex-lawman. His security had only improved slightly when he was moved from the Murfreesboro hospital to Little Rock. Bransom figured the two had to have devised some kind of a plan to get together and escape. They wouldn't care what they had to do in order to gain their freedom. The Little Rock office dispatched a task force which reached the hospital just as Thomas was being admitted. Immediately, the conspirators were separated and returned under extra security, to jail cells.

The fact that the escape plan had been thwarted was hardly a comfort to the agency. If Bransom hadn't gotten the call from Mallory's staff in the middle of the night, the two probably would have succeeded in escaping!

When Erik Bransom notified Daniel Faulkner and John Anderson of the escape plan, he could tell they were nervous, too. All their efforts at safety for Mallie seemed to be failing. Faulkner knew life was made up of one trial after another, but he had whispered to the Lord that he wished he could pass this trial and move on to something else. Then he had laughingly admitted to the Lord that maybe that wasn't a very smart prayer. He thanked the Lord that the "escape" scheme had failed, and petitioned Him for wisdom and continued safety for everyone.

Bransom ordered that no privileges or change of routine be granted the two alleged felons. Anything was to be regarded as suspect. He reinterrogated them both on Thursday morning. He informed Melville about the decision to repeat the autopsy on Patrick O'Shaughnessy, including a toxicology screen.

The man didn't flinch. He informed Bransom that he had wanted that done all along.

Bransom had Melville's written orders in the case. He was lying; he seemed to have been hurrying for a closure of the case with the 'natural death' finding. He asked the former sheriff when he had been aware of Patrick's immense wealth that Patrick was trying to subterfuge with the appearance of poverty.

Melville insisted he didn't know anything about any wealth or any diamonds!

Bransom then readdressed the subject of Martin Thomas's truck. He asked Melville again, how he could have been in the truck without noticing the blood, which had even transferred onto his clothing.

He said his "worker" was just messy, and he didn't know what all the mess was. He said he had never driven the truck or tried to hide it. He claimed to have grabbed Mallory by the throat in self defense. Bransom asked him about all the gaps in his life; where he was born, where he went to school, what law enforcement experience he had prior to Pike County. He claimed not to know about all the pictures of Mallory in Martin's room, even though the various pictures had all been found on his computer, and his fingerprints were on Martin's wall and on the photos in question.

David stayed in Murfreesboro for Wednesday night's service at his dad's church. His sister had been trying to get him involved with her fight with Mallory about Kerry Larson. He felt miserable enough about the entire situation, without his sister drumming at him constantly. He spent the night at his mom and dad's house so he could be at Murfreesboro High early in the morning. Mr. Haynes had some final exams ready, and David was supposed to go to the study hall so that Miss Richmond could monitor him. He felt ready for the tests, but at breakfast, his dad had told him that Martin and Melville had practically pulled off an escape from Federal custody.

Now he sat in the study hall, perplexed. How could such goons manage that? His gaze wandered to the window, and the study hall teacher made a threatening, revolting sound in her throat. Like "Ahem!" but worse.

"I'm waiting for my sky-writer guy to fly by with the answers," he explained mischievously.

She stomped over and huffily closed all the blinds. "Better watch yourself, Mr. Anderson," she hissed at him.

"Yes, ma'am," he mumbled, trying to neither laugh at her nor show his annoyance. "I'm done with this one."

She snatched it and brought him another one, smacking it down on the desk in front of him.

He managed to tell her thank you in a fairly civil voice. He finished the Geometry and began the Calculus one. He liked math, and he whipped through the lengthy test with ease. That seemed to make her madder than ever. He had always thought it was fun to make fun of her with his friends. Now, he was just ready to graduate and get away. Especially since Mallory was gone.

Tears had begun to sting his eyes. He was trying not to be overwhelmed by the separation. That was bad enough. But then he had to listen to his sister's nutty obsession. On top of that, the danger persisted. He wished he could write her a letter. Just to tell her he missed her and was praying for her. He thought of all the times she had told him she wished he would write her notes.(He had found the few he had written to her over the years, tied in a ribbon, on the little dresser in her room in the little house.) He had seldom slowed down to do it. Now that the opportunity was gone, he regretted it deeply. "If you love somebody, let them know." Maybe if he had told her more, her heart would be better protected now, from guys like Larson. He sighed and took the second exam up to the monitor's desk. She glared nastily and gave him his English exam.

English drove him nuts; not because he "didn't get it", but because he had "gotten it" the first time, in second grade. The eight parts of speech hadn't changed much. The lit. part was harder; he was taking both American and English lit. in order to graduate a year early. The American authors, he found fun and entertaining-for the most part. He thought the English lit. was a little dull. Beowulf, Chaucer, Milton, Shakespeare! He had enjoyed Milton, but that wasn't the kind of thing you confessed to openly. He had cracked his family up acting out Macbeth, playing all of the parts, including, and especially, the old crones.

He finished the test and turned it in. Miss Richmond told him to go open the blinds back up. He did so, acting like he was waving good-bye to the sky-writer! Then he couldn't resist asking Miss Richmond if he could change some of his answers.

He escaped the musty building and sprinted to his truck, grabbing his phone to check for messages. He had missed calls from Shay and Bransom. He called the federal agent first, but the call went straight to voice mail. He tried Shay.

"Hey, Dave," Shay answered immediately. No one called David, "Dave". He didn't know why; they just never had. It didn't seem like his name.

"Shay, I saw I missed your call. What's happenin'?"

"Usual stuff; what about there? Who was at church last night? Were those two Forestry Service guys back?"

"Yeah, matter of fact. Guess they haven't found any of the guys yet. Did you hear that Martin and Melville almost got away from the Feds?"

There was a shocked silence. "No, how did that happen?" Shay finally responded.

David filled him in. "I better give Mallie a call then," Shay decided. "Do you know how I can get in touch with that Trent Morrison? My security saw that odd-looking thing cruising around at Daisy Campground a couple of weeks ago. I wanted to let Morrison and Porter know. I don't know if that van was casing out me and grandmother, or if it showed up because Mallory had come up there that day. I need to go visit my brother in jail here, but I don't want to get his friends stirred up against us any worse than they already are."

"Yeah," David interjected hastily. "Bransom tried to call, and I missed him. Don't do anything to risk yourself or Delia. If you think the stuff here may still relate to Shannon, I'll have Bransom shake that tree some more. Let me know what you hear from Mallie!"

"Sure thing!" Shay responded conspiratorially.

Chapter 15

TRUST

Proverbs 3:5&6
Trust in the LORD with all thine heart; and lean not unto thine own understanding. In all thy ways acknowledge him, and he shall direct thy paths.

MALLORY DIDN'T SLEEP very well for the remainder of the night. She finally quit trying. She grabbed her Bible and journal and headed to the music room. Turning on a cute table lamp that had a "treble clef" worked into the base, she sank into a huge black, velvety recliner and opened the pages. Having given up, temporarily, at least, on the Old Testament, she opened to Colossians. She really loved the little epistle. She had been delighted when Diana had pointed out to her that the town of Colossae was located near the sites of the seven churches they were going to be visiting in Turkey. She read the little book through, then read her Proverbs chapter for the day.

Opening her journal, she wrote in some new needs and requests that had come to mind. She filled in spaces on some of the pages about dramatic answers to prayers. Tears of gratitude began streaming down her cheeks. David seemed to have seriously recommitted to the Lord. Her mom and Erik Bransom were already getting really involved in church. Mallory thought it would be easier for them, if they just joined the church in Hope where the Sanders went. But, her mom felt a lot of loyalty to the

Andersons and Faith Baptist. Maybe she didn't want to wear thin on her employer and his family. Whatever the reason, they were faithfully making the drive back and forth. Her mom had told her that Tammi thought Mallie was trying to get all the diamonds for herself, and that Tammi had complained about the Mustang when Mallory had a Jaguar. She wished her mom hadn't told her; but that was just her mom~who really did seem to be trying harder to be discreet. And truthfully, on the Friday afternoon when Mallory had signed the checks for all of the Anderson family's vehicles, she didn't know she owned a four-car garage housing luxury vehicles! She just had a little high-mileage used car.

There was a really cute throw with the musical score of "Amazing Grace" woven into it. Mallory had started to snuggle under it so she could ward off the chill and fall asleep. Instead, she moved to the piano. She played by ear, but she was already planning to order gospel arrangements for the piano. She thought about the Faulkner children, already being so proficient on stringed instruments. She wondered if she could learn violin. That brought her back to the thoughts she had been trying to bury; her school work! She knew she needed to get to her office while her new system was being set up. And she had to face whatever Mr. Haynes had cooked up for her for curriculum. Daniel Faulkner had already told her she would have to finish Geometry.

She got ready quickly, slipping into the soft yellow denim outfit with the coordinating sweater, featuring Dinky. Since security followed her in one of the Suburbans anyway, she suggested that they simply chauffeur her to the office. They acquiesced to her wishes. She liked driving the Jaguar, but she didn't enjoy the commute in traffic.

In her office, she deposited the brief case full of papers and headed down to the little café. Grabbing a bagel and a latte, she returned to begin her workday. Marge had left a memo about the "china" order; it was being shipped express. There were some texts and e-mails on her phone. The computer person was supposed to arrive by ten. Shay had texted that he was going to try to visit his brother in Federal custody in Boston. He wanted her to pray for him to be able to witness, and that Shannon would get saved.

He told her that their grandmother sent her love.

Mallory texted Delia, telling her grandmother to call or text her any time. She couldn't figure out why her grandmother was still only contacting her through Shay.

Then there was a missed call from Callie, wondering if Mallie had time to get together with her.

Mallory called her back. "Hi, Callie," she began, her voice still somewhat hoarse and whispery. "I really want to get together and get better acquainted. I'm waiting for this hammer to fall on me about my school work. I should know something by noon. Maybe we can at least get together for a coffee."

"Oh, that would be so much fun," the other girl responded. "What do you mean, 'Waiting for the hammer to fall'?"

Mallie laughed, less of a ripple than usual. Kind of a wheezy sound, like a grandpa, or something.

"Well, that might have been a little melodramatic! I hate to encapsulate my entire life in a phone conversation, but my school principal from Arkansas is fixing me up to finish my junior year on-line; I'm behind, so I may be buried."

"Well, when will you know about coffee? If we can get together, you can fill me in more. Are you dating that attorney?"

"Oh, good grief no!" Mallory responded. "He was my dad's attorney, so I guess I inherited him, with a lot of cool stuff, besides. My friend from Murfreesboro has it bad for him! She goes ballistic if I even have to talk to him."

Marge buzzed the intercom; the tech had arrived.

"Oh, no! Here it comes! I'll call you around twelve-thirty, ok?" She ended the call. She wondered if she had confided too much; she had barely met the girl! All the more reason to meet for coffee to ask her to keep things quiet! She powdered her nose, then stepped out to greet the tech.

"Hey, Tater Tot!" he greeted her cheerfully.

"Hello, Sam, uh, was it?" She was stunned to see him. "I thought you worked for the Treasury Department!"

"I did! Just finished my notice and started for GeoHy and DiaMo yesterday morning. I'll have you up and going in no time! Well, by early afternoon! I'm good, but I'm not that good!" He chuckled.

"Ok; you can have it. I have an appointment. I'll have Marge call me when you're done. Will you have to teach me the system?"

"Maybe an hour to go over things. I'm supposed to make sure you access your on-line classes and sign in before I go."

She made a face at him. "Still have to act like a detective, huh? My name is Mallory." Grabbing her handbag, she exited smoothly.

Now, she wished she had driven; she could go meet Callie. She phoned her. "Sorry I'm being a pest. The guy said it will take him between three and four hours. I guess now is as good a time as ever, if you're free. Where would you like to meet?"

"Where are you?" Callie asked. Mallory explained that she was at her office, giving her new friend the address.

"I know exactly where that is! On the way to Galleria from here."

"Yeah! Right off the toll way. You mind meeting me at the little mezzanine café here in the building?"

"Should take less than thirty minutes. I'll call when I'm close."

Mallory had barely disconnected, and her phone rang. It was Delia.

"Good morning, Grandmother," Mallory answered respectfully. "How is everything going for you in Boston?"

"Mallory, have you heard anything from Shay?" Delia was attempting to keep panic out of her voice.

Mallie wasn't sure what to say. She had wondered if it was a good idea for Shay to try to visit Shannon. Now it really seemed like a bad idea; if he had failed to confide his plan to their grandmother!

"Mallory? Are you still there?"

"Um- Yes, Ma'am," the girl's voice was hesitant. "He texted me earlier. I haven't answered his text; it was a prayer request, so I've been praying about it."

Silence! "He wasn't trying to see Shannon, was he?" The fear in Delia's voice gave Mallory a chill!

"He wanted to win him to the Lord," she finally responded.

"He always tells me where he's going! When he left without saying anything, I figured he was up to something like that. He promised he would call Mr. Bransom first and find out what he thought, before he just went and paid a visit! You take care of yourself, too, Mallory. Will you let me know if you hear from him?"

"Sure! Now I wish I had texted him back not to go. Try not to worry; I'm sure he'll be fine. I'll call if I hear anything!"

Shay's inheritance from his Uncle Patrick had funded into his account. He could hardly believe it. His grandmother had given him a credit card in his name that he was using for their business ventures. She had never really discussed any salary arrangements with him, at all. Now, using the credit card, he had tried to rent a car. No one was renting to sixteen year olds; even if they were really close to being seventeen. He felt compelled to see his brother; Grandmother had been too nervous about it. He tried to call Erik Bransom, but Erik hadn't answered or called back. He slipped out of the house and hailed a cab.

The confusing one-way streets in the downtown area were causing the cabbie to do some circling. Shay wasn't sure if he was just trying to run up the fare. He scanned the buildings, trying to figure where Federal detainees might be held. The cab driver jammed the brakes on, honked, and let go with what sounded like a string of expletives in some mysterious foreign language. A strange-looking vehicle had cut in front of him; then it had just stopped! The cabbie was still honking; but the vehicle, although, blocking a traffic lane, was not moving forward.

Shay was stunned at the sight of the sought-for vehicle; that was before he noticed his brother, Shannon, and Oscar Melville dart toward it! Giving furtive looks around them, they had hopped into it! It had finally lumbered forward, while the cab driver had continued to carry on. Shay tried to tell the driver not to pull beside the thing: but the cabbie was still intent on telling the other driver off. Shay sure didn't want his brother, out of custody, to see him. His mind was trying to analyze the information about Oscar Melville! How could he have possibly gotten out of jail in Little Rock to make it to Boston and get Shannon out?

Shay hadn't told the cabbie to "follow that car", but it did work out that way. They had continued alongside the vehicle on a one-way street. A garage door on a warehouse opened, and the strange bus veered out of traffic, disappearing from sight as the door glided down behind it.

Shay traveled a couple of blocks farther before he paid and tipped the driver. Running into a downtown hotel lobby, he disappeared into the restaurant. He ordered coffee and eggs benedict, then attempted once more to contact Erik Bransom.

"Erik here," the gravelly voice answered. "Shay, you ok? You have your grandmother in a panic about you! Did you manage to see your brother? I just received word that he got cut loose."

"Yeah, by Oscar Melville! Thought he was still locked up in Arkansas!"

There was a silence. "Melville is still locked up. He isn't connected with your brother. Where did you think you saw Melville?"

"I took a cab downtown; the cabbie couldn't really find where I needed to be. Then that big, crazy-looking thing they thought was in the National Forest swerved out in front of the cab and jammed on the brakes. Shannon and Melville sprinted into it. It traveled about a mile, then pulled inside a big warehouse. Can you call anyone to check out the warehouse?"

"How close were you? It couldn't be Melville. I was just re-interviewing him, no more than thirty minutes ago."

"I was too close; but, I'm pretty sure they didn't notice me. If that wasn't Oscar Melville; he has an identical double; maybe he has a twin! Would he have needed to sign in when he picked Shannon up?"

Bransom could hardly believe what he was hearing!. He was pretty sure the part of his case that he was being allowed to continue, was about to morph into the one he had been instructed to leave alone. He couldn't send the Arkansas agents or the Forestry Service guys into downtown Boston to check out Shay's story. If he were being allowed to pursue the leads, he could have agents stake the place out. Shannon certainly wasn't using a low-profile car.

"Shay, I'll look into what you're saying. You get as far away as you can. Don't try to gather any more intel, or anything. I'll make a call and find out what I can about who might have visited your brother. I'll stay in touch. Delia's worried about you, and so is Mallory."

Bransom disconnected and called one of the agents he knew in Boston. Within twenty minutes, he had gotten Bransom's information and called him back. Several guys had visited O'Shaughnessy; one name stood out! Otto Malovich!

Bransom roared for one of his subordinates, who was beside his desk immediately.

"You never filled the blanks in for me for Oscar Melville! Try Oscar and Otto Malovich!"

Leaving the office, he began running. He needed to clear his head. Twin brothers! That could be absolutely the worst. If Mallory said Oscar tried to strangle her on the mine property, and he had an identical twin; that could create enough reasonable doubt to bring a hung jury, or even an acquittal. They had to assemble criminal cases against both men, and find a foolproof way to differentiate them. Out of breath, he paused in his run and pulled out his phone. Calling his superior, Jed Dawson, he filled him in on the latest developments. Dawson wasn't sure what the exact parameters were surrounding the case. The strange, armored-looking, paramilitary vehicle on the streets of Boston, being driven by armed felons, alarmed him.

Mallie's new friend arrived within the thirty minutes, driven by her father. He was tall, distinguished looking, and very well dressed. Mallory apologized for bringing him out of the way; she had assumed that Callie could just come join her. He was nice about it, though, and said he had some more work that he could do from his car.

When the two girls were seated, Callie began trying to explain her dad's obsessing about who her friends were.

Mallie could tell she was embarrassed. "It's no problem for me. I understand completely. My dad was the same. Sometimes I resented it. Now that he's gone, I'm really sorry I was ever bothered by what he did."

Callie didn't know how to respond to that. She didn't know about Mallory's recent loss. They began visiting, and an hour flew by. Callie had found the Lord through a series of events, but it became clear to her when she found a "Chick" tract. Her dad was very unreligious, but he didn't mind Callie's pursuing her faith. He prided himself on being open-minded. He had actually been relieved that some of his daughter's rebellious tendencies had vanished before her new-found faith. He didn't want her to get "too extreme" about her faith, and he turned a deaf ear when she attempted to witness to him.

She was pretty shy, but Mallory drew her out. Callie was eager to grow in her faith. When Mallory had mentioned the upcoming journey to Turkey, the other girl's amber-colored eyes had widened in amazement. "Oh, that sounds fabulous. How did you ever decide to travel there?"

Laughing, Mallory had said it was kind of an involved story; maybe they could get into that when they got together again. Their coffees finished, Callie hurried to join her dad for the drive home. Being both quiet, and sheltered, Callie hadn't had any real girlfriends. She was still amazed that the beautiful girl took time for her and seemed ready to extend genuine friendship. Her dad was glad to see a happy glow. He pretty much wanted her to have whatever she wanted. Friends were one thing that could be difficult for a doting dad to supply. He sometimes wished he had a real friend or two, himself. Often, it seemed, people were only interested in what they could get out of him. Callie rambled about the Arkansas girl all the way home. Everything about the girl sounded nice, and she seemed to have good sense. He couldn't help hoping the girl's sudden wealth wouldn't hurt the values she held. He was surprised he cared.

After paying for his breakfast with the credit card, and making an expense note on the receipt, Shay returned to the cab stand in front of the hotel. The bell captain hailed a taxi for the tall, slender, young man. Shay was just sliding into the back seat when his phone jingled that he was receiving a text. From Shannon! It read: "Shay, stay out of this; go home to grandma!"

At first, he was annoyed at the "big brother giving little brother an order" tone of the message. Then he felt a strange emotional response. It seemed like more of a warning than an order, or a threat! Maybe Shannon did have some feelings! Maybe it was a warning that Delia was in trouble. He forwarded the text to Bransom and gave the driver the address for his grandmother's elegant estate.

Mallory returned to her office and watched as Sam finished the new setup in her office. The man held more admiration for Patrick

O'Shaughnessy now, than he had before. He said so to Mallory, and she beamed with pride. She seemed to grasp the essentials of what he explained to her. He showed her the icon for opening her curriculum; he had assumed that she would access it immediately. Then he could return to Tulsa and report to Daniel Faulkner what her reaction was to it

Mallory was fairly determined that she wasn't going to log on with smilin' Sam standing there grinning at her.

"Thanks, Sam, I'll get right on it!" She was leaning back against her desk, her arms folded determinedly. "Glad you came right down to fix things up."

He stood there, not being sure how to insist.

"Once you log on, you kind of start a timer for finishing the course work."

That kind of made her madder than ever! She wasn't sure what he meant, but she didn't want him to expound on his comment. It didn't sound good!

"Thanks again, Sam!" she had restated it in her most dismissive voice, but he wasn't moving toward the door. "Live long, and prosper!" She gave a Vulcan, Star Trek hand signal.

He even laughed like a tech nerd. "You're a 'Trekkie'?" he questioned in amazement.

"No, but I figured you are! Bye, Sam, I'll get started on the curriculum! Here, don't leave your tools."

When the door closed behind him, Mallory whispered a prayer. She pressed the icon, and an introduction to her work appeared on the monitor. Mr. Haynes was telling her she still had to get the troublesome geometry assignment turned in, but she would receive a "0" because she hadn't turned it in on time. Then there were assignments for the remainder of the term with test dates highlighted. Tears were already stinging her eyes. English/lit didn't have any big bad surprises, American History was summing up with the twentieth century, Biology was all the way up the evolutionary scale to "Humanoid". She scoffed softly; she was glad she knew she was made in God's own image, to do His will, and fulfill a specific purpose He had for her. Her eyes seemed fixed on the screen, but her thoughts had flown to David. She wondered where he was, what he was doing. She wondered if he could possibly have done all this and an entire senior year at the same time. The only thing that was shoring up her spirit was, that if he could do it, so could she! It had been over a week since she had seen him. A long time before six months were up! Mr. Faulkner hadn't guaranteed she would see him then; it just had to be, at least that long. She pulled a calendar from her desk drawer, and tears dropped onto it. And he was so cute, all the girls really liked him a lot!

Thinking she was at the end of her courses, she pressed the "Advance" button again, out of curiosity. There was a Chemistry course! She dissolved into despair. Callie texted her to ask her if it was bad, but Mallie didn't respond. She wished she had a Bible here. It always brought comfort and balance to her when she was distressed. Spinning around, she began searching the reaches of the credenza behind her, then the book shelves! Surely Daddy would have kept a Bible here! At last, she found one, in a decorative magazine rack beside the deep leather recliner. "Chemistry! And a research paper on a "chemical compound" due before the departure for the trip to Turkey! How could anybody be that mean? And a "0"! She had never received a zero in her life!" She was glad she had sent Sam on his way! "No wonder they were curious about what her reaction would be!"

She opened the beloved volume reverently, sobs still escaping. The tissues were out of reach, so she wiped her nose with her hand. She turned first to Psalm 104 and Job 28. The passages had always fascinated her! Her dad had understood that, trying to nudge her into that direction of study. She had resisted him, because his plan would be hard. He was right. She had been coasting! She was doing far less than she was capable of! The riches buried in the earth had always intrigued her! But "Geology" would be a difficult course, crammed full of evolutionary thought! Her dad thought she could take a "Creationist" stance in a "dark" (both figuratively and literally) discipline, because he had been watching Daniel Faulkner do it.

Tears still glittered on her eyelashes, but the old fire was back, flashing in her expressive eyes. She sent the awaited response to Tom Haynes. "I'm set up and ready to start! Can you add a course in beginning Geology?"

"Lord, I'm really going to need Your help! Please direct my paths." she whispered, and entered the "send" command.

Shay's glance swept around anxiously as the cab neared his grandmother's. He was praying that his grandmother hadn't been harmed! His brother's cryptic message set off alarms in his mind. He paid the cabbie, and watched until the cab was out of sight. Drawing his gun, he advanced through the back gate, where deliveries came and went, and trash was picked up. Easing his way along the manicured shrubs, he thought he had made the approach unobserved. Fifteen feet, and he would gain the steps down to the basement, where Delia had installed an elegant fitness area. He hadn't seen or heard anything out of the norm. Maybe he was being silly-

"FREEZE! FBI! Drop the weapon!"

Shay did as he was instructed, and found himself at the bottom of the "dog pile". He was cuffed before the agents pulled out his ID and his license for the gun. Uncuffing him, they urged him into an agency vehicle and raced away. "Is my grandmother ok? Was she still home?" he questioned anxiously.

"We moved her to a safer place, somewhat against her will," one of the agents informed him. " We raided the warehouse you told us about, just in time to stop your brother from being executed! He's in custody again, and we think he's relieved. He didn't want out before. Think he knew they had plans for him that were less than pleasant."

Otto Malovich was holding the gun to the back of Shannon O'Shaughnessy's head when Boston SWAT and FBI agents swarmed into the warehouse. On his knees, bound, and blindfolded, Shannon had tried to pray. "Hail Mary-."

Bransom could hardly believe the story as it unfolded. God had answered his prayers! There was plenty to nail both twin brothers with! The big bus/truck had been swiftly moved to "impound" for techs to go over!

Daniel Faulkner hadn't been pleased with his conversation with Sam Whitmore. He had told him to make sure Mallie accessed her school file before he left. The girl continued to amaze him with her ability to manipulate people and situations to her advantage! She had rushed Sam from her office so she could check her regimen out in privacy. Faulkner had argued with Haynes, the Murfreesboro High School principal. He still worried that pressure on the bereaved girl would stampede her back to David! He was pacing nervously, watching his computer screen. He agreed with Haynes that Mallory was bright and capable of a lot, and he had tried to encourage her that Diana would gladly help her. The longer the elapsed time, the more worried, the GeoHy CEO grew! Diana had called, the suspense weighing on her, too. They wished that she would just e-mail that she wasn't going to do it. Did the silence mean she was escaping from it all? Her security reported that she was still enclosed in her office!

He got the surprising developments from Boston! He had heard nothing of that entire scenario. Needless to say, all of that had come as a shock! He was relieved that the whole thing was resolved before he had become aware of it. Melville had a twin? Melville wasn't Melville, but Malovich! Crazy!

Finally, Haynes forwarded him Mallory's e-mail response! Tears were clouding his vision as he forwarded it on to his wife. "Patrick was right! She was a trooper!" He closed his system and headed home. Once in his car, he placed a call to David Anderson.

"How's your passport process advancing?" he asked as soon as the kid answered.

"Didn't know I was one of the ones that was supposed to get one," David responded hesitantly. "I hate to be a tattle-tale, but I don't think my mom and dad have started on theirs and the other kids' yet, either."

Faulkner tried to hide his annoyance. Janet Walters had already sent Brad in to tell him that the passport was a hassle and foreign travel too dangerous; she wondered if they could just receive the cost of their trip in cash and go to Las Vegas. He had been pretty astounded by the sheer stupidity of that request! He was surprised Pastor John Anderson wasn't excited about the prospect of the trip. Surely he could see visits to the New Testament sites could enhance his ministry!

David could tell by the pause on the other end, that his admission wasn't being well-received. "I guess everything is hard for us to grasp!

It's such a drastic change!" He felt like what he was saying was lame. The guy was so intimidating!

"I'll call your dad and talk to him about it. It's really a pretty straight forward process. David, could you meet me at McKenna's for dinner about eight o'clock?"

'"Yes, sir! I guess so. Have you heard about all that crazy stuff in Boston with Shay and Delia?"

"Yeah! Unreal! See you at eight!"

Mallory returned to the Geometry assignment. She scrunched her eyes and tried to remember her last time in the class; right after the revolting incident with Martin Thomas! She had fainted, and the school nurse wanted her to go home. Since Mallie hadn't wanted anyone to know her mom had left for Hope, she insisted on returning to her classes. If only she had just stayed in the infirmary, she wouldn't have this assignment past due! She reworked the first problem of the assignment for at least the tenth time. There were twenty problems on the page, and the answer was filled in for the first one. That way, you could tell if you were doing them right before you went on. Each time she worked it, she came up with the same answer. But according to the book, her answer wasn't right! She couldn't tell how they had come up with their answer; she didn't "get it".

Her cell phone kept ringing! Shay, Delia, Erik, Callie; Shay, Delia,... Then Kerry called; she figured she should answer him.

"Mallory!" she answered crisply, forcing tears and frustration from her voice.

"Hi, Mallory, you planning on spending the night in your office? It's time to call it a day! Why'd you volunteer for extra? You just a glutton for punishment or something?"

"Word spreads fast," she observed cryptically. "Guess I can head home; Sam has this set up to access from there, too. I'm not sure how I'm supposed to get home; I rode in the Suburban with security. They went back when the office guys took over."

"I'll give you a ride," he offered. "Time they get here for you, you'll be another hour leaving."

"I have plenty to do for an hour, and I don't want to hear it from Tammi. Thanks, anyway."

"I'm walking your way right now, to insist. I have your portfolio to go over again. Daniel told me to."

"Nothing to make my head spin any worse, please," she begged.

Once in his car, she began to return the phone calls; Delia first, who gave her a breathless recap of their day. It was hard for her tired mind to absorb. She was relieved that Shay was all right; and amazed at Shannon's last second rescue by law enforcement! Erik's calls were about the same incident; he was worried when she wasn't answering her phone. Wearily, she apologized to him. Callie was calling back before Mallie could get her number up.

"It was that bad, huh?" her friend questioned.

"I can't really talk now," Mallory responded. She figured one of Kerry Larson's jobs was to report back to Mr. Faulkner about her. "I'll call you when I get home."

David entered the steak house, glancing around for Mallory's Mr. GQ guardian. The guy made him nervous. The hostess rescued him, showing him to a table where Daniel was already seated. David had shaved and changed into nice slacks and the alpaca sweater from Shay. He was no match for the CEO, but he sank into the chair across the table.

Daniel encouraged the teen to order a large steak; he opted for an entrée salad, himself. Diana hadn't been terribly happy about his hop down to Arkansas, and she always worried about his health.

"I called your dad about the passport process. He cleared his slate to fly to Houston for the expedited process. They've been working on locating birth certificates; that kind of stuff is hard to keep up with. You need to go with them. They're trying to get Tom Haynes to give permission for the kids to get their work done early. That guy's tough!"

Dinner rolls arrived and Daniel asked David to bless the food.

David said a short prayer, resuming the conversation, as he buttered one of the fragrant rolls. "Tell me about it! I had a ton of tests the other day! I really have a lot to do by the end of next month."

"Haynes can cut you some slack. I wanted to meet with you to talk about the trip to Turkey. Have you accessed any of the sites?"

David shook his head, "No".

"I've been trying to figure out how to include you in the trip and keep you and Mallory apart. I considered dividing our group in half, and having one group start in the east and work west; the other half going west to east."

David listened, miserably. He guessed he was glad for the guys candor. Not knowing what to say, he waited for the man to continue.

"None of those plans were working. Then, today, Mallory showed such a good spirit about her schoolwork. And she has already really picked a nice friend from church. I want you to be on the trip with us. Promise me you won't try to jump any fences!"

"I'm not sure what you mean. I'm pretty sure I can do whatever you want me to. I really want to go on the trip; I figured I couldn't. Just spell it out for me."

Their food arrived, and with the difficult conversation finished, the rest of the meal was enjoyable. When the server presented the check, Faulkner pushed it toward David.

"Your turn to buy!" Then he laughed and shoved a credit card across the table. It was different-looking. The teenager had only ever seen one like it on a Travel channel program. It was exclusive! And it was in his name! He presented it to the server, then signed and made a notation on the receipt.

"Find some good clothes for the trip! In all your spare time! Haynes has really been bearing down on you, hasn't he?"

"I'm the one who wanted to do it; he hasn't made it easy. He was really mad at me for starting that fight!"

They were in the parking lot. "Good thing you did start it! Bransom working on getting you some reward money for Martin?"

"I'll be rewarded enough if they just keep him from ever getting out!" David jumped into his truck, waved good-bye, and headed toward Murfreesboro.

It didn't take Kerry Larson very long to navigate his way to the suburbs. A couple of miles from Mallory's home, he pulled in at Chili's. Max was there, and several other young people from church. Mallie was still worrying about her schoolwork, but she was starved. Being in a group made her less nervous about being with Kerry. To her surprise, Callie was there, too. Then, Mallory noticed Mr. Cline already seated unobtrusively in a small booth.

The restaurant was crowded, so they had to wait fifteen minutes for a table for ten. The group was fun, though, and the wait seemed shorter than it was. Callie and Mallie had headed for the rest room. "The school work came in that bad?" Callie asked again when they were alone. Mallory checked her reflection in the mirror. She had forgotten how much she had cried during the afternoon. She was trying to fix her face. Once the waterproof mascara transferred itself to the wrong areas, it was there to stay. She tried to powder over it, but the results were pretty grim. She had the "Panda-look" going on this time.

Callie laughed at her. "Panda's are cute! I love that outfit! Where do you find such cute things? You really have good taste! What a funny-looking dog!"

Mallory laughed; her laugh was starting to sound slightly more normal. "I guess it's just the Lord! I mean, I always wanted to be elegant and have good taste. We were really poor; or I thought we were. It's a long story, but the Lord threw me into a batch of fashion designers. They are incredible. Diana designed this and got it made for me. The picture is of my dog, Dinky. The Lord gave him to me, too. Let's go see if they have a table yet."

"No! Your curriculum! Are you going to keep me in suspense forever?"

"This is going to be fun. I'm not even going to think about it until I get home! It's not your problem; quit worrying about me! Let's get some food! I'm starving!"

The group ended up fairly close to where Mr. Cline was seated. None of the rest of the group seemed aware of the fact that Callie's dad was watching and listening. Kerry was probably the adult of the group, but he acted as silly as the rest. Max had started mimicking the song that

Mallory had thought was so funny the previous night. As soon as he started, the two girls, once more, dissolved into giggles. After that, Mallie and Callie couldn't look at one another without collapsing again. Mallie had wondered if Callie liked Max when they had been drinking their coffees earlier. Now, she was sure of it. He was a junior and went to a Christian school nearby. Finally, the party was ending with everyone needing separate checks. The server seemed relieved they were leaving, even though they had been fun and were leaving nice tips. Mallory had picked up some gospel tracts from the church, and she handed one to him. "I'm Mallory, Callie, Max, Kerry ..." she pointed around the table. We go to Calvary Baptist Church. Some of us are in the teen department, and some from the college/career class. We have fun activities. You should come sometime."

"Maybe, sometime! Between work, classes, and studying, I don't have much time."

Mallory gasped, glancing at her watch. "Why did you have to say that word?" She had clasped both hands over her face. Her jewelry shot sparkles!

"What word?" he asked puzzled. "Studying?"

"A-a-h," she moaned dramatically! "You said it again! Kerry, I need to get home; I'm sorry."

"I need to, too. I have an early case in court." He pulled out her chair, and the rest of the group rose, too. Mallory gave Callie a hug. Her dad was already pulling the car up to get her.

Mallory raced to her library and turned the computer on. The clock in the foyer was bonging out nine when her cell phone rang again. It was Callie.

"Hi, Callie," she was waiting for the computer anyway. "Wasn't that fun? Your dad probably thinks we're all really a bunch of psychos!"

"He was glad you guys invited me. I had fun. You aren't really still going to do schoolwork now, are you?"

"You can't imagine! You should see what I have on my plate before I leave for Turkey in two weeks. If you don't hear from me, it isn't that I don't like talking to you! I haven't found out anything about you, yet."

Callie hesitated. With her shyness, she never had many real friends. With her mental acuity, she had experienced quite a few "so-called" friends using her to help them academically.

The computer was up, and the same Geometry assignment was in Mallie's face, again.

"What are you stuck on?" she plunged in.

"Geometry! It doesn't make sense!"

"Read me the first problem," Callie commanded.

"I don't think I'm supposed to get help," Mallory replied glumly.

The other girl considered that a good sign. The other people who always demanded her help didn't care whether things were fair or if they were cheating.

"I won't do it for you. Maybe I can explain it."

Not having much hope, Mallory read off the first problem. Then, she explained how she thought it should be solved.

"That's right!" Callie responded. "That answer the book gives for that first problem is not the right answer. I never figured how they came up with that."

"Well, the book can't be wrong!" Mallory was tired, and she realized her voice sounded whiny.

"The book is wrong! You've been stuck for over two weeks because of that? Do the next one!"

Callie checked her out for the next three or four, then hung up.

Mallory worked each problem, finally pressing send, to turn the assignment in to Mr. Haynes' office. She was in bed by ten-thirty. What a relief!

She was asleep before she finished praying.

Chapter 16

TRUTH

John 14:6
Jesus saith unto him, I am the way, the truth, and the life: no man cometh unto the Father, but by me.

THE SUN WAS shining brightly, and reflections from the swimming pool below her terrace were creating shimmers on the ceiling when Mallory finally opened her eyes. She lay, blinking, trying to think where she was and what she should be doing. Stretching, she scooted the pillows up behind her and propped herself against them. By habit, she reached for her Bible. She let it fall open to the colored pictures of Ephesus, the landmark photo of the "Library of Celsius". She wondered who Celsius was, and decided it was the guy who invented Celsius temperatures when Fahrenheit was good enough for most people! Yawning, she reached for the intercom to order coffee and some breakfast. The clock said ten-thirty! She had slept for twelve hours!

Friday morning! The kids at school would be starting third hour. She wondered if Mr. Haynes had checked his emails, and if the Geometry assignment contained any right answers. "If it's all wrong, he'll probably give me a double zero!" she told herself pessimistically.

She gazed at the beautiful pictures longer before she flipped pages backwards to John chapter fourteen. Pastor Anderson had read the first six verses of the chapter at the graveside service for her father. The first week in January was more bitterly cold than usual, and the wind had been whipping savagely at the little pavilion. In the freezing cold, she had bidden her daddy a hasty good-bye.

Her eyes took in her lovely surroundings, warm sunlight, and tranquility. Almost four months of terror and uncertainty had brought her out to a quiet resting place. She wasn't sorry she had slept too long. She felt rested in both body and spirit.

Her thoughts returned to her curriculum, even as she pulled her daddy's picture into her embrace. When she had first seen the photo, she wondered when it had been taken. She didn't have many pictures of him. This professional portrait of him was a real likeness. His smile, usually impish, seemed more enigmatic and distant; but his eyes still looked lively, full of fun and mischief! "Diana, of course!" She answered herself aloud.

Mallory somehow knew that the peaceful feeling she was experiencing had come because she had surrendered! As a Christian, she thought that she tried to stay surrendered. Smiling through tears, she reread the letter her father had written to her. It hadn't specifically come out and ordered her to be a Geologist, but he had encouraged her in that direction.

Of course, she had preferred her own plan! She thought it was far more spiritual and in tune with the Lord than what her dad wanted. She assumed he wanted her to pursue Geology because of the diamonds that were sprinkled around Pike County.

"Of course, none of the "Christian Colleges" she was considering offered such a major! As with many "scientific" disciplines, this one was really entrenched in "Evolutionism". To Mallory, it seemed pretty male-dominated, too. Besides that, the course matter would just be hard! The scholastic standards wouldn't be a joke! One of the reasons she had resisted was the fact that campus life anywhere besides a Christian environment, would really require her to stand alone for her Biblical values! The Lord had resolved that for her! With the security issues, she wouldn't be attending any classes on a campus; she wouldn't be experiencing dorm life and collegiate partiers.

"You have done all things well!" she whispered, sweeping her gaze Heavenward.

Rereading verse six, she knew that any science that pursued "truth" would dead-end the seeker into the reality of an omniscient, omnipotent, omnipresent God!

Her breakfast and coffee arrived. Large, flaky, steaming, buttery biscuits and four slices of bacon. She daubed a thick layer of Apple Butter on half of a biscuit. Smiling, she guessed it was a product of "Larson Orchards". She planned to ask. Her coffee arrived, already white and sweet! It was delicious!

She replaced the portrait, but continued to glance over at it. She had mentioned once to Patrick that she was considering studying Psychology. Often, he would argue with her; more often, he would say nothing! She would know that he disagreed with her, but it was hard to argue with silence. Finally, she had burst out with, "Well, what's so wrong with Psychology?"

Just the opportunity he knew she would give him eventually! "It's just a bunch of philosophers chasin' their own tails! They spend tons of money in government grants and stuff, trying to find the answers to questions that are plain as day in the Bible!

"Like what?"

"Where we came from, where we're goin', why we're here. What makes people bad? Is it genetic? Will a murderers kids have to become murderers? Is it environment? The Bible is very clear that we all have the same sinful nature; have had since the Garden of Eden. But they won't admit to the real problem, or the real Solution! They make up medical-sounding names for spiritual and sin issues, then prescribe treatments that usually involve medication. Alcohol and drug abuse are attempts by people to avoid their eternal issues, rather than facing them."

Mallory tried to patiently explain that there were a lot of really good Christian Psychologists and Psychiatrists; good people who gave Bible-based advice.

When he would nod, still unconvinced, the conversation would be closed-until next time.

She turned to Proverbs and read her daily chapter from it. She took quite a bit of time with her prayer journal. The Lord was expanding her life, and experiences, and circle of friends and acquaintances. She wrote down the new church; she hadn't met the pastor yet. She felt like she should probably join there, but she didn't want David and Tammi to think she was chasing Kerry. She even considered the church in Hope, but even with all of her fabulous and expensive transportation, that commute was impractical. She already liked Callie and Max; and Kerry's being there was helpful and comforting. She asked the Holy Spirit for leading. She had included the Faulkner family, her mom's new husband, and Delia and Shay when she first started this journal. Now, she added the Sanders, her cousin Shannon, and her new friend Callie. She wrote in Mr. Cline's name, and wondered if Callie had a mom and what the story was about that.

Devotions finished, she turned her computer on. Her email from Mr. Haynes acknowledged receipt of the math assignment, but no word as to whether any of it was right. There was a somewhat terse reminder that the problems on the next two pages were now due. She had twenty sentences to write using her vocabulary words, a chapter to read in Biology, some other stuff. He also wanted to know what topic she had chosen for the Chemistry research paper. It was supposed to be about a chemical compound, which she thought that was the topic!

She brought up her screen saver and ran the Jacuzzi full of bubbles. She sipped on another cup of coffee, and she was nearly finished dressing and ready to resume the work when Callie called. After visiting briefly, they arranged to get together to swim and play tennis the following morning. Mallory remembered guiltily that she had invited Tammi to come. That was before her hospitalization. Neither had mentioned it since. Maybe it wouldn't come up again. She called her mom's cell phone, figuring she would be at work.

"Morning, Mallie," her mom's voice sounded reassuring. "Guess what?! Connie just had her baby! You should see him; he's darling!"

"Wow! That's exciting! Tell everybody I said 'Congratulations'! Everybody doing okay? Now I really need to go shopping!"

"Like we need an excuse," Suzanne agreed, laughing. "You doing okay? Working on your school stuff? You need any help?"

"You have a minute, Mom? I don't want to get you in trouble with Roger."

"It isn't a problem, but you can call me any time. You sure you aren't upset that I got married so soon?"

"Mom, I'm not upset! I like Mr. Bransom a lot. It's just that I don't want to interfere in your new life."

"It isn't a new life, Mallory; it's a continuation of the old one. You're part of it! What do you need?"

"It's the Geometry, Mom! I just turned in an assignment that's two weeks late, that I got a zero for. I hoped I could find out if those were right, before I do the next assignment the same way!"

"Oh, I guess they were right! Tom and Joyce were just here to see the baby, and he mentioned you were on the clock. Guess everyone was worried about whether you plan to finish, or not. They all acted pretty relieved. The zero made me mad! You've lost your dad, and you've had people trying to kill you! Then you were in the hospital, and you're running a corporation. Then trying to go to church and have time for friends, too! It's not like you're just goofing off! I'll call Tom and ask him if the assignment was done right; he better give you credit for it!"

Mallie was surprised. "I don't mind the zero, Mom. I did play Russian Roulette about getting it finished. I miscalculated, and it serves me right! I called to ask you what you think I should write a paper about for Chemistry. I wanted to write it about 'Diamonds', but they are Carbon, which is a single element; not a compound. The first chapter did explain that much! I thought maybe since you work for a big chemical company, you might have some insight."

"Roger gave me a set of DVD's for you. I thought I might come see you tomorrow and bring them then. I haven't seen your house yet, except the pictures on-line. The films are about a lot of science stuff. He said the one on water is exceptional. That's what he thought you should write about"

"About water? Is that a chemical? Oh, yeah, I guess so! H20; Hydrogen and Oxygen. Sounds kind of boring."

"You don't have to do it on that; you should see the video, first, before you decide."

"Okay! Thanks, Mom! You've been a big help! I'll see you tomorrow. What time you coming?"

" I should be there by ten or ten-thirty."

"I can't wait, Mom! Bring your swimsuit and something for playing tennis. My new friend is coming over. I can't wait for you two to meet! Love you."

Mallory returned to the computer and quickly composed sentences that indicated she understood the meanings of the vocabulary words.

She read the Biology chapter from the on-line copy of the text, then clicked that she had read the matter. A "pop quiz" popped up, and she laughed out loud. Mr. Haynes was so-o-o predictable! She answered the one-word answers. She read quite a few selections from her American Lit book; she had fallen behind. Mr. Haynes responded! Her previous submission was done correctly. It took her an hour and a half to complete the two pages of similar problems. Even after sleeping late, her work was completed by the time school would normally have dismissed.

Humming softly, she headed back to the nail salon for fills and a fresh pedicure. That errand completed, she headed toward home. Hoping she wouldn't interrupt dinner, she phoned Diana.

"Hope I'm not catching you at dinner," she began.

"Not at all, Mallory. We're eating later. Daniel went to Hope to eat at McKenna's with David last night; then he's been gone to Houston all day today to help all the Andersons get their passports. I miss him when he has to be gone."

Mallory was curious why her guardian left his family to go have dinner with David. She was thinking to herself that she needed to be more like her grandmother, and hire a private detective. Not that David would care about having her spy on him. She had missed what Diana was saying, being lost in her own thoughts.

" I had a few more ideas about designs," Mallory began. "Either for jewelry or clothing, or both. Do you have time? Or do you have more ideas than you can sketch?"

"Always interested, Mallory. It's just that cell phones aren't necessarily secure. Why don't you e-mail me your ideas when you get a chance? It probably seems strange to you, but secrecy really does matter!"

Mallory liked her laugh. "The trip is coming together!" Diana was continuing. "There is so much to see! First the trip was seven days, then ten; now it's up to fourteen! Delia and I put our feet down, that that has to be long enough for one trip! We start in Istanbul, or course, with the sights there. There's a Topkapi Palace that is a museum now with exquisite artifacts. Then there's a ferry trip up the Bosporus; Europe on one side, Asia on the other; up to the Black Sea. From there we go south through the Dardanelles. Pastor Anderson is excited about the Gallipoli Peninsula, where there's a big World War One Memorial and battlefield. Then we go to the Asia side, and visit Troy, before we do the seven cities of the seven churches and Colossae. Daniel wants to go to Ankara, then Cappadocia, (the apostle Paul mentions it), Tarsus, where Paul was from; and then all the way east to view Mr. Ararat!"

"Wow!" Mallory was amazed. She had no idea there was so much to see in one country! Before discovering her Daddy's Bible, she had assumed Turkey was a small country. It was huge; with many significant historical and Biblical sights! The excitement was contagious!

Diana was dying to tell Mallory that David would also be on the tour, but she figured Daniel planned to do it, also presenting the ground rules. She hated the fact that Mallory was alone in the big mansion on Friday night; she wished they had arranged to have her come to Tulsa for the week-end. She expressed the sentiment.

Mallory's turn to laugh. "Thank you; that's nice! I love it here! Establishing a new normal. I got school work done, then my nails. Red Sox are playing in about half an hour. Then, my new friend, Callie is coming over for a while tomorrow, and my mom's coming. I'm almost sure I'm joining Calvary Sunday morning. I'll let you go, and I'll get an e-mail sent to you before the game starts."

Mallory became so engrossed in capturing her ideas in words for the e-mail, that she missed a couple of innings of the Boston game.

One of her ideas was based on *Proverbs 14:1a Every wise woman buildeth her house:*

The idea was to create a pin/slide-pendant of a "house" with children's faces in the windows. Each child would have a birthstone, to represent the month of his birth. The foundation of the house showed the engraved portion of scripture. It was possible to have additional children added, as a family would grow. The piece of jewelry would be available in 14kt YG or sterling silver. A coordinating bracelet, available in the same metals, featured the house, smaller in size, again engraved with the Scripture. "Children" links would complete the circle, customized for boys or girls with the appropriate birth stone.

Her next set of ideas was also based on one of the verses she loved from the "Wisdom" book of Proverbs.

Proverbs 14:24a The crown of the wise is their riches:

This plan included clothing, as well as jewelry. The girl was a little less sure of the best way to incorporate the idea into garments, but she knew Diana would know. First, the pin/slide-pendant would be a beautiful crown, set with diamonds or other gems. The scripture would run along the base of the crown. Coordinating pieces would include a charm bracelet of an assortment of crowns and tiaras, again sparkling with gemstones; ring, and earrings. Feeling like her plans were totally fuzzy, she sent them anyway.

Then she watched the game with Dinky, and they shared pizza again.

When the Sox lost, she checked her e-mails. Diana's just raved about the ideas! Mallory still thought the lady was just always exceptionally kind. Diana said she had never noticed the phrase before about the "crown of the wise being their riches". Mallory could sense the bubbling joy Diana always exhibited coming through her message. "If some Christians ever see this verse, they'll have to adjust their thinking!"

Mallory fell asleep thinking about becoming a Geologist. Mr. Haynes had answered her that he was researching the best course for her on-line pursuits. She thought about:

> *Luke 19:40. And he answered and said unto them, I tell you that if these should hold their peace, the stones would immediately cry out.*

She had searched her concordance until she found the reference. How could stones cry out? What was Jesus saying exactly? The verse was written, according to her Bible's timeline, around A.D. 33: long before man had discovered a way to record data on quartz chips. Her dad had wanted her to delve into another mystery of Creation. The rocks would speak volumes to anyone who would honestly seek for the Truth they were created to reveal.

Chapter 17

TRIUMPH

DANIEL FAULKNER HAD moved the Andersons into high gear about their passports. He knew his indecision about David must surely have offended them; he felt the same about his children, and perceived slights to them. The trip was exciting to him, but all the little romantic situations still had him concerned! Shay and Emma; Tommy and Alexandra!? (He didn't like it; he guessed it was a reality he was going to have to figure out how to deal with.) Kerry and Tammi; that really struck him as a ticking time bomb! Besides the situation with David and Mallory! "Maybe Diana was right," he acknowledged to himself grudgingly. "Maybe hormones should be outlawed!" He called her from the Houston Galleria.

"Afternoon, Beautiful," he greeted when she answered. "All of the Andersons have passports now, and we have been at the mall so they could shop for the trip. Their kids have been cute trying to ice skate. We're all about to head your way. Why don't you and the kids head to Saltgrass? They'll let you put our name in ahead of time for a table. There are twelve of us. Try to get a table for twelve, or four and eight; whatever works. We should be there by eight. Love and miss y'all."

Diana laid out fresh clothes for her children, then gazed into her walk-in closet. Decisions, decisions! She selected a beautiful, brilliant, orange-yellow, mango-y looking, silk suit. It was a radiant color! She had decided to "go for it" after seeing Mallory's Easter dress. The color looked like orange juice mixed with sunshine! Yummy! Showering quickly, she slid into it, wearing it with an ocean-aqua, silk-knit top, screen- printed with an underwater scene. A bright fish in the foreground tied the brilliant colors together. She styled her hair, then stopped and made an appointment for cut and color before the trip. After applying make-up, she changed to a large aqua leather handbag with matching high-heeled pumps. Opening a large safe, she withdrew one of her jewelry boxes, opting for pearls twisted with gold clamshells. Lipstick, gloss. She was ready!

Alexandra was ready, and Louisa was helping Jeremiah and Cassandra. The three kids were excited to see their dad, and they were quickly making friends with the Anderson kids. Jeremiah was hungry; already planning in his mind what he planned to order. He seemed to be in a real growth-spurt, and Diana had noticed she could hardly keep him full. She gave him a hug! They were growing up so fast!

They loaded into one of the corporate SUVs and headed toward the restaurant, Diana in the second row with Alexandra, and the two smaller children all the way back. They had begun with a movie, but the kids were talking to her so excitedly, that she muted it; and they all laughed and talked during the thirty minute ride.

She had called to get on the list for seating: Daniel and the Andersons actually arrived first. All three kids ran to hug their dad; Diana caught up, joining the group, to receive her hug and kiss.

Daniel hugged her affectionately, then held her away, surveying her in amazement! "You look absolutely gorgeous, Honey! Jer, Buddy, is this the sweater you were telling me about?"

Jeremiah was already checking out a toy that Jeff Anderson was showing him, but he turned and nodded.

"I don't see a shark!" Daniel looked at his wife, puzzled.

Embarrassed that he was studying her tummy in front of a large porch-full of people, Diana was trying to pull herself free and tell him she'd show him later.

He thought it was funny. "No, I want to see now; show me the shark, Honey," he wheedled.

"Daniel Jeremiah!" She was exasperated.

The hostess called out "Faulkner!", and they followed her to a large round-top.

John Anderson knew Lana would be upset, again, about being upstaged by Diana. They had just been shopping at the huge Houston shopping center, but their packages were all somewhere in the helicopter. Not that any of the new things compared to what Diana was wearing. Like a brilliant, shining sun, she literally eclipsed everyone in the entire restaurant. He wondered what the joke was about a shark.

By the time all twelve of them had placed their orders, Cassandra needed the ladies' room. Lana started to say Tammi would help her, but Diana had already risen. They disappeared, and Diana's phone began jingling in her bag beneath her chair. Daniel was searching frantically, finding it in time to note that it was from an unknown number. He decided not to answer it. If it weren't related to his family, his business, his church, or his friends, he wasn't interested. With his having been busy in Houston all day, he hadn't heard anything about Mallory. Bread and their beverages arrived, and they prayed.

"You had a phone call, Honey," he told Diana as she returned to the table. "An unknown number."

"Did you answer it?" she questioned. She was already checking the call log.

"No. Don't worry about it now; let's eat and visit with the Andersons."

Diana had already begun the call to the number. A woman's voice answered, "Hello".

"This is Diana. Did you just try to call me from this number?"

"You probably don't remember me, but--"

"Of course I remember. You're Nell, aren't you? Mallory just asked me if I had heard anything more from you. Are you doing okay? How are your boys?"

The conversation at the table among the adults had died so Diana could carry on the phone conversation. Daniel was giving her one of his exasperated looks. But she had already been returning the phone call before he told her not to. She smiled at him, and shrugged her shoulders. She was so cute!

The people at the table couldn't understand what the other woman was saying.

At last, Diana broke back in. "Did you read that little booklet I left with you?"

More conversation. Diana wasn't sure if she should go out on the porch so Daniel and the Andersons could talk. It might take her a while to deal with the woman. "I'm afraid I'm not sure why you called me, Nell. Have you prayed that prayer? It's really a very simple transaction. You just ask Jesus to come into your heart and be your Savior."

"That's just it," the other lady responded. "It's too simple; there has to be more. I mean, I prayed the prayer, and something happened. I just feel like there's something I should do next. Am I supposed to dress up all fancy and start going to church?"

Diana laughed. "I'm having dinner right now with a pastor and his family; he has written several books. I'll send one right away about what you need to do to start growing in grace. You don't have to dress up fancy, though."

"Oh, you don't? That's too bad. You make it look kind of fun."

Diana laughed again. "Serving the Lord is fun. Give me your address, and I'll either mail the book tomorrow, or someone will bring one by. Nell, I'm so excited about your decision! Mallory will be excited, too. We are just about ready to eat, but call back if you need to." Diana tucked the address into a compartment of the her handbag.

David was trying to keep track of a baseball game; he could half-way watch it across the crowded restaurant. His iPhone helped, too. He figured Mallory would at least be keeping up with the score; he knew she was watching it, if it were possible at all. His passport in his jacket pocket was a thrill to him! The picture made him look like a mutant; but he, David Anderson was taking an international trip! He figured it just had to be the Lord that had made the Faulkners decide to let him travel along with the group. It was because of Mallory's submissive spirit, too. She was pretty incredible. David's dad had always preached that, when you please God, and he blesses you; the blessings extend to everyone around you. Conversely, if you disobeyed, and received chastisement, you brought pain to other people, too. Looking back, he could see, at least partially, the havoc caused by his rebellion.

And the blessings because of Mallory Erin! Like, when had he ever had thirty dollar steaks at nice restaurants? Never! Then, in the past two weeks! Well, it wasn't all because of Mallory! His mom and dad had been really faithful in their commitment to the Lord, too.

"David, you're quiet, tonight." Diana's lilting voice brought him out of his reverie.

"Yes, ma'am," he responded. He felt more tongue-tied around her than he did around Mr. Faulkner. He was impressed with her, though. He was pretty sure that Nell that just got saved was one of Mallory's nurses. He was sorry he hadn't been sensitive to her need for the Lord. His steak was incredible!

The conversation ebbed and flowed; some of it was enlightening about Mallory. Evidently she and Diana were working on some fashion designs together. But, then, Mallory was going to be a Geologist, too! David wasn't sure where that had come from! He didn't want Mallory to change. He liked hearing about her, but he was worried.

After the meal, Daniel asked the rest of the party to excuse them, and he led John to another table. He still needed to deal with one more issue with the pastor, in order to have the travel arrangements solidified.

"Is this still about David?" John questioned apprehensively when the coffee came.

"No! Worse!" Faulkner replied. Might as well get it out in the open. "It's about Tammi."

The pastor met his gaze. "What about her? You mean Haynes and her school work? He's giving Mallory and David and Tammi a hassle about their work and the trip, but then when it's Tommy-"

"No, it isn't that. He is serious about education. Tommy's about three years ahead of himself academically, anyway. It's about Tammi and Kerry Larson."

John Anderson frowned, not angrily, so much as quizzically!

"He doesn't have a clue," Faulkner surmised. He could tell the other man was trying to process information, that, to him, was inconceivable.

"Tammi and Kerry Larson." The pastor had finally repeated the phrase blankly. "What are you talking about, Faulkner?" Revelation was dawning slowly, and the man wasn't liking the picture. "What are you saying? Tammi's just fifteen. How old is that guy? You're saying he's after Tammi? I'll kill him, if it's true!"

John Anderson's voice hadn't risen in volume, but Daniel knew he meant what he was saying! He met the man's angry gaze steadily and shrugged.

"Kerry's twenty-six," he answered softly.

"I haven't seen him back around much. I'm sorry, Faulkner, I can't tell what in the world, you're talking about! When did he tell you he likes my daughter? I notice he hasn't been man enough to talk to me!"

"Yeah; he's been pretty confused," Daniel admitted. "I probably told him not to talk to you about it, or to anybody. I told him to get over her. Now, I'm pretty sure that isn't happening."

Daniel was pretty miserable, wondering why conversations like this kept falling on his shoulders. He plunged in again.

"He's an attorney. If anyone is aware of the ramifications of this, he is! If anything happens, he risks his career! And going to jail!"

"Well, let's not forget what it would mean for Tammi! And my family!" Now Anderson's voice had risen.

"Sorry," Daniel apologized. "I know that! There's a ton of stuff at risk here. Believe me, I would have preferred not to bring it up." He told Anderson about Diana's comment 'that hormones should be outlawed' ; he didn't laugh!

Tears of frustration and disbelief were trying to fall. Anderson blew his nose, brushing away the annoying tears. He wanted to taunt Faulkner about his little girl and Tommy Haynes, but he knew that would be a childish response.

"Look, my family's waiting, it's late, it's been a full day, they're tired, so am I! Just put it on the table!"

"Okay. We all came to Murfreesboro because of Patrick and Mallory. Kerry got into town on that Wednesday night before the will. Tammi had just been rescued from Adam's sites by a nest of wasps. Kerry said his gaze met Tammi's, and they were in love! He had to stay through Friday for the will and the corporate meeting. Then he ran for home."

"So, you think Tammi is aware of this?"

"That's the problem; Kerry is trying to put the brakes on, but Tammi, well she's just young," Faulkner ended lamely. "I hate for Larson not to make the trip. He's really an integral part of the group."

Anderson was rising from the table. "I'll speak with my daughter! You take care of your attorney friend: or I will!"

John's facial expression was strained as he rejoined his family on the large circular porch of the nearly deserted restaurant.

"Ready to go?" his pleasantness was forced. "G'night, Mrs. Faulkner, kids." He strode toward the vehicles that had arrived to ferry his family to the helipad. "Honey, ride with Tammi and the little kids; David can come with me!"

Lana wanted to know what on earth Faulkner's problem was now! It had been a really fun and happy day! John's expression was totally unlike him, so she didn't argue, but loaded up according to his terse order.

David climbed silently into the second vehicle with his dad, wondering what he had done this time.

"Is there something I should know about your sister?" John Anderson usually tried not to speak freely around the drivers. He didn't know them, and they worked for Faulkner. At the moment he didn't care! He could sense his son stiffen.

"You do know!" he accused, his whisper both angry and disappointed. "It's true? Why haven't you said anything to me?"

"Right Dad, tell you about Princess Tammi? She can do no wrong! 'David, don't tease your sister'! I started to say something to Mom the other day, but then, she seemed to be happy. I hated to 'rain on her parade'. At least, Larson's acting like a grown-up!"

"He's twenty-six, and he likes a fifteen year old girl; and you think he's acting like a grown-up?" Anderson was trying to control his volume and his emotions.

David stared miserably out the window. "Figured!" he thought. "Faulkner yelled at his dad about his sister, and he was the one riding in the hot seat with his dad! Getting yelled at! Why didn't Dad ever yell at Miss Tammi?" He was trying not to cry.

"I'm sorry, David. I'm acting like it's your fault."

"I know, Dad! Everything's always my fault! I get tired of it!"

"It isn't your fault, Son. That's why I was trying to apologize. What should I do?"

"About what? What did Mr. Faulkner say? He wants Kerry Larson to be able to go on the trip, without Tammi throwing herself at him?"

"Yeah; guess that was what he was getting at."

"Why don't you start by taking a look at Tammi's phone? Oh, yeah, I forgot! You don't know how to work 'em. Get her phone, and I'll show you what's on it!"

"David, cut the sarcasm and watch your tone of voice. What's on her phone?"

Now his voice was laden with dread.

David sighed. "Nothing, Dad. Get it, and I'll show you. Mostly that she tries to call him twenty times a day. I mean, in a way, I don't blame her. How many cool guys are there in Murfreesboro? Not many; then good Christian guys, too? Zero! Kerry rides into town; an attorney, with a Porsche, handsome, single, carrying a big worn-out Bible. He seems to be her ticket out of the sticks! I've tried talking to her, but she gets all witchy on me. I don't think he's ever answered one of her calls, but when I spent that Saturday night at his house, he told me he does like her, too."

"Son, why haven't you said anything about this?"

"I already told you! You never believe anything I say about her, and I didn't want to make Mom sad again."

The vehicles stopped at the helipad, and the family rejoined in the spacious helicopter.

Lana could tell John and David had both been crying, and she figured the Faulkners must still not like David. She felt like people were always examining her and her entire family like bugs under a magnifying glass. Figuring she wouldn't find out anything with all the kids around, she buckled in before beginning to pull out the purchases they had made earlier in the day. She hadn't felt really satisfied with her selections before; now she really didn't like any of it. But there weren't even the same stores in Arkansas. She figured there was no way to go back to the Galleria in Houston for exchanges. A sigh escaped.

"Sugar, we can go back tomorrow when there's more time."

Lana glanced over at her husband in amazement.

John's baritone laugh filled the cabin. "Don't look so shocked! I think we definitely need to shop some more. It was the middle of the afternoon before we left the Federal building and got started; then you kept checking on the kids. You kind of had to snatch and grab. That's what you've had to do for twenty years. Grab what you could, with no time, and no money! Lady, I'm taking you shopping! It's already late on Friday night, and I know everyone likes to sleep late on Saturday, but will y'all think I'm mean if I get you up at the crack of dawn to spend the day shopping in Dallas?"

His family's eyes were all alight as they chimed a "No, Sir!" in unison.

Daniel asked Alexandra to ride with him, and their SUV pulled quickly into position behind the one carrying Diana and the other two children.

"You excited about the trip, Al?" he asked his daughter, giving her hand an affectionate pat.

"Yeah, it sounds like a lot of fun! Mallory is really super-cool!"

"She is" he agreed. "Not as super cool as you and me though, right?"

Alexandra laughed. "Of course not, Dad. We're the coolest! Why don't you like David?"

"I like David a lot, Al. You know that. I wasn't talking to the pastor about David, if that's what you thought."

"About Tammi, then?" she asked him curiously.

"You just interested in gossip?"

"No, Sir; I don't think so. Just they're all my friends, and you're against us all being together."

"Being together- what do you mean by that exactly? As couples? I'm against it. You're all too young to be 'couples'. You all get to be together as a group, for fourteen days, on a fabulous trip. At this stage of your life, Alexandra, you just make friends! Everyone going is your friend, from Delia to Sammie and Sarah Walters. You make friends across the spectrum; across gender and age differences. It enriches your life and your experiences. Believe me, I like the Andersons and their kids. I like the Haynes, including Tommy. You're not going to be alone with him; don't try to get alone together. Do you understand me?"

"Yes sir, but I'm getting tired of hearing 'I'm too young.'"

Daniel laughed and gave her shoulders a squeeze. "Too bad! You're just getting started hearing it!"

They pulled into the garage, and he unfolded his long legs with a stiff groan. "Look on the bright side, Al. Better to be too young than too old!" He slid out and held the door for her to slide across.

Diana stopped to examine the mail on a polished table in the foyer before skimming lightly up the marble, curving, staircase. The polished dark wood of the banister contrasted dramatically against the gleaming white. She loved her home! Never had she dreamed of anything this beautiful! More than the stone and glass, though, she adored her family who made the mansion "home" and made life worthwhile.

"Any interesting mail?" Daniel was asking from the high, arched, dark-wood trimmed doorway of their master suite. He had removed his tie and loosened his collar. She thought he was more handsome than ever. She handed him the pamphlets and circulars.

"Come on kids; let's step it up! It's late!" Daniel was moving into the hallway as he spoke.

In less than five minutes, all three, in pajamas, with their teeth brushed, had bounded onto their parent's bed. They played and wrestled for a few minutes, then prayed, before tucking the kids in tight, and giving good-night kisses.

"Honey, come back downstairs with me, will you?" Daniel asked when they had watched a few minutes of late-edition news, and the kids were asleep.

"Surprised," she followed behind him, and he led her into the music room. He sat down on the piano bench, pulling her down next to him. His hands moved across the keys, playing the introduction to "Can't Help Falling In Love". He sang the first verse and the chorus; then wanted her to sing the second verse. She didn't know it. Her dad, a second-generation missionary to Africa had never encouraged her much to listen to Elvis Presley. Laughing at her, he sang the second verse to her, too. Tears filled her eyes; the love song was beautiful, and he meant it.

"I did a little shopping today, too." He pulled out a beautifully wrapped gift and pushed it into her hands.

"I don't understand why the Andersons couldn't just go get their passports and shop without your having to go," she sighed. She knew hanging out at a mall wasn't his favorite thing! He always did have a lot to do.

"Well, Honey, they really can't get used to the idea of plenty, and being able to shop!" he defended them.

Diana smiled brightly. "That's true! I was the same way, when you first brought me here from Africa. You remember? I didn't know how to shop, either!"

His laughter echoed around the music room, booming through the house.

"Yeah, I did forget. Well you're way ahead on the learning curve, now! Maybe there's hope for the Andersons!" He squeezed her. "Open your present, Diana. I love you! Hope you like it!"

She was picking delicately at the Scotch tape. "I hope I do, too. If I do, I may show you my shark!"

His eyes, serious, met hers. "I finally saw it! That's scary to me, Diana! I'm not sure I know how to handle it. The outfits you put together with the pictures are incredibly beautiful and creative. You are incredibly beautiful and creative! I certainly had no idea we were in such imminent danger. I guess we always, are, really! The Lord must have decided to show me how useless my plans are, ultimately, without Him! You need some help getting that paper undone?" He had reached for the package back.

"I can do it myself," she mimicked Cassandra.

Opening the box from a high end jeweler, she gasped with delight! "Oh, Daniel! Oh, Honey!" She kissed him, her eyes sparkling with love and delight at the gift!

"That is so beautiful! It's just perfect! Oh, Daniel!"

The gift was perfect! The necklace was an eighteen karat yellow gold circle, similar to a classic Omega necklace. But this piece featured five emerald-cut emeralds, mounted horizontally in sleek, modern rectangular frames. The centrally mounted stone, approximately eighteen by twelve millimeters was framed with diamonds. The other stones, set at intervals on the gold, decreased slightly in size. A coordinating hinged bracelet featured a matching emerald, surrounded with diamonds. An emerald solitaire ring, also rectangular, completed the set! The deep, lovely green was mesmerizing.

She tried it on, loving the way it circled her throat. The ring and bracelet shimmered as she moved her hand in the ambient light, surveying the treasures with awed satisfaction. Ashamed, she realized that she had been annoyed at her husband's need to accompany the Andersons.

Her attention, drawn once again to the sparkling gems, she admitted that "All things work together for good."

They filled large glasses with ice water and ascended the stairs for some sleep, themselves.

Jed Dawson called Erik Bransom's cell phone late Friday night. Some of the lab results had come in on the 'War Wagon' (as they had affectionately dubbed it), as well as from evidence gathered at the Boston warehouse. Some of the mud pulled from the wheel wells was indicating that the vehicle had been in rural Arkansas. It wasn't definitive, at all, for Dallas. They had guessed that there were two of the vehicles. Bransom thought they were some kind of old military surplus stuff from Eastern Europe. They were armored, and had, at one time, been armed. The large caliber guns had been removed. The advantage of being bulletproof was obvious; it seemed to Bransom that that advantage was more than outweighed by the disadvantage of calling so much attention to themselves. And, they were big! Plenty of room to hold a large group of captives! So much evidence about the missing staff; so much frustration at failing to locate them!

Erik phoned Morrison, asking if they had checked geological maps of the Ouachita Forest. Morrison admitted they hadn't; that was the only data they hadn't analyzed. Morrison felt frustrated; he couldn't begin to guess what the FBI guy was thinking. He hung up and filled Porter in.

Porter, increasingly homesick for his family, was ready to bail on the entire project. His boss kind of kept pushing the religion stuff on him, too. When Morrison suggested geological maps, he had nodded.

"He thinking there are caves or abandoned mines, or something like that we don't know about? Do Geological maps show that kind of stuff? How do we requisition something like that? Don't want anyone to think we're prospecting on Federal Lands, or we'll lose our jobs! We may, anyway!" He shook his head. "Call him back. If he thinks his idea is so great, he can find the maps and show up tomorrow with three saddle horses. If those guys are hidden in this forest, I'm past ready to find them! I'm ready to head home!"

"Good idea! I agree!" He called Erik back, and to his surprise, the Fed good-naturedly agreed with the plan.

Daniel turned off the bedroom light, and the phone rang. Bransom's land line. Faulkner grabbed the phone, praying nothing else had happened to Mallory! He was relieved she was okay. Bransom filled him in about his idea about Geological maps. Faulkner, listening, was agreeing it might be worth looking into. He was as amazed as Erik had been about the tie-in to the Boston crime-syndicate. He didn't know why; Patrick hadn't been paranoid without good reason! When Bransom revealed the rest of their plan, to further the search into the forest as a casual trail-ride, Daniel asked to be included. He had hired most of the people; he felt responsible!

"Can't do it! We three are law-enforcement; you aren't. Just supply us with the maps and keep praying."

"Honey, I have to go back to the office," he began. "Maybe not!" He headed toward his study. Maybe the maps he was using for the DiaMo Corporation project extended far enough north. He pulled one out, and unrolled it. Patrick O'Shaughnessy had hired GeoHy Corporation to chart currents and subsequent deposits of alluvial diamonds. Figuring any additional pipes would be in close proximity to the one at the Crater State Park, he hadn't been as interested in the Little Missouri at its origins in the north. Still, one of the maps did extend upwards into the Ouachitas.

Since Daniel had gone back downstairs, Diana pulled her robe on and went to her design studio. She was too excited about the beautiful gift to sleep. Daniel told her he chose emeralds because she didn't have any. She brought up the sea floor photo, once more. People were probably getting tired of it, but inspiration had seized her. Moving the cursor to the seaweed, she changed the color of the green, slightly, to match the green of her new emeralds. She played with lightening and darkening the blue of the water and left it slightly paler. Pulling out a sketch pad, she sketched the photo with the new colors, illustrating it with an emerald-green silk suit and the new jewelry. The jacket of the new suit had a definite flare, to accommodate her growing waistline. Squinting critically, she tried to decide if emerald shoes and bag were too much of a good thing. The only other possibility was metallic gold! Much better! The foreground fish, still mango-orangey, seemed a little garish. Moving the cursor to him, she zapped him to an electric blue-purple. Too dark! She zapped him again, and he was red-orange; another click, a bright, pure yellow! Perfect! She scanned and e-mailed! Another breath-taking outfit would be on the way! It was so much fun! She smiled as she flipped the pad shut and put it away.

Daniel pored over his map. He wasn't sure Erik or the Forestry guys knew how to decipher the geological data. Combining some quick internet research with the data on the maps, he felt like he was actually coming up with a grid that might be useful. Pleased, he scanned a couple of the maps, section by section, with some of the areas highlighted with sticky red arrows. He forwarded the internet info, along with his assessment of what appeared to be a couple of cave-systems, as well as a couple of abandoned mines. He warned Bransom that the areas might be dangerous for cave-ins, not that he would care. Then, he reminded himself that though the seasoned agent was a risk-taker, he wasn't fool hardy. He turned off the office equipment and the light and headed back upstairs.

Bransom gazed at the information from Faulkner with amazement. If the people they sought were really in any of these places, they had been nearly on top of them the entire time. As he sat at the kitchen table with the pages spread before him, a powerful sensation swept over him. The apartment had been too hot, but a chill swept over him, raising goose bumps. He began forwarding the data to his superior, Jed Dawson, and to the Forestry Department agents. Then he called all the local agents to get in ASAP.

Dawson notified the governor of Arkansas, being quite sure the FBI was still supposed to be off the case. He couldn't understand why, but he knew the governor would have the ABI run the raid! He didn't care! Just so someone did it! The more he gazed at the data, the more he felt the same certainty that Erik had experienced. Horses and tack were being loaded into trailers. Guns and ammo checked. Medical supplies, food, and water. As they were mustering, a plane had flown high, with heat-seeking imagery. Looked like there were living bodies; if the raid were successful and the hostages didn't get killed by panicky captors!

Mallory opened her eyes; daylight was barely beginning to seep into her room. She sat up, then turned on a lamp next to her bed. The phone rang. Trying to see her clock as she reached for the receiver, she answered groggily,"

"Hello-"

"Morning, Mallie!" It was her mom. Mallory was instantly worried that something was wrong and her mom wasn't coming. "Someone has something to say to you," her mom continued.

"Hello, Miss O'Shaughnessy?"

Mallory, trying to emerge from sleep, didn't recognize the guy's voice at all. She was thinking her mom could at least wait until the sun was up to play games.

"This is Tad Crenshaw," the voice continued.

"What? Mr. Crenshaw, where are you? People have been searching for you, high and low!" she stopped, totally confused!

"I know!" He laughed. "I'm glad no one gave up on us. Sorry to call so early; your mom's the one who did it."

Suzanne took her phone back from the dehydrated mine foreman who was being assessed by an agency medic.

"Mallory, are you still there?" she questioned.

"Yeah, Mom." As the realization of what was happening dawned on her, she began to cry. Her mom was jubilant! Everyone found, in reasonably good condition! There hadn't been anyone guarding the prisoners, so no arrests had been made. That was disappointing, in one way; but it had made the rescue operation safer and easier. Everyone wanted Mallory to be the first to know! The second she had turned her lamp on, they had placed the call.

Mallory thanked her mom and Erik and began placing calls to everyone else!

All rescued! The eleven mineworkers, and the four from her home!

When she finished the calls, she picked up her Bible. She still felt totally overwhelmed with relief and gratitude for the answered prayer.

It had been hard not to give in to despair, as the time had passed. She was curious about lots of details she hadn't thought to ask about. There would be time for that, though.

II Corinthians 2:14a Now thanks be unto God, which always causeth us to triumph in Christ,

Mallory quickly found the verse that had come to her mind. In spite of everything, God had caused them to triumph! Maybe some guilty parties still needed to be apprehended! DiaMo had sold off the fifteen acre O'Shaughnessy property. But they had already voted to purchase the property that bordered the Faith Baptist land.

The shareholder meeting wouldn't pull together, so Kerry Larson had called and polled each voting member.

She pulled on a swimsuit and cover-up. Taking her Bible and prayer journal, she requested her breakfast poolside. Callie was coming over, and her mom was still coming, too!

Chapter 18

TREATS

KERRY LARSON WAS awake early on Saturday morning. That wasn't the norm for him. First, Mallory had called with the unbelievably good news that all of the hostages were safe and receiving medical treatment. The conditions during their captivity had been far from good, but at least none had suffered anything imminently life-threatening. As Mallory's attorney, he knew that one or two, or all, of the men might end up trying to sue her. Well, sue DiaMo! He was already praying for none of that to happen. He considered calling her to work out a pre-emptive package to offer the guys. That had still been on his mind when Daniel Faulkner called to talk to him about going to Turkey with the corporate group. The guy was really lit up about it, and he put the hard sell on. It sounded amazing! Big chartered jet with the whole bunch! All the Biblical sites! Kerry had taught a series of lessons on the Apostle Paul and his missionary journeys, but he had failed to grasp the significance of how much his Bible maps fell within the borders of the modern day nation. Turning to the maps at the back of his Bible, he mentally super-imposed Turkey's borders over the map which showed the Apostle's travels. Troas, Assos, Lydia, Troy, Tarsus, Cappacochia, Bythinia, Galatia, Colossae, besides the cities of the seven churches. Daniel said Turkey also claimed to be the birthplace of Abraham. The Tigris and Euphrates rivers had their headwaters there. That was without the wonders of Istanbul (Constantinople) with it's mysterious and historical sites! The Black Sea, the Bosporus (once called the Hellespont), the Golden Horn, the Dardanelles, The Gallipoli Peninsula, The Aegean Sea, and the Mediterranean. Long ago names from his history books were jumping from forgotten pages, summoning him seductively.

Some of the other things Daniel told him were troubling; mainly that the big-hearted, mild-mannered Arkansas pastor was threatening to kill him! He poured a tankard of iced tea and carried it and his Bible out to the pool enclosure. It was a pretty morning. He called his dad.

"Hi, Kerry," his mom answered. "Dad's gone already, and he forgot to take his phone; he forgets it more than he remembers. You okay? We know how busy you are, Honey, but-"

"I know, Mom. I should answer your calls. I've been trying to get some stuff worked out in my mind. I'm sorry! Basically, things are great here."

"Everything went okay that you were telling us about that little girl?"

He couldn't help laughing. "Yeah, Mom. It went fairly well! She's hardly a little girl. She's seventeen, and she's picked up the corporate reigns like you wouldn't believe! I've been offered a really exciting trip to Turkey, and I wanted to talk to Dad about some of the issues. Have him call me; will you, please, Mom?"

"Turkey! Isn't that a terrorist place? What does the State Department say? If you want to take a trip, why don't you come see us?"

"Because Turkey and central Oregon aren't really the same, Mom," he laughed. "It isn't terrorist, although it is Islamic."

"It's all the same," she cut in, sounding panicky.

He laughed. "It isn't all the same, Mom. Turkey's a NATO nation with a secular government. We always travel with good security! And, we'll have you praying for us! Will you have dad give me a jingle?"

"He should be back in about an hour. Honey, there's a real nice single lady that's been visiting at church here. If I send her address, will you write to her?"

He chuckled. "Nice try! Love ya, Mom!" He hung up.

Forty minutes later he was on the toll way to the Galleria. He didn't hate to shop, or love it. But, if he were going to Turkey, and if he were going to be seeing Tammi every day for two weeks, and if he were traveling with such a stylin' group, he should find some new threads. He parked and jogged into Nordstrom's.

Suzanne was the first person to land on Mallory's newly completed helicopter pad. She was dazed by the estate. The on-line photo gallery rundown hardly did the mansion justice! The most amazing part to her, was the fact that Patrick had done it. "Who would have guessed?"

Mallory, in a cute cover-up and sunglasses had rolled up in a golf cart with Dinky at her side. She hopped out and gave her mom a kiss on the cheek.

"Wow, Mom, you were up all night? You must feel just awful! You look great! I'm glad you decided to come on. I've been excited since you said you were coming."

Mallory threw her mom's light, day-trip luggage into the cart, and they zoomed toward the house. Suzanne was eating a light breakfast and catching up when Callie arrived. They swam and played in the water park, which was a blast! Then, they tried tennis. Mallory had never played, but was pretty naturally athletic. Callie still beat her bad. Suzanne had played before, but it had been a long time. She played a set, but worn out, she had crashed laughingly, onto a poolside lounge chair.

"You two, have at it!" she laughed. She really liked her daughter's shy, little, new friend. She seemed a fit for Mallie. Callie and Mallie! They were cute. She was relieved, too, that Mallory seemed to be recovering; both from her grief, and from the injuries Oscar Melville had inflicted. Her gaze returned to the lines of the elegant home.

"Maybe Erik and I will just move in with you. Then we won't have to build!" she laughed.

"I wish you would," Mallie responded, unhesitatingly. "There's plenty of room."

Suzanne scanned her daughter's face. Mallory had meant what she said. She was the warmest, most loving, and sincere person Suzanne had ever met. "Chalk that up to Patrick, too," the mother was forced to admit.

She laughed. "That's nice, Mallie. The place is beautiful. I like my job at Sanders Corporation and Erik likes the Hope office. I'm not sure I was ready to turn you loose so soon, but I'm proud of you."

"Are you excited about the trip?" Suzanne changed the subject.

Chips, salsa, and guacamole had appeared, along with tall iced teas. Mallory scooped up a generous mouthful of guacamole and shrugged. Her expression registered frustration, then she laughed.

"You know what, Mom? When we were poor, I always wanted to be rich. I thought rich people never have any problems. Now, I'm rich, but Geometry's still the same!"

"Pay someone to do it for you," Suzanne suggested. "Maybe money hasn't solved your problems because you haven't learned to use it right."

"Mother!" Mallory's voice was shocked.

Suzanne laughed. "I thought the same thing, and I'm older than you are. Rich or poor, there are still struggles. And, you still need the Lord. You're frustrated about the Chemistry paper before the trip, too, aren't you? Watch Roger's DVD's and then just get it done! Why did you ask for another extra course, too?"

"I'm crazy, I guess."

Fat, stacked up, gourmet cheeseburgers, oozing with grease, materialized. They all three eyed one another, before, laughing, they all threw on onions. What was a burger without the onions? Dinky popped to life, whining softly.

"I was thinking about maybe doing some shopping here, before I go back to the sticks." Suzanne suggested a change in the plans, tentatively.

"What will your dad say, Callie?" Mallie questioned her friend. "My security will be all over us. You think he'll let you go to Galleria?"

Callie wasn't sure. Her dad had the bucks, for sure, but he didn't encourage frivolous shopping. Then, Callie was already dreading having Mallory gone on her trip for two weeks. When Suzanne and Mallory talked about the big, upcoming trip, she felt really left out. She called, and almost to her chagrin, her dad gave permission. Finishing their burgers and getting ready super-fast, with shopping as a motivation, they were past the gates, being driven in one of the SUVs, in under an hour.

Daniel had been too wired about the caves and the new leads in the investigation to sleep well. Bransom had texted him when the raid was under way. Diana was up early, too. She usually was. She loved mornings and sunrises. They were enjoying an early morning cup of coffee and a light breakfast in bed when Mallory's call came. Daniel had complained good-naturedly that Bransom could have called him first, since he had provided the map and interpretive data. Truthfully, they were both just immensely relieved that the worst of that ordeal was finally over.

"Let's get the kids up and all go to Dallas today; you want to?" Daniel suggested. "I'll ice skate with the kids, and you can shop. You hardly had any time Monday night when you met Shay and Mallory. You can start finding stuff for the trip. Remember, we only have a 747; and eighty-nine other people need room for a suitcase, too."

Laughing, she made a face. He was usually a pretty good sport about shopping if she really wanted him to accompany her. He didn't usually offer. She hurried toward the bathroom to get ready while Daniel went to waken the kids.

The Andersons were already en route to Dallas when they got word from Mallory that the DiaMo workers had been found a short distance north of where eleven of them had been grabbed. Evidently, the mine workers had been outnumbered and surprised. Overcome, they were placed into the pit beneath the floor of the shed. Evidently, Oscar Melville had been aware of the space (they hadn't found out yet, how he knew it was there). They were pretty certain Patrick O'Shaughnessy hadn't wanted anyone to know about the mine pit he was hand-excavating.

It appeared that the miners' cars had been used by the kidnappers in order to flee from Murfreesboro. Melville, very much at the center of the plot, must have just been finishing up, preparing to leave, when Mallory happened by. Adrenaline must have really been pumping! He would have tried to kill her, even if she hadn't taunted him!

Later, after Melville was transported to the hospital, and the FBI agents had finished investigating that crime scene, the captives had been relocated to the cave system to the north. By the time the ABI found the hole beneath the shed floor on Sunday morning, there was evidence that the men had been imprisoned there, but then moved.

When Pastor Anderson ended the call, he filled his family in on some of the details. He was still explaining and re-explaining everything when they arrived at the large, elegant shopping center. The large family had broken into two groups to travel the short distance from the DiaMo helipad to the mall in a couple of SUVs.

David thought he noticed Larson's Porsche in the Nordstrom's parking garage; so had his sister!

They all moved together, accompanied by their security, down to the skating rink level. There was a la Madeleine bakery, and they ordered in the line before finding a rink-side table. David prayed, and then John turned his attention to Lana. Presenting her with a select credit card in her name, he basically told her to go have fun. She didn't have to stop to meet the kids at intervals; he would keep up with everybody. He told her not to worry about returning any of the previous purchases. He basically felt that she had chosen things she liked, and that suited her. But then, being around Diana Faulkner filled her with self-doubt. He was telling her to keep the stuff, but expand on it, and get accessories, whatever she needed to feel put together. He told her he loved her, and so did the kids, and so did the church members-- just like she was.

Without waiting for her latte and omelet, she was gone. Not having much choice, Tammi started helping her little brother and sisters. When they had eaten, John paid for the three little kids to skate and got them started.

"Can David and I go look around?" Tammi questioned hopefully when he returned to the table.

His eyes met his daughter's. "Let me see your phone, Tammi." He held his hand out, expecting a stammering explanation, or immediate compliance. David sat there, uneasily.

"Your phone, Tammi!" Her father's voice wasn't necessarily louder, but more authoritative.

She had been looking everywhere for it, hoping she could find it before her parents found out it was lost. It was an expensive phone! She knew she would be in a ton of trouble. She started to cry. That made David mad; his dad never could stand to see her cry!

"Tammi, turn off your waterworks! I've asked twice for your phone!" Her dad was losing patience.

She sobbed harder. "It's lost! I've looked everywhere! I keep calling it, but no one answers it!"

David snorted derisively, and she shot him a killer look. "You're probably hiding it from me to get me in trouble!" she accused. "You're always mean to me, anyway!"

He shrugged at her indifferently. "Whatever! I don't have your stupid phone! If I did have, I would have showed it to Dad last night," he shot back.

"When did you notice the phone was gone?" the pastor was trying to deal wisely with his kids, but their incessant fighting got on his nerves.

Tammi blew her nose in a napkin and dabbed delicately at her eyes. "This morning, before we left home. I had it when we left from Saltgrass last night. I think it might have fallen out of the helicopter!" She had started crying harder.

"Well, isn't that convenient?" David couldn't believe what he was hearing! She was either the luckiest person on Earth, or she was even more devious than he had given her credit for!

Anderson was thinking, amusedly, that his daughter still didn't realize she might be in trouble about what was on her phone! She was just worried about being in trouble for losing it! Which, under normal circumstances, she would be. The light dawning on him, was that with the phone gone, the Lord wasn't just helping Tammi, but him as a dad.

"You sure it fell out?" he questioned

"Yes, Sir, pretty sure! I'm sorry, Daddy!"

David went to refill his dad's coffee mug and his Dr. Pepper.

"Tammi, dry your eyes, and stop crying! Go ahead and wipe off the eye make-up! You know we've been over this before. Give me the make-up. People are saying you've been calling Kerry Larson incessantly! Is that true?"

She pulled the little cosmetic bag out, releasing it reluctantly. It hit the trash bin from where Anderson was sitting. She glared at David for telling their dad about the calls.

"Go shopping, David. Faulkner gave you your credit card already. I'm going to watch the kids skate from here and visit some more with your sister."

David jumped up eagerly! He almost felt sorry for her!

❧ ❧

Callie seemed even quieter than usual. Finally, she confided to Mallie that she wasn't really looking for anything to buy. Since she wasn't traveling, she didn't have any specific needs.

Mallory wished Callie could go on the Turkey trip, but it hadn't really clicked with her to check into it. She just suggested that her friend buy something extra-cute for church the next day.

"You do sort of like Max, don't you?" she questioned teasingly.

"He's never even noticed me," was her blushing response.

Picking up a lovely medium-tone orchid sweater, Mallory held it up by her friend's face. It looked good. "Make him notice you!" Her tone was half-joking; half-serious.

"I don't want him to notice me because of clothes!" Callie's response was indignant.

Mallory really liked her new friend; she never liked to hurt anyone's feelings; she certainly didn't want to hurt their growing friendship.

"Well, no," she agreed. "But there's nothing wrong with always looking as good as you can. Don't do it because of Max; do it because of Callie.

"But externals are so phony. Being judged by your clothes or labels is totally superficial. I can't stand that. Why doesn't anybody care about who I am?"

"Do you think I'm phony because I try to look nice?" Mallory questioned.

"Of course not! You don't know what I mean. Skip it!" She was about to cry.

"I do know what you mean. Our clothes and bank statements aren't all there is to us. But, they are part of who we are; the key word here, being 'part'! There are lots of facets to both of us; to everyone. I want my clothes to be an outer expression of my inner person. I don't want them to be a disguise, and I don't want them to misrepresent me. I want them to show that I think I'm important enough to take care of. I want them to reflect God, and His Goodness, and Glory. And, I want them to reflect who I am."

Callie sighed and rehung the sweater. "Let's focus on the world-traveler here," she laughed. Mallory and Suzanne found a few items, then they all went in search of soft drinks. They were still full from the gourmet burgers, but decided to all try a gelato.

They were still sitting at the table when Kerry Larson passed by. Always good-mannered, he asked if he could join them. They talked briefly about the rescued employees, and he shared with Mallory, his concern about lawsuits. He asked her opinion about a preemptive offer. She hadn't thought about it. Just off the top of her head, she suggested that all of their medical costs resulting from the captivity definitely should be covered; as well as therapy, if they had ongoing issues as a result of the strain. She wanted them to receive their full salaries, as well as double over-time pay for the entire duration of their captivity. Any other lost time and income should be generously compensated, also. She knew one guy was a musician, who had missed playing his baritone in a suburban orchestra concert. One of the Arkansas guys hadn't been able to run his paper route.

Kerry turned his attention to Callie. "Hey, glad you could make it to Chili's the other night. We should try to get a bunch together more often. It's really fun getting acquainted with each other. Do you have any particular evening that works better for you than others?"

"No, I don't want to go meet with people without Mallory. She's planning to study every minute until the jet lifts off, and then be gone for two more weeks."

Her morose tone temporarily silenced the loquacious attorney.

Mallory laughed. "I'm not the bad guy, here! Blame Mr. Haynes!" She had temporarily forgotten that her mother was sitting beside her. Her mom had gotten pretty cool, but she knew she shouldn't have criticized the principal. "Sorry, Mom!" she apologized.

"Mallory, you're letting it overwhelm you, when you shouldn't. You still have nearly two weeks." Suzanne wrote out a schedule on a napkin. "You can finish the paper in less than a week. Plan to get together with your new church friends next Friday night, when it's done." Her mom's plan did look totally do-able. Organization was one of her strengths.

Kerry glanced over the railing to the ice rink three levels down. Amazed, he noticed the Anderson kids trying to skate. His eyes sought for Tammi. He didn't see her, and was amazed that he was relieved and sad, at the same time. John Anderson sat alone on a bench, watching his kids fall around on the ice. Kerry needed to talk to him. He excused himself from the ladies and made his way down to the rink.

After thirty minutes of serious discussion with his oldest daughter, Anderson sent her to shop, also. He had spoken with her, again, about the cosmetics. He talked to her about the attorney, forbidding her to call him. Her lost phone wasn't going to be replaced for awhile, anyway. Finally, he addressed the way she had been trying to dress. He tried to convince her that she was far too precious to cheapen herself. She seemed in better spirits and more cooperative when he sent her to find some new clothes, within the newly established parameters. He was just about to sigh with relief when Kerry Larson appeared in front of him, seemingly from nowhere.

"Pastor Anderson," Kerry began. "I know you're spending a day with your family. I need to speak with you. If this isn't a good time, I can make an appointment to come see you when you're in your office."

"No! Now's good! Let's get a table over there."

He moved back to the spot he had recently vacated. He wanted to look the guy right in the eye as they spoke!

"Daniel called me this morning about going on the trip," Kerry began. "I hadn't even considered going, but he made it sound really great. Of course, he knows I'm in love with Tammi, and all the complications that brings to the table. That's why, I just figured I wouldn't really even be invited to travel with the group. Guess he looks on the trip as one huge chaperone job for him."

He paused, uneasily, but Anderson didn't jump into the conversation to make things any easier for him.

"I guess, I don't know what to say to you, Sir. I mean, I'm not usually at a total loss for words. Your daughter is just beautiful; I didn't mean to fall in love with her. I've told myself I'm crazy; Faulkner's told me the same thing. I finally called my dad in Oregon. I think I could have heard him without the phone, when I told him she's just sixteen."

"Fifteen!" Anderson corrected. "Why didn't you tell your father she's fifteen?"

Kerry's face reddened. "I-I guess, because, she's almost sixteen. Saying it, he knew it was lame. He had lied to his father. Feeling the tears stinging his eyes, he shrugged, too choked up to speak; not knowing what to say, anyway.

"Guess Faulkner's got it right about the chaperone job. Are you asking me if you should bow out of the trip? Are you asking my permission for loving my daughter? I don't know what to say to you, either. You seem like a fairly decent guy. I don't think you should miss out on the trip. I think Tammi will be in seventh heaven for fourteen days, and then she'll pout until she sees you again-- which won't be soon. She says she lost her phone. She isn't getting another one for a long time. I don't want her to marry anyone until she finishes college, although, you know better than I do, that once she turns eighteen, I can't stop her. I haven't worked any of this out in my mind. Seems like I'm the last one to know you two have a thing for each other."

He saw Jeff fall on the ice and start to cry. Giving the attorney a dismissive nod, he moved toward his son. Hugging him, he looked at the bumped place sympathetically. It was heart-wrenching to see his older kids having to deal with some of the real bumps in life. He wasn't ready for it. He guessed it didn't matter. It was bearing down on him like a freight train!

Daniel offered to watch the kids at the skating rink, but all three needed new tennis shoes. Their feet were growing so fast, and they would be doing a good bit of walking on the trip. When that task was completed, they opted for lunch. They always had so much fun together; the kids were so much fun, saying such funny things, and asking such cute questions. People always noticed their family. As Daniel was paying out for the meal, he noticed a gentleman, staring at them more than usual. He nodded pleasantly. The guy didn't seem like a freak, but "in this day and age, you never know" Daniel had surmised.

"You Daniel Faulkner?"

Daniel stuck out his hand. "That's right, and you are?" he questioned courteously.

"Donovan Cline. We've never met before. My daughter met Mallory O'Shaughnessy at church."

"Oh, yes, Callie? She seems like a great girl!" Daniel picked up enthusiastically. The guy hadn't cracked a smile, and his cold expression gave Daniel a chill.

Diana had started away with the children, but they came back when Daniel got sidetracked.

"Yeah, you should really be proud of Callie. Nice meeting you, uh-Don, did you say?"

"Donovan!" Mr. glassy-glare corrected. Daniel just wanted to get away. Maybe the guy had a problem with Mallory.

Diana laughed. "He does the same thing with everybody's names," she intervened. "My name's Diana, but he must come in fifteen times a day, telling me to 'Die'!"

Relieved for some help, Daniel answered her innocently. "I don't tell you 'to die', Honey! Di's your name. I'm saying, Di, D-I! not Die, D-I-E!"

"He murders our children's name's too," Diana continued brightly to Mr. Cline. "Honey, the gentleman said his name is Donovan."

"Yeah, nice meetin' ya, Donovan." Daniel nodded, trying to steer his family away from the unpleasant man.

"Buy you coffee?" Mr. Cline spoke again, not accustomed to being brushed off.

"Go ahead, Honey," Diana encouraged. "I can get the kids started skating."

"Sure thing, Cline!" Daniel fell into step beside him. Diana had ignored the desperate appeal in his eyes as she scurried the children ahead of her.

"What's on your mind? The girls up to something I don't know about?" he demanded when they had purchased beverages and found a table.

"Tell me about this trip to Turkey!"

Daniel tried to be an easy-going kind of guy, and a good Christian. But this had to be the coldest, most arrogant guy he had ever met. "And that's your business, because?" He hadn't meant to respond in kind, but the guys whole demeanor put him off.

"My daughter wants to go!"

"Big jets go there several times every day! Work it out! I'm with my family!"

"Callie wants to go with Mallory!"

"She get everything she wants?" Daniel couldn't believe the guy was demanding for his daughter to be included with someone else's group.

"If I can, I try to make her happy. I know for a fact that every seat isn't filled on that chartered jet!"

"You don't know anything! We're still working on all of the arrangements and the details of who can go. We travel with a security contingency; they'll occupy quite a bit of room, too. It's Mallory's trip, and if she wants to include her friend, she can talk to me about it. If you don't mind, I want to go play with my kids!"

Donovan Cline sat motionless, watching the other man stride away. "Play with his kids!" He'd never thought of that. He made a phone call and Callie joined him, her team a few feet behind her. "You shop long enough?" he asked. His tone let her know she had. "You haven't bought anything," he observed.

Then, Erik picked Suzanne up, so Mallory headed home, herself. She had seen Lana and Tammi Anderson, but if David was with his family, Mallory never saw him. Then, she had noticed the Faulkners down at the ice rink.

When she got home, she watched the Moody Science film that her mom had brought her. Some of the properties of water really were amazing. She wasn't totally sold on the topic, but it seemed easy. She did the two hours of work on it her mom had scheduled for Monday, so she was already ahead on the project.

Boston was playing, and she watched the game, listlessly. She suddenly missed her dad, and her mom, and the little house in Murfreesboro. She walked from room to room, but the lovely mansion seemed unreal, and she felt like a clumsy guest. She tried to be excited about the trip. Evidently some of the Anderson's were going on it, but she was pretty sure David wouldn't be going. She called Callie, but, once again, her friend didn't answer. Her dog beside her, she sank onto the beach chair her mom had used earlier.

When she went back in, she started to iron out some of the wrinkles in her yellow, linen, damask dress. Someone grabbed the iron from her hand and shooed her away.

Callie still didn't answer, so she climbed into her big bed and tried to fill the loneliness with reading her Bible

The Lord had filled her life with beauty, and friends, and more than heart could wish for. Then she tried playing the piano and singing.

Going back to bed, she cried herself to sleep.

Chapter 19

TREACHERY

SUNDAY MORNING! RAIN splatted loudly against the doors and windows of Mallory's suite. Usually she loved the powerful voice of the thunder. This morning, she just pulled blankets and pillows around her ears, trying not to hear any of the noise of the storm; trying to keep from waking up and facing the day.

She couldn't figure out what her problem was! Everything was great, beautiful, fabulous! She kept asking the Lord to forgive her for her ingratitude and whininess in the midst of His marvelous blessings. She had already been feeling a little bit blue, before whatever had happened with Callie. Unable to fall back asleep, she threw the covers back, frustrated. Opening one of the four curtained French doors which opened onto her terrace, she stood morosely as raindrops stung her, and a brisk north wind made her shiver. So much for wearing her springy "tablecloth" dress to church. Even though she felt pretty bummed out, the thought hadn't even occurred to her, of missing Sunday School and church.

She asked for hot chocolate and toast, and sank into a deep double-recliner, where she could watch the storm through wide plate glass. From where she watched, she could see a large portion of the elegant mansion, as well as much of the beautifully landscaped grounds. The flowers stood out, more brilliant than ever, against the gray monotone of the stone and the heavens. Digging out her camera, she zoomed in on some of the beautiful roses, tulips, jonquils, and pansies. No wonder her mom had taken comfort in growing things. She was putting her camera away when a double rainbow swept across the dull neutral that was the sky. She stood, transfixed! Tears filled her eyes again! She shot picture after picture. Finally, she decided she'd better get moving, unless she wanted to show up late: she definitely didn't want to do that.

She was putting the finishing touches on styling her hair when her phone rang. Diana's musical voice, calling from Tulsa!

"Morning, Mallory! How are you this morning? Alexandra just told me that she thought she saw you at the Galleria yesterday. Then, I was talking to your mom, and she said the two of you and your friend Callie were there. Wish I had known you were there. I just thought you had plans. I didn't want to bother you just because we were coming to Dallas for the day."

"You guys aren't ever a bother. Feel free to let me know whenever you're coming. I like you to stay here, when it works out."

"Still, I'm sorry I didn't know you were right at the mall when we were. Are you sure you're okay? Have you been crying? Is it cold and rainy there?"

"I have been crying, but I know I shouldn't be. It isn't anything for you to worry about. I can't figure out what my problem is." She sighed, and she was struggling not to cry again. "I mean, look what the Lord has done for me!"

Diana laughed, but it wasn't mean at all. Like grown-ups could laugh at teen-agers' problems, dismissing them as trivial. Her laughter was sympathetic.

"Don't be too hard on yourself for crying, Mallory. Crying is important. It's one of the gifts God has given us. Tears are an escape valve, mentally and physically. Don't chastise yourself, that if you're where you need to be spiritually, you won't cry. Think about Jeremiah, in the Bible. He was known as the "Weeping Prophet". That didn't mean his relationship with God was wrong. It really meant it was right. We know that Jesus wept. I mean, when you think about it Mallory, look what you've been through this year! And it isn't even May yet! You have reason to cry! Go ahead and cry!"

She already was, even before Diana's permission.

"Yes, the Lord has been good to you, and He has safeguarded you and cared for you. But, you have still lost your father, and you've nearly been murdered twice, and abducted. Just the injury you sustained from Melville, and the viciousness of his attack would be enough to affect you emotionally for a while. You aren't clinically depressed, or having a pity party. You really need to heal. Actually, your heart has been hurt with grown-up pain for more than a year. When David got rebellious, you really felt personally betrayed by him, didn't you? I mean, we take hits to our spirits, and we try to go on like nothing happened. And it has!"

Mallory was listening eagerly, trying not to cry so hard she couldn't hear the tender, comforting voice. It seemed like Jesus was talking directly to her heart, through the lilting voice of her treasured new friend. The sun was coming out again in her heart, as it began to chase the clouds away from the leaden sky outside.

She dressed quickly in an ivory skirt she had bought the day before, a soft aqua silk blouse, and the navy blazer. Surveying herself in an ornate, full-length mirror, she managed a smile. Her damaged make-up needed repair. Then, she slid her feet into aqua pumps. She carried a metallic gold handbag, adding her pearls, and some gold and diamond jewelry, before heading to the garage.

Callie wasn't at Sunday School. Then, she didn't show up for church, either. Max asked Mallie if she knew where she was. She didn't tell him anything, except that she didn't know. She didn't call or text her friend again. She had tried that, and left quite a few messages.

She was heading for her car, when Kerry caught up with her. She had seen him from across the auditorium, but they hadn't spoken. She wondered if Daniel and Diana had called him about her tearfulness, earlier. It was hard to tell; he was just usually pretty nice.

He was treating the pastor and his family to dinner at Macaroni Grill, and he invited Mallory. He figured Mallory should get acquainted with the new pastor and his family. Mallory laughingly accepted the invitation and followed her attorney to the restaurant. She was so used to the Andersons that she figured she would be really nervous around a new pastor's family. She was quite bemused, as she realized they were nervous around her. They were trying not to act too interested in her jewelry and money. It just turned out to be a little odd and awkward.

Overall, though, she liked them. Paul Ellis, his wife, Mary Beth, and his two younger children, Paige, aged fourteen, and Evan, twelve.

"I want to get busy right away," Mallory confided to them. "In Arkansas, I helped in the nursery and was an alternate pianist. My dad and I helped with the cleaning every third week. I worked in AWANA and Vacation Bible School. You guys have that, don't you?"

The pastor laughed. "We do. There's always plenty to do for anyone really willing to work."

Mallory was aware that Kerry was trying to slow her down. "My attorney wants to be sure I don't get so overcommitted I can't do my Geometry!" She laughed. "Like I would allow such a great joy to get shoved aside!"

The two kids had finally laughed. The teen-aged girl, whom their parents had been hoping would join the church, seemed pretty normal and friendly.

The chilly rain dampened the spirits and the attendance of the college/career class Daniel Faulkner taught at the Honey Grove Baptist Church in Tulsa. Trying not to become overly discouraged, he placed a call to Roger Sanders. Sander's spirits had been pretty buoyed up, especially since the entrance of his first grandchild, Anthony Brent Watson, Jr. Faulkner hoped to catch his friend between lunch and a Sunday afternoon nap. All the Sanders, including Connie and Brent were just finishing their Sunday afternoon meal.

Sanders commiserated with his friend about having attendance go down, even when you worked hard at making it grow. He bragged on all the cute new things his grandson was doing.

"Walked home from the hospital, did he?" Faulkner couldn't resist sticking a pin in grandpa's ego. Diana, listening in, frowned at his meanness; but then she couldn't help laughing. Sanders laughed, too, after a pained interval.

Faulkner wasn't usually much of a telephone yacker, but he continued the conversation with his new business acquaintance. He knew Sanders had concerns about leaving his business for a two week trip. Especially, since Suzanne was coming along, too.

Besides, Faulkner had been troubled since the previous day, after his encounter with Donovan Cline. So much so, that even though it was getting late by the time they had returned home, he had still googled the name. The guy had a degree in chemical engineering. So did Sanders, so Faulkner just wondered if the two men were acquainted.

When he mentioned the name, Sanders went silent.

Roger had been holding the baby. Suddenly, he handed him off to Beth as he rose from the table to head for his study. Beth gave her daughter a startled look. Connie had heard the name; it had brought an event to her mind that she had forgotten! Something she should have told her dad!

Once in his carefully-appointed office, Sanders closed the door before responding. "Where did you hear that name?" His voice came out hoarse and strained. Faulkner couldn't believe the difference in Sander's demeanor. More worried now than before, he recounted the encounter with the man at the mall. He finished with, "I take it, you've met him!"

Sanders still hadn't spoken again.

"I told my security to double up, and watch my back. Guess I wasn't overreacting, huh?" Faulkner's dread continued to skyrocket in measure with the other man's silence.

Sander's voice sounded ominous. "That's not the kind of back-stabbing you need to guard against. That guy will own your company! Get Whitmore on site, your attorneys, CPA's, shareholders! The guy's a shark. He chews up companies and spits them out! You think it's too late to call and tell him his kid can go anywhere she wants with us?" Roger queried.

Faulkner laughed uneasily. He thought of the man's cold, unblinking gaze, and the shark on Diana's sweater. A chill went through him, and tears sprang to his eyes. His company! It was his dad's too! Had he blown three lifetimes of work? Three generations of careers? Even as terror was catching him in a vice, he was trying to remember his own "FEAR" sermon. Now, his own voice would barely make itself audible.

"Calm down, Roger. Tell me what you know! Stick to facts!"

"Those are the facts! How did you know I know him?"

"He's a chemical engineer; so are you. I didn't know for sure you had met."

"Yeah, that's one of his degrees. We have known one another since back in the days. Not sure how many other degrees he's gotten since. Marketing, MBA. He must own fifty businesses. Most of them not acquired under the most pleasant circumstances. He designs golf courses; he designed the one at the country club, here in Hope. We used to golf together. He's a great golfer; has a real psych game; messes with your head. I never came close to beating him. I thought we were kind of friends. It was mostly before I got saved.

"Then, my entire family got saved, because of Patrick and Mallory. We all started serving the Lord. We were all happier than we'd ever been. My company was on the brink of taking off; I thought revenues were going to double that year. Then, it all just fell apart. We even lost our house, but we held onto the business."

"That was because of Cline?" Faulkner interrupted. "What happened?"

"No, that was because of the Lord! I couldn't understand it! It made me mad at God! I was tithing and serving Him, and then there's this huge setback! Looking back now, I can see it! When my company looked like a big plum, just ripe for the picking, Cline had everything in place to raid it in a hostile takeover!"

"While pretending to be your friend?" Faulkner demanded indignantly.

Sanders laughed for the first time. "If you consider his behavior 'pretend friendly'! Don't ask me why I was shocked! He only ever acted like a predator. If I considered him a friend; it was because I was naïve."

Faulkner's turn for stunned silence! "How could an adversary like that appear, poof!? From nowhere!? You're having a fun lunch with your family! Laughing, Talking! And the rug gets ripped from under you!"

He listened numbly to the rest of the story. "Cline pulled the plug on the hostile takeover when my profits took the dive. God saved the Sander's Corporation to spring back at a later time."

When the conversation ended, both men continued to sit staring, unseeing, out the windows of their offices.

A timid tap on his office door brought Sanders back to reality. "Come in," he replied.

Connie opened the door a crack, and peeked around it. Her dad smiled a welcome to her, but the expression seemed forced. He looked pretty pale.

"Mom made some coffee, and there's lemon meringue pie. Are you in? Was everything okay with the Faulkners besides his Sunday School class' being down?"

"Yeah. Tell Mom I'm okay for now. I'll be down in a little bit." He smiled at his daughter again, but she wasn't leaving. "Shut the door, will you, Honey?" He meant as she left, but she stepped farther in, closing it behind her. He adored his family, and he was always glad to visit with his spunky, personable first-born! But he needed to think! Faulkner's call had him rattled! He couldn't decide what to say to his daughter.

"Um, Daddy," she began. "There's something I forgot to tell you about, that happened when you and mom were in Hawaii. I think it might be important. I'm sorry I forgot. It happened right at the same time as Suzanne's coming in. We got so involved with contacting her back, that I forgot until just this afternoon."

"It's okay, Connie. Why don't you tell me about it later? I kind of have a lot of stuff on my mind right now. Tell your mom to enjoy getting such a long turn with Tony. I get an extra long turn next time." He was trying to sound anything but as panicked as he felt!

She stood there, her eyes filling with tears. "Is it about that Mr. Cline?" Her voice was a soft whisper. "That's what I forgot to tell you. He came into the corporate office, asking for you, on that same Monday. He just said he'd come back by another time. What did he do, Daddy? Is he why you're so upset?"

"Don't worry, Baby. Tell Mom I'll get that pie later."

Daniel Faulkner continued to sit in his big leather swivel chair. The house was so quiet that he was pretty sure the kids must be asleep. Hostile takeover! Never in all of the myriads of things he spent his time worrying about, had such an awful thought occurred to him! Now the vague worry that had been tugging at the back of his mind all morning had turned into palpable fear. He felt paralyzed! Should he call his dad? His attorneys? The computer systems guy? Was Cline really after

GeoHy? Would he be after Mallory's enterprises, too? Sanders' again? Delia and Shay's? How could this happen in America? You could spend three generations to build something up, and lose it overnight to bottom-feeders? Of course, he had heard of its happening. Just not to him!

Dropping his head onto his arms on the inlaid, antique desk, he sobbed.

He felt something touch his shoulder. Startled, he began a reflexive upward swing with his fist. It was Diana. He had figured she was napping. He hadn't heard her soft tap, followed by her approach. Pausing in his upswing, his eyes met hers, and he dropped his gaze guiltily. How could he tell her what his stupidity was about to cost everyone? His arrogance?

She continued to stand, frightened and perplexed. The nurse in her could tell everything was wrong. Rapid breathing, pounding pulse, dilated pupils, the fight reflex! She had never seen him so distraught. Tears were filling her eyes. What concerned her the most, was that something had been bothering him that he hadn't confided to her. She thought they handled things together, as a team.

Prayer was usually a normal response for her, but she was temporarily so stunned that she hadn't even thought of that! It seemed that she had stood helplessly, gazing at him, for a long time. She heard the clock in the foyer chiming two. Five minutes hadn't even passed.

"What am I gonna do, Di?" he questioned hoarsely. "What's gonna happen to us?" He pulled her into his arms, and she clung to him while he sobbed. She could feel his heart pounding, hard and fast, under her hand. Instinctively, she counted.

"Daniel, calm down, Honey! Whatever it is, we can deal with it! The Lord will help us. What happened?"

"We're ruined! That guy, Cline! My mom and dad, too! They thought they were taken care of for the rest of their lives! How can I tell them, Honey?" His anguished gaze met hers.

"It's only money," she began. "Your heart's working too hard. Please calm down. Nothing's out of the Lord's hands. You know that!" She was really worried about him.

"It isn't 'only money', Honey. It's sustenance! It's security. What we've had represents three generations of men giving themselves to something. It's who I am; who we've all been. If I lose, GeoHy, I lose myself!"

His voice was lost in sobs. Harder sobs, and he had started to shake uncontrollably.

She pulled free, and sat on his desk, facing him. He was starting to hyperventilate, and she felt totally helpless. She glanced around at the items on his desk. A real neatnik, he kept the surface pretty clean and organized. Nothing on his computer screen presented any clues to what was happening either. Picking up his phone, she scrolled his call log. He had been talking to Roger. She started to push call back, but Daniel was holding his hand out for his phone.

"I'll tell you, Honey," he gasped. "Just give me a sec!"

Moving into the half-bath that adjoined his office, he splashed water on his face. Still toweling his hands and face, he sank heavily back into his chair. His breathing continued to be ragged, punctuated with sobs. Diana began to cry. She liked the beautiful house and cars, the elegant clothes and jewelry, the corporate life-style they lived. But that wasn't why she was crying. She was crying because she loved him so much, and something had shattered him. And he was looking at her with an expression, of lostness, like she had never seen in his eyes, before. It was heart-breaking!

At last, he had been able to get most of the story gasped out. His wife listened, sympathetically, without interrupting him. Even as he confided in her, his confidence began to return. In the middle of recounting Roger's words to her, he stopped and said a prayer. He didn't even slide to his knees. Just a breathless, "Lord, we need your help, please."

He called for coffee, then he urged Diana into the comfortable desk chair, and he perched where she had been, on his desk. He smiled at her and winked mischievously. He placed a call to Dan Vaught, one of his attorneys. He really hated doing any corporate business on Sunday. He apologized for calling, but he had gotten a little glimpse of hope. Vaught told him that GeoHy's stock was pretty well tied up by investors who were close to the Faulkners and the corporation. Few, if any, of them would be willing to sell to Cline, regardless of what he might offer. He was quite sure that there wasn't enough stock available for Cline to obtain, to gain a majority vote. He was familiar with Cline, though, and he suggested Daniel not cross him again, if it could be avoided.

"Hope you aren't charging me extra for that advice!" Faulkner laughed as he disconnected.

His next call was to Larson, and he apologized to him for the Sunday call about business matters.

"That's okay," Larson responded jovially. "I'm already defiling the Lord's day by doing laundry"

This time, Daniel's laughter had brought some color back into his ashen face.

Kerry listened, amazed, to what his friend was telling him. He thought Mallory's assets were all safe. Patrick's corporation belonged mainly to Mallory. The remainder of the stock held by Suzanne, the Faulkners, Kerry, Shay, and Delia, the rest, was a pretty small fraction. Nothing there for Cline to get his hooks into. He was surprised that Faulkner didn't want Callie to go on the trip with them to Turkey.

"It wasn't anything against Callie," Faulkner responded. "I guess it's just the way her dad acted. I can't even describe--"

"Yeah, I've heard the guys a total charmer! But, hey, you know this trip is mostly on Mallie's dime. We should include her friend if we can work it out."

Diana called Shay about their business interests. Shay told her they had considered issuing additional stock to raise capital for expansion, but they hadn't acted upon it. Diana suggested that they might consider offering a private offering to the immediate circle.

Roger Sanders sat silently, reflecting on his past association with Donovan Cline. Reliving the past episode had caused him, once again, to be awed by the way God had saved his business. Since then, he had been far more careful, less trusting. He thought he had everything better protected legally, but the guy's name still caused a panic response with him. Connie's apologetic revelation hadn't calmed his nerves any. He figured the guy would be on the golf course, but he phoned the old number he had accessed. An accented voice answered. He figured it was house staff. He left his name and number before going in search of Andy and a slice of lemon pie.

Connie was sleeping, with her new son in the crook of her arm. Roger kissed both heads. An empty pie plate in the sink seemed to say he had come too late, but Beth appeared.

"Everything okay?" she asked, searching his face carefully.

"Yeah; except I missed out on the pie!"

Her folded arms and stern expression told him she didn't believe him.

"Remember Donovan Cline?"

Her startled expression answered his question. "Guess he followed the Faulkners around the Dallas Galleria yesterday to try to get Callie included in the trip with Mallory.

He was his usual arrogant, overbearing self! Anyway, Faulkner ended up telling him to get lost. Then Cline acted so creepy that Faulkner got worried. I told him what he tried to do to us. Anyway, guess Connie heard Faulkner say Cline's name, so that made her remember that Cline came to Hope looking for me a couple of weeks ago. Whenever we were in Hawaii. He told her he'd come back another time. She forgot the whole thing until today. I called and left a message at his house. Maybe I'll hear something from him when he finishes his golf game."

Beth shook her head slowly. "He was here, and Connie forgot?" She pulled a large slice of pie from the refrigerator. Saving it hadn't been easy. He sat down at the long kitchen counter with a cup of coffee. His cell phone vibrated.

Mallory moved her computer out to one of the patio tables to work on her homework. The sun and the clouds were still fighting over the sky. A cool breeze frisked around her. Dinky lay napping next to her, and her iPod played her favorite music, blending with the soft murmur of the shimmering blue water in the swimming pool. Trying to concentrate on her Geometry problems was always difficult. Now, she was worried about Callie. She guessed she must have hurt her feelings more than she thought, about getting something new and cute. She sighed. Worried or not, she had to do her work. She finished the math, then had to label some muscles on a picture for Biology. She studied the diagram before sending the answers. To her surprise, no pop quiz followed. Then, she worked for an hour on the Chemistry paper, getting even further ahead on the schedule her mom had worked out to help her with the project.

Kerry called to talk to her about Callie's going on the trip. It was the first Mallory had heard about it. She hadn't known Mr. Cline had been at the Galleria the previous afternoon. She figured he had finally trusted her security. He was uptight about Callie's safety! Mallory couldn't figure out how he could want her to go on their trip, when he wouldn't let her out of his sight! She finally confided to Kerry that she thought Callie was mad at her, anyway.

On the return trip from Galleria, Donovan Cline was still angry about Faulkner's treatment of him. Callie was mortified! She couldn't believe her father had tracked Mallory's guardian and his family to a restaurant. Then, he had eavesdropped on the family's lunch with his phony 'Bluetooth' listening device, before ambushing the man to demand that Callie be allowed to travel with him. Callie burst into tears when her dad told her that he had checked, and there were seats available on the charter jet.

"That doesn't mean I'm entitled to one, just because it's there. How do you know who's going and what they're doing, and how many seats will be empty? I'm so humiliated now, I never want to see any of them again!"

When she got home, she went to bed and wouldn't talk to him.

He was annoyed in response. She had told him that she felt left out, and she wished she could go on the trip with her new friend. Trying to make her happy wasn't easy! Those so-called Christians could have acted a little nicer. Sometimes, Callie acted so much like her mother--!

Sunday wasn't much better. Recently, Sunday had been a lift for his daughter. Her faith and the church had brought life and excitement to her. Now, she had refused to get out of bed, still claiming she couldn't face anybody.

He poked angrily at his dinner, then indulged in an extra drink.

Before turning in, he returned to her door. Usually, he knocked! This time, he didn't! Callie sat at her computer. Stunned at his sudden appearance, she desperately hit some keys. Her work disappeared from the monitor.

"What were you looking at, Callie?" he demanded.

"Nothing!" her response was sullen. " I was just looking at some puzzles."

She had a genius IQ, and she did like solving things, but Donovan knew she was lying. Grabbing the laptop, and striding onto the terrace, he flung it into the pool three stories below. He nearly lost his balance in doing so, but managed not to go over the low stone railing himself.

"Don't think you'll have another one soon," he sneered drunkenly before storming out.

Callie cried, and cried, and cried!

Six months previously, she had seen a story about her mother on the local news, and had been transfixed by it. Carmine, a divorcee, had begun as a clerk in a law office. Now, she had fought her way through all the phases of becoming an attorney, and she had passed the bar exam! The story mentioned Kerry Larson, as someone who had mentored and encouraged her in her struggle. Callie had gone to the same story on-line and saved it in her laptop. She liked to reread it, and just look at the picture of her mother, whenever things seemed bad. That was the site she was on when her father burst in. Her dad told her often that her mother didn't care anything about her, but Callie still idolized her anyway. She never spoke to him about her mother.

Earlier in the week, at Chili's, Callie had mentioned Carmine Henderson to Kerry. He had beamed with pride, so Callie asked him for her phone number. It caught him by surprise, and he wasn't sure about giving it out. Then he decided Callie was probably okay.

It was nearly midnight when Callie composed a text:

"Hello, Miss Henderson.

My name is Callie. You may not remember me. I am very unhappy. I am almost eighteen. I have money. Can you help me? Thank you. Callie Cline."

She agonized over whether to send it. Mallory had brought happiness to her for a week, before her father had destroyed that, too. Mallory had explained to Callie how she always read her Bible when she felt lonely and unhappy. Callie decided to try it-- after she sent the text!

Chapter 20

TRASH

WHISKING BY HELICOPTER to her office on Monday morning, Mallory was the first one to arrive. Mixing a hot chocolate packet in one of her new colorful, pottery mugs, she made her way to the spacious corner office. She had confided her plan to Diana, about some changes in the décor, to make it more feminine and reflective of Mallory's personality. Of course, Diana had thought it was a great idea, but she suggested waiting until after the trip. Evidently there was a bazaar in Istanbul which was one of the oldest and largest in the world. Diana was really pumped about the shopping, and her enthusiasm was contagious. She was pretty sure there would be some mementos from the trip, that they could incorporate into a new décor. Smiling to herself, Mallie was imagining what her office might end up looking like. Not knowing for sure what Diana was thinking about, she hoped it wouldn't end up resembling the 'harem' in the Topkapi Palace!

After her Bible reading and prayer time, she checked her emails. Her Sunday afternoon schoolwork had received good grades. Mr. Haynes had also sent an introductory view of Geology and related careers. Mallory studied it, fascinated. Some of the options, she was aware of. It was definitely a vast field. She laughed at herself. "Vast" was an understatement! Geology covered the entire face of the Earth! Including the sea bed! She guessed it must cover celestial bodies, too. Geologists were the primary scientists to study the rock samples brought back from the moon. She wondered, curiously, if Daniel had ever had access to the "moon rocks". Her other e-mails were from Shay, Tammi, and Calvary Baptist where she had joined the previous evening. She was glad for the welcoming message, even though she knew it was a formality. She responded to Shay and Tammi, before calling Marge in to work on some corporate correspondence.

Carmine Henderson arrived at Kerry Larson's law office at nine-thirty. Since passing her bar exam, she had interviewed with various firms. For a corporate attorney, Kerry's firm was at the top of the list. Since Kerry was only a junior member, Carmine hated to ask him to risk his aspiring career to help her any more. While she awaited her appointment with one of the senior attorneys, she idly scrolled through her phone. For the first time, she noticed the message from her daughter. Terror seized her, and she was momentarily frozen with indecision. The interview was of the utmost importance! But compared to Callie!

Trying to remain calm, she accessed information for the Southlake police department. Speaking softly, she tried to explain the situation, but the man on the line told her to speak up. Feeling like everyone around her could hear her, she still raised her voice slightly. She explained about the text from her daughter, explaining that Callie might be in danger.

After accessing the address and the property-tax level, the impersonal voice said there would need to be more proof of a problem than the text indicated. He informed her the police didn't knock on the doors of residents because their minor children claimed to be unhappy. Callie hadn't claimed to be at risk.

Fighting back tears, she hung up. Her ex-husband terrified her! But she had assumed her daughter was safe! Dread flooded over her. She wondered if Donovan were aware of the text yet. She was certain he would find out!

Kerry Larson and William Jacobson, a senior partner, entered the upscale office suite at the same time. Larson started to give Carmine an encouraging nod prior to her interview. Her anguished expression alarmed him instantly. This interview was so important! He knew the firm wouldn't be interested in Carmine if their first impression of her was "Damsel in Distress"! You pretty much had to prove to them that you could chew people up and spit them out!

"William, this is Carmine Henderson," he introduced hastily. "Carmine, one of the senior partners, William Jacobson!"

Carmine rose with a disarming smile, and shook the other attorney's extended hand.

Kerry Larson poured two cups of coffee and followed his associate to the conference room. He handed the first cup to Jacobson; and then, in what he hoped was a smooth maneuver, he handed the other one to Carmine, at the same time, pulling her phone free.

Once in the privacy of his office, he started searching her phone. Callie's text came right up. He reread the terse text a couple of times, as the light began to dawn. Callie's words were, "You may not remember me." She had met Carmine before! The shy girl seemed unsure she had made a memorable impression. Why would Carmine look so stricken?

Still confused, he called Mallory. If Carmine couldn't help the girl as an attorney, maybe he and Mallory could, as her friends.

"Hey, Mallory," he greeted. "You hear anything from Callie? Just wondered if you knew why she wasn't at church yesterday. You think it could be 'cause Faulkner tried to give her dad the brush off about letting her come to Turkey with us?"

Mallory was caught off-guard. She didn't know anything about Mr. Cline's conversation with her guardian. She told Kerry about not getting any response to calls or texts from her friend since they parted at the mall Saturday afternoon. She told him she thought Callie's feelings were hurt over their disagreement about outer appearance and real depth. The possibility that Callie might be in trouble had never entered her mind. She immediately wanted to call Erik Bransom, but Kerry suggested she begin calling Callie's cell. He was going to call the hard line at the house and speak to Mr. Cline, if he could.

Callie still wasn't answering Mallie's calls. Donovan Cline spoke with Kerry, just saying Callie wasn't feeling well. The man's voice sounded hard and non-committal, but Kerry desperately pushed a little harder. "She's okay, though?" he was trying not to sound panicked.

"Like you people care!" He responded gruffly and banged the receiver down.

Frowning slightly, his steepled fingers tapping together at his chin, Kerry breathed a hasty prayer. When Mallory called back, fearful and frustrated, he asked her to meet him at the little in-house café. By the time Kerry arrived, Mallory was already at a table, talking on her phone. He hoped Callie had finally answered. To his surprise, she was reaming Daniel Faulkner out for telling Callie's dad, "No" about the trip without even talking to her about it. Usually, she was so meek and quiet around Faulkner, that Larson could hardly believe what he was hearing. Evidently his client could be a Jekyll and Hyde; a lot like Patrick had been! She wasn't giving Faulkner much of a chance to explain himself. The only reason the guy got a break at all was because her phone was ringing with an incoming call! Callie!

"Callie's on my other line!" She cut off Daniel's explanation, and responded to the other line.

"Mallory, I'm fine! Tell Mr. Larson I'm okay! Please just leave me alone!" The call ended. Kerry signaled a server and ordered iced tea, then soup of the day and Caesar salads. It was a little early for lunch, but after a short wait, the meal arrived.

They were relieved that they had heard Callie's voice, but they still didn't know what to do. Finally, Kerry agreed to call Bransom, at least for advice.

Donovan Cline awakened on Monday morning, with a headache and a groundskeeper presenting him with the dripping, ruined laptop computer he had just scooped from the pool. Sitting up with a moan, he accepted it gingerly. He sent the guy on his way with the usual warning to keep his mouth shut. Surveying his devastation woefully, he dropped his head into his hands. He vaguely remembered the episode with Callie. He rang for coffee and summoned his daughter.

When Callie received the word that her father wanted her in his suite, she was filled with dread. He never sent for her to visit him there. She should have already hidden her phone, but she had continued watching it, eagerly, hopefully! For any response from her mother! "Maybe Kerry had given her a wrong number," she tried to encourage herself.

Defeatedly, she slid the phone with the incriminating text into the pocket of her robe. She didn't even delete it; his staff could get the entire history off of it, if he wanted them to. She tapped softly, and he told her to come in. She followed the maid in, who had responded with coffee, and waited until his cup was poured and served.

"Have you eaten anything this morning?" he asked her when the door had closed.

"No, Sir, not yet." She wasn't hungry, but she didn't want to make him mad by saying she wasn't. She stood nervously, trying not to start crying.

"The gardener pulled your computer out of the pool; what happened to it? Sit down!"

She sank down on the steps that adjoined the high, four-poster bed. Nothing she could think of to say, seemed wise. He wouldn't want to hear that he was drunk! He wouldn't want to hear that he had done it in a rage. She couldn't think of a logical explanation about how she had inadvertently dropped it at an angle that would have caused it to land in the pool! Her gaze met his helplessly.

"I'm sorry, Daddy. It was all my fault!"

His head hurt so that he could hardly stand to move. "What was on the computer?" he asked again.

Tearfully, she told him about the story and picture of her mother. She finished by pulling her phone out and showing him the text, dreading the rage that was certain to come.

Instead, Donovan Cline began to weep. "No wonder your friends are worried about you. You really should call them and tell them you're okay. I'm sorry I embarrassed you with Mallory and your other church friends. Guess I always mess everything up. I'm sorry, Callie. I really love you. I want you to be happy."

The behavior was so bizarre for him, that Callie was totally nonplused. The only thing she could figure out was that with his realizing she would be free when she turned eighteen in a few months, he was taking a new tack to bind her to him with a guilt trip. She had never seen him cry; the crack in his thick crust had a significance that was temporarily lost on her

Even with his head pounding painfully, and his stomach churning, he called for breakfast to be served on the terrace outside his sitting room.

Pulling on a robe, he led his daughter out to the table. He courteously pulled a chair back for her: a first!

"Call your friends," he encouraged again, making a little impatient circle-gesture with his hand, before he shoved it back into his robe pocket. That was when she made the terse call to Mallory's cell phone.

He shook his head. "You accused me of being rude to all your friends; what was that? I actually think they all genuinely care about you." He sipped cautiously on some tomato juice.

Erik and Suzanne Bransom grabbed breakfast together on Monday morning before Suzanne headed to her job. As usual, Bransom had a busy day planned, too. He had spoken to Ivan Summers and Janice Collins at church the previous day. They were getting accolades for the rescue raid of the DiaMo employees. Of course, the FBI and the Forestry Service had played big parts in it, too. Now, to Bransom's surprise, Janice Collins had come to him about leaving her position in the ABI for a place on Mallory's personal security team. He had mixed feelings about it. He felt like working personal security should be for ex-law enforcement and ex-military personnel who had somehow lost the privilege of serving the public and the greater good. It was his feeling that law enforcement was the most important work there was. Leaving it for personal gain was like abandoning your post. He was pretty sure she was quitting in order to push Summers up the ladder, and that the two of them were planning on getting married. He was happy for that. She would definitely be an asset for Mallory. He shook his head.

He was planning to reinterview Herb Carlton, too. The Westeran Arkansas Paw Shop owner had acted less than delighted about it. Bransom had agreed to meet him at the Starbucks in Target. A Federal agent hanging around a pawn shop could hurt business; previously, he wouldn't have cared.

He kissed Suzanne good-bye, and she hurried out to the sporty Jaguar. He watched her retreat. She was so beautiful. Her fragrance lingered after she was gone.

He still had an hour before the interview with Carlton. He paid the cashier for their meal, witnessing briefly, and leaving a gospel tract.

Maneuvering the big agency car from its space, he called Faulkner about Collins and her desire to switch from the public sector over to private.

Once in Starbucks, he hooked up his laptop. Everyone else was hyped about the upcoming trip. Now that his cases were winding up, he planned to take a look at some of the on-line sites, for himself.

Kerry Larson called him about Mallory's new little friend. Kerry had finally realized that Carmine was Callie's mother; and Donovan Cline's ex-wife. Bransom asked him a few more questions. Kerry kept stressing how much danger there could possibly be. Carmine was terrified.

Bransom listened carefully, reminding himself that there are always two sides to every story. Finally, he got Cline's phone numbers, promising Kerry that he would talk to the guy. The attorney thought Bransom should have the police show up with battering rams and CPS.

"Whoa, slow down there." Bransom's gruff laugh followed. "You said you were calling for advice. Sounds like you're giving me orders. Last I knew, I was taking orders from lots of people, but you weren't one of 'em. I said I'll talk with the guy. Then, I'll call you back. I have an appointment, so it might be early afternoon before I get back with you. Leave it alone until then. Thank the Lord, the police can't just charge into people's homes for no reason. You didn't learn that in law school?"

He hung up, enjoying leaving Larson at a loss for words. He called Cline's cell number first, and he answered right away. Bransom told him what he knew; Callie's friends were worried about her, and her mother was in hysterics.

"I know," the guy confided. "I've never harmed my daughter! At least not physically!"

"I know!" Bransom responded. "I already checked. Never any record of physical abuse or suspicious injuries. Nothing about physical abuse with your ex-wife either! You've used your money and contacts to strong-arm your way into sole custody. How'd you keep Carmine from having visitation privileges?"

"It's a long story! I told you Callie's fine!"

"Bet it is long, and not very pretty!" Erik shot back. "How you planning on staying in control, once your daughter turns eighteen? That worries me. Why don't you take Callie and meet with your ex-wife someplace public? Seems like she's earned a visit."

There was silence. "Maybe I'll give that a try!"

Mallory returned to her office and called Daniel Faulkner back. She had just found out that the pilgrimage to Turkey was being provided by DiaMo. Daniel was CFO, and she didn't have a problem with the arrangements he was making. She just wanted to be more aware of all that was going on. All she knew was hearsay. This person was going; this one might. So and so had been invited. First class tickets on Turkish Air from New York City had been lined up; but then with the flux of the arrangements, the seats had been relinquished, and a jet had been chartered. She figured Mr. Faulkner had plenty of other business going on, so she asked him to have someone assemble all of the facts so far, and fax or e-mail it to her ASAP.

Marge buzzed her on the intercom. Carmine Henderson, finished with her law-partner interview, was asking to meet her.

Eager to meet her friend's mother, and concerned for Callie, she dashed out to the lobby to meet her. Kerry was with her, and he made the introduction. At first, Mallory thought Carmine didn't look like Callie, at all. Callie pretty much prided herself on looking as plain as possible: her mom was really cute, high maintenance! As they interacted further, she could see some of the same expressions and mannerisms. Kerry asked for iced tea and Carmine for hot, in response to Mallory's offer. Kerry was miffed from his talk with Bransom. They hadn't heard whether Bransom had talked to Cline because Bransom had another interview to conduct in the meanwhile.

Carmine's cell vibrated. She blanched! Donovan! She braced herself for the vulgar, cruel tongue lashing she expected to receive! She wanted to jump up, find a private place to listen! But she was rooted to the spot, unable to rise! Sure her legs wouldn't support her!

"Carmine!" she answered breathlessly.

There was a pause, then, an actually civil-sounding voice.

"Carmine, this is Donovan. You're an attorney, now? Wow! Good for you! I'm impressed!"

His tone didn't sound sarcastic, but he always was. Was he trying to throw her off-base?

"Where's Callie?" she demanded, ignoring the greeting that didn't square with her expectations.

"Callie's fine! Some guy just called me who's a friend of Mallory's. He told me everyone's in a panic. He suggested that I bring Callie and meet you someplace in public. Will you meet us at the French Room at eight for dinner? I already reserved."

Rage swept through Carmine Henderson! However nice he was sounding, it was a trick! One thing she could count on about her ex! He was never nice without a reason! He was just so shrewd! Now, she wondered why she had ever thought her attainments would make her a match for him! For one thing, she wasn't ruthless enough! He had been presumptuous enough to make a reservation before he called to ask her!

"Please come," he continued, since she hadn't responded. "Or, you and Callie can have dinner together, and I'll eat at a table by myself. Surely you want to see her and catch up."

"Eight!" she snapped

Herb Carlton noticed the images on Bansom's computer screen as he joined him at Starbucks. The two men were surrounded by young moms who met for coffee before shopping at the big retail outlet. Carlton was pretty much of a slave to his small profit-margin business. He had convinced his son to oversee his shop while he talked to this agent. But he didn't trust his son too much! When Bransom extended his hand for a handshake, Carlton noticed the diamond ring! And the wedding band!

"You married my cute customer with the big diamond, didn't you!" Carlton accused.

Bransom looked startled, then laughed. "Quick as I could! The big diamond wasn't hers, though. You did the right thing by calling the police. You ever deal with Barton before?"

"Nope! He was there to rob me! Then he saw the big diamond! Figured it was worth more than everything else in the store put together! Followed her out of the store to take it from her. When I called the Hope police department, I didn't know you Feds were listening in. Glad there was a fast response!"

"Yeah, me too," Bransom's gravelly voice. He had sensed the man's resistance to meeting with him. He hadn't had a clue it was over Suzanne.

It made him feel luckier than ever. He really was glad he had been able to rescue her, too.

"So, what's going to happen to Barton? Do you need me to identify him, or testify, or anything?"

"Don't know. I've been so caught up in these other cases that I haven't done much homework. Guess right now, it's with the local DA. If you hadn't seen the guy before, and you're right about the robbery thing, it may go interstate, making it Federal."

"Oh, I'm right about the robbery thing! You don't get robbed as many times as I have, not to see it coming. It was just, that I was so caught up with both her, and that diamond! Did the girl get it back? I heard it got lost."

Bransom chuckled. "It didn't get lost. How many times you been robbed? Why don't you sell and do something else?"

"Twenty-seven times. It pays the bills. I got to hold that diamond!"

"Twenty-seven times!" Bransom took it as a personal failure! He always did! Maybe he should give up on law enforcement and start preaching. He could go all over America hollering, "REPENT"! One businessman, robbed twenty-seven times, in the United States of America! And people would think he was crazy for begging people to repent and do right! Most Americans didn't have a clue the direction everything was heading! He wished he didn't know!

"Have you been to Turkey before?" Carlton questioned curiously. "I see you were looking at the "Spoonmakers' Diamond and the Topkapi Dagger."

"That what I'm looking at?" Bransom laughed. "Going in a couple of weeks. Why do you care so much about diamonds? They give me a royal pain!"

The quiet pawnshop owner's turn to laugh. "I said, 'that diamond was worth killing over,' and you corrected me, 'No diamond is worth killing over!' You are right, but they are very beautiful stones. Your ring is very nice."

"Thanks!" Bransom felt awkward. He wasn't sure guys were supposed to talk to other guys about diamonds. "Mallory's company gave me the ring and the Mont Blanc. I'm really proud of the pen, too."

"The gold in the ring is as valuable as the pen. The diamond, six, seven thousand. You ever get hard up for cash, come see me. Enjoy your travels."

Donovan Cline's headache was finally easing up. Usually, by this time of day, he had already had several drinks. But he was afraid. Maybe he was in more trouble with alcohol than he had cared to admit. He gazed again, at the ruined laptop. He was on a precipice, with no one to care. "But he didn't need anyone! Never had! He could master this, too!" But his reflection looked old and haunted. He dressed with care. He always dressed well! But for dinner at the five star restaurant, he chose his best. Of course, It wasn't for Carmine. That relationship died years ago. He brushed his hair; it looked thinner on top than ever. He wished he had gotten it trimmed.

"Wow, Daddy! Where you going?" Callie had wandered in, looking for him.

She had slightly startled him. His nerves were on edge. She looked tiny in the huge white robe. Like a little disembodied spirit with huge eyes. He was fairly certain she hadn't taken a bite of food all weekend long.

She was scared. That the hammer hadn't fallen yet, about her texting her mother, didn't mean it wasn't going to! It wasn't a matter of "if", but "when"!

"Callie, go get dressed. We're meeting your mother for dinner later. Wear something nice. Do you have any make-up? Have you eaten anything yet? Why don't you at least drink some juice?" He tried to pour her some orange juice, but his hands were shaking too hard.

Forty minutes later, showered and dressed in what she hoped would pass for "basic black", Callie joined her father in his Mercedes convertible, and they headed through the double gates, with security vehicles ahead of, and following behind. Shrewd, Cline was immediately aware of an additional car, lagging behind his convoy, but still following. His security called him about it. "Looks like some kind of cops," he observed. "Guess we should all observe the speed limit." He glanced sideways at his daughter. Carmine wasn't taking any chances that he might try to flee with their daughter. He couldn't figure out why his hands kept trying to shake. By the time they reached Galleria, Cline was ready to admit he shouldn't have been behind the wheel. His plan had been to insist that Callie shop! Both for something nice for dinner with her mother; and for some beautiful things to wear on the trip. He was still determined his daughter was not going to be left out of something she wanted to do! However, he felt so ill that he sent three security people to accompany Callie, and he sank down heavily onto a bench

"I don't even know where to start," Callie had protested softly. "I'm kind of hungry now; what time are we having dinner?"

"Meeting at eight! It'll be awhile. Let's go in Nordstrom's and have something."

He willed himself to rise to his feet and make it that far. Nothing sounded good to him until Callie ordered a French Dip Sandwich. He asked for the same, and it was actually pretty good. Callie nibbled unenthusiastically. Cline was feeling a bit better by the time Mallory arrived.

Callie sighed. "I seem to have been set up!" She tried to express her displeasure with her father's actions by giving him a scolding look. He was so impossible! But she was so happy to see Mallory that she couldn't even be upset! Mallory looked beautiful, as usual. Dressed in a chic, pale gray linen tweed suit with self-ruffled trim, she captured the perfect balance of tailored femininity. Gray high-heeled pumps and a large, flat, matching bag finished the look. Her elegant jewelry flashed dazzlingly.

Cline sent the two friends to shop, trailed by watchful body guards

"Are you sure you're okay?" Mallory asked again, when they were on their way to Macy's. "Why wouldn't you answer my calls? I didn't mean to hurt your feelings, if that's what happened. I left you messages, apologizing."

"I wasn't mad at you. I've just been mortified by my dad's behavior! He's unreal! Like he would let me go that far, without being on top of me!"

Mallory's startled gaze met her friend's. Then her expression looked troubled. That was something she hadn't considered! She had told the Faulkners that Callie was coming! She had never considered the fact that Mr. Cline was planning to crash the party, too! Now, as her gaze met Callie's again, she was certain of it!

"So, what are we looking for?" she asked. "Stuff for the trip?"

"Mallory-" Callie began.

"You are coming! Don't worry so much! This trip is going to be incredible! You need something really cute for the flight! Maybe comfortable, too. But remember, style before comfort!" She laughed. She was trying to act zany. Her friend's countenance seemed even more downcast than usual.

Rather than laughing, Callie burst into tears. "First, I need to find something to wear to the French Room at the Adolphus tonight. If I live through that, I might worry about whether I'm going to Turkey and what I'll wear. Where did you get that suit? I do shop and look around, but I never find anything like that! It's gorgeous on you! With your figure and your eyes!"

"My grandmother! Here's how you tell! If it's linen, it's my grandmother! If it's silk, it's from Diana! If it's wool or Alpaca, it's from Shay!"

"What am I supposed to do without a troupe of personal designers?"

"Get a team of personal designers! Go to their web sites. You have enough money to afford them! You're looking for designers; they're looking for a following! Now for dinner tonight, though, we better pray. Lord, please have something perfect prepared for Callie, and lead us to where it is! In Jesus Name, amen!"

Callie looked horrified. "That was a prayer?" she asked. "I never heard of praying like that before. Shouldn't you slow down and be more reverent?"

"Well, we're kind of pressed for time here!"

A rolling rack of new merchandise nearly knocked them over! Trying not to be indignant over the stocker's rudeness, Mallory followed with Callie in tow. The rack stopped, and Mallie grabbed a slender, mid-calf, ivory skirt. Callie noticed a silk tunic with a black and ivory 'newsprint' motif. It was stunning looking! Callie was amazed that Mallie had prayed, and the answer had come immediately, almost running over them! They found cute, ivory, high heels, trimmed in black patent piping, and a small black evening clutch.

"Do you have pearls?" Mallory questioned. "I think pearls would be good. Or a gold Omega? A jewelry store will have better deals than the fine jewelry department here will!"

"My dad didn't say get jewelry!" Callie's voice was alarmed.

"Sure he did! He said get some outfits! Jewelry is part of outfits! I'm not sure that's good grammar."

You think jewelry is a must because you have a diamond mine," Callie accused. But she was finally laughing!

"Make-up time!" Mallory indicated a place in line where a high-end cosmetics rep was doing make-up makeovers. Callie submitted helplessly. Maybe, if she could look really good, it would make her mother want her. If it was shallow, it was better than nothing! She tried not to cry; it was making it hard for the lady to make up her eyes.

The results did look pretty good, she decided. She bought one each of all the cosmetic items, and added a fragrance.

Mallie purchased two more tubes of the lipstick she liked, and couldn't help remembering how worried she had been the Thursday night at the mall in Hope, when she had bought an extra tube. The night before her daddy's will and letter had been read, a feeling of dread had hovered over her.

"Don't be afraid, Callie." she told her friend encouragingly as they headed toward a jewelry store. "Things are going to be okay about your mom and dad."

"You don't know what it's like!" Callie's voice was hurt and shocked sounding. "My mother doesn't care for me at all! Your mom's so nice."

Mallory stopped to face her friend, and they moved out of the foot traffic. "Your mom cares for you, Callie! What makes you think she doesn't? My mom was fun the other day, but she's kind of different, too. Like, she can take me or leave me! I still haven't figured out if my dad tried to exclude her from us, or if he was covering for her because she really didn't care. She's kind of a detached person. The whole Campbell side of my family's like that. But, your mom's been in a panic about you all day!"

"My dad told me she doesn't care about me! Since the divorce was finalized seven years ago, I haven't heard one word from her! Seven years! They were separated for eighteen months before that, and I could see my mom for some week ends and vacations. I lived for the time I could be with her! I begged to go with her when the divorce was settled! Guess she wanted to start over without any baggage! I'm so nervous about dinner! Can you come with me, please?"

"I don't think so, Callie. I haven't been invited."

"I'm inviting you! Oh, you mean by my dad? If he's crashing us into your Turkey-trip party, you can come with us to the Adolphus! Maybe they won't fight in front of you!"

"Maybe not," Mallory sighed. "It never stopped my mom and dad. I hate hearing people fight! I'm never going to fight! Every night, year after year, the same thing! It never resolved anything!"

Once at the jewelry store, Mallory spotted a beautiful, classic, sixteen-inch, necklace made up of yellow gold links set with graduated diamonds. It sparkled gently along the neckline of Callie's cute new top. Then, a set of yellow gold and diamond in-and-out hoop earrings, a diamond tennis bracelet, and a gold bangle. One thing about the jewelry purchase that helped Callie go for all of it, was the fact that it could be returned within thirty days for a full refund. She was pretty sure her dad wouldn't allow her to keep it.

As they returned to meet Mr. Cline, Mallory confided to her friend about Carmine.

"I can't explain what happened, but she does love you! I think your dad lied to you about your mom so he could have you all to himself. I think she studied law, so she could figure out a way to fight against his money and power!"

"I wish that were true!" Callie's tawny eyes sparkled with unshed tears. "I'm pretty sure she wanted to pursue her own goals, unhindered. For seven years she's treated me like I'm less than garbage! I'm sure my dad was right about her!"

Chapter 21

TREADMILL

CARMINE AND DONOVAN seemed relieved to have Mallory join them for dinner at the exclusive Dallas restaurant. Mallory was dazzled by the lovely décor and the confusing array of dishes and silverware. She was relieved that Mr. Cline ordered all of the different courses for the entire party. First, Caviar arrived, accompanied by an ice sculpture and an elegant presentation. Mallory thought the Caviar was a little too strong by itself, but with plenty of toast and all the accompaniments, it was enjoyable. The conversation seemed tense, but at least the couple remained civil. Callie was extremely quiet, making Mallory wish she had stressed the point more with her friend, how panicky her mother had been about her.

Finally, with desserts and coffee finished, Mr. Cline slipped his credit card discreetly to the Captain. Mallory found the man to be a source of education. His coldness was somewhat terrifying to her, but he knew how to be correct. As a seventeen year old girl, from small-town USA, she was eager to study his demeanor. She figured if she had a heart like Diana's, and a shell like Mr. Cline's, she would probably be pretty balanced. Rather than trying to argue over the check, or offering to pay for her own meal, she simply thanked the man as graciously as she knew how. Their cars were awaiting them, so Mallory bid them all good night and headed for home.

She hadn't accomplished any school work all day, so she hit the ground running! Opening her curriculum, her fingers flew on the keyboard, writing a synopsis of one of the Literature selections. Then she unscrambled some words for a spelling test, of sorts.

Pausing briefly to raid a Diet Coke from a mini-fridge concealed in the library cabinetry, she wrote a thank you note for the dinner. She called Callie to ask for the mailing address, and to check again, if she was in a war zone.

Callie's voice was barely a whisper. Actually, Mr. Cline felt so ill by the time they left the restaurant, that they had gone straight to Baylor's emergency room. His heart was acting up, and he was shaking and perspiring profusely. He thought he was having a heart attack. The problem was, that, with his determination to stop drinking on his own, he was in the onset of alcohol withdrawal. The attending physician recommended checking into a treatment center, once his dangerous, initial symptoms were under control.

"Don't come," Callie seemed to have read her mind. "My mom told me you and Kerry spent lots of time, today, helping her about me. I know you need to do your work. Just pray for my dad to be willing to do whatever is best."

Mallory quickly prayed for her friend's situation. As a new Christian, Callie still thought that there should be something more mystical about prayer. But- she was still wearing the beautiful outfit Mallie had asked the Lord's help in finding. Her dad had been happy with it, and her mother had raved over and over again about how beautiful she was and how she had grown up!

By the time she returned to her father's side, he was signing the consent forms for alcohol treatment. Crying softly, he kept mumbling that he had thought he could "handle it".

"It's okay, Daddy," she tried to console him. "Sometimes things come our way that we can't handle on our own. It's a strength to admit it; not a weakness!"

Donovan Cline was amazed at the wisdom of her words. They helped!

Mallory tried to do some problems out of a new chapter in her Geometry book. Having finally grasped the previous chapter seemed to have no bearing whatsoever for understanding the new one. Raking her fingers through her hair in frustration, she reread the chapter. Tears welled in her eyes.

"Lord, please help me," she breathed softly.

Her cell rang; Callie!

"Thanks, Lord," she whispered.

"Hope I'm not calling too late! I'm just calling to let you know prayer works! My dad signed papers to get help! You can't imagine what a miracle it is! I mean, you don't know my dad! I thought you had to get in an 'attitude of prayer' and say 'thee' and 'thou'!"

Mallory's tears dried quickly as her laughter rippled. "No! Prayer is just normal conversation with God. You'd think I was nuts if I started talking to you, 'O thou, Callie, thou art such a kind friend. Could it please thee to explain some geometry to thy humble, undeserving servant? If thou wouldest give me thy gracious help-"

Callie's giggles interrupted her friend's petition.

"Guess you must be on chapter twenty-two. It's kind of a new ball game from the previous chapter."

"What? Like you have this book memorized about all the chapters?" Mallory's tone was incredulous.

"Well, I do have kind of a photographic memory," Callie reminded her modestly. Explaining the new concepts in a graspable way, she was able to get her friend unstuck from her seemingly hopeless situation. Before disconnecting, she gave Mallie the same lecture she had just given her dad.

"Sometimes, things come our way that we can't handle on our own. It's a strength to admit it; not a weakness!"

Mallory's days were demanding. Work on her paper for Chemistry was still ahead of the schedule her mom had worked out, but the more she researched the topic of "Water", the more confused she grew. She thought she had narrowed her topic down to a manageable size, but even her limited topic was still vast. Like spilled water, it wanted to run all over the place and make a mess. It was pretty frustrating.

Thinking of sitting at a computer doing research papers for the next five years was making her feel overwhelmed. She reminded herself that the material really was fascinating, and that Proverbs was full of instruction to be interested and curious, always being hungry to learn! And, to take one day at a time!

She stopped long enough to e-mail Diana some more ideas.

She wrote, "I know it's way too early to think about Christmas, but I have some more ideas for jewelry. I'm not sure they are entirely original, but they will be a way to witness. One piece of jewelry could be of the Wise Men on camels, all sparkly with paved precious stones. It would say, 'Wise men still seek Him' I heard a song by that name in a Christmas Cantata that Roger's church put on one year. It was a really pretty song. Do you know it? It would be a nice one for you and your family to do. Speaking of that, I've been wondering if you think I would be able to learn violin.

Also, I was thinking about a 'Nativity Scene' charm bracelet. Available in both gold or silver; it could feature a little Baby in a manger, a star, Mary and Joseph, a sheep with a shepherd, and a Wise Man; maybe one charm that says 'Merry Christmas'. With people trying to leave Jesus out, some of us can make our own statement. Then, finally, what about a 'Ten Commandments' charm bracelet, or a pin? It says to wear it on your heart!

Also, Callie found a really cute outfit; I'm attaching a pic to this e-mail. Could you design something similar for me, but different? Instead of the newsprint, maybe a piano keyboard and some musical staffs? I'll pay you. Don't worry about any of it, though, before the trip. I know you have to be really busy getting ready.

Well, back to my school work.

Mallory"

And, she did get back to her schoolwork.

Diana responded to the e-mail that, in fashion and retailing, it's never too early to think about Christmas! She loved Mallie's ideas; but she said with design, production, and marketing, they would do well to have the items available by the next Christmas. She had already e-mailed Beth and Roger about finding and sending her a copy of the song: she wasn't familiar with it. She was delighted Mallory was interested in learning violin, suggesting they get lessons set up immediately upon returning from the trip.

Mallie's days raced by! Sometimes she felt as dazed and dizzy as she had when watching Nascar with her daddy! Wake up, have breakfast and devotions, get dressed, go to the office to take care of DiaMo business, lunch, schoolwork, go home. She was settling into a disciplined routine, actually feeling like she was getting things accomplished. Still dissatisfied with the chemistry paper, she finished it and pressed the "send" command.

By Friday night, she was more than ready for the get-together with Callie and Kerry and some of the other young people from her new church. She headed down the drive, feeling satisfied that she had earned the privilege by being diligent. Tears filled her eyes, thinking that her dad would be proud of her for trying to do what he wanted.

She had kept in touch with Callie enough to know that Mr. Cline was in rehab. She was glad that he had agreed to the treatment, but she knew he really needed Jesus and His Resurrection power!

The group met at Macaroni Grill, where they laughed and had a good time, but also shared burdens and talked about different things that were important to them. Mallory and Callie shared a dessert, then Callie rose to leave.

"If you're going to visit your dad, can I come with you?" Mallory questioned. "Will he be out in time for the trip? Do you want your mom to come, too?"

Callie was hurrying toward the door; her security pressing close, actually pushing Mallory aside; but she followed her out anyway.

"Look, Mallie, I don't think the trip's going to work out for us this time. I hope you can still cancel the rooms. I'll pay whatever, if you've paid deposits that can't be refunded. It sounds like fun." She started crying. "I can't just go off and leave my dad! He needs me! I don't think he'd want you to visit him. He's pretty embarrassed."

Mallory started crying, too. She prayed another one of her quick prayers as Callie ducked into the vehicle.

Callie buzzed in through security and raced to her dad's room. He had been raging all afternoon about the confinement and everything else about the treatment center. When she returned from the get together with her friends, he was calmly working a crossword puzzle. He smiled when Callie entered, asking if she had fun and why she hadn't stayed longer. Then, he noticed she had been crying. Callie's phone jingled before he could ask her about what happened.

It was Mallory, asking Callie to speak with her Mr. Cline. Callie was trying to state that it wouldn't be a good idea to talk to him. With a quizzical glance at his daughter, Donovan Cline reached for her phone. He was disappointed that it was Mallory. He had been horrified at the thought of his ex-wife's finding out he was drying out, yet at the same time, he hoped she might care. At the French Room on the past Monday evening, she had looked even more radiantly beautiful than he had remembered.

Mallory plunged headlong into the conversation. She still very much wanted Callie on the DiaMo tour of Turkey. She was also expecting Mr. Cline and their security. Pausing briefly, she plunged ahead, asking him if he would mind if she invited Callie's mother. A quick cynical smile flashed across his face, disappearing quickly. He told the girl she was free to invite whatever guests she wanted to; it was her trip.

Callie cringed, thinking he sounded hateful to her friend.

Donovan Cline was pretty sure Carmine would refuse the offer! But he thought Mallory was kind to think of it. Winking at Callie (a first for him), he assured Mallory that Callie and two of her bodyguards were definitely traveling with her group. He told her he wasn't sure he could be free to leave by their departure date. But he asked if he could catch up and join the group farther into the tour, if necessary.

Callie and Mallie were both overjoyed at his decision!

Carmine Henderson had been on edge all week! Her career hopes were really pinned to Kerry's firm. She hadn't heard anything; from any of her other applications and interviews. Angrily, she assumed Donovan had moved into action to block her. She knew he wasn't just being nice! He was never just nice! Still, she had enjoyed being with Callie for an entire evening!

Pacing her small apartment, she was desperate. Student loan payments were coming due, and her legal-assistant position didn't pay enough for her monthly expenses and the loan payments. Kerry hadn't heard any word from his partners about accepting her. Tears streamed down her cheeks! Rage and frustration! She had felt like she was so close to success! To have it sabotaged by her cold-blooded ex-husband!

It was late Friday evening when her phone rang. She jumped. It was too late to be a business call.

Trying to sound as normal as possible, she answered.

"Hello. This is Carmine Henderson."

"Hi, Mrs. Henderson, this is Mallory O'Shaughnessy. How are you? I know it's kind of short notice, but we are taking an exciting trip in about ten days. Mr. Cline just gave us permission for Callie to come. I would like to invite you to join us. I know Callie wants you to come."

Carmine didn't have enough money for a bus ticket downtown; she wasn't expecting to travel internationally any time soon. She knew she had to decline, but thinking about spending fourteen days with Callie made her listen. Mallory, excited about all of the sites, was really doing a great sales job.

"Sounds marvelous, Mallory," she broke in laughing. "The hotels you're talking about, and fourteen days--too rich for my pocketbook, I'm afraid. Thank you for thinking of me."

She was ready to hang up, but Mallie was saying, "Wait! Don't hang up!" She explained that the trip was paid for, and Carmine would be a guest of DiaMo corporation. The only money she would possibly need would be for shopping she might want to do.

Carmine guessed her experience with Donovan had turned her into a cynic, but she couldn't believe it! Besides, one of the firms might want her to start before the scheduled end of the trip.

"You should come! We want you to, please! It would be a huge favor to me. We have a jet chartered, that isn't full; and we have an entire floor reserved in each hotel, for security reasons, mostly. At least promise me you'll think about it. There are two new coaches for short distance travels, and we'll split up into them, with our security. Some of the sites have religious significance for a lot of us, but you'll still enjoy everything! It's all beautiful, and exotic, and exciting!"

With a laugh, Carmine promised to consider the offer and let her know soon.

Mallory knew neither of Callie's parents were saved, but she was praying they would be, before the trip ended. She was praying for another big miracle, too! She not only wanted Carmine and Donovan to get back together, but to be in love and not fight. Tears filled her eyes, remembering the nights she had cried herself to sleep, praying the same prayer for her mom and dad. She hoped her mom was being nicer to Mr. Bransom, and her mom's recent commitment to the Lord really seemed to be making a difference. Mallory had to admit to the Lord that she still didn't understand His timing and workings. She would have chosen for her mom to respond earlier, and her daddy still to be alive, with the three of them finally being a happy family. Sighing, she gazed for a long moment around her palatial surroundings.

"To whom much is given, much shall also be required," she whispered the part of a familiar Bible verse to herself. Rather than telling the Lord "thank You" again for the fortune she had inherited, she thanked Him for her mom and daddy. They weren't either one perfect, and they never got along; but they had invested themselves into her and taught her the important principles she needed to build her life on. She knew the wealth could be more destructive unless she lived by Biblical standards.

David Anderson had finished a busy week. Not much sleep, but he had finally completed his course work, and was officially a candidate to graduate from Murfreesboro High! He would miss the ceremony! But, hey, he was going to be in Turkey! Nothing wrong with that! He was Valedictorian! Not an easy accomplishment, when finishing two years in half of one. Still, in a small high school, there wasn't a whole lot of competition. Even though his dad was a pastor, who spoke in front of people all the time, David was relieved he wasn't going to be at graduation to deliver his Valedictory address. He had written it out, then taped it, to be played at the ceremony.

Things were also moving along for the Bible camp. Reasonably good security had been established, so the construction was about to get underway. Plans were being drawn for the first phase, which would be the large, main building. This would contain the kitchen and dining hall, which would also double as the chapel and assembly area at first. Restroom facilities, the Camp Director's office, a snack bar, and an infirmary, were also under the same roof.

And, they had been hauling materials! His every muscle ached! "No gym membership needed," he laughed to himself, as he stood under a hot stream of water in the shower. It was a good tired, though. He was planning to drive down to Murfreesboro to eat one of his mom's home-cooked meals, then come back and crash until about noon.

Wearing jeans, a t-shirt, and sandals, he headed his pickup towards home.

The beautiful spring evening, his iPod music identical to Mallory's, the smooth new pickup truck, combined together to make his heart sing. Mallory smiled at him from a photo he had placed against the steering wheel! The drive was enjoyable, unbelievable, really! Arriving at the parsonage, he hopped from the truck and sprinted up the back steps. Fried chicken and yeast rolls! The aromas greeted him before he even pushed the back door open. The crispy chicken was already heaped on a platter, the gravy in progress, and his mom was removing rolls from the oven. He gave the gravy a stir so she could tend to the delectable rolls.

Lana had looked up as her first-born pushed the back door ajar and bounded into the kitchen. He looked like he had grown again, visibly, since she had seen him the previous Sunday. Tall, bronzed, and muscular, he filled the door frame. She suddenly wondered if two chickens were going to be enough. Milk splashed all over the range-top, as he attempted to help with the gravy.

"You don't know your own strength; don't stir so hard you slop it all over! You shouldn't wash t-shirts in hot water!"

He laughed! "Just trying to be a help! Nice to see you, too, Mom!"

The meal was great! Mashed potatoes(not from a box either), sliced tomatoes, cantaloupe, roasting ears, snap beans, and cherry pie ala mode. His mom was a great cook. He played wii with his little sisters and brother, in spite of his sore muscles. Even Tammi acted pretty decent. Once he had finished watching the "Sports" with his dad, he headed back to the camp site.

A front had swept in, and he was driving in such a deluge, he could hardly see. His spirit, which had felt so light a few hours before, suddenly felt like lead. The windshield wipers, operating on high, couldn't keep up with the rain. His tears made it even harder to see!

Pounding the steering wheel in frustration, his sobs tore loose! How could they have all kept from mentioning her? Even once? Had the rules tightened down so much, that no one could tell him anything about her? He wished he could call her, or send her a funny card! Of course, when he could, he seldom had. He had been careless of her, assuming she would always be around when he was ready.

A deer was suddenly illuminated in the beam of his headlights. Jamming on the brakes, he careened crazily toward the animal. Finally, the truck stopped, and the graceful animal leapt up the hillside. David sat, shaking. Finally he straightened around on the road and continued toward the camp.

Dismally, he viewed the site. The deluge wasn't helping the earth work any. He was hoping to actually have some roads underway before leaving for Turkey in a little over a week. He wondered how long the rain was going to last. He wished that Brad Walters were staying to keep the work going. Janet had finally agreed that they would take the trip to Turkey, since she couldn't get her way about Las Vegas.

He pulled up as close to the little house as possible, hoping his truck wouldn't get stuck. He was just now realizing they should have hauled in some gravel for a driveway.

"I'm only seventeen; what do I know about all this?" he grumbled wearily to himself.

His phone vibrated. It was kind of late. Ever since Mallory had been hurt, every call alarmed him. Kerry Larson was the caller

"Evenin', Larson," David greeted. "What's going on in Dallas?"

"Not much now," the attorney responded. "A bunch of us from the church got together earlier for dinner. Then the ladies left, and we guys played nine holes of night golf. You a golfer?"

"I tried playing with my dad and some of his preacher friends a time or two. I did pretty bad; I don't have clubs. I think my dad sold his."

"Wow, that is a sacrifice!" Kerry was really impressed. "No wonder Patrick O'Shaughnessy thought your dad was such a great man!"

David laughed. "Yeah, for more reasons than selling his clubs. Don't tell him I said so; it might go to his head and ruin him."

"My attorney lips are sealed," Larson responded. "Just a little over a week until we leave. Everything still looking good there for everyone to make it?"

"Oh, everyone here! Yeah, even Tom Haynes is missing officiating at high school graduation so he can go."

"Oh really," Kerry tried to sound like he cared about Haynes and his dedication to learning.

David was enjoying the moment. He named most of his family members, then Tommy and Joyce Haynes. "Yeah! Guess that about accounts for all the Murfreesboro contingency. "Oh, my little sister Tammi isn't going now," he finally added.

There was confused silence.

"Tammi isn't coming?" Larson was trying to sound nonchalant, but it wasn't working.

"Nah, I sold her to the gypsies, and they wanted to take immediate possession. Oh no, here they come now, bringing her back!. Yep, they want their money back!"

"Anderson, I'm gonna get you for that!" Larson was sputtering and spluttering, but it was pretty funny.

They talked for a few more minutes. Finally Larson got around to at least mentioning Mallory. She had been part of the dinner group, and she had left fairly early with her new friend, Callie. She was working hard on her academics.

The rain and the conversation died out at the same time. Removing his sandals, David waded through the mud the short distance to the house. As he crossed the back porch to grope for the light switch, sharp things dug into his bare feet. Yelping as he went, he continued another two or three feet across the small enclosed area. Flipping on the light, he noticed a sprinkling of broken glass on the sagging floor. He sank down where he stood, trying to scrape away the thick ooze from his feet, as well as the sharp stuff!

Puzzled more than alarmed, he was trying to figure out where the glass had come from. He hadn't broken anything. He was quite certain no one else had entered the premises and scattered glass around. There was a crack in the plaster ceiling, but the light fixture didn't seem to be broken. As he returned his attention to the crystals around him, he realized that the transparent matter didn't look exactly like broken glass. They looked like what they were! DIAMONDS!

Rubbing away as much of the mud from his feet, as possible, he slid his sandals back on. Then, stepping onto one of the aluminum-framed, fifties-era, dinette chairs, he pulled at the plaster along the crack. As the gap in the ceiling widened, more of the precious stones dropped down around him. He stood transfixed.

In his mind, he was back at the banquet room of Hal's lodge. It had been three weeks earlier, although, it seemed much longer. Mallory, still pallid from a harrowing week, had presided over a corporate meeting. At the end, she had been questioning Larson and Faulkner about where more diamonds were stashed. They didn't know there were more, but Mallory had been certain of it. He could still see her sitting there! Like a queen! Her expressive green eyes mirroring the soft tone of her suit. The elegant outfit fitting her- Well, she had looked cute in the high heels, and everything!

Finding an old broom and dustpan, he swept up most of the diamonds and dumped them into one of his socks.

Daniel Faulkner's secretary e-mailed the trip details to Mallory, and she liked what there was, but she had lots of questions. Her first panel of questions fired off to the Air Charter Company. Daniel and his corporate pilots had already looked into the details of the company's air safety, and the capability of the crew. Mallory was checking on interior creature comforts. Making sure the menu was special, but also more than sufficient snacks, juices, and soft drinks. By the time she was finished, she had elicited promises for special sound and entertainment, and a state-of-the-art business center. She finished by wanting to know when she could inspect everything, personally. When the agent told her Monday, May fourteenth, just prior to departure, she patiently explained that that wouldn't allow time for remedying unsatisfactory situations. After some good-natured wangling, she managed an appointment for Sunday afternoon, the thirteenth. With the normal church schedule, and the newly-scheduled appointment, plus Mothers' Day, she wasn't quite sure how she was going to manage. She was trying not to get so exhausted she wouldn't be able to stay awake for the trip.

It was getting late; even an hour later in Boston, but she called Shay anyway. He answered immediately. He had just finished a deal with one of the Colorado Alpaca breeders. Mountain Daylight Time was two hours earlier than Boston, requiring Shay to work late some evenings. He was still wide awake, and he loved talking to his newly-found cousin.

She was calling to ask him if he would like to furnish a corporate gift for each of the travelers. He jumped on the opportunity eagerly. He wanted to provide an Alpaca throw for each person. Delia had retired after the news broadcast, but she had already told Shay she was planning to have an embroidered linen neck roll for everyone. They were kind of waiting for a final list.

That was kind of a problem. The Walters were really into the last minute frenzy about passports! Carmine hadn't replied. Mallory had been begging her Aunt Linda Campbell to join them, but she hadn't yet given in. Bransom still had a couple of "mystery guests" he was working on. For the throws Shay was bringing, the name list wasn't crucial; but for Delia's embroidered work, time was really beginning to matter.

Shay let it slip that David was one of the confirmations they knew of for sure. Mallory was so shocked that she felt like she barely had any presence of mind to finish the conversation. When the conversation ended, she continued to sit, staring across the expanse of the library desk. David! What did that mean? She had been told not to see him for six months! She wondered if the Faulkners knew he was planning to come! Surely, they must not! Tears filled her eyes. Would they think she had schemed to get him in, against their wishes? Would she be in trouble?

She couldn't figure out what to do. She thought about calling Daniel, e-mailing Diana, calling her mom, calling Tammi. None of the options seemed good. It was probably just a rumor!. There was no way David would even be interested in any of this stuff anyway! Was there?

When she couldn't fall asleep, she read her Bible for awhile. At last, she fell asleep, after deciding to try to "run into" Kerry at church on Sunday, or at the office café on Monday.

Tom Haynes finished a walk-through practice of the Murfreesboro High School graduation. He had arranged graduation ceremonies for fifteen years, but each one was important to him. He hated missing an event as important as graduation, but the upcoming trip! He was excited about it! It kept getting better every day! Beyond anything he could have ever imagined! But, then that was how the Lord worked! Just the names of the sites thrilled him! Wow! But a huge chartered jet and luxury hotels! With like-minded people! What friends the Lord had sent them! Tears tried to escape, but he was meeting a few stragglers in the wide, polished corridors as he headed for his office. Before closing down his system, he gave his e-mails a final check. He glanced over Mallory's submissions. Everything seemed to represent her usual diligence and humor. Glancing quickly at the Chemistry research paper, he frowned, then smiled. He wondered how soon she had realized that she was in trouble, and should have started over. He quickly composed an e-mail.

"See you in Dallas on the fourteenth!"

Diana, thrilled with Mallory's new ideas, was already working to bring them to reality. She loved bringing things from the realms of thought into the material. Callie looked lovely in the picture Mallory had forwarded. Diana immediately created a gorgeous and artistic silk sweater, utilizing the musical theme, rather than the "News Headlines" of Callie's top. Diana was the one who had selected the throw for Mallory's music room, thinking it cute! But the idea still hadn't made the jump for her to incorporate it into clothing. She was annoyed at herself for not thinking of it.

Beth Sanders had contacted their music director about locating the song Mallory had remembered. As quickly as possible, she scanned it and sent it to her designer friend.

Diana's hands trembled as the pages printed. Already, the lyrics were speaking to her powerfully:

"Though fools, have said, in their hearts, there is not God-
Wise men still seek Him, today!

She could tell she liked the melody, too, just by sight-reading it. From the Steinway Baby Grand, the melody filled the house!

"What a song!" She stated it aloud, amazed!

It had been in print for a long time! Why did every Christmas CD have the same songs, while ones like this didn't make the mainstream? She was praying to change that!

She contacted the music publisher for permission to record the song, but also to use the music in the design motif she was working on for Mallory. She signed a royalty agreement, and singing softly, scanned the first page of the music, including the title, as the focal point of her design. Ordering rapid delivery, she sent the design. Then, she added embellishments to make another, more Christmasy version. Changing the song title to calligraphy, she drew beautiful stars to dot the I's on wise, still, and Him. Diamonds shimmered as the centers of the stars. Sketching wise men riding camels, she carefully illustrated the gemstones that would add their sparkle. Then, she played with various ideas for representing "present-day wise men and women" seeking Him. She was still immersed in the project when she realized Daniel was standing at the doorway of her studio, watching her.

"You're home early!" she exclaimed, startled.

He laughed. "Actually, I'm late. Thought I might be in trouble. Looks like you're as involved in projects as I was. Where are the kids?"

"Kids?" she questioned blankly. "We have kids?"

He laughed. "Well, we still did when I left this morning. Hey, kids!" he hollered.

Returning his attention to her drawing board, he whistled in amazement. "Di, that's beautiful! What's this song? Where'd you find it? Wow!

What a theme, Wise Men Still Seek Him"! Honey, that's the most powerful thing you've done yet!"

His amazement deepened as he scanned over the lyrics. "Honey, we need to do this song!"

He was already moving toward the music room.

"If you insist!" she acquiesced.

When Mallory checked her e-mails mid-morning on Saturday, relief flooded over her. Mr. Haynes' e-mail was a welcomed and unexpected respite. He hadn't commented on the "Chemical Compound" paper, either way. Knowing the principal for her entire academic career, she was pretty sure he was planning to talk to her about it in person, on the trip. Resolutely, she began reworking it. She knew he would want her to rewrite it!

"Dummy!" she castigated herself. But, the reworked information was already yielding itself to a more managed style.

"That's where they came up with the idea of 'rough drafts'!" She was talking to her reflection. "And- where they came up with, 'Haste makes waste'!"

At least, she didn't have any more assignments. Maybe her mad dash on the treadmill was at least slowing down.

She scrolled to the contract that the charter company had resubmitted. They really had a lot of nice features available, if you pursued it! She clicked to accept more amenities during the flights: facials, shaves, shoe shines, nail salon services, hair cuts and styles! She was delighted. She made some calls to ensure that her corporate gifts were going to be ready, well before departure. Mothers' Day gifts, special ordered for her mother and Diana, had already been shipped; expedited- and insured!

Checking the time, she decided it was late enough on Saturday morning for her aunt to be awake!

A groggy voice answered on the last ring before the call would roll to voice mail.

"Mallory, you don't give up do you?" Her Aunt Linda was laughing.

"I will, if you tell me too," Mallory responded. "I kind of thought the door was still open a little. Do you still really not want to come? It's almost too late for a passport, anyway. I'm sorry I woke you up. Can you fall back asleep easy?"

She knew her grammar was more colloquial than proper, and that her aunt would probably correct her. She felt kind of stupid, sometimes, trying to sound like an "Oxford Scholar", when she lived in rural Arkansas.

Linda Campbell passed on an opportunity to correct the grammar.

"Actually, I have a passport."

"You do?" Mallory responded before she even realized she should have tried not to sound so surprised. "When did you get it?"

There was silence.

"You'll probably laugh at me; it's kind of stupid. I've been keeping a current passport since I was in my early twenties." She chuckled self-consciously. "I always had this fantasy of a handsome, dashing someone, sweeping into my life and whisking me off to exotic locales. Guess I've kept a passport up so I could be ready!"

Tears had sprung into Mallory's eyes, and all she could say, was, "Oh~"

She could feel her aunt's pain at still being single.

"Is that dumb, or what?" Aunt Linda's voice, trying to cover the awkward silence.

Finally, Mallory found her voice. "Well, the only really dumb thing is that you expect a handsome prince to charge your mountain of books to find the little mole, buried deep. You have lots to offer, but nobody knows you're there. I love books, too! They're great. But they shouldn't make you content to live your entire life vicariously!"

Linda Campbell hadn't seen Mallory since she was a little girl. She didn't quite know how to deal with the spicy wisdom she was receiving. Almost offended, but recognizing this was a chance to step out of Dullsville for two weeks, she responded suddenly.

"Count me in! See you a week from Monday. I'll e-mail you when I get a flight to Dallas worked out."

Chapter 22

TRENDS

DIANA FAULKNER KISSED Daniel good bye, and he headed toward his office in downtown Tulsa. The five of them had enjoyed breakfast together; then, the kids had begun their schoolwork. The May morning sparkled alluringly, so Diana grabbed her Bible and another mug of steaming coffee to enjoy her time with the Lord by the outdoor pool. One week until the departure for Turkey! Her eyes danced at the prospect. Then clouds of doubt swirled in. She was worried about Daniel. Tall, handsome, athletic, he seemed the picture of health and vitality! A world removed from the first time she had seen him. Her soft chin cupped thoughtfully in her hands, she gazed unseeingly across the sparkling aqua and soft, colorful kaleidoscope of manicured flower beds.

His long, emaciated body had extended beyond the foot of the worn, soiled hospital cot. Ravaged by fever and hemorrhaging blood, he had been at death's door. Diana, having just been certified as a nurse at a small college in Nairobi, had returned home to take a position near her parents' nearby mission station.

She stirred from her reverie to sip some coffee; then her thoughts traveled back once more. The young geologist from Tulsa, Oklahoma was there to help search for water and get drilling started for wells. He hadn't been on African soil twenty-four hours when the chills, fever, and hemorrhaging began. His body hadn't responded to any of the treatment. With the limited facilities, no one really knew for sure what they were dealing with. Tests for Ebola were negative! His frantic father in Tulsa tried to arrange an airlift, but everyone was afraid to come near the patient with the vicious, unidentified illness.

That was when Diana walked in and fell in love! Remembering, she smiled, shaking her head in wonder.

"How crazy was that?" she questioned herself softly. Now thirteen years later, surrounded by luxury, the rural, Third-World backwardness had retreated far away. She sighed. "Third World!" What was that? She wondered, somewhat sadly, if there were a "Fourth World" or a "Fifth"! Tears fell onto her open Bible.

Africa! It still broke her heart. Her grandparents, and then her parents had labored with the motto, "Dispelling the Darkness"! And because of their dedication and determination, darkness had been dispelled forever in many an individual heart! She shivered suddenly, unexplainably. By and large, though, the Continent as a whole seemed darker and more hopeless than ever. Sadly, so did Asia, Europe, South America, and yes; enlightened North America! Usually, she read her Bible, then prayed. This morning, with her mind on the past, her petitions were already issuing forth. She prayed for her family, still in Africa, and all the gospel witness there; then her family here, especially Daniel. She prayed for their church and pastor, then the Andersons and their Work. For Bransom, trying to uphold righteousness by his diligence in law enforcement. Then she prayed for Mallory and all their other new friends. Then, she prayed for herself and the Lord's help in accomplishing her to-do list.

Her thoughts once more returned to Africa. She could see herself that morning, heading out to work, in the heat! She wore a starched white uniform, a little on the short side. She could remember trying to ignore her daddy's disapproving countenance. Thick white nylons, and some orthopedic-looking, hideous, white nursing shoes. Her white nursing cap, with the ribbon she had just earned, sat strangely on her long, long, mousy brown hair. No make-up; no jewelry. Between her strict parents and the strict nurse's training, no primping was allowed.

She reported a few minutes early for her shift, the only white face in a sea of black ones. During "Report" Diana puzzled over the patient's chart. The staff had nearly pronounced him dead, already, eager to burn his body to prevent spread of whatever it was!

Bracing herself for the awful sight they were warning her about, she stepped into the small, stale room~ and fell in love!

Daniel Faulkner thrashed and fought violently, hallucinating and delirious! Then, he would lapse into semi-consciousness. The fever was high! Staying high regardless of fever reducers! IV's replaced fluid, blood transfusions tried to keep pace with the hemorrhaging. When he survived to the end of her shift, everyone was amazed.

All day long, as she took care of her other responsibilities, she would make a point of stopping by his room, to say his name and speak softly to him. She didn't expect him to survive, either. Maybe she would get a chance to tell him about Jesus.

When her shift ended, she called her mom to ask for permission to stay and work another shift. She had smaller brothers and sisters, so she had responsibilities at home after work, too.

Grudgingly, her mother had granted permission, and she had raced back to her patient, certain that he had already expired.

Running a basin of water, she sat beside him, speaking to him, praying for him, sponging him with the cool water. By ten-thirty, she was on the last run of a decrepit bus, heading out of town to the mission. Barely sleeping, she rode the earliest bus the following morning! As roosters crowed, she dashed into the clinic. Then, paralyzed by fear, she paused, sinking into a heap in a dim corner of the squalid lobby.

Tears filled her eyes as she sat remembering.

Still begging God to heal him, she had at last tip-toed to room four. She could hear his breathing before she reached the doorway. He needed oxygen, but the administrator didn't want to waste it, nor did he want to waste any more of the limited blood supply.

Desperate, she called Mr. Faulkner to ask him to wire money to the financially strapped facility. He had sworn at her for trying to extort money from him at such a time. He was about to depart on a flight into Johannesburg.

Knowing Africa better, she suggested an easier route for him and Mrs. Faulkner to reach their son. Then, explaining again, that she was an American missionary's daughter, she asked for money again. When she honestly admitted to the man that she thought Daniel still wouldn't survive, it seemed to soften him. By now, she had the Director next to the phone. The call ended with the Director's promising whatever they could do to alleviate Daniel's suffering and keep him comfortable, in exchange for Mr. Faulkner's covering some of the cost when he arrived. The Director was crying. He wished they could meet people's health needs, without the constant financial pressure. Diana didn't blame him for caring about his fellow compatriots more than he did some rich, white, American kid.

She clocked in and listened to report as the night shift made her patient more comfortable. Throughout the day, she continued to look in on him, in addition to caring for the other patients and performing her usual routine.

He didn't seem aware of her or any of his surroundings, although, unexplainably he seemed more stable. She spent her lunch break sponging, talking softly about Jesus; she couldn't remember what all. When her shift ended at three-thirty, she was by his side, once more. Calmer now, with more regular breathing and less fever, he slept, snoring softly. His face looked drawn, with a stubbly growth of whiskers. She stroked his face gently, then pulled her hand back, startled, when brown eyes opened to study her questioningly.

"Hi, Daniel," she greeted him. "I'm Diana. You came here with your corporation to help find water, but then you became very ill. Your parents are on their way here from Tulsa."

Louisa refilled her coffee, and she smiled.

Daniel got better, miraculously! The illness was never diagnosed, but he returned to health and to Tulsa, with the beautiful nurse he credited with saving his life. His health seemed fine, until! Alexandra was born, and they returned to Africa to show her off to Diana's family. Once more, Daniel hadn't been there a day before the same awful symptoms nearly robbed her of him again! As mysterious the second time as it had been the first, she nursed him through it again.

"It was the Lord," she whispered softly. When they made it back to the U.S., they hadn't left her soil again. They had traveled to Hawaii, for one corporate meeting and golf tournament. The illness didn't come back then. She still couldn't help worrying about Europe and Asia, and if some mysterious virus might be waiting for weaknesses in his immune system.

She opened her Bible to the place where she had been reading:

> *Isaiah 41:10 Fear thou not; for I am with thee: be not dismayed; for I am thy God: I will strengthen thee; yea, I will help thee; yea, I will uphold thee with the right hand of my righteousness.*

Her heart lighter, she went in to check on the progress of her children and their schoolwork. Humming the new song softly to herself as she skimmed up the curving stairs, she allowed herself to give way to the mounting excitement! She spoke briefly to the children and their teacher, before going to her studio.

She loved the studio! It was a vast space, with large, slanting, widows allowing light to stream in. She loved the way the walls slanted down from the high ceiling, reflecting the way the room fit beneath the slope of the roof. Dark hardwood floors gleamed around the edges of a large antique Persian rug. A marble fireplace and mantle created a focal point at one end of the room. A large area bordered by three-way mirrors, brightly lighted, occupied the other end. The grandfather clock in the foyer chimed eleven deep bongs, the volume of the tones softened slightly by the distance and furnishings.

Time to place some finishing touches on some projects and get them ordered. This was the deadline to send designs to her staff so they could complete the projects for delivery by Saturday. They were all nearly ready.

She smiled as she carefully examined Delia's. The sweater of soft ivory silk, featured a whimsical motif of Delia's sleek, silver, classic Rolls Royce. Delia was visible through the lowered window of the back seat. Shay stood beside the car, bending down toward his grandmother. It was cute! She sent it off!

Lana's had been harder for her. Now, she examined it carefully, frowning slightly. She reworked it, and the clock bonged noon. She still wasn't pleased, totally, but she sent it. It was kind of cute. One sleeve was a soft aqua-green, the other a soft orchid-mauve, which blended into a gentle yellow back. Then, the front worked the various pastels into a rather impressionistic piece of artwork, featuring the faces of her five children: David, Tammi, Jeff, Janni, and Melody.

Mallory's idea about a musical theme, then asking about learning to play a violin had given Diana more inspiration. She illustrated a sweater for Alexandra, of soft ivory, with a rich brown violin, and a few bars of a classical music score. She lettered "Stradivarius" in elegant brown script, making the dots over the "I's", decorative and set with "Chocolate" diamonds. It was elegant!

She pressed "send"; that one was on its way, too

Then she turned her attention to designing the top she was planning to wear on the flight. She had a beautiful photo she had shot from the beach on Maui. White sand faded into soft blue surf, which ultimately blended into sky. The blues ran the gamut from aqua, to blue, to periwinkle, serene and infinite. She sighed slightly, designing it into a decided maternity look. Then, she laughed at herself. All of them were praying desperately for her to be able to carry the baby. Now, with everything looking good, she should be more grateful, not minding her expanding shape! In the sand, along the bottom edge of the garment, she added:

Psalm 95:5a The sea is his, and he made it:

The verse, in attractive, legible lettering, appeared to be written in the sand.

Then, Mallory had given her a cute idea for something for David. The fine-gauge silk, long-sleeved crewneck would be business casual. A photo from a ski trip showed beautiful snow drifts; white, sparkling against deep Blue Spruce. Diana inserted a silhouetted, somersaulting, Extreme snowboarder against the wintry sky. Black lettering said "CATCH THE DRIFT'! She ordered it in men's extra large.

The tops designed, she quickly placed orders for various outfits in the soft, comfortable denim she often used.

Silver-gray skirt and softly shaped blazer for Delia; ivory skirt and hoodie-vest for Mallory; black for Callie, who could wear it with the Newsprint top she had found shopping with Mallory; brown for Alexandra with the violin crewneck; the soft mauve color in a different style for Lana; and Diana's would match the sand of her sweater.

With those items ordered, she sent swatches off to order soft leather loafers. Daniel kept telling her to bring comfortable shoes. She made a face, thinking about it. She knew the shoes would be right to the wire for time. She double-checked the colors with the sizes, pressing "send" one more time before shutting down the system.

All of the tourists were busy trying to plan what to take. The Anderson's had wall to wall suitcases in the crowded parsonage. Work continued to progress on their new house. Lana and John had chosen some of the interior design material: tile, carpet, hardwood flooring, wallpaper, paint, lighting. For now, though, they were still pretty wedged in, trying to get organized for a fourteen day international trip! For seven people!

Delia and Shay were ready. Rather than traveling from Boston to Dallas for the Monday morning flight, they were traveling to New York City to meet the chartered jet and the rest of the group. Shay was a little disappointed. He didn't want to miss out on any of the fun! Or any of the time with Emma! But there were going to be fourteen days, so he guessed a few hours trimmed from each end of the trip wouldn't be that bad.

Callie continued to be in a panic about her father. She was certain that he would change his mind about allowing her to go, unless he could be right on the jet, keeping an eye on her, himself. His rehab wasn't progressing smoothly at all. She was kind of at a loss. Finally, she took her own advice, calling Mallory about it, who e-mailed Diana, who called the director of the rehab program. The director wasn't particularly interested in discussing Mr. Cline. Diana understood patient privacy, but she felt like the facility was hiding more information than necessary. She felt like they planned to keep Mr. Cline for a long time. Why not? He had infinite insurance, and a fortune! Even after she explained that she was a nurse with a current Oklahoma license, and that she would take responsibility for the man and his meds, she continued to meet resistance!

Stiff resistance! The man had practically threatened Diana. She was threatening back, mentioning checking with an attorney, when Daniel overheard her.

"About Donovan Cline," she mouthed, in response to his puzzled expression.

Frowning, he sat down to listen in on the conversation. His amazement grew as he listened. He didn't know that Mr. Cline planned to join them; he hadn't even heard of Carmine until now. Seemed to him like that could get dicey. It was Mallory's trip, though.

Mallory still continued to amaze him. As the Chief Financial Officer of DiaMo, he had allowed the trip to include a growing number of guests, then more elaborate transportation, accommodations, and security. Then, Larson had, he thought, kind of spoken to Mallory about it out of turn. Kind of accusing Daniel and Diana of going through her money.

That was when she had demanded to know the details of the trip. From that point, she had contributed to the planning, expanding on it, rather than cutting back. They were planning a shareholders' meeting one of the nights at the Hilton in Izmir. That would turn most of the trip into a tax write-off. She needed all the tax help she could get. The added amenities were unbelievable. The long flight seemed to be turning into a seamless part of the fun! But Donovan Cline?

Diana gave up arguing with the rehab person and called Kerry to locate an attorney to get Cline released.

Erik and Suzanne were aware of the fact that they could invite another friend or two to join them on the trip. Suzanne was happy with Mallory and other friends who were already going. Erik really didn't have any friends except for the new Christians from within the past month. His former cronies and drinking buddies from the Bureau, no longer held any attraction for him at all. He couldn't get Herb Carlton out of his thoughts; he didn't know why. The guy was married to his store; if he would barely leave for an hour, he sure wouldn't go anyplace for two weeks! But the way he had seemed so longing when he saw the items on Bransom's laptop, had stuck with him. He dropped by the pawn shop, under the guise of checking out ways he could help him improve his store security. The store wasn't well protected. Bransom gave a couple of suggestions that wouldn't be costly to implement. Trouble with most security advisors was that they were usually just trying to sell expensive gimmicks and systems.

Carlton still figured Bransom had something more on his mind, so he asked about Barton, then the rest of Bransom's suspects.

Finally, Erik Bransom just blurted out, "You know about the trip to Turkey next week. All the spaces aren't taken. If you can leave your store, you'll have a great time! All paid for! You got a passport? You were making over some of those museum pieces on the laptop. Be your chance to see it, in real life!"

Herb Carlton couldn't believe what he was hearing. "How can a trip like that be free?"

"Well, I guess it isn't really free; Mallory's company's paying for it. But it's a free gift to us, if we receive it. Kind of like salvation. Jesus paid for it, so all we have to do is receive the free gift." He figured he was really confusing the suspicious man. Embarrassed, he shrugged, turning toward the door.

His ears burned as he ducked into the big car. "That was dumb, Bransom," he told his reflection in the rear-view mirror. His cell rang! Carlton possessed a current passport, and he wanted to seize on the opportunity!

Carmine called Callie at the house number, surprised that Callie was there, and her ex-husband wasn't. Callie immediately asked her why she hadn't agreed to travel with them yet. Carmine had reasons she didn't feel at liberty to mention. When Callie found out that her mother could be free for lunch, she asked to get together.

"What about your father?" Carmine asked. "Is it okay with him if you have lunch with me?"

"Yes, it's fine, Mom!" She knew her dad didn't want her mom to know about his treatment. She had already visited him, and he had been such a raving maniac that she left almost immediately.

Callie chose the café in Kerry Larson's office building. It wasn't far for either one of them. They enjoyed the quiet, and the flavorful soup and salad. Even though they didn't run into either Mallory or Kerry, William Jacobson was finishing lunch. He stopped by their table and assured Carmine she hadn't been forgotten. Then, he gave her the disappointing news that they wouldn't need her before the attorney she would be replacing, actually left. His guess was six weeks. He smiled when she introduced Callie, then excused himself and left.

Carmine was so devastated she wanted to cry.

"That's good news, isn't it, Mom?" Callie was trying to fit her assessment of the situation to the crestfallen expression on her mom's face.

"I guess," Carmine replied guardedly. "I was hoping for something sooner."

"This gives you time to come to Turkey!" Callie's voice was triumphant. "Do you have a passport?"

"I can't come, Callie! I have to stay here and work my other job until something opens up with one of the firms."

"Do you need money, Mom?" Callie asked suddenly. She was surprised she thought of it. She had never known anyone who needed money.

"You don't have any, either, Callie. Your dad has you on a really short leash!"

"You checked?" she asked her mom, shocked.

"I've tried to keep up with everything relating to you, that I could. The financials were relatively easy to get to, compared to anything else about you."

"Wow!" Callie's voice was shocked, but soft. "I thought you didn't care anything about me. Can you go shopping with me when you get off? I'll get us some money."

Carmine returned to work, and Callie returned to the center to visit her dad again.

"Daddy, I need some money," she announced. "You need to settle down. I could hear you yelling from the elevator. We're trying to get you where you can come to Turkey. If you're this crazy, they can't get a court injunction. Are you taking your medicine?"

"Enough medicine to gag a horse!" he responded feistily.

Something about his demeanor caused her to pause and meet his gaze.

"Daddy, I'm really sorry I asked you to come here. I really thought they would help you to stop drinking. Mrs. Faulkner was trying to talk to them about your getting out long enough for the trip. She's a nurse, and she offered to help with your meds. Now, she's afraid they're making you crazy, on purpose, with some of the drugs; because you have lots of insurance and money. Maybe you should try to get by without taking the medicine." She began to cry. "I don't know what to do."

"Why do you need money?"

"So, mom can quit that law clerk job, get some cute new clothes, and go on our trip with us!"

Somewhat dumbfounded by her sudden boldness and complete transparency, he told her where to find credit cards and an ATM card in his billfold at the house. He used her cell to call Tony, his valet, to approve it.

With a quick kiss on the cheek, she was gone!

Meeting at the Galleria, as quickly as Carmine could get there after work, they shopped like fiends until the stores closed, and the P.A. systems were telling them it was time to stop. They had a blast~ Callie helping and encouraging her mom, Carmine doing the same for her daughter! By the time they drove separately and met for a late dinner at a near-by restaurant, Carmine was in a panic, again. She couldn't imagine Donovan really giving Callie permission to use the credit cards so lavishly, even for herself! Now, she was certain Callie would get in trouble~ for spending so much, and on her, too.

Tears filled her eyes as she pled with Callie to take everything back.

"Don't make him mad, Callie, you don't know what he's capable of. In less than six months, you'll be eighteen. He'll still always be able to control you by threatening to cut you off. But, he'll give you a little more autonomy then, I hope."

Callie's earnest gaze met her mother's. "He's in a treatment center, Mom. It's a miracle. I told him I needed money to go shopping with you, and he just gave me his ATM and credit cards. I was scared when I let Mallory talk me into buying jewelry last week. He just took the receipts and told me "everything looked very becoming".

"I don't think a "treatment center" can make that much difference. Sorry to be a "Doubting Thomas" when you have this new faith! If he does manage to unpickle himself, he'll still never turn into a human person!"

Callie didn't argue with her mother. If any two people knew what was wrong with Donovan Cline, it was the two of them.

They ordered and sipped on iced tea while they waited for their food. They had worked up some serious appetites!

"I don't want to hurt your feelings, Callie, but you're so smart! What made you decide to try this Christianity bit?" Carmine had been trying to work out a tactful way to phrase the question. When it spilled out so badly, she wished she could pull the stupid words back.

One general rule was, "When you get yourself in a hole, stop digging."

As she tried to explain herself, she was making it worse. "What made you decide to go to church and 'get saved'?"

The server was approaching with a large tray. Callie waited until the food was placed, and the server gone, before she bowed her head and silently blessed the food.

"Wow, Mom, we ordered a lot!" she laughed. "Is it okay if I call you 'Mom'?"

Tears filled Carmine Henderson's eyes. She couldn't speak, so she nodded.

Callie ate silently for a couple of minutes, trying to collect her thoughts so she could answer her mother's searching question. She dabbed her lips with her napkin, and swallowed some tea.

"I didn't decide to go to church and 'get saved'. I think I 'got saved' at the bar in the Adolphus Hotel!"

"What were you doing there?" Carmine demanded. "You know it's illegal for you to drink!"

"I know, Mom," Callie responded patiently, still caressing the word, 'mom'. "I go there with Daddy a lot. I just drink Cokes or orange juice, but Daddy wouldn't care if I drank alcohol; and I don't think anyone would ask for my ID when I'm with him."

Carmine hated the guy so much that she hadn't realized hatred could deepen.

"You know Daddy has lots of companies and lots of projects going on," Callie continued. "One of the 'biggies' of the moment is 'Robotics'. I think he kind of wants me to get a degree in physics or nano-technology, or something to benefit some of his endeavors. He had me help with some robotic-arms and hands technology. What we had, Mom, was so half-baked! I mean, in the field, I guess it was a breakthrough. So, we were at the Adolphus to 'celebrate' this sophisticated triumph, with several of the key development people. So, they were all drinking and toasting and slapping themselves on the back."

"I can see that, now! I can't believe he had you there! Carmine's tone was fierce. "What happened?"

"Well, I always just accepted evolution as truth, and never thought about questioning it. But, there was a pianist in the lobby bar, and I was watching his hands move. Then, I thought about our 'engineering marvel' in comparison. I told Daddy that we would really have something to celebrate if we could get a robotic that could play a piano. Think about the circuitry and fluidity of movement that would take."

Callie's laughter rippled at the idea. "But, if we did it, it would still just be a replication of something already conceptualized and designed long ago. Well, then, I started thinking, not just of the nerves, muscles, bones, in the hand; but the motor center issuing the commands. The information enters as musical notes, through the complexity of the human eye! Something else that defies duplication! It is processed faster than~ I don't know how fast. The musician doesn't even use conscious thought to execute the music. The eyes see the notes, and the hands respond. Then, think about music. It's so mathematically perfect and scientific. No one ever tried to explain where it evolved from.

So, all these guys are drunk, and I'm sitting there with revelation dawning on me. That's when I knew for sure that there has to be a Creator! Then, I thought, 'If there is a Creator, it's God! And, if there is a God, I must be in trouble'!"

Carmine Henderson's heart contracted into a hard knot of fear. She was surprised it could still work, but she could both feel and hear its hard pounding! Trying to steady her shaking voice and hands, she rose quickly from the table.

"Look how late it's gotten," she murmured. "I have to be up early for work."

She literally ran from the restaurant, leaving her daughter staring after her, with her heart breaking!

The server gave Callie a perplexed look. Holding back tears, she requested the check. Ignoring all of the scarcely touched food, she jabbed a fifty dollar bill into the plastic folder, and handed it back. She didn't say, "Keep the change", but she fled before he could offer.

Carmine hardly remembered the drive back to her cramped apartment. She was in a panic! She wanted to hide! Hide from an angry God! Her genius daughter's line of reason made sense to her. If Callie had known she was in trouble with Him, where must she be? She had lived longer and committed worse sins than her daughter had!

It was eleven o'clock, but her phone rang, further jangling her frayed nerves. She hoped it would be her daughter! But it was Donovan. He might be in lockdown, but he still had people reporting to him! Callie's security couldn't hear the conversation, but they reported the events of the entire afternoon and evening to him.

He sounded tired. His voice doused her with its usual iciness. "What was that about, Carmine?" he demanded, trying to control his rage. "I may be locked up, but I could have kept you from getting with her! And I would have if I had any idea you were going to act like that! She wants you with her on this trip, and she bought you clothes and dinner! What did she have to say to you that you couldn't deal with?"

Carmine didn't know how to respond. The truth wouldn't make sense to him. And she shouldn't have just run out the way she did! She had asked Callie about the religion thing. She was afraid! Afraid she had ruined the trip, afraid she had ruined being allowed access to Callie. Afraid of God and His judgment, afraid of arousing the wrath of Donovan Cline!

"I'll take everything back tomorrow, first thing." Her voice was barely audible.

Eight years! Eight years since she had defied him enough to move out! She was still as much of a slave to him as she had ever been!

"No! You're keeping the stuff, and you're going on the trip! You call her now, and apologize. Quit that stupid job so you can go. Get whatever else you need to look really good, and help Callie look really good. This is a really great opportunity for Callie, but these people are really sharp! I don't know why you couldn't keep from fighting with her. Try to be the bigger person, here!" The savage tone of his voice increased, then the call ended.

Chapter 23

TRAVEL

THE FAULKNERS TRAVELED to Dallas after church on Sunday night to spend the night in Mallory's luxurious guest suite. Daniel and Diana, accompanied by a colleague of Kerry's, were planning on getting Donovan Cline released from the treatment facility early Monday morning.

Mallory was meeting her Aunt Linda, who was flying into DFW, at approximately the same time.

The chartered jet, inspected and passed by Mallory the previous afternoon, was fueled and prepared for takeoff from Alliance.

Mallory's luggage was already loaded into one of the SUV's that would carry the Faulkners and Mr. Cline. They all had lots of luggage. Mallory had squealed with delight when she had received even more, new , beautiful items, designed by Diana. She had found lovely things during her shopping expeditions, too.

She was wearing the "Wise Men Still Seek Him" sweater with the soft ivory denim outfit and the cute, comfortable shoes. Excitement had prevented her sleeping well, but adrenaline was compensating. She looked beautiful as she raced away in the Jaguar convertible, her security following closely, to get her aunt.

Donovan Cline had somehow managed to free himself from his confinement, and he was in the lobby of the establishment waiting, when

Daniel and Diana arrived. He looked more like he had just stepped from the cover of Gentlemen's Quarterly, than he did like someone who had escaped from alcohol rehab. An angry charge nurse had basically thrown several bottles of pills at Diana, and told her she could figure his treatment out for herself.

Even though it was still two hours before the scheduled departure for New York City, everyone was already assembled in the elegant private departure area ,when the Faulkners arrived with Donovan Cline! Erik and Suzanne, with one of their guests, Herb Carlton, were enjoying a coffee. The Andersons were checking out the various amenities the facility offered. Kerry Larson; Callie Cline; Carmen Henderson; Tom and Joyce Haynes, and Tommy; Roger and Beth Sanders, with Emma and Evan; and Brad and Janet Walters with Sammie and Sarah, had assembled. Everyone was chattering at once, as luggage was being moved onto a baggage truck for transport across the tarmac.

Mallory called to see how things were working out about Mr. Cline, and was relieved that things had worked so smoothly there. (Diana, trying to look up the various powerful prescription meds was more concerned). Mallie's aunt's flight out of Kansas City was delayed by at least thirty minutes, which was causing a little bit of alarm.

Lana Anderson appeared, wearing the lovely mauve outfit featuring the soft pastel portraits of her children. David was sporting his new shirt. The rest of the family was demanding to know where theirs were.

Nervous and edgy, Donovan Cline sat withdrawn from the group. Callie sank into a chair beside him.

"Are you okay?" she asked him softly.

"I feel like I'm coming out of my skin! I can't describe it! I thought you said that woman's a nurse! She doesn't know squat! Trying to look stuff up on some on-line pharmaceuticals web-site. I could do that!"

"Take it easy, Daddy. She knows what it all does, she just can't understand how it's supposed to help with alcohol withdrawal. She knows you're having really uncomfortable symptoms. She wants to help you; not make you worse!"

"Well, I don't like her sweater!" Cline growled.

Callie was amazed. She thought it was beautiful, and Diana looked beautiful in it.

"What don't you like about it? The Bible verse?"

"Oh, that's a Bible verse? Think about how preposterous that claim is! "The sea is His, and He made it"? Do you know how many square miles of the earth's surface are covered by oceans?"

She did, and she spit the number out. One hundred thirty nine million, five hundred thousand square miles! She agreed the claim would, indeed be preposterous, if it were not true!

Everyone did a little more last-minute shopping for books and magazines, then Daniel issued the order for the guests to show him their passports and begin boarding.

Diana was holding onto her handbag and her Louis Vuitton overnight bag. Since it seemed a little heavy, Erik offered to help her with the overnighter. Thanking him with a bright smile, she declined.

Daniel grabbed it. "Send it with the rest of the luggage, Honey. These guys have already been tipped very nicely. Let them handle it."

Ignoring whatever message she was trying to telegraph him, he placed the bag down with others that were still waiting to be hauled to the open cargo bay.

Mallory had called again to inform everyone that she had her aunt, they were stuck in a bit of traffic, but they were fifteen minutes out.

Nearly in vain, Daniel was trying to shepherd the chattering group aboard. It made him feel sorry for Jesus, and for Pastor Anderson. Maybe he had made a mistake by not already asking the pastor to pray. He had figured when everyone was on board, and the doors secured, the pastor could pray for a safe flight. Getting the security guys to pay attention seemed futile, too. They seemed less disciplined than the rest.

When Mallory had checked on the amenities the previous afternoon, she had somewhat assigned seats, placing each alpaca throw and embroidered pillow where she planned for people to sit. Daniel figured it wouldn't be hard and fast, but a guideline for getting started. Everyone was basically picking wherever they wanted and pushing the nice gifts onto the floor, out of their way.

Giving up on the boarding and getting settled, he returned to the terminal, to watch for Mallory and her aunt, and to help with Linda's luggage. Exactly according to her ETA, her car sped toward the private terminal. Her security, in a vehicle ahead of her, pulled into a parking space and began unloading their luggage.

As Mallory's path crossed the empty baggage truck, something caught her eye. She waved to get the driver's attention, then blew her horn when he wouldn't acknowledge.

He seemed to be speeding away on purpose. Faulkner stood helplessly watching, as Mallory spurted away in pursuit of the vehicle. Her security didn't have a clue they had lost her! Daniel stormed over to tell them to go after her, but they had managed to unload their luggage in such a way that they had to move it all, in order to back from the space.

Alarmed, Daniel stood and watched as Mallory attempted to block the speeding truck by pulling into its path. When it would have barreled into her, she punched the gas in time to squeal away. By now, all three vehicles were racing along the runway. From the jet's interior, Bransom and David noticed the scenario at the same time. Eyes riveted on the speeding truck, Bransom could see one piece of luggage stashed, almost out of sight. Looked like Diana's piece he had offered to help her with.

Mallory's car easily outperformed the airport vehicle, and she was in front of it again. A cry escaped David's lips as he saw Mallory raise her arm and aim a pistol at the truck. She put four in the grill, and two in the tires, bringing the vehicle to a groaning halt.

The security pulled up last, and the guys sprang out to tackle the other driver.

"She either needs to lose the convertible, or not shoot at people, Bransom!" David dropped back into his seat, visibly shaken.

Erik agreed with him. If the guy had fired on Mallory, she would have been an easy target! He wasn't overly fond of convertibles, either! They were barely safer than motorcycles, in his opinion! He wondered if Faulkner had seen the incident.

He sprang into motion! Racing back down the jet way, he rounded up Faulkner, Mallory, Aunt Linda and her luggage, the security team, and the Louis Vuitton!

"Let's get going while everyone's still hiding under their desks. That guy was trying to steal, but we're the ones they'll treat like criminals. These small municipality cops will take this jewelry as 'evidence'! It'll get 'stolen', and we'll never see it again."

Faulkner spoke with the flight crew as nonchalantly as possible. To everyone's relief, the jet taxied and was airborne a few minutes later.

"Pastor, will you pray for us to have a safe trip?" Faulkner's voice directed toward Anderson, above the hum of the engines.

"That's a good idea. Wish I'd thought of it, and sooner." His voice resonated through the cabin, as he prayed for safety and God's blessing on everyone.

The atmosphere in the cabin was tense. Diana figured Daniel was mad at her for not keeping better track of the suitcase carrying her jewelry. Daniel felt terrible about jerking it away from her! Everyone was annoyed by the security people jockeying for position instead of being vigilant. David was mad because the whole thing had scared him. Humiliated because she realized her determination to stop the guy had placed her and her aunt in danger, Mallory had sunk into a seat next to Callie! Then Callie asked her who the tall, handsome guy was, and if he was taken! Coldly, Mallory responded that his name was David Anderson, and, as far as she knew, he wasn't!

Gradually, everyone relaxed and settled in for the four hour flight to New York City. Several pulled out their Bibles. Mallory wasn't surprised; that was what she had planned to do, too. Take care of business, have devotions after take off. But she realized that the "Bible Hour" was making their unsaved guests nervous.

Having regained her composure, and with the seat-belt sign off, she moved over by Carmine. This isn't an enforced quiet hour! You can talk or use your phone, and it won't interfere with this plane's navigation. There's a business center, and snacks and beverages. Feel free to move around and talk to people. If anyone needs silence, they have headsets."

"Mom, did you even say, 'Hi,' to Aunt Linda?" she asked Suzanne as she passed by her seat.

"I waved at her when she boarded."

"Okay, just checking." Mallory was always baffled by her mother's disconnectedness with people. Suzanne hadn't seen her only sibling in over two years. No hug! No, Linda, great to see you? How ya been?"

Mallory felt bad, almost wishing she hadn't insisted on her aunt's making the trip.

She moved back by Mr. Cline, telling him the same thing about the availability of the business center. She could tell he felt bad. And he did, but not as bad as he had felt before that pastor prayed. Funny coincidence!

Mallory extended her hand to Herb Carlton. "I don't believe I've met you before, have I?" she questioned amiably.

"Herbert Carlton. Pleased to meet you Miss O'Shaughnessy. I have had the pleasure of viewing your beautiful ring before. Mr. Bransom invited me because he said there is extra room; is that correct?"

Mallory glanced behind her, to Erik and Suzanne, all immersed in one another. She didn't mind their acting like newly weds; but what was she supposed to do with Aunt Linda and this guy? Bransom didn't invite a friend he liked? Just someone to fill up empty space?

"Mr. Carlton, he was absolutely correct. Lots of space and lots of fun! You don't have to be quiet so people can read their Bibles. They have headsets. There are some different books and games toward the front, if you want to check everything out. Lots of food and beverages. I'll look forward to talking to you some more."

She shoved pillows and throws aside and sank down next to her aunt. "Sorry for the wild ride," she apologized. Thinking about it made her want to cry again. "I'm so happy you agreed to come; when was the last time I saw you?"

"Twelve years ago! You were just a little girl. I don't know why I never came to visit."

"You couldn't leave your cats," Mallory reminded her flatly. "Speaking of the cats, how are they?"

Linda Campbell couldn't help laughing at her niece. "Well, actually, they were both very old and very sick. I had both of them put down. It was inevitable. I didn't know how I could stand it, but having the trip to think about was really a help. I actually haven't grieved as much as I thought I might."

"How long ago did you do the makeover?" She couldn't wait any longer to ask.

Linda laughed. "Maybe twenty-four hours. What do you think? I'm still not sure it's me.

"I love it! You look fantastic! Come around with me, and I'll introduce you to everybody!"

"No!" she whispered. "Everyone's busy!"

Mallory could tell her aunt felt uncomfortable, too, with everyone sitting around reading their Bibles. Even David and Tammi were reading theirs. She introduced them first. They both said, "Hello," then returned their attention to their Bibles like they never did anything else.

Daniel had been watching with amused interest. Leadership wasn't easy, but she was making a good attempt. He decided to help her out. "I'm Daniel Faulkner. I tried to introduce myself when you first boarded, but everything was a little crazy." He was speaking to Linda. "Did Suzanne introduce you to Erik, yet?" He pulled her back toward where they were seated. Bransom rose courteously to acknowledge the introduction. When Suzanne had waved, he assumed the two women were acquainted. He was a little amazed to learn they were sisters.

He caught Carlton's eye, but the pawn shop owner had already noticed.

"Well, the plane's off the ground," Mallory acknowledged to herself. "But the party isn't."

She grabbed the four little kids: Cassandra, Melody, Sammie, and Sarah; and got them started playing a children's game, in an aft area she had designated for that purpose. They all wanted to win, so there was some crying and whining.

She emptied a jig saw puzzle on another table, then started some gospel music, various styles and artists, playing through the sound system. Figuring everyone was still too up-tight to raid the snacks and beverages, she asked a member of the flight crew to arrange an assortment of the various treats where the travelers could see them and get to them easily.

To Mallory's relief, some of her friends were stashing their Bibles and getting into some lively interaction. Part of the problem, of course, was that she was afraid to even look David's direction. She figured Kerry and Tammi felt the same, and she didn't have a clue about Tommy and Alexandra. She was trying not to think about how awkward two weeks being around David were going to be.

"One day at a time," she reminded herself.

Her aunt, drawn inexorably toward the puzzle, had found some coffee, and was assembling the border. Carmine moved to the puzzle table, too. She wasn't a jig saw enthusiast, but she wanted to get acquainted with another non-Bible member of the group.

The two women visited, somewhat stiffly. Then, Carmine rolled her comfortable chair to the children's game. Immediately, she had the four little ones eating out of her hand. Amazed, Mallory acknowledged that Callie's mom had a gift with little kids.

Hearing the fun, the next level of kids surfaced! Jeff and Janni Anderson, Jeremiah Faulkner, and Evan Sanders started assembling a Lego spacecraft. Janni soon bored with that, but she spotted a book and curled up where she could read it and boss the boys. They basically ignored her, but none of them seemed to mind.

Erik contacted his supervisor, knowing his confession wasn't going to make him very happy. When Dawson's voicemail came on, instructing him to leave a message, he was actually relieved. He left a terse message about the attempted robbery in Dallas. As a federal agent, he should have waited for LEO's to arrive and investigate. He was aware of that! He tried to explain how the proceedings would have criminalized the victims. Their travel plans would have been skewed; Diana's valuable jewelry would disappear, probably forever, and the guy could just claim he didn't realize he still had a suitcase in his trailer, and he couldn't figure out what the lady's problem was that tried to flag him down!"

He ended his message, sighing! This would probably mean his career!

Dawson listened to the message, then pressed seven to erase it!

Mallory joined her aunt at the puzzle, fitting in several pieces. "Wow, you're going to have it done before we get to New York! Then what are you going to do?"

Linda laughed. "I may sleep. I was pretty scared of flying, but by the time I got to Dallas from Kansas City, I was actually enjoying it. I see you have some really good books stashed, too!"

Mallory nodded thoughtfully. Her head-librarian aunt had noticed the classics that lined a book case. Barely a month earlier, Mallory had grabbed the volumes desperately, terrified about what the following day might bring! Somewhat terrified that Daniel Faulkner would throw her into a dungeon or something, she had cleared out Books-a-Million . They had probably changed their name to Books-a-Thousand after she left!

She could laugh at herself now, and the groundless fear. The Faulkners had transported her to a beautiful home (not a single bar on a window) where she was enjoying more freedom than she had ever dreamed of! Freedom she didn't want to abuse!

She heard a "ding" from the business center and glanced around the corner. No one was waiting for documents. So far, only Roger Sanders had availed himself of any of the services: not for his business, but to receive more pictures of his new grandson!

A lighted display announced, "receiving images". Mallory stood smiling, expecting to be able to razz the Sanders some more.

The file, though, was to the attention of Erik Bransom. It didn't say "Secret" or "Confidential", so she stood there, watching the first picture print.

Her smile faded and tears stung her eyes. Trembling, she stood waiting for the transmission to end. She was praying Erik wouldn't come looking for his paperwork. The high-speed equipment seemed to be slowing with each image! Finally, it blinked, "transmission complete" and the soft whirring, clicking ceased! Not being able to think of a good excuse for seeing his incoming file, she simply sailed through the cabin, her eyes straight ahead, and thrust the papers into his hands!

Noticing her stricken expression, but not knowing how to respond, he thanked her, then watched as she made her way to one of the lavatories and slammed the door!

His eyes met Suzanne's! He was almost afraid to look at the papers in his hands. He had been expecting Dawson to call back and cuss him out about the situation at the Dallas airport. But maybe there was a warrant for Mallory's arrest for shooting the gun; maybe the thief they had sent on his way decided to press charges against her!

His gaze returned to the closed door, then he cautiously began leafing through the printed material. Relieved in the extreme, that it was only a report he had requested on one of his suspects, he continued to scan it. Oscar Melville's (or Malovich, or whatever the guy's name was) computer photo file. Bransom had requested it in order to figure out if Martin

Thomas had a fixation about Mallory, or if Oscar did, or if Oscar had tried to make it look like Thomas did. The file was thick, going back eighteen months. Evidently the former sheriff had too much time on his hands!

"You know what's wrong with Mallory?" he asked Suzanne.

Tears in her pretty blue eyes, she nodded, reaching for the sheaf of papers.

Bransom had fanned the file quickly, but Suzanne had noticed the photo that would have affected her daughter so much! She pointed it out to him, then focused her attention out the window!

Tears filled the hardened agent's eyes, too! Melville could sure keep the pot stirred!

The photo showed David carrying a baby up some steps, and a girl carrying a twenty-four pack of beer. Bransom realized the picture could mean any numbers of scenarios across a broad spectrum!

"Have you seen this before?" he asked Suzanne.

She nodded. "Melville sent it to Patrick," she whispered as softly as possible. "I'm not sure if it was posted on the internet like the one of "the kiss". I don't know if Pastor and Lana ever saw it. Patrick began trying to steer Mallory away from David because of that! David was already missing church and talking about quitting school. Patrick didn't want Mallie to ever see the picture! Too bad it came through now!"

In the ladies' room, Mallie was drying her eyes, and trying to regain her composure. Maybe she could arrange her face long enough to get to her place and bury herself in the alpaca throw! The spacious cabin area didn't provide for privacy. Head held high, she made her move. Tell-tale rosy spots on her cheeks were a give-away!

"She's hot about something!" David noticed. "Best to steer clear!"

But he was in possession of something she needed to know about. Aside from this trip, he wasn't sure how he would be allowed to communicate with her.

"Now or never," he told himself as he unwound his frame from the luxurious seats and headed toward her.

From her place, Mallory watched him get up; maybe he would go help build the Lego spaceship. Terror seized her when he headed her direction. Near the back of the cabin, there was no escape! He loomed over her!

Cornered, she faced him defiantly! Cheeks more flushed than ever, her eyes blazed into his!

"Not just hot! But mad at him, as usual!" But it was too late for him to turn back. The whole group was going to witness whatever spectacle this was morphing into!

"Have a weather report for you!" His practiced line sounded really stupid! "Windy with diamond showers!"

He dropped the sock of diamonds beside her, then stood there. The top of the sock was tied with a string to secure the stones.

"Ew! What's this? Your dirty sock?" The loathing in her tone was for more than the sock; he wasn't sure what!

"Dirty ones are all I have!" he responded evenly, watching while she picked delicately at the knot, being purposely cautious not to touch the offensive sock.

Pulling it back from her grasp, he cut the string and poured the gems into her hand. The profusion was dazzling!

"Stashed in the house!" her voice was soft with wonder. "When the wind blows around the house, they dislodge? Is this all of them?"

"Well, that's what I need to explain," he squatted next to her. "The first couple of times it happened, I thought broken glass had fallen from someplace; I just swept it up and threw it out."

Bransom, overhearing the confession, laughed. "Suzanne throws them in the river; David throws them in the trash! Let's throw them all away and get back to normal!"

"Hear! Hear!" Diana echoed from her watchful position near Donovan Cline!

Mallory shook her head in amazement at their opinions. The incriminating photo of David pushed from her mind, she met his gaze again.

"How many do you think you threw out? Do you think there are still more in the house?"

"Lots less than what's here, maybe an eighth as many. I'm not sure! I think there are still quite a few hidden different places. When I realized the problem, I moved in a construction trailer to work from, so I could seal the house up. Hope everything will be okay until I get back. Then we need to move the house into a secure warehouse and take it apart board by board."

Daniel Faulkner hoped people would leave the little house alone, too. David had really needed to be able to communicate with Mallory when he discovered the stones, but he hadn't been able to do so.

Herb Carlton gazed at the diamonds in amazement! Drawn inexorably, he rose from his seat to gaze awed, at the wealth the girl held so carelessly in her hands!

Diana was the one to notice Carlton's demeanor. The only thing she knew about him was that he was Erik's guest. Her first thought was that he was a diamond-cartel spy who had worked his way in with Bransom. Now she watched him closely.

Her nursing school in Africa, where technology was extremely limited, focused the care-givers' attention on close observation of the patients; barely perceptible variations in pulse and respiration. Daniel called her "a walking lie detector", laughingly saying he could never get anything past her!

Seeing the wonder in Carlton's eyes, Diana followed his line of vision toward the sparkling stones Mallory was reconsigning to the sock.

"Mr. Carlton, is it?" Diana questioned.

Almost as if emerging from a trance, the gentleman turned toward her voice.

"Yes, Mrs. Faulkner. I'm very sorry; were you speaking to me? I was very absorbed with the stones. I think some of them might have fallen on the floor."

"You like diamonds?" she questioned, surprised!

"Oh, yes Ma'am, very much! They are God's masterpieces! Do you not agree?"

"No, I don't." Her response was quick. "I mean, I guess they are. I think people are His masterpieces! He allows us to adorn ourselves and be surrounded with all of His beautiful creations. He made all things for His pleasure, and we can enjoy it, too!

Carlton nodded soberly. "Yes." he replied softly.

David returned to his seat. Whatever Mallie was mad about seemed to have blown over. He hoped.

Diana returned to check on Mr. Cline, who, feeling worse than ever, was demanding to receive at least some of the medication! The strange assortment of drugs seemed both dangerous and fraudulent. Her opinion was that the facility seemed to be trying to induce psychotic symptoms in Mr. Cline so they would continue to find it necessary to "treat him". Since she wasn't certain which agency had the oversight of "clinics" like this one, she asked Bransom. He wasn't sure, either. He wanted investigations into every sneaky, underhanded scheme in America! There simply weren't the resources for that!

She returned, studying Cline's twitching, and obvious discomfort.

"Give me something!" His voice was insistent, although whispered. "Even if it's only a sugar pill!"

"Mr. Cline, you don't seem to have a suggestible mind. I'm not sure a placebo would benefit you very much. Sugar might not be a bad idea; there are quite a few different sugars in alcoholic beverages. Have you eaten anything today? Do you have Diabetes or problems with sugar assimilation that you're aware of? Did they order many tests in the ER?"

She sent Daniel around to the group to ask if any of them had apparatus for checking blood glucose. When he returned empty-handed from the search, Mallory went to her mom. Still an hour and a half out from landing in New York, she asked her mom to get on-line and find a testing kit in the city, and have it delivered to them at the airport. Suzanne ordered two, to be on the safe side. Having testers delivered to them at the airport on such short notice wasn't going to be cheap; it didn't matter.

The dirty sock loaded with diamonds rested next to Mallory in the wide double, reclining seats. Carlton kept looking backwards toward the strange bundle, anxiety etched all over his face.

Mallory shrugged at him. "What?"

Taking that as the best opening he was going to be offered, he rose from his seat and moved toward her.

"What are you doing about those diamonds?" His puzzlement and concern were both genuine.

Mallory picked the sock up gingerly. "Please sit down," she invited politely. "We really don't know what to do with them," she confided, her laughter musical. "They're kind of hard to move without the cartel's blessing. Guess we'll just pull the rest from the house and keep mining. Maybe we'll get another offer."

"Yes, but with these, here on this airplane. These haven't been inventoried? Surely you plan to remove them to a safe place in New York City! If you try to move them into Turkey, you~we will be accused of smuggling! I think Turkish jails are not nice!"

Kerry, asleep since he tucked his Bible away, sat up, startled!

"What's that about Turkish jails?" he questioned. "Who's smuggling stuff?"

"David is!" she accused. "It's <u>his</u> sock! Full, I'm sure of his DNA, among other-um-stuff! He can go to jail for all of us!"

David made a childish face at her, and she laughed.

Erik, hearing the pawn shop owner's warning to Mallory, spoke out. "Hey, Faulkner! We got a problem back here!"

Daniel strode back. "Thought you were our problem-solver, Bransom! What are you hollering at me about?"

Bransom's eyes danced. "I can solve the problem! Just give me the say-so, and I'll flush these rocks all across the eastern US!"

"Spoken like a true FBI agent! What's the problem?" Daniel rubbed his hands together. "I can probably solve it with a little more finesse!"

Bransom, Kerry, and Mallory all focused their gaze on Carlton, so Daniel zeroed in on him, too.

As he explained the problem again, he emphasized that the stones must be deposited in New York City.

The original plan was to stop in the city for two hours. Refueling the plane, changing crews, adding the staff for the "frills" package! Now, they had to meet up with one or both of the blood glucose kits, load Shay and Delia, their luggage and security personnel, and accomplish something else inside the private terminal that Bransom asked if Diana could help him with.

The corporate team devised a plan. Daniel and Kerry, with two security members would find the nearest bank, rent a safety deposit box, stash the gems, and return. Bransom and Diana would have three security guys with them to do whatever Bransom was scheming. The remaining passengers and security could deplane and look around in the terminal, in preparation for the transatlantic flight.

Before the preparations for approach and landing, Carlton once again approached Faulkner with a problem about the diamonds. They should be carefully sketched, described, and inventoried! Without time to complete such a task on so many stones, he insisted that the diamonds should be weighed, at least!

When Faulkner acquiesced, Carlton dove immediately into a battered, expandable, leather bag, pulling out a scale, a loupe, and a magnifying jeweler's visor.

Saying, "Excuse me, dear lady," to Linda, he poured the diamonds carefully onto the jigsaw puzzle. Grasping some of the larger stones with gem tweezers, and holding the loupe by his eye, he gazed for long moments. Finally, he placed the entire treasure trove onto the scale, carefully recording the weight. He then requested four of the officers to verify the weight: Mallory, Diana, Daniel, and John.

"Anything good there, Herb?" Daniel finally questioned, unable to control his curiosity any longer.

Carlton gazed at him strangely.

"I know they're pretty small," Faulkner continued awkwardly "Any guess as to the value of this sock-full?"

"No guess at all," Carlton stated honestly. "Very beautiful, very nice! No "small" stones; only large and larger. Smallest stones here, probably cut to nearly a carat. Maybe, one to three million; I do not know!"

Mallory was the only one who wasn't shocked by the estimate.

As quickly as they could deplane, Daniel, Kerry, and two of the most seasoned security guys crowded into a single cab and gave a bank address they had hastily located on-line. The sock-full of diamonds, stashed in Larson's briefcase made them all nervous, to say the least! Faulkner was praying for the Lord to help them seem more relaxed than they felt. They had already discussed what a miracle it was that David had presented the stones to Mallory before the New York layover. Asking the cabbie to wait for them, they hurried into the bank.

Diana followed Erik from the plane, where they were met by a couple of agents Erik knew. After greeting Diana, they quickly led the way through a twist of corridors that seemed to grow narrower and less important with every turn. Arriving at a metal door, one of the agents pounded, and it opened, admitting them to a small, bare room. A table stood in the center, a young man seated dejectedly in one of the ladder-back metal chairs.

Diana gave Erik a questioning glance.

"Daniel told me you can tell when people are lying," Bransom explained briefly. "This is Shannon O'Shaughnessy. Thought he could give you a quick rundown of his story; then you can ask him whatever questions you want, and give me your take on him."

Diana could hardly believe it. "You couldn't just give him a polygraph? I'm not sure any assessment I make would be foolproof. What's at stake here? Surely, Diana Faulkner's unofficial lie-detector testing ability won't stand up in court."

"Just wondering if you think it would be a good idea to bring him on the trip!"

She could hardly believe what she was hearing! No wonder the wily agent had acted so sneaky, not letting Daniel know what he had on his mind. She shot Bransom another incredulous glance before sitting down.

"Can you make the room any brighter?"

"Nah! This is as bright as it gets!" Bransom perched on the corner of the table.

Mallory grabbed Callie so they could stick with Mr. Cline; they were both afraid he would make his way immediately to the bar. He knew what they were up to, but he followed them around, relatively good-naturedly, anyway. He did crave a drink, but part of him desperately wanted to complete the drying out process.

Callie was sorry she had asked about David. That hadn't set well with her new friend at all! In all of their yacking and confiding in one another, Mallory had never breathed a word about being emotionally involved with anyone. She didn't blame Mallory for liking the guy! He was fun, and really good looking! She was curious what the story was!

In the bank, Daniel Faulkner filled out paperwork to rent a box. For simplicities' sake, he filled the form out in his own name. Having Mallory present would probably have been better, but the diamonds had been weighed properly with the stockholders. This was still on the up and up. With the box paid for and assigned, Daniel and Kerry stashed the diamonds away, before rejoining security and taking the cab back to the airport. No problems, but no one knew they carried millions of dollars worth of diamonds! Paying and tipping the cabbie, they sprinted back inside the terminal.

Delia and Shay joined the excited group, watching carefully that no luggage was mishandled. Suzanne took possession of two blood glucose testers, and returned to the boarding area. Mallory was beginning the task of keeping everyone assembled for the reboarding process, reminding them to keep their passports handy from this point forward. After warm hugs for Shay and Delia, Mallie stepped back to admire her grandmother who looked stunning in the outfit that featured her classic car. She was more proud of Shay, though, than she was the Rolls.

Few people were around, but a couple of well-dressed men seemed to be intrigued by the group. Finally, one of them approached David, handing him a business card. They were Seventh Avenue advertising executives who commuted daily from Connecticut.

They were intrigued by David's shirt and its *Catch the Drift* slogan.

Daniel and Kerry rejoined the group in time to catch the conversation. Kerry figured the two guys were going to discover that the phrase was unprotected, and they would sell it. He introduced himself as the corporate attorney, and was stunned when they asked to purchase the rights to the idea on the spot! They offered two hundred fifty thousand!

David was shocked!

"Two hundred fifty thousand plus royalties," Kerry countered. "One percent!"

They agreed. Having already learned that David had only worn the garment for part of one day, with few people having seen it, they wanted the shirt immediately. Shay sprinted toward the gift shop, returning with an extra-large *I Love New York* t-shirt. David swapped shirts. Then Kerry, Mallory, and Daniel and the other execs disappeared into a business center, where they received and signed a temporary contract. Shaking hands, they went their separate ways.

"You seen Diana?" Faulkner questioned, not seeing her in the group.

"She's on board; so's Erik and another guest," Mallie responded conspiratorially. "Everybody show your passport as you board. Let's go!"

Chapter 24

TRANSATLANTIC

MALLORY TRIED NOT to allow her disappointment to show when she wasn't able to see the Manhattan skyline or the Statue of Liberty. By the time they all reboarded and took off in a northeasterly direction, conditions hadn't improved. At least the low visibility didn't create any delays. Maybe she could see the sites of New York City in the near future. She was already aware of a huge Gemstone Show to be held at a convention center in the City in December. She could meet some important contacts in the industry by attending.

Huge boxes of New York Style pizza, hot and tantalizing, were delivered. Mallory asked Shay to bless the food, and the pizza began disappearing! It was great pizza! The group seemed to be melding together.

Allie (as Mallory had nicknamed Alexandra), Mallie, and Callie staked claims to the three double seats at the back of the cabin. Alexandra was in seventh heaven to be "in" with the teens.

The Anderson family members were hunkered into several rows toward the front. Donovan Cline, was situated where Diana could monitor his condition, while still being with her family.

Herb Carlton repositioned a little closer to Linda Campbell. Kerry moved where he could talk to Carmine. She had lots of questions for him. Even though he was young and not terribly experienced, he was pulling her along. She was still eager to learn more from him.

A family movie played in the toy and game area, which captured the attention of some of the little ones as they played.

In the main cabin, an audio-visual display began, featuring information about Turkey, showing some history~from the Hittites to the present day nation. Mallory knew some of the information from her personal study, prior to the trip. It all amazed her! Like, she had read in her Bible about the Hittites, but she didn't know who they were, really, or where they came from. Troy was pretty fascinating, too, with a recap of the Trojan War. Schliemann, the archeologist who unearthed the ruins, was nearly as colorful as his find! Quite a focus was on the sites in the city of Istanbul, itself. Some of the treasures from Topkapi Palace shone dazzlingly from the big screens. Many items Mallory viewed fired her imagination with ideas she couldn't wait to share privately with Diana. Everything in the video was interesting. Some of it related heavily to Greek and Roman mythology. Not surprisingly, to the Greeks and Romans and those they reigned over, the little deities and myths pertaining to them were not considered myths. It was truly a wicked and idolatrous religious system! The group would be viewing the remains of temples built to the gods and goddesses where sacrifices were made! Under Roman rule, which also included Emperor worship, other religious practices, especially Christianity, were not tolerated! Some of Topkapi's most treasured objects were those relating to the Prophet Mohammed and Islam. That brought some irreverent comments from the group

Kerry Larson actually halted the presentation to give a serious, well thought out warning to everyone.

"Whatever you have to say for jokes about all this, get it out of your system. This is part of the Topkapi Palace Tour. Most of us want to see various parts of it. Unfortunately, when it's time to tour through these rooms, we can't just say we don't want to see the Islamic part. We have to pass through without one smart-alecky comment! Not even whispers. In these huge stone buildings, whispers carry! And phones and video equipment pick up, too. Remember a few years ago, there were riots in Denmark about insulting Islam! Denmark isn't even a Moslem country! We don't want to get into any trouble here! That goes for obeying all the laws. Turkey doesn't have a legal system like ours. Believe me, it's easy to get into trouble you can't get out of!"

Daniel nodded agreement. "Good point, Kerry! Anything so cute that y'all can't resist saying, say it now; get it out of your system."

John Anderson simply added that it grieves Christians when their beliefs are ridiculed. The way to reach Moslems wouldn't be by offending them, anyway.

Kerry reentered the conversation. "Speaking of converting Moslems, that isn't legal here either. There are churches; we'll attend one in Ankara. Our witnessing should mostly be through our conversation to each other, that people overhear. But Americans have a reputation for being a bunch of noisy obnoxious drunks, so we need to show that American Christians are nice, polite people."

The display ended with a documentary about Mt. Ararat and the hot disputes, pro and con, for evidence of the Ark's having been spotted on the slopes. Fewer and fewer expeditions were being permitted by the Turkish government for the search for the ark. Daniel laughed, not that any of them had any desire to climb the peak, if they could. At over sixteen thousand, nine hundred feet, climbing it was a challenge for experienced climbers!

Shannon O'Shaughnessy, seated with the security staff, enjoyed the pizza and the group surrounding him with a silent awe. Ashamed, he hadn't met the gazes of anyone, especially his grandmother and brother!

With the completion of the video, Daniel started through the cabin with a goodie box of gift-wrapped items. Instructing them to hold onto them until all were distributed, he presented a gift from the DiaMo Corporation to each traveler. Nearly everyone had received a diamond ring in April. Now the gifts were gold and diamond in-and-out hoop earrings for the ladies and gold and diamond cuff-links for the men. They were very nice! Carmine, Donovan, Herb, and Linda were particularly amazed to be included in the lavish gift-giving! Like the trip wasn't over the top, already! Each kid received a new toy or game and a thousand dollar certificate of deposit in his name.

David liked the cuff links, but he didn't have any dress shirts, let alone any with French cuffs. They were hard to find, but with his height and long arms, it was impossible. Then he realized his dad was confiding the same thing, so Diana was giving out business cards for a custom shirt maker. Custom-made shirts! Never in his wildest dreams, would that have occurred to him! A couple of Scripture verses came to his mind.

> *For my thoughts are not your thoughts, neither are your ways my ways, saith the LORD. For as the heavens are higher than the earth, so are my ways higher than your ways, and my thoughts than your thoughts.Isaiah 55:8 & 9*

Since the heavens are light years above the earth, he knew God's plans for him were light years better than his plans for himself.

Occasionally a readout would appear on the screen showing the jet's progress. From New York City, the course carried them northeasterly along the coast of Newfoundland. Clouds continued to obliterate the view of the Atlantic Ocean, but the flight was smooth.

Shay moved where he could visit with David, and Allie struck up a conversation with Delia. Daniel's talk with her seemed to have gotten through.

Tammi had already been helping with the little kids, and generally all round, acting better. The new clothes she had chosen were all cute, making her really fit into the group, while still reflecting her own personality and taste. Shay and David were turning into a real comedy duo, their showing off not lost on Emma and Mallory!

With the pizza devoured and the travelogue finished, Callie challenged anyone to a Chess game. With her "genius" reputation, no one was willing to take her on. Finally, Daniel accepted the challenge. Callie was surprised; he lasted longer than most of her rivals. Defeated, and having drawn a group of spectators, he demanded a rematch. When he lost again, he conceded defeat. To his surprise, John Anderson picked up the challenge. A match was on!

Linda Campbell, intrigued at first, realized it was going to be a long game. She decided to be the first to take advantage of the salon service. A reclusive, shy lady who had been head librarian in a small Kansas town for twenty years, encouraged by her niece, had decided to cast off the long worn-out cocoon, and emerge! With the loss of her cats, she sold her house and jalopy, quit her job, and withdrew some of her savings, to launch into anything new and different! Surely there was more to life than watching yourself and your cats grow old! In less than a day, she had more friends, more fun, more excitement, than she had experienced in more than a decade! The cute new hairstyle and cosmetics were a beginning! Now, it was time to break the nail-biting habit and cover up the damage!

To her amazement, Herb Carlton pulled a chair up next to hers at the manicure station, stating he was curious what the process was to "make fingernails". He really was curious about the process, but he was even more intrigued by the cute, single lady.

Donovan Cline's glucose test did reveal low sugar. After enjoying the pizza, he was able to fall asleep.

Relieved by his improvement, Diana stopped by Shannon's seat to visit briefly with him. Her assessment of him was in complete agreement with Erik's. With his loss of both parents, his last-second rescue from a gangland execution, and the jail time, he was at the end of his options. The government was in the process of seizing what little property his father, Ryland, owned. The corporation was working to protect Shannon's inheritance from his uncle's estate, from being seized, too!

Diana smiled brightly as she sank down next to him to ask if he needed anything.

Overwhelmed by her kindness, he simply mumbled something she couldn't understand.

"Don't forget, I'm a walking lie detector," she laughed. "You look kind of miserable just sitting here. Would you like a Nintendo game, or a book, or anything? There's ice cream and desserts. You can get up and move around. I guess Erik wanted these guys around you until he can watch you a little bit more. Are you nervous to talk to Shay and Delia, or did Erik tell you to wait?"

Noticing Diana talking to her cousin, Mallory moved forward to join them.

"Hi, Shannon," she greeted. "I haven't seen you in a long time. Sorry I don't remember it!"

Having barely taken his eyes from his cousin since boarding, he really felt bashful! She was one gorgeous lady! Of course, Shannon had always thought his Aunt Suzanne was really pretty!

"I remember you," he rejoined. "You gave me a black eye one time."

Diana's laughter rippled.

"I'm sure it was an accident," Mallory spoke quickly.

"I don't think so! You really had a temper!"

Mallory was blushing. "You probably deserved it!" was her response.

Diana moved on, getting a bottle of water, before returning to check the progress of the Chess match. It was pretty even. Diana wondered if the girl had ever played an equal before. She returned to settle into her own double-seat area across an aisle from Daniel. He was reading a Geology periodical, so she leaned across to ask him how all the rocks were doing.

Smiling at her, he took her hand and kissed it.

"I don't know. Maybe I've studied rocks so long I'm turning into one! I'm sorry about your bag, Honey! I don't want you carrying heavy stuff; but I would have wanted us to hang onto your jewelry and keep it with us in the cabin. The insurance company should thank Mallory. I knew you were trying to tell me something, but I ignored you. Forgive me? Please?"

"I thought you were mad at me." was her response.

After sitting a few more minutes, Shannon decided to take advantage of Diana's invitation. *Moby Dick* seemed like the best choice among the books. He was hardly an avid reader, but he couldn't really spot where the games were that Diana had mentioned. Then he paused to watch the Chess players in their match of wits. He understood the game a little bit, and the girl was pretty cute!

Mallory introduced him to her; her name was Callie. Callie responded with a shy, "Pleased to meet you." Then, noticing the volume in his hand, she spoke a little more animatedly. "Oh, you're reading *Moby Dick*? I love Herman Melville!"

"Oh, yeah! Nice to meet you, too, Callie." He backed away awkwardly, disappointed!

He wondered how such a cute girl could be in love with a guy named Herman, but it sounded like Callie was already spoken for!

Since desserts and beverages were being served, he returned to his seat in time to ask for Turtle Cheesecake and coffee. Suddenly, he was overwhelmed! Such elegant dessert, served on fine china, and he was traveling overseas in an exquisite private jet! He couldn't figure out how he was in federal custody one minute, then the blond lady asked him a few questions, and here he was! His Aunt Suzanne's new husband was the FBI guy who had been in his face for the past month!"

Sipping the fragrant coffee, he opened the classic novel: *Moby Dick* by Herman Melville. He nearly laughed at his own ignorance!

Lana and Joyce, with their desserts, moved back toward the "Beauty Station". Joyce had pretty fingernails, so she had them manicured. Lana's hands were pretty disastrous from cleaning the little parsonage non-stop after the seven of them. Choosing a soft mauve polish to match her outfit, she sat and visited while waiting for Linda's new set to be finished.

Herb Carlton wasn't giving up on trying to talk to Linda. She was extremely shy, and with her hum-drum existence, she felt like she was pretty uninteresting, even if she told him everything. The pawn-shop owner continued revealing information about himself. A widower of twelve years, he had one married son. They didn't usually get along very well, but the son, who went by Merc, was taking care of the shop during the trip.

Joyce Haynes asked him about his interest in the diamonds, and jewelry, in general.

The jewelry part of the pawn shop was his passion. Even though diamonds mesmerized him, he had never visited the Crater of Diamonds State Park, not far from his home. Shrugging, he admitted he lacked faith to think there could be anything that spectacular, nearly on his front step! He did know and understand gems and jewelry. As a trained jeweler, his real dream was to someday become a designer, producing his own jewelry line.

Diana came into the area in time to hear the last of the conversation. What an answer to prayer! With her clothing designs becoming reality; her jewelry sketches remained on paper! With an entire team of talented and trained garment industry employees, she had no one in place to bring the jewelry designs to finished products.

She was pretty certain Herb was unsaved. Not that everyone she worked with knew the Lord, but she wanted a little more information before she could reveal any of the secret design ideas. He seemed like a genuinely nice guy, so she visited with him a little more without revealing the fact that she was interviewing him. Linda tried not to be miffed by the beautiful and friendly woman's entrance into the conversation. Diana already had an extremely handsome husband; and no one ever paid this much attention to her.

Mallory retreated to her seats. With her efforts to get people introduced and mingling, she still needed to read her Bible. Forcing the picture of David from her mind wasn't easy. She turned to a special verse she loved.

Thou wilt keep him in perfect peace, whose mind is stayed on thee: because he trusteth in thee. Isaiah 26:3

"Lord," she breathed softly. "Please help me to stay my thoughts on You and trust in You. If David is the one you have for me, the picture doesn't matter; if he isn't the one, then it really doesn't! Help me to focus on You so I'm not bitter at Sheriff Melville, for sending out pictures of people that are nobody's business, and for choking me. Help me just to trust You and not be worried. Don't let David's being along, or the picture, ruin this trip."

Even as she read and prayed, she was aware of David's voice amongst the happy hum as the jet hurtled across the Atlantic. David's laugh, his presence! He was really a personality! Then she heard his guitar! He certainly wasn't one to be ignored! A few chords. Then a soft song floated back toward her.

"Welcome to my world,"

Then Tammi chimed in, repeating the phrase with a beautiful counter-melody.

It surprised Mallory, who had no idea her friend could sing so beautifully.

Evidently, Tammi shocked her brother, too. He hesitated only briefly before continuing~

"Won't you come on in?"

Tammi echoed. "Won't you come on in?" It was beautiful!

"Miracles, I guess,"

"Miracles, I guess,"

"Still happen now and then."

"Still happen now and then."

They sang through the song until the final phrase when Tammi harmonized with David, rather than repeating.

"Welcome to my world!"

Everyone had stopped what they were doing to listen, then everyone in the cabin broke into applause. A couple of people knew it was an old Eddie Arnold song; most thought it was new.

The crowd asked for an encore, but the guitar was already back in its battered case. Instead, David started the DVD of the Easter Sunday evening concert by the Faulkner family. Those who had heard it before were delighted to get a repeat performance. It was thoroughly enjoyable.

Daylight had long since dropped behind them as they surged eastward, but everyone seemed too hyped to consider sleep. By now, everyone seemed plugged in. Shannon, engrossed in Moby Dick, still surfaced occasionally to laugh at the antics of the people around him. Carlton continued to watch the fingernail process, while expounding on his favorite subject of gemstones and jewelry.

John Anderson's patient strategy finally won out in the Chess match, to Callie's total humiliation. Little rich girl wasn't accustomed to defeat. Still, she tried to shake off the loss.

"That's long enough in the Bible," she announced to Mallory. "Come on Allie, let's go work on the puzzle and find more to eat."

Laughing, the three moved aft through the cabin.

"Oh-oh, here come the Three Musketeers," Shay warned David and Shannon, managing to be both loud and conspiratorial at the same time.

"En garde!" Callie laughed, feinting toward Shay with a fork. All three girls laughed, then turned their attention toward the DVD that was still playing. Daniel's sermon came up, with the pictures of the little sparrows.

Donovan Cline tried to stay asleep! Between the scripture on Diana's sweater and a sermon playing, this stuff was getting on his nerves. His hands shook really hard as he poured himself a cup of coffee. Callie seemed to be having a really good time, though, he told himself, satisfied. That was the main thing. Carmine sat alone, going over some legal stuff.

"Can I get you something?" he asked her. "There's all kinds of desserts and pop and stuff. Are you moving around any? It isn't good for you to sit still too long."

Carmine stared at him suspiciously, trying to figure out what his angle was now.

"Is all this religion stuff getting on your nerves?" she questioned. She still trembled every time she thought of her daughter's testimony. She figured Donovan didn't like any of it at all.

"My nerves were shot before the sermon got started," he confessed with a wry laugh. "They all seem to be pretty nice people. Callie's enjoying herself. You want a snack?"

"Not a snack; my pizza's worn off. What smells so good?"

Donovan returned to his seat, elated. At least she talked to him.

The guys weren't too interested in helping with the puzzle, but they pulled chairs up so they could hassle the girls.

Emboldened by them, Tommy joined the group, too.

Allie swept him a sideways glance, blushing. A giggle escaped. Evidently contagious, Callie and Mallie dissolved into gales of laughter. That brought Kerry to join the party in the game area. Tammi didn't join the group, but her gaze met Kerry's briefly. It was an electric jolt.

The cabin crew appeared with an extra midnight meal; a delicate puff pastry filled with chicken and mushrooms in a divine sauce. The kids could opt for Mac cheese. When Kerry chose the kids' selection, the teens mocked him mercilessly. He thrived on the attention.

Mallie asked Shay how everything about his business ventures was progressing. Using his iPhone, he showed off some of the beautiful Alpaca garments that were in the works for fall.

"Wow, let me know when I can order it!" she laughed, impressed.

"No kidding!" Callie was amazed. She was copying Mallie's example of finding beautiful garments on the racks in the stores, while at the same time, taking advantage of the lovely designs coming from this group.

Everyone was excited by the deal Kerry had struck in the New York terminal over David's sweater.

Diana, passing through, noticed Alexandra's flirting with Tommy. She joined the group, admiring Shay's iPhone images and fitting in a couple of puzzle pieces. Her bright personality didn't dampen the party at all. Excitedly, she added ideas for completing looks featuring the Alpaca garments. Sketching on napkins, she added boots, belts, handbags, and finally jewelry. Once again, she mentioned some of the shopping available in Turkey. After hearing about beautiful leather goods, she added that shopping excursion into the itinerary. There was just too much to see and do!

"Let's don't forget the wool," Mallory reminded. "I was watching the History Channel the other night. It was something about whether the Norse were in America before Christopher Columbus. The Norse raised sheep and used wool and traded it, from Greenland, or Iceland, or someplace like that. Anyway, it said that 'Wool was white gold for the Norse'."

"Yeah, and it would be for Shay and all of us, if PETA would pipe down," Diana inserted. "They have out a campaign 'that it's better to go naked than wear wool'! Shearing sheep doesn't hurt them, but even if it did, it's no different than using other animals for our benefit. In Proverbs, it says not to be wasteful in hunting; it doesn't say not to hunt. It's no different than eating meat, fish, and poultry! I don't think they should have the right to choose for all Americans, but they have really impacted the fashion industry!

"Well, let's impact it back! Mallory responded. "I think we are! Your fashions are beautiful and lady-like, and it's amazing the way they glorify the Lord as the Original Architect of Beauty and Design."

David thought Mallory was losing sight of herself to become a little "Diana clone".

"That's kind of a stretch about God," he contradicted.

"Not really!" Diana came in smoothly. This was her passion, and she was eloquent about it.

"Look at the description of the Tabernacle and the Priestly garments in the book of Exodus! Everything was a beautiful combination and integration of materials and artistry, precious textiles carefully worked with jewelry elements of gold and gemstones. The Tabernacle was the luxury fibers we all deal with. Silk, Linen, embroidered with rare and expensively died threads. Maybe the goats' hair was cashmere! Then leather, and I think, finally, a fur coat!"

David gave her a sideways glance, his expression conveying his opinion that she was speaking, 'great swelling words of blasphemy'!

"Maybe you should bounce some of your thoughts off my dad," he suggested. Then directing his conversation back to Mallory, he asked why she was watching the History Channel, anyway.

" Because Boston wasn't playing!" Her response was quick, and she made a face at him.

"What do you think 'Badgers' skins' means?" Diana asked him.

She enjoyed a lively debate. She knew Bible dictionaries and footnotes in most Bibles, translated the expression as 'porpoise'. She thought that was a stretch! Made by men! As a woman, she could see the obvious. The Tabernacle in the Wilderness, like the later Church, represented the "Beloved Lady" the Bride of Christ, who was adorned with linen, embroidered and embellished silk, cashmere, then leather, then fur. Even today, the badger family included the luxurious Mink, Sable, and Ermine. She figured the word was translated "badger" because the Hebrew text meant "badger"! The Tabernacle was covered by "Rams skins dyed red." Why would it need two leather coverings? Why did leather with the fur left on it make men so nervous?

David was forced to admit that he hadn't ever thought of things this way.

Shay was studying Diana's sketches, amazed.

"Can you show me what some of my designs would look like with fur trim?" he asked her.

Closing his book, Shannon drew closer, too.

Mallory loved watching Diana sketch.

"I liked your coat you wore to church that Wednesday night when I first saw you," Mallory confided to Shay. "Was that wool?"

"Yeah, wool herringbone," he responded.

"I liked it, too," Diana agreed. "That gives me a great idea!"

Giving up on the napkins and ball point, she pulled out a sketch book and large set of colored oil pencils.

Having already sketched a basket of Larson Apples on an ivory-white sweater, inspiration fired up, where she had been stuck!. The apples, a rich rosy, pink-red, she designed an accompanying suit in gray-blue herringbone, with tweed dots of the rosy pink worked in.

"Ah! That is so adorable!" Callie squealed.

"It is good, Mom." Allie admitted.

Mallory loved the big, firm apples, so she asked if the suit would look too wild if the silk lining featured an all over pattern of them. Diana loved it! Bold and stunning, but not too over-the-top!

She sketched some variations on the theme, showing the suit with a solid, matching, blue-gray silk pullover sweater. Then, adding a silk scarf that matched the lining, she illustrated the ensemble, showing it with matching rosy heels and slouch bag.

Everyone ooh-ed and ah-ed over it. At Mallie's suggestion, Diana redrew the same outfit reversing the colors, making the herringbone rose and white with blue gray tweed dotted throughout. A solid-color rose sweater looked beautiful with the "Apple" lining and matching scarf.

Diana told Mallie she was a genius to think of repeating the prints in the lining material. Mallie was pleased. Everyone always needed compliments, and she really coveted Diana's favor.

That reminded Mallory of her pastor's teasing Diana that she hadn't designed him anything. He really did like the cute pictures of his children that Diana had designed for Lana. Mallory suggested a brown leather bomber jacket for him, lined with the same artwork, but in browns and tans, rather than the pastels. Diana was delighted with the idea of repeating some of the same themes, using different color combinations.

David left the group and wandered back to ask Daniel if he could talk to him.

Daniel wasn't particularly thrilled with him at the moment. Erik had finally shown him the photo of David from Melville's file, wondering if Patrick had told him about it or shown it to him. Nevertheless, he moved some periodicals so David could sit down.

"What's on your mind?" he questioned.

David asked several questions about the Bible Camp. There were questions about whether it would be primarily available to church groups, or if it should be an outreach for inner-city kids. Daniel assumed it would be for church kids, junior age, teens, maybe family week, and a few retreats the rest of the year. That was what David thought, but Brad thought it should be more of an outreach for the tough, gang-type unsaved. Daniel wasn't for that at all. To his amazement, Donovan Cline, who was listening intently, spoke up. He thought the camp should do both! Have the nice, civilized kids there during the early part of the summer. They needed the reinforcement of Bible Camp. Then, bring in the tough kids and have the winter to repair their damages to the facility.

Sounded like a reasonable solution; maybe the guy would be useful, after all!

Daniel showed David the picture: he wanted an explanation.

David viewed it in consternation and shock! He had never seen it before, had no idea of its existence!

"Where'd that come from?" he asked. "Did Mallie see it? I thought she was mad at me earlier."

"It came off Melville's computer for Bransom. He said Suzanne and Patrick saw it when it first appeared. You mind explaining to me what it's about? You don't have to; it might clear some stuff up."

David took a deep breath and plunged in!

Janet Walters had sort of kept to her husband and herself. Her initial concern about the trip was because of Sarah and Sammie. So far they had been entertained and were pretty happy. Finally worn out, they had fallen asleep with their new pillows and blankets. The other little ones seemed to have succumbed to the Sandman, too. Janet shyly moved back to get her hands and feet prettied up, too. Suzanne joined her, finally leaving Erik's side-temporarily, at least. Both were amazed how much nicer their beautiful new rings looked on manicured hands.

Daniel was the first to try a shave, joking with the barber about how steady his hands were with the straight razor in turbulence. Since the flight was smooth, he needn't have worried. David followed next, then his dad. Erik got his shoes shined, then his hair trimmed. He kept it cut close, gray sprinkled lightly into the brown at his temples.

In the cabin, Daniel started the *Star of Bethlehem* DVD. The main cabin was primarily darkened now, with a few of the adults napping a little, too. Anyone who didn't want the documentary could read by the individual overhead lights. All had noise-filtering headsets to block out cabin noise if they chose.

Mallory moved immediately to her place to watch it! It reminded her of Easter Sunday, the previous month, with the Faulkners in the motor coach. Looking back on it, the memory was good. At the time, though, she had been filled with dread and uncertainty. The DVD had captured her interest then, but too much was going on for her to concentrate. Now, she followed it, amazed.

An attorney, Rick Larson, growing curious about what the Bethlehem star really was, set out to uncover the mystery. Purchasing Astronomy software, he was able to track the movement of all the celestial bodies back throughout history! It was amazing! Using Kepler's Laws of

Planetary Motion, he had unraveled quite a revelation. Mallory sat stunned, tears rolling down her cheeks. The science and math! The heavens were a literal clock! God's timing and purpose in the Advent of His Son; and then also for the Passover and the Crucifixion! There was an explanation of the "signs and wonders" she had always read and heard about. It gave unfathomable new depth to Psalms 19:1~3

> *The Heavens declare the glory of God, and the firmament sheweth his handywork.*
> *Day unto day uttered speech, and night unto night sheweth knowledge.*
> *There is no speech nor language, where their voice is not heard.*

She always thought the heavens declared His glory in a general way! By the vastness of the expanse of space and the unfathomable number of stars! Now she was amazed by the specificity of the message! A message understood clearly by the ancients, deliberately shunned by humanity, as they tried to deny their consciousness of Him! Their accountability to an omnipotent God!

She decided she was going to get a telescope when she got home, and the software. For now, though, she focused her attention rapturously on the large screen. And, she was going to order her own copy of the DVD. She could invite people over and show it; she could play it for some of her employees. Momentarily, she wondered if she should become an Astronomer instead of a Geologist. To her amazement, she still felt great peace about her chosen path. Her studies of the Earth would reveal the same awesome and powerful Creator that Larson found studying the Heavens.

"If you truly want to find God, He's pretty hard to miss!" she decided.

As Callie realized the significance of what she was watching, she moved to the vacant seat next to her dad.

"I'm seeing it," he growled at her. "They could have seen all this happen and then worked it into the story. A lot of fiction gets real events incorporated into it. Like *Gone With the Wind*. Just because there was really the Civil War, it doesn't mean the whole novel was true.

Callie only nodded. No matter how compelling Jesus and salvation were, the believer still has to come by faith. She was still glad when he continued to watch it. And she was glad for the way Delia and Shay finally got saved after Mallory and her dad and mom prayed for her for ten years. She sat praying her dad would live long enough to be saved. And her mom!

When the video ended, Mallory turned her attention to the window again. After a short night, due to their easterly travel, the sun was beginning to rise ahead of them. Far below, she could finally see the Atlantic Ocean! What appeared to be tiny ripples from this altitude, were undoubtedly significant swells on the surface.

And the sky! A line of radiant orange defined the hazy melding of sky and water ahead of them. She was trying to capture the moment on film when Daniel told her to join him and Diana. He had requested permission from the crew to enter the cockpit for a more panoramic view of the Eastern sky. Mallory and Diana snapped happily away as the colors spread, deepened, lightened, expanded, disappeared, to leave the sky a solid blue canopy above them. Finally, Mallory turned to leave the cockpit, but found her way blocked by David's massive frame.

Since he was in the initial stages of learning to fly, he had immediately moved forward to view the controls in the cockpit. The sight of the display was fascinating, but seeing Mallory backed by the radiant color and light took his breath away! She looked like something from an illuminated manuscript! She was so beautiful! Dazed, he stepped aside.

In a few more minutes, the jet's shadow zoomed onto the European Continent!

Mallory's spirit outsoared the plane!

Chapter 25

TREASURY

THE CHATTERING GROUP deplaned in Istanbul, Turkey, midmorning, clearing passport control, purchasing visas, then moving cooperatively to their assigned places in the luxury coaches. They crowded in good-naturedly. There was plenty of space, but not the spacious comfort they enjoyed on the jet.

They met their Turkish guide and bus drivers before heading for the famous Topkapi Palace complex. The curve of the property, called Seraglio Point, was located on the Sea of Marmara right where the Golden Horn curved westward from the Bosporus! Wow! Talk about real estate! Far away names with hazy meanings manifested themselves into the reality of the here and now!

Leaving the coaches parked, they disembarked to walk along a broad sidewalk toward some cone-shaped cupolas flanking the entry before them. The weather, pleasantly warm with breezy whispers, enhanced the courtyard garden they passed through. Then, an old, dark red church was pointed out to them, because surprisingly, it had escaped ever becoming a mosque!

Then there was a large "fountain" which reminded Mallory of some old-fashioned movie theater ticket kiosk. The group around her, chattering excitedly, and with exhausted silliness, was preventing her hearing the guide. She worked her way to the front! She didn't want to miss out on anything!

As the group progressed through the Palace Treasury where priceless, antique treasures rested behind thick glass, they quieted. Even though the objects spoke volumes by themselves, the group now hung on every word uttered by their guide! It was hard to absorb everything! Due in part to her having stayed awake for so many hours, but also to the unfathomable nature of the treasure, Mallory felt like her head was spinning!

The exhibit housed many objets d'art that would have elicited oohs and ahs by themselves, but were somehow eclipsed by other objects, more valuable or more famous. The Topkapi Dagger, stunning with its three huge emeralds, surrounded by myriads of other set gemstones and pearls, twinkled enticingly at them. Crystal quartz decanters, embellished with gold and precious gemstones must have gleamed from the dressing table of a favored one of the court! Mallory paused as long as possible gazing at The Spoonmakers' Diamond: the most valuable single item in the entire treasury collection! An eighty-six carat, pear-shaped jewel, it was surrounded by a double row of diamonds. The story was a confused supposition of a silver spoon-maker's having found it in a pile of trash in an alley-way, sometime in the nebulous past. Bransom couldn't help teasing Suzanne about throwing her fabulous ring into the Little Missouri! Joining into the banter was Diana, who quoted a once-famous actress, famous for having had several husbands, making the statement that, "She had never gotten mad enough at a man to throw his jewelry away!"

Herb Carlton spent at least fifteen minutes studying a suit of chain mail studded with diamonds, the chain mail in itself being a cross between the art of a jeweler and that of a blacksmith!

Mallory thought the diamonds were a nice touch, remarking that "putting on the whole armor of God" would elicit a different picture in her mind from now on Laughing, her pastor's wife agreed with her.

They toured through the large area which once housed the harem. Without the lavish interior elements that surely adorned it at the height of its splendor, it indeed seemed dismal. It seemed like life must truly have been bleak for the women enclosed here.

Shay said he felt sorry for the eunuchs, and the girls who heard him blushed. Pastor just picked up on the conversation to comment on the dark, wickedness of humanity not enlightened by the Word of God. Even in modern day America, slave trade continued, wicked undercurrents that people didn't know about, and didn't want to know about.

Before departing Seraglio Point, they stopped at Sirkeci Station. Its claim to fame was that it was the train terminal of the famous *Orient Express*. It continued to serve rail traffic from Istanbul to Thrace and the rest of Europe. They lunched at the station café, trying to imagine the travels of the rich and famous of a bygone era.

After lunch, they traveled to the Sultanahmet section where they viewed the remnants of the Hippodrome, an ancient stadium with a long oval track, that was the city's focus for more than a thousand years. They stood there, amazed, thinking about chariot races from long ago, laughing about the Indy Five Hundred and Nascar! Some things hadn't changed much; just the speed and power!

The next site was the famous Haghia Sophia, the Church of Holy Wisdom, one of the world's greatest architectural achievements. Later, it was converted to a mosque, and minarets were added. Now, it was neither church nor mosque, but a museum. They wandered beneath the beautiful domes, admiring the shimmering golden, Christianity-themed mosaics. Everything showed great wisdom and sophistication, showing the Americans they didn't own the market on intelligence and design.

Of course most of the group was clicking away with their cameras wherever photography was allowed. They snapped up souvenir books and picture postcards, also sampling the different street foods sold from cute carts and stands. There was a nice crunchy bread that Haynes bought, passing it around for everyone to sample. Once outside the Haghia, the tourists took photos with different groupings of them smiling in front of the famous international structure. The Blue Mosque, across a garden from Haghia, was well-known also, with its cascade of domes and half-domes, and the group photographed it as well. The interior of it was heavily tiled with the famous Iznik tiles, which were predominantly blue and white, giving it the name, "Blue Mosque". Actually a mosque, the tourists stepped quietly inside to view the tile work; they could see several Moslem men praying, their faces to their prayer rugs.

Beyond exhaustion, they reboarded their coaches to travel to the Bazaar Quarter. Actually, considering the lack of sleep, everyone, including the little ones had enjoyed the day's tours. Entering the maze of the Grand

Bazaar, tired bodies rejuvenated. Fresh adrenaline brought renewed excitement and stamina. In the "Gold" bazaar, they encountered their first experience with the "hard sell" of the determined merchants. Not sure how to barter, and with "no," meaning nothing to the hawkers, the experience was intimidating. The carpet sellers were the same. Everyone claimed to sell the best "Turkish Delight"! After an hour of laughing at the funny ones and apologizing to those who were hostile, they gladly escaped to the shelter of the coaches for the ride to the hotel. A few of them had managed to come away with a purchase or two, and during the ride through the city to the hotel, the rest of the group either admired or ridiculed the "prizes".

Tom Haynes, having shared his bread purchase, now produced a box of the Turkish Delight confection. Available in differing varieties, most of it was sticky, nutty stuff, cut into small cubes, and sprinkled with powdered sugar. "Not bad", was the decision of most of the samplers.

Traffic in the city was congested. Ten to thirteen million was the estimated population. In less then thirty minutes the coaches rolled to a stop in front of the Ritz~Carlton. The drivers and uniformed bell men began removing luggage, closely supervised by security, while Daniel and Mallory sprinted inside to collect electronic keys for each guest. Daniel returned quickly, bounding onto the first coach with keys for the Andersons, Haynes, Sanders, Walters, and his own family.

Mallory handed keys to Delia and Shay, her mom and Erik, Donovan Cline and Callie, Carmine, Kerry, Linda, and Herb, keeping the one for her own luxury suite. For now, Shannon was still with the security personnel, who were in double occupancy rooms. Their schedule of rest and vigilance would be worked out during the dinner hour.

Congregating briefly in the impressive lobby, the travelers agreed to go to their rooms for freshening up and unpacking. Naps were not recommended. International travelers were aware that it was best to try to stay awake until "bedtime" for reestablishing "body clocks" according to local time. The time was a few minutes past five, and the group agreed to meet for dinner at seven fifteen in the lobby. The lavish hotel was a convenient walking distance to shopping and dining, so the coaches, drivers, and guide were sent home for the night. With a recommendation to remain inside the hotel, everyone was dismissed to their suites.

Daniel offered to unpack their suitcases, allowing Diana the opportunity to shower first. After quickly stashing the hanging garments into the closet, he went to work setting up electronics, checking on business back in Tulsa. He made a couple of calls to answer some questions, then e-mailed his mom and dad briefly about the flights and the first day of touring. He had tried to get them to come along. His mother was relieved that he was still symptom-free of any terrible illnesses! He laughed, then realized it was a blessing that the entire group seemed pretty healthy.

Mallory entered her suite, gazing around the custom interior appreciatively. Grabbing the remote, she turned on the TV, checking for baseball scores and US news. Feeling like her eyes had been sandblasted, but hoping to stay awake until midnight, she brewed coffee. After adding her usual amount of creamer and sweetener, she carried it to the balcony to watch water traffic on the Bosporus. She was still anticipating Ephesus! But this wasn't too bad! She tried to miss her dad, but she wasn't sure he would have cared for any of this, so she sat alone, enjoying the coffee, the view, and the pleasant afternoon air. It dawned on her that she was sitting in Europe, staring across into Asia! It was the coolest!

At seven fifteen everyone reassembled, promptly and in good spirits. Daniel had put Roger in charge of dinner plans, so he was just finishing talking to the concierge as the group assembled. Trying to decipher a map, he announced that they had a reservation about three blocks away! Walking was very safe! The food would be very good, with plenty of variety for everyone from the brave to the fainthearted.

Bransom arranged the group, placing everyone's personal security where they could be most watchful. Maybe "safe", but Americans always stood out as possible targets! This group looked pretty prosperous; he didn't want to take any chances.

Taksim Square was a happenin' place; the streets alive with people; locals, and foreigners! Plenty of businesses and, restaurants. Almost everybody in the DiaMo group had been awake for the better part of thirty or forty hours, but the ladies and kids were still planning to shop on the walk back after dinner. The menu featured a variety of Turkish and western cuisine. They enjoyed the food, but it was fun, too, visiting with the Turkish people and quite a few different Europeans. Many people spoke pretty acceptable English and seemed to enjoy the gregarious Americans.

Mallory slid the proprietor a credit card, adding gratuity the way the concierge had instructed Roger. She signed, adding her notation to the receipt for the CPA.

Leaving the restaurant, they wandered along the street, in and out of shops, finding this or that. Mallory spied a hand-carved Chess set with Knights carved of Malachite and Moslem Warriors of Lapis, representing the opposing sides. The Chess board was inlaid mother of pearl and onyx, with the Lapis and Malachite inlaid attractively around the border. She purchased it for her game room, even though it would be heavy to carry around for the remainder of the night. She ran into Diana, who led her back into the shop and set everything up for having the heavy set shipped home. Then Diana fell in love with a similar set, asking Mallory if she minded her getting the same thing. Mallory laughed. She was flattered her friend liked her choice, and she didn't mind Diana's having the same thing. Diana arranged for the other set to be shipped to Tulsa. About nine thirty, they all rejoined for coffees or soft drinks and desserts. Some carried treasures to show off to the group, others, like Mallory and Diana, had arranged to have their choices shipped.

Finally dragging back into the hotel lobby, everyone wearily bid each other good night. The plan was to load up at eight thirty the next morning, ready to travel by ferry up the Bosporus to the Black Sea. Everyone should have already eaten breakfast or else have snacks along. Their room rate included breakfast.

Awake early, Mallory slipped into the Turkish terry-cloth robe and the Aladdin-like satin slippers with slightly upturned pointed toes, which were included in her suite. Preparing her coffee, and carrying a chunk of bread from a street vendor of the previous evening, she returned to the balcony. She was grateful the area provided privacy. In her most soaring dreams, she had never contemplated being in such a luxurious hotel, in Istanbul, Turkey, watching the sun rise over the Bosphorus. One of her favorite travel posters showed the beautiful mosques silhouetted against an impossibly orange and golden sky. She had decided there was no way the sky actually ever was really those colors! Of course, she was wrong! God's artistry needed no enhancing. The glorious sky far surpassed any attempt by man to reduce the glory to a photograph. Everything was better than the pictures!

She still tried to capture it on film, thinking what a marvel photography was. Thursday, May seventeenth, she read Proverbs 17. Then she read Ephesians, still thrilling at the color photographs. The golden morning brightened into cloudless blue, and she praised the Lord for that. The cruise would be far more enjoyable with nice weather. She was hoping they would have good weather every day.

She dressed in time for a little bit of the hotel breakfast, wearing an indigo denim outfit with a hot pink top, printed with diamonds spilling from a velvet bag across it.

Diana wore the cute top again, with the kids in the Lunar vehicle on the moon's cratered surface. The Earth beyond them, suspended on nothing, didn't appear to be spinning. Mallory smiled. Alexandra now smiled from the photo with her brother and sister, and this sweater flared more than the one from a month before. Diana was amazing; the picture of Alexandra blended in seamlessly.

The luxurious ferry cruise was amazing. The water was calm, and Diana had dispensed tablets at breakfast to anyone who thought they might suffer from seasickness. Mallory enjoyed the gentle rocking, and a few of the smallest of the children soon fell sound asleep.

Mallie, Callie, and Allie, rested and excited, raced up and down and in and out, to keep from missing anything. There was so much to see, on both sides. The Fortress of Europe across from the Fortress of Asia! A huge bridge spanned the Golden Horn, and, in a few minutes their ferry passed beneath an even more wondrous engineering feat, The Bosporus Bridge. Two hundred ten feet above the water, it literally joined the two continents!

Most of the group had already taken advantage of the hotel breakfast, which was profuse and delicious. They snacked on the fare available on the ferry, then disembarked for lunch at the northernmost landing on the Asian side. Laughing, Roger had confided that he and Beth had expected to lose weight on the trip, due to the amount of walking! So far, there had been a lot more food than exercise!

The lunch was outstanding, on the water's edge, beneath the shadow of the Genoese Castle.

Reboarding, they all took turns using binoculars to gaze to the north for a glimpse of the Black Sea, as the ferry headed back south.

The final stop was the Dolmabache Palace. Newer than Topkapi, it retained more of its splendor. Pastor Anderson pointed out the sad decline, though, of the Sultans of the Ottoman Empire. Historically, nations rose and fell, their edifices left to collapse and ruin over time. The Kingdom they all served was eternal. They were grateful about that, but they still all had heavier hearts about the plight of the U.S.

The treasures on display were still marvelous to behold! One of the wonders was a Baccarat crystal stairway, and they all took as many pictures as possible, before purchasing postcards and tour books. The lovely situation of the palace was right at the water's edge.

Leaving the palace behind, they walked to their hotel. Not a long walk, it was somewhat steep. Complaining good-naturedly, everyone was teasing Roger that they hoped he was happy about the exercise. Daniel carried Cassandra the last couple of blocks, while Brad carried Sammie, David carried Sarah, and John carried Melody.

Entering the lobby windblown and disheveled, Daniel dispatched everyone to their own devices. Erik agreed that they should be able to explore the Beyoglu neighborhood surrounding the hotel safely, as long as they were accompanied by their security. The concierge said he could arrange taxis for anyone who wanted to return to the Bazaar or other shopping areas.

It seemed that none of them, though tired, had any plans to simply return to their rooms.

Dinner was to be served at eight in the Ritz restaurant followed by a corporate meeting in an adjoining conference room.

Chapter: 26

TRUSTEES

NO ONE HAD specifically issued the order to dress up, but people did it instinctively, following the example of the leading corporate figures. Mallory wore her flattering pastel yellow Damask dress, enhanced by more Canary diamonds set in white gold. Matching linen heels and a small silver clutch completed her look. Her hair had decided to cooperate with the clip, so her hair was 'up' except for a few tendrils framing her soft features.

Diana, in the emerald green, silk suit with the new emerald and gold jewelry suite, smiled radiantly at the members of the group as they reassembled, and at the Turkish hotel employees who scurried to meet the needs of the Corporate Americans. Daniel, in a black suit with his usual white French cuff shirt, wore gold and emerald cuff links, and a silk necktie, striped in black and emerald.

All three kids were squeaky-clean, dressed to perfection, and polite, able to visit pleasantly with any of the group who spoke to them. Looking at Sammie and Sarah, in comparison, Mallie knew the Faulkner children's deportment hadn't come naturally. Daniel and Diana both worked on it constantly.

She said a prayer for the Walters. They were new to the corporation and new Christians. She didn't want them to feel like they didn't fit in, even though they really didn't, yet! She protectively moved to greet them, saying something calming to the kids, and showing them to their places. The group, including half of their security, covered about a third of the restaurant. The rest of the space seemed to be occupied by business men and a Turkish wedding party.

One of the men prayed at each table, then people began ordering. Carmine and Donovan were actually at the same table, by choice, with Callie. Herb and Linda seemed to be finding more and more to talk about. Erik and Suzanne joined them. As the week progressed, Erik thought more and more that the two sisters resembled each other. He was amazed that, although they weren't close, they didn't seem to hold any animosity for each other either. The meal was fun; he enjoyed the pawn-shop owner's wit and wisdom.

David sat with Shay, Delia, and Kerry. Mallory had grabbed Shannon, and she joined her mom's group.

Shannon was emerging. He was still working on *Moby Dick*, so Linda was impressed with him. She suggested several other books she thought he might enjoy, and he was pleased to have an identity as a scholar. It was something no one had ever accused him of before. Strangely, he liked it! And he loved the history and mystique of their travel destination.

Suzanne and Erik enjoyed veal; Linda and Herb tried a herb-crusted fish, thinking Herb-crusted was the funniest joke in the world. Their selection was delicious. Mallory, remembering the fabulous, gourmet meal prepared by the Faulkners at Easter, ordered rack-of-lamb. Shannon decided on the Beef Wellington. When the beautifully presented entrees arrived, they surreptitiously sampled one another's food. It was all superb!

Once the meal was finished, the children, accompanied by their moms, were taken to Mallory's suite. The little ones, changed into their pajamas, brushed their teeth, and sacked out on the king sized bed and sofas. The older kids could play with toys and games, and watch a video until a little later. Linda insisted on overseeing the little ones during the meeting, since she enjoyed them all, and she wasn't part of the corporate entity.

Security kept watch at the elevators since the corporation controlled the entire floor. The moms returned for the business meeting.

The first floor conference room they had arranged for was extremely nice. There was a dais with a podium and sound system, and comfortable chairs at tables for all of the members. Corporate minutes and different material already lay at each place. A piano sat next to the dais. The only thing wrong with the room was that hinges protruded where a door should have hung.

With a need for privacy, even secrecy, for some of the corporate business, Daniel was trying as politely as possible, to remedy the problem. The hotel's shift manager seemed to understand English, but still couldn't understand what the 'problem' was. Roger tried to help, both reminding themselves not to be "ugly Americans". Still trying to be courteous, they asked if another room, that had a door, might be available.

Annoyed, the manager pointed out that his people had set this room up to Diana's exact specifications. She hadn't said there had to be a door. There were no more rooms!

Trying to remember that the cause of Christ was the most important thing, they smilingly thanked him for setting everything up so nicely.

Showing his graciousness, the manager sent in pitchers of iced water and trays of fruit.

Daniel stood to turn the microphone over to Mallory. As before, she asked pastor Anderson to pray for the meeting. He did so, following his earlier precedent of calling the meeting into session.

She requested David and Tammi to sing the song again, that they had sung on the flight. Almost with the first chord, smiling faces appeared at the opening where the door should have been. By the time Tammi echoed the second phrase of the song, people were crowding into the room.

When they were finished, they had to squeeze their way back to their seats. Daniel and Diana came to the mic and sang "It Takes a Storm Now and Then", "Tell Me the Story of Jesus", and their new song, "Wise Men Still Seek Him."

The smiling crowd that had gathered applauded enthusiastically. The corporate members weren't trying to break the laws about proselytizing. Overwhelmed that the Lord must have sent the door out to be fixed for this reason, they continued to sing.

The manager pushed his way in to apologize for the encroaching crowd of local people. They ended up moving out to the baby grand piano in the lobby, at management's request, providing an impromptu concert on a slow Wednesday night. Daniel was sorry their stringed instruments were all back in Tulsa and that his children had been sent to bed.

Finally, they relocated to the Faulkner's suite, where they reconvened with their documents in the limited space. After praising the Lord for the opportunity to sing His praises as a testimony to so many unsaved people, they held a briefer meeting than had been planned.

With the sale of the O'Shaughnessy property having funded, they discussed the disposal of the funds, voting to continue exploration along the river system and into the gulf. They also unanimously voted to infuse capital into the fashion and textile corporations held primarily by Delia, Shay, and Diana. Diana reported on the secretive lines she was developing for the coming seasons, in both, ready-to-wear, and also home interiors. Even those less interested in the fashion aspect agreed that the designs were not only appealing, but Christ-honoring. Delia's linens, always primarily for the home, were branching out into the fashion apparel industry.

Mallory originally credited Delia with the cute Damask dresses several of them owned, and she had written her grandmother a thank you note for hers. She discovered that Diana had designed the lovely fabric into wearing apparel.

Conversation centered around the jewelry designs. The diamond exploration and mining were totally different from the design and manufacture of jewelry. They wanted their primary emphasis to be in "fine jewelry" with Christ-honoring themes. There was Christian jewelry and fine jewelry; they didn't seem to meld together, and the corporation could see a window of opportunity in the combination. The problem was with finding someone with the expertise to launch the endeavor. Their owning "for profit" corporations made hiring tricky. They were subject to "fair employment" laws they didn't totally agree with. They tried to stay low-key about hiring, inviting people to join their companies who held similar values and views. For this reason, they couldn't just advertise for someone with a jewelry background. Diana could barely conceal her excitement as she mentioned the possibility that Herb Carlton seemed like a gift from God.

Shay reported on the wool, Alpaca, and Vicuna, mentioning the problem with attempts of animal-rights activists to boycott the fibers.

This pulled Erik and John into the spirited conversation. They were the least interested in style and fashion of anyone, but they agreed Americans should have the right to wear what they liked, whether it be animal or vegetable fibers, leather, or fur. And eat what they liked. They agreed that the lobby group was becoming too powerful!

At one time, there had been laws about "indecent exposure". Americans had expected people to be modest and covered to a reasonable degree. Now, it seemed like decency and good taste were practically being abolished. They designated funding for their own counter-advertising, realizing it would need to walk a tightrope of not being too insensitive.

After discussing the Bible Camp and the Anderson's ministries, they entertained ideas for furthering the cause of the gospel, reminding themselves of Matthew 6:39

> *But seek ye first the kingdom of God, and his righteousness, and all these things shall be added unto you.*

Roger Sanders prayed, and then, with the meeting adjourned, everyone hurried to their suites to get some sleep in preparation for the coming day.

Chapter 27

TRIVIALITIES

MALLORY WAS STILL sleeping when the alarm began its annoying racket. She couldn't figure out where she was, or where the beeping clock was! She finally managed to smack it into silence! Weak gray light seeped through a slit where the heavy draperies didn't quite meet. Rising slowly, she switched the coffee maker on. She could hear rain drops pelting out on the balcony. Drawing back the drape, she stared out at the grayscape. It was awesome-looking, actually. Ghostly gray mosques and minarets seemed more like fantastic clouds than solid structures. The Bosporus Bridge, nearly invisible in the gray, seemed to suspend strings of headlights in air. Ship's horn's mooed at one another through the soupy daybreak air! It was awesome! She grabbed her camera, hoping to capture the subtle nuances of the grays.

Coffee brewed, she read her Bible, facing out toward the drizzly weather. She prayed through her journal. So many answers to prayers! Little and big. She filled in the story about the complicated way the Lord had worked for Callie to be along on the trip. She was still praying for Donovan and Carmine to both get saved and get back together. Now, three days had already passed and she hadn't entered all the exciting stuff about Shannon. She sat thinking about the smiling faces of the hotel staff and guests who had been introduced to the Savior through the music the previous evening.

If you could keep from getting annoyed at some of the circumstances of life, you could see that God has reasons for them. They had all been pretty mad about their meeting room with no door. She quoted Romans 8:28

And we know that all things work together for good to them that love God, to them who are the called according to his purpose.

Then, she copied it into her journal, musing on it. People had said the verse or parts of it to her when her dad died until she wanted to scream. They meant well, she knew. Even now, though, she was realizing the verse didn't just mean devastating situations, like her heartbreaking loss. But all things! Little things! Big things! Bad things! Good things! All the happenings of our lives arranged to work out the purposes of God! For our good and His glory. Tears streamed down her cheeks as she finally thanked God for taking her dad. She still wasn't happy about it; her finite mind still couldn't understand it. She thanked Him by faith that He was working her life out to be the best it could be for accomplishing His purposes with it.

Pastor and Lana had tried to explain that sometimes Christians suffered heartache so they could eventually comfort others who endured the same thing. Too painful to deal with at the time, she now considered her grandmother and two cousins: Delia, losing her only two sons within a short timeframe; Shannon and Shay both losing both parents. She asked the Lord to use her to comfort them and bring Shannon to a decision for Him. She thanked the Lord again for all the people who had come to know Him, at least partially, through her dad's death.

She wasn't sure how she could be hungry again, but she hurried to get ready in time to sample the breakfast fare. She quickly dressed in the soft yellow denim outfit with matching yellow sweater that pictured Dinky. She paused, liking the yellow sandals better with the outfit, but thinking the cinnamony color that matched Dinky were more practical in the rain. She was still frowning when someone tapped on her door. She figured it must be someone from their group, or security wouldn't have allowed anyone to approach her door. She still looked cautiously through the "peephole". Callie! She opened the door.

Callie ducked into the suite, shutting the door behind her. She looked awful, like she had cried all night. She was sill crying.

"Mallory, you have to help me get back home this morning! Just lend me enough money for a taxi and plane fare. I'll pay you back as soon as I can." She got it out coherently before she dissolved into sobs again.

Before Mallie could respond, the phone on the desk jingled. She answered it, "This is Mallory."

"Mallory, this is Donovan! Are you talking to Callie? I can't for the life of me, figure out why she's such an emotional basket-case. Got it from her mother, I guess."

"Maybe you just have the same effect on both of them!" She had spoken without thinking, but for the moment she wasn't sorry.

"Well, try to talk some sense into her. I try to make her happy, but she just always ends up being mad at me!"

"Yes, Sir, she just now got here; we haven't had a chance to talk. I'll talk to you later.

She hung up. "Calm down, Callie. I guess this has something to do with your dad. Why do you want to go home before the trip's over?"

"He just humiliates me so bad!"

"He's not the most sensitive person I've ever met, but you should be used to him by now. What did he do?"

"When I think nothing he can say or do can shock me, he sinks to new lows!"

With the prospect of the breakfast buffet fading, Mallory motioned her overwrought friend to sit down across from her and tell her about it.

Finally, Mallory was able to piece the story together, but she could hardly fathom it! No wonder Callie was so humiliated and heartbroken!

Mallory thought that Shannon and Callie were starting to like one another a little bit. She had been nervous about it, because of Shannon's record. She figured Mr. Cline thought like her dad- that no one would ever be good enough for his little girl! She figured he would really be mad that Callie got exposed to a "low-life" guy like Shannon on the trip. But, no!

While most of the group convened in the Faulkner's suite for the business meeting the previous evening, Donovan, Callie, their security, and Carmine, had invited Shannon to join them for a late dessert. With Callie and Shannon just starting to like one another, Donovan had told him that he should marry Callie, and be part of the family, and handle, "some of the dirty work".

"I'm just a piece of meat to him! For him to offer in exchange for what he wants!"

Mallory just sat, eyes wide with shock.

"What did Shannon do?" she asked finally. She thought it was kind of an insult to him, too. Everyone in the group wanted Shannon salvaged, but Donovan Cline wanted him as a family member, to do what? "Doing dirty work", she was pretty sure, didn't mean gardening!

"I have no idea what he did! I jumped and ran! I never want to see him again! I never want to see anybody again. I just want to go home and hide! I always tried to overlook lots of stuff about my dad, cause I thought he loved me! In his own way, he loved me! He did things he shouldn't do for "me" because he loved me! Please help me leave," she pled in an agonized whisper.

"Do you have your passport? I can get some cash out of the ATM in the lobby, and I can get you a ticket on line with one of my credit cards. I don't blame you for wanting to hide, but getting you out, I don't know. If you were eighteen!"

Callie wailed! "You're right! He has my passport, and he won't let me leave unless he goes with me. I can't face Shannon! He probably didn't even like me a little to start, and my dad's pushing me on him, to marry me!"

Mallory could hardly fathom the entire situation. Callie was a beautiful girl in the looks department, and a beautiful person. How she had avoided being just like her dad was a miracle. Why would he be pushing the first person who seemed interested in her? She was only seventeen, too! Too young to get married! Just being a genius wasn't real preparation for getting married and establishing a home!

Another tap on her door; it was Carmine. She had been crying too!

"Callie told you about the latest, new low? And he can't even figure out what was wrong with his proposition! He thinks we have emotional problems! How can a Father~?"

She couldn't even think of any terms descriptive enough. "How can such stupid things just fall out of his mouth like that?"

There's a verse in the Bible that says something about "out of the abundance of the heart the mouth speaketh". He has a dark heart and mind, so that's just the kind of thing that issues out," Mallory responded thoughtfully. "It makes sense to him because that's how he thinks. He doesn't just need to withdraw from alcohol. The Bible says people say perverse things when they're under the influence, but he says stuff like that when he's sober."

Carmine couldn't help laughing through the tears. Mallie pretty well had him pegged.

Callie didn't laugh, but Mallory helped her perspective, as usual. She couldn't run away! Guess she would have to stay and face Shannon! Her spirit kind of soared at the thought!

"Come with me, Mom, I need to go in there so I can clean up and get dressed."

"Only for you!" Carmine allowed herself to be pulled along.

"Come join me for breakfast when you're ready," Mallie instructed them, grabbing her bag and room key.

She had planned to call Shay and Delia's room to tell them she wanted to join them for breakfast. With the interruption, she failed to do so. She was hoping Shay wasn't already clowning around with David; she needed to comfort him!

The atmosphere at the buffet was a definite chill! Not weather related, but evidently with the spiritual victories of the previous evening, the Devil was working to make everyone get on everyone else's nerves!

Evidently, when Callie had jumped and run from the late dessert, Cline had sent all three of his security guys after her. Seeing the other three left vulnerable, a team of sinister looking thugs encircled Donovan, Carmine, and Shannon, demanding their valuables. They had already grabbed Carmine, and then weren't releasing her, even though she had handed over her bag. Under the guise of pulling out his possessions, Shannon pulled a switchblade, getting a good slash at one of the assailants! Shocked by the resistance, they ran, leaving a trail of blood. Cline was crediting Shannon for his heroism!

Bransom was furious about the switchblade! In their quick visit to the Grand Bazaar, the kid had purchased the dangerous weapon! While Chip Johnson watched him! When Erik reprimanded the new security man, he laughed it off, saying if Shannon had come at him with it, he could have easily disarmed him. Daniel, witnessing the interview, was pretty mad, too. He didn't blame Bransom for losing it.

"You could have disarmed him! You're sure! In all my years, I've never had that much confidence about how stuff turns out! I've seen better guys than you taken down with a knife! But what if he didn't buy it to escape from you? What if he's still trying to kill Mallory, or his grandmother, or his brother? Or any of us? I told you to keep tight tabs on him, and you stand there and watch him buy the biggest switchblade in the country!"

They didn't fire him on the spot because they didn't want a disgruntled ex-employee with them for the remainder of the journey. Erik and Daniel were both pretty discouraged with the prospect of trying to hire people with even a minimum of good judgment.

Then the Haynes seemed to have some kind of problem about the Andersons! Room to ice skate on that rink! Mallory wasn't surprised about that! She always thought Joyce Haynes had been a little bit jealous of her pastor's wife! Of course, Mallory always heard the stories from David and Tammi's perspective. But her dad had always listened sympathetically. He never really said so, but he always thought Joyce drove Tom about keeping the Anderson's from getting better pay and benefits. Maybe they were kind of mad now, that the Lord had taken away part of their control. She sighed. She didn't want anyone to let their petty jealousies ruin the trip.

Diana, accompanied by her children, entered the restaurant, and the hotel manager approached her, smiling broadly. He asked if they would be willing to entertain in the lobby again, but he wanted the stringed instruments and the children, too. Pleased, Diana laughed.

"We are actually checking out at one," she reminded him. "Otherwise, we would love to do another concert? How did you find out about the stringed instruments and our children?"

He responded that the tall boy, David, had told everyone in the crowd, as they were dispersing, that if they wanted to hear more, they could go to a certain website. The manager had already checked it out! The web-site concert that included Daniel's preaching! The move on David's part was pretty much genius! Diana handed the man her business card, inviting him to stay at their home if he ever had occasion to visit Tulsa.

The plan for the day was a little lighter. Shopping at the Bazaar, exploring Istiklal Caddesi and Taksim Square, or relaxing in suites until check-out. Some of them planned to go up into the Galata Tower, although the view would be pretty much non-existent because of the weather. Mallory wanted to ride the Tunel and vintage street tram that traveled back and forth on Istiklal. It seemed like the best, most touristy choice, so quite a few adopted the same plan.

Around two or two-thirty, everyone was to load back onto the motor coaches to travel southward from Istanbul along the Sea of Marmara, then along the European side of the Dardanelle Straits, where they would cross at the narrowest point, via a ferry, into Asia.

Mallory carefully selected from the many choices presented on the buffet. She didn't see Delia or Shay, but she didn't want to join the warring factions either. She picked a table and sat alone, hoping Callie and Carmine wouldn't take long. She blessed her food and was fixing her coffee when Shay and David, with heaped-up plates, joined her.

"Can we sit here?" Shay asked. "We need to ask you something."

Diana and the kids were trying to decide where to head with their plates, so Mallory asked Shay and David to pull another table over. They did so, but after Diana joined them, they seemed reluctant to discuss whatever it was.

Diana said good morning to everyone, then complimented David about his Internet announcement. He was pretty pleased that the manager had already accessed the site, and was still asking for more music. He was pleased for Diana's nice words to him, too. He was pretty sure Daniel hadn't totally believed him about the picture. He really wanted the Faulkners to like him, and not just because of their authority and influence over Mallory! He had a lot of respect for both of them and their Christian testimony.

"What were you guys going to ask me?" Mallory plunged in. She didn't want to look like a guilty party for sitting with David. And he always made her feel so flustered.

Shay went ahead, asking if she knew about the attempted robbery and Shannon's heroism.

She nodded, not sure she liked where the guys were heading. Bransom didn't consider him a hero at all; he was trying to make arrangements to take him back to lock-up in Boston. Not surprisingly, they wanted her to intervene. Evidently, Delia wasn't having much luck.

She quickly bowed her head and said a prayer.

"Lord, we don't know what's best. We want Shannon to come to know you. If he should finish the trip, please intervene. In Jesus' Name, Amen"

"That's it? That's all you're going to do?!" David was mad.

"That's enough," she flashed back. "I know the Lord a lot better than I know Erik! I don't know Shannon's heart, but God does. I don't know if Shannon poses a threat. Why did he need a knife?"

"Well, it's a good thing he had it!" Shay was angrier than David was. "For all we know, he saved Carmine Henderson's life!"

"That's what I mean." Mallory shrugged helplessly. "Only God can sort it out. Erik's a good guy. I wouldn't go against his judgment, or ask him to. But, maybe he's wrong, and the Lord can override him if he is."

Jeremiah was listening, awed. He already adored Mallory. The prayer of faith made an impression on him.

David, trying to regain his self control, asked Diana if they could, maybe, get another concert together in the lobby before checkout. He knew some of the group still wanted to do more sightseeing and shopping, but~

"But none of that is important, if there's an opportunity to share the Gospel," Diana finished for him. She was already texting Daniel.

He had been listening to Erik's calls, trying to help make arrangements to ship Shannon out. Nothing was working. The airport was socked in, for one thing. The group was scheduled to leave the city; they wouldn't even be near another airport for a couple of days when they would reach Izmir!

A text from his wife interrupted him, and he was heading for the restaurant when Darrell Hopkins knocked. Darrell was head of Mallory's security, one of the ones who had been held hostage in Arkansas. His experience seemed to have sharpened him, although he had seemed pretty savvy from the start. He was embarrassed by Chip's failure, and he was there to offer his personal oversight of Shannon. Dismally, Erik agreed. For now, there wasn't much choice! But when they got to Izmir~

Daniel hurried to the restaurant, not happy about Shannon's reprieve!

He gave his wife a peck and high-fived his kids. They were all so beautiful! His heart swelled with pride in them. Diana explained about the manager, and his visiting the Faith Baptist website after David's announcement. He had asked them for another concert, but she had declined, figuring he meant for the evening. She wasn't sure she could resurrect the invitation for something mid-day.

"That was a good move, mentioning the website," he complimented David. "Can you and Tammi sing something sacred, too? We like the "Welcome To My World" and want you to do that again. If we mix in some secular we might have more people, and it might seem less evangelistic. Where can we come up with stringed instruments, though? Mallory, can you sing with us?"

"No, she can't!" Diana's firm voice.

Mallory, pleased and flattered was about to agree.

"Her voice isn't back yet! Mallory, you're still talking too much. You're always hoarse again by mid-afternoon. You can play a couple of piano pieces; that would be great! But please, take it easy on your voice. That really was a very serious injury!"

Herb Carlton showed up, surprisingly, without Linda. The pawn shop owner, hearing the manager's conversation with Diana earlier, had taken a taxi to a pawn shop he had located on line. He had come away with some amazing deals! Two violins and a cello!

With the bellman's help, he had deposited the instruments at the bell mans' station in the lobby.

He figured when he got home, he would be able to resell the instruments for approximately what he had paid. And the talented fellow-passengers would have the use of them for now!

Daniel gave him a clap on the back! The cases were beaten up, but the instruments were nice and in good shape. The guy knew his merchandise! Evidently he didn't limit his knowledge only to the jewelry end of his business!

Diana laughed. "I wouldn't have minded going out in the rain to shop or see sights, but it's amazing the Lord has given us a rainy day and something awesome to do here in the hotel. Come on kids, we need to get something together."

David went in search of Tammi, and she agreed to try to find a song. She really liked a song Mallory had often sung as a solo, "My Father Planned It All". She wondered if it would be tacky to sing "Mallory's song" when Mallory couldn't sing it because of Melville's attack

"It's a good idea, because we know it already, and it isn't really hard. Call her and ask her if she minds," David agreed.

"I don't have a phone," Tammi reminded him, making a face at him.

"Not my fault," he reminded her. "You're the one that was abusing it, and Faulkner's the one who told Dad. She probably won't answer a call from my phone." He gave it a try anyway.

"This is Mallory!"

"Hey, Erin, Tammi has a question for you." He handed the phone to his sister, who glared at him again.

"Just ask her!" he mouthed the words.

"Hi, Mallory, David and I are supposed to sing something sacred together. It's kind of short notice. Do you care if we sing, "My Father Planned It All"?"

"No, not at all. Sounds like a good choice. I may cry through it because my dad liked it, and I know my Father did plan it all, but I'm still trying to understand it."

Tammi's eyes filled with tears because of the pain and bewilderment Mallory was going through.

David hadn't understood the whole conversation, but anguish reflected on his face. He had hoped that the money, and the house and cars, and the trip, had somehow eased her grief.

He knew one of the reasons-one of the many reasons-she had been upset with him, was that he hadn't "been there for her" in her grief. It kind of made him mad back! Sometimes it seemed like people expected things of him he didn't have to give. Like since he was a pastor's son, he should have been born with the ability to pastor, and to do without what other people had, and like it! To know what to say to your best friend, when nothing he tried seemed right. When everything made her cry more!

"What did she say?" He was forcing back tears.

"It's fine! Let's get to work on it!"

Roger Sanders, a chemist, and not a graphic artist at all, was attempting to do some makeshift business cards to place on the piano for anyone who cared to pick one up. With software on his computer, he managed a respectable-looking design to point to the Faith Baptist website.

Donovan showed up at the restaurant just in time to grab some breakfast before it was cleared away. He honestly couldn't understand why what he said and did always seemed to make Carmine and Callie go ballistic! He rubbed his face with both hands, sitting dejectedly. Sighing, he smeared some jam on a hard roll. Carmine was still beautiful! The thieves' grabbing at her had affected him more profoundly than he cared to admit! They must have been watching for a security breakdown to make their move. He was grateful for Shannon's intervention.

He sipped at his coffee thoughtfully. What they called American coffee seemed to fit the description he had always heard of for "Turkish Coffee". He wondered how thick the brew they drank must be! He requested a pot of hot water, diluting the stuff. His resolve about alcohol was weakening when Mallory appeared in the deserted space, looking for him.

She sat across from him to tell him Callie had been trying to get on a flight home.

"Maybe someone should write a book on being a dad," he spoke dejectedly.

Mallory couldn't help laughing! "I think God did; it's called the Bible! I'm not sure how many other people have taken what it says and written best-sellers. Anyway, Callie feels better about everything now. The musicians in the group are doing another concert at noon. They're working to put it together now. Some of the rest of us are going to see some of the nearby sites, in walking distance. The Pera Palace Hotel is a world famous hotel that catered to rich people who traveled on the Orient Express in its heyday. You want to come with us?"

"Yeah, sure." He was glad she made the comment about the Bible and passed over it. And he was glad people were going to go look around instead of being expected to attend the Gospel concert. Diana was wearing another sweater today that made him madder than the one about the sea. This one showed a night sky, and was lettered with another Bible verse.

He telleth the number of the stars, he calleth them all by their names. Psalms 147:4

He couldn't explain why it got on his nerves so bad. She was really a pretty nice lady. He agreed to meet the group in the lobby in ten minutes.

The Haynes, Erik and Suzanne, Herb and Linda, the Walters, the Sanders, and Carmine and Callie all assembled. Roger distributed amazing little packets that actually held little rain ponchos. Lightweight and breathable, they were great! They bore the logo for the Sanders Corporation. Don't tell Delia and Diana on me. They seem to hate anything not made of "natural" fibers."

"Delia heard that," she spoke as she and Shay joined the group. She was trying to get over the fact that her appeal about Shannon with the FBI agent had fallen on deaf ears.

"Your artificial stuff may be useful for repelling rain. I can't say much for the aesthetics!" But she was smiling as she held her hand out for one.

They had fun! Mallory and Callie hung with Delia and Shay. The walk was quite a distance; the three teens were amazed that they sometimes weren't keeping up with Delia.

"She runs on the treadmill every night," Shay told them proudly "I never can keep up with her, mentally or physically. I hope she lives forever."

Mallory met his gaze. Without his mom or dad, he really needed her! And she needed him! It was perfect. She couldn't help wondering where Shannon would fit. She nodded her agreement.

Sammie and Sarah loved the Tunel and tram ride. They were cute. Mallory thought everything was pretty cool, but seeing it with their wonder made everything extra memorable. They snacked their way up and down the street. They were already kind of tired of "Turkish Delight" and kebobs, so they stopped for pizza. The Pera Palace Hotel was a treasure of ambience and history, recently totally renovated. They wandered through the public areas, buying more post cards, taking more pictures, shopping for more souvenirs. One of the most prevalent items, found in jewelry and nearly everything else was the "Evil Eye". Carmine had bought quite a few things with the motif; it seemed so typical of Turkey.

Mallory figured it wasn't anything she should get as a Christian. Sure enough, it was linked to superstitious belief. She finally asked one of the street vendors the significance. It was a trinket worn to protect the wearer from the envy of others. She smiled to herself grimly. Maybe Christians did need it, after all.

When Tom and Joyce Haynes paused by one of the windows, Mallory joined them.

"Where's Tommy?" she opened. "Did he stay to watch the concert?" She figured he did, since Allie was playing her violin and singing.

They nodded yes. Mallory could tell that Joyce was still upset about something.

"Mr. Haynes, I owe you an apology for skipping out of school. I was coming back to apologize the next day, but then school got cancelled. I'll apologize to the student body if you think I should. And I'm sorry for telling you I wanted copies of that picture! I was pretty shocked to see it. I'm sorry it's a bad testimony, and I'm sorry for my response when you asked me about it. And I know my Chemistry paper wasn't very good. I was starting to rewrite it before we left, if you'll let me do it over."

"No problem, Mallory. I've just been real worried about you. Then, you already seemed to be in a tailspin before your mom took off, and Melville made the implication he made. I didn't say anything about the Chemistry paper; what do you think's wrong with it?"

"Well, I didn't realize the immensity of the topic of water, so, when I thought I had narrowed it to a manageable scope, there was still way too much information to organize."

He laughed. "And you were aware of this, when?"

The question annoyed her; he had struck a nerve. Since she was trying to be humble, apologize, and mend fences, she answered as respectfully as she could.

"Well, I was kind of mad about the course to start with! I can't even do the Geometry and stuff I already had all year! Then, I was excited about this trip, and I just wanted to concentrate on it. My mom could tell I was bummed out about it, so she wrote me out a schedule so I could take the paper in bites. Well, then I got a good start, and I was ahead of the schedule. But right away, I guess, I knew I should start over. But everything was so interesting I couldn't decide what to omit. So then it was all just a jumble."

He laughed again. "That's about what I thought happened."

He glanced around. The loosely knit group were in and out of shops and checking out stands on the street.

"Could we ask your opinion about something?"

"I guess," Mallory responded. Might as well find out what the deal was.

"Did your dad leave all that money to the church or to the Andersons?"

Mallory was still shocked. "I'm not sure," she evaded. She was guessing that if money officially belonged to the church ministry, Mr. Haynes, as chairman of the board of deacons would still have quite a bit of authority about how it should be used. She knew her dad was in favor of a church's being "pastor-led" rather than "board-run". It was more scriptural, but he was also for accountability.

"Am I being set up?" answering a question with a question was a good way to avoid a direct answer.

"We heard John asking Daniel about buying Lana a fur coat!" It was Joyce, impatient with her husband's pace. "Do you think your dad left money for them to waste on something as frivolous and unnecessary as that?"

"You know, I had a lot on my mind when the will was being disclosed. Most of the detail is fuzzy to me now. I need to talk to Kerry Larson, and have him get back to you if it's necessary. I need to catch up to Delia and Shay."

She escaped.

The concert went well. Several uniformed, official-looking people had paused, frowning, but the concert wasn't broken up. Kerry Larson was pretty nervous about the whole thing, though. He would be relieved to load onto the coaches and head out of the city.

Mallory had returned early to close her luggage up and have it carried down to the lobby for departure. The hotel staff was preparing for the three o'clock high tea in the lobby. She knew Delia would love for them all to stay for it, but then also her pastor wanted to travel all the way down the Gallipoli peninsula for the World War I Memorial that was there. She wished there were time to see what everyone wanted! Not that anyone was complaining!

She found Kerry; well really, he found her. She was really still too upset with the Haynes and their attitude to care about finding out the answer to their question. It was another thing- where she simply did not know! Would her dad have wanted Pastor to buy Lana a fur coat? She was sure the thought had never entered his mind! And! He was pretty tight-fisted! She guessed she was shocked that the Andersons could be considering such a thing! And that Joyce Haynes would be attempting to block it! Maybe she should run back up the street and buy out all the "Evil Eye" stuff they had!

"Hey, Kerry, what do you need?" She was trying to sound cheery, but the red spots on her cheeks gave her away.

He told her about the attention they were drawing from the government, asking her if she would try to get everything lower key from now on.

She stared at him helplessly, fighting back tears. She was only seventeen! Her dad always helped her sort everything out until the past four months! She didn't want any or all of them to end up in a Turkish jail, any more than he did! But if God opened doors (or lost them) for His Name to be proclaimed~

"Yeah, I know what you mean," he agreed. She hadn't said a word, but he could see her dilemma.

Their guide encouraged the group to enjoy the tea, stating that a later departure would actually help avoid the heaviest afternoon traffic. The delightful event, coupled with the lightening weather, seemed to lift everyone's spirits. Mallory was glad for the pleasant camaraderie, but she knew the underlying tensions would still need to be dealt with. She prayed for wisdom, believing God wouldn't have given her the responsibility unless He planned to help her deal with it.

Before departing the interesting city, the coaches carried them to the remnants of the city walls. What was left of the fortification was pretty interesting. How many times the walls had been breached and rebuilt through the centuries, with remnants from the different eras still visible. Some of it was relatively recent restoration.

Istanbul went on forever! If they had managed to avoid some of the heavy traffic, it was hard to tell it. At last, the coaches escaped the congestion, as the blue overhead escaped the gray. They traveled along the Sea of Marmara, bright sparkling azure, causing everyone to rummage for sunglasses. The coaches ground to a stop at a little gas station/store, like at home, yet totally different! Coins were required for the WC stalls. On their way once more, a few of them pulled out Bibles, books, or games.

Mallory, too excited, tried to take in absolutely everything, referencing one of the maps in her Bible to keep track of their progress: south along the western edge of the Sea, then continuing the southerly direction along the European side of the famous Straits.

She was trying to imagine if it would have looked much different nearly two millennia earlier when the Gospel was first spread into the area. She was pretty sure the modern highway system had been added since that time! The glistening water visible from the left side of the bus continued to look the same, so she risked glancing at one of the travel books.

John Anderson, using David's expensive binoculars, gazed inland toward the famous battlefields of Gallipoli. In his wildest dreams, he had never imagined being even this close! As a history buff, he was amazed to be motoring along the peninsula! As a Bible scholar, he could barely grasp the significance of what he was about to see in the coming days. Then, the Faulkners and Sanders were talking about taking a trip to Israel in the near future, too!

Suddenly they were in a lazy-seeming, small Turkish town, and the coaches were stopping in a small parking lot near the water's edge! Time for the ferry ride!

Kilitibahir didn't offer much to travelers waiting for the ferry's return. Faded Coca Cola signs tried to lure shoppers into derelict shops which offered a few pitiful postcards. John felt like if any of the merchants were enterprising at all, they would take advantage of their location to offer merchandise relating to the World War I Battleground. Evidently, they weren't enterprising at all!

The ferry bumped and swayed into its dock, and they all boarded. It wasn't new or luxurious, but adequate. The thrill here wasn't the vessel itself, but the fact that everyone was crossing onto a continent none of them had ever visited before! And across such a scenic and historic waterway, known in ancient times as the Hellespont.

They hadn't minded the rain, but the gorgeous water and sky gave the crossing a special shimmering atmosphere. Everyone's photos were gorgeous!

They bumped their way into Asia, then watched as their coaches materialized from the cavernous belly of the ferry. Watching amazed, Mallory wondered how they had stayed afloat. For her paper about water, she had touched on buoyancy. But still, two coaches loaded with everyone's luggage, plus cars and semi-trucks, and people!

Reboarding the coaches, they rode another thirty or forty minutes to Canakkale, where they checked into their hotel. Far less luxurious than the Ritz, the hotel was still fairly nice. And the views and the sunset were stunning!

Following an enjoyable meal included with the lodging, the group once again opted to hit the streets for shopping, desserts, and coffee. The prize items offered in Canakkale were those of a famous local pottery. All of the ladies managed to acquire at least a few pieces to have sent home.

Mallory was the first one down for breakfast the next morning. Without coffee in her room, she had gotten ready first thing, deciding to read her Bible while she ate. She looked gorgeous wearing a peachy colored denim tiered skirt and vest with a natural-colored, ruffled linen blouse; stunning sterling silver and turquoise conch belt; and coordinating Southwestern jewelry. Silver moccasins and the silver hobo bag polished off the look.

Starting with coffee and juice, she read the Book of Revelation's warning letters to the Seven Churches they were finally about to visit.

She could see the sky brightening into a beautiful day. She was glad! She really, really, really wanted to be able to take some great pictures!

She turned back to Proverbs and read her daily chapter.

She smiled as Daniel and Diana joined her, asking them if they had rested well.

Since they had directed the kids to a different table, she figured they must have something on their minds.

"Let me guess! The Haynes and the Andersons!" She laughed, scooting her Bible and journal onto the banquette beside her to make room for their plates.

"You know about it?" Daniel questioned.

"Trying not to, but the Haynes brought it up to me yesterday. I wish they hadn't; I hardly slept trying to sort everything out. I mean, I'm just a kid, so I've been pretty unaware of the undercurrents. Think my dad tried to keep me that way. But last night, as I looked back over some things, it made a little more sense. It's still kind of hard to realize that Christians who have been saved so long, and who have been your heroes are still so petty at times. I mean, I'm sure I am too." She sighed.

"So Joyce Haynes has been envious of Lana Anderson for being able to have children," Diana prodded.

Tears welled in Mallory's eyes. "I guess. And I'm not sure the Andersons have always been really ecstatic about the additions to their family. I mean, they love all their kids, but they're always pretty strapped financially. And then, no one really offers to help do a lot, so Pastor and Mrs. Anderson do everything. Then Mrs. Haynes says Lana's just trying to be in the limelight! And she gets mad if she thinks the Anderson kids get more Goldfish or cookies at treat time than Tommy gets. But the Anderson's have sent out letters asking other people to contribute for treats, and no one provides any. So, it comes out of their little grocery allowance. I guess Mrs. Haynes flaunts their good salary and nice house at the Andersons to compensate for not having more kids."

Daniel sipped his coffee, frowning as he listened to the information. Sometimes he thought the only difference between Christians and non-Christians was that Christians were forgiven for their bad behavior.

"Did the Haynes tell you that John wants to buy Lana a mink coat?" he asked her.

Her gaze met his, piercing and direct. She shrugged her shoulders helplessly.

"They did! They pretty much caught me off-guard about it. I mean, I heard what you were saying the other night about the Tabernacle and badger skins," she directed the comment toward Diana. "It was a pretty new concept for me to muddle over; and David really wasn't buying into it. Mrs. Haynes asked me if my dad would have wanted Mrs. Anderson to own a fur with 'his' money. I mean, I don't know! He probably wouldn't have, but he didn't like the way the Haynes tried to 'keep them in their place' either."

She laughed. "God had to force diamonds on us; maybe He wants to open our eyes to some other things, too!"

Diana, blue eyes alight, smiled knowingly. She looked sensational!

Chapter 28

TROY

THE ENTIRE GROUP eventually filtered in for breakfast. Callie and Shannon shared a table with Linda and Herb. Carmine was talking to Kerry Larson, David, Shay, and Delia. Donovan Cline had pulled Roger aside, so Joyce was sitting with Emma and Evan, eyeing her husband and his nemesis warily. Mallory had indicated for Brad and Janet to fix up their kids with the Faulkner children and then join her table. Sammie and Sarah both gave her big hugs before digging hungrily into their pancakes and eggs.

By nine AM they were loaded, luggage and all, and traveling from Canakkale toward the ruins of ancient Troy.

Daniel asked John Anderson to pray and bless the day. Then he also added that the pastor had a few thoughts to share about the famous battle of Troy and the Trojan Horse, once they arrived at the site. Of course, their Turkish guide would be explaining everything from his standpoint.

When they arrived, their first view was of a humongous wooden horse! It had been built for a recent epic movie. Their group pulled into a tight knot to listen to John's talk.

He began with a relaxed laugh. "We were always told the story of the Trojan Horse, kind of tongue-in-cheek, that it was probably just an incredible myth. Now, more light on history indicates that it might have been an actual happening. All I want to say is that if it really did happen as we have heard, then the 'Horse' would have had to look better than what we see here and other depictions of it. I mean, think about it! What city would bring a big hollow thing with a hinged door inside their walls without checking for infiltrators within it? Were the Trojans that dumb? I mean we hear that they thought it was a 'gift from the gods', so they received it.

I'm trying to make a point, and I'm not sure I'm doing a good job. What I'm trying to say is, the Greeks didn't throw together some crude apparatus and roll it into view. They were clever, and sophisticated, and patient. The door had to have been very artfully concealed, and the sculpture needed to be beautiful enough to be desirable to the Trojans. The enemy was more clever than history has given them credit for being, just as our enemy is clever, patient, and seductive to get us to pull him into our midst. We don't just open the gates and say, 'Come on in, Devil!' So, we all know he uses desirable-looking traps to take advantage of us. He makes alcoholic beverages look sophisticated and enticing; he makes immorality seem like it's acceptable and everybody's doing it; he makes vulgarity and profanity seem normal, and preachers and the Bible seem extreme. He makes evolution and atheism seem scholarly. If we take the Biblical position on homosexuality, we're the ones who are considered guilty of 'hate crimes'. America, in opening her arms to all religions and philosophies, has given entrance to the enemy to spread every ism and doctrine, while silencing Christians. If there ever was a Trojan Horse, ladies and gentlemen, it didn't look like that!"

The guide and drivers had taken the opportunity for a smoke. When John's talk was finished, their guide led them to some points of interest in the excavated ruins. The site was important, historically, although it had less Biblical significance. The Greek Empire, although of great historical importance, had basically enjoyed its heyday during the Bible's approximate four hundred years of silence between the close of the Old Testament and the advent of Christ. It had been foretold by the prophets, specifically by Daniel, and it had fulfilled the prophecies of defeating the Persian Empire and spawning Rome.

The ruins were exciting, and the situation on the Aegean Sea was exceptionally beautiful. The site was the pivotal point of Homer's *Iliad* and dated back as early as four thousand years BC. To the Christian group, that date meant the ruins were nearly as old as the history of Earth and man. The headwaters of the Tigris and Euphrates, mentioned in Genesis in relation to the Garden of Eden, were located several hundred miles to the east. Adam's immediate descendents had spread out quickly, already being metal workers and musicians. If there were cave men, they came later, when mankind's minds became darkened by their deliberate rejection of God.

There was a Roman theater, the first Mallory had ever viewed. For some reason, she had the impression that the Coliseum in Rome was the only one to survive. That assumption was about to change!

They viewed portions of the nine excavated layers, then paused at what was assumed to have been the palace of king Priam, known historically for his immense wealth in gold! Everything was so interesting it was hard to absorb.

More pictures, more souvenirs, more excited chatter! Then back on the coaches for the drive to Assos. Situated on the Aegean Sea overlooking the Bay of Edrimet, it had a reputation for being the most beautiful spot in Asia Minor. The Greek Isle of Lesbos(the capital city of which was Mitylene of Acts 20:14), visible across six miles of sparkling sea, enchanted. Maybe a cruise amongst the Greek Isles could be arranged sometime. The Isle of Patmos, where the Apostle John was exiled, was located in the Aegean, off the Turkish coast. A day trip to Patmos was available, but the group had longingly forsaken the idea. So much to see; so little time! They lunched on seafood along the bay, realizing the Apostle Paul had walked along this same beautiful bay. How his spirit must have thrilled at the scenic beauty as theirs did!

Plato's protégé, Aristotle, had founded a school of philosophy here in 540 BC. Since U.S. history was pretty sketchy until late in the seventeenth century AD, it was hard for some of them to grasp such antiquity.

Their next stop was Pergamum, their first visit to one of the Seven Church sites! Although the third church addressed in Revelation chapter two, its ruins were the first to be visited along their route. Mallory was shocked! She guessed she expected to see a church there! There wasn't one! Probably the historic church had met in a house! If there had ever been a church building, it wasn't grand enough to have survived through the two millenia! As the church itself hadn't survived the onslaughts of Satan, neither had Christian structures survived the onslaught of time and its destructive forces! But, there were lots of interesting Roman ruins, the most predominant of which were massive temples to pagan gods and goddesses

Pastor Anderson read from Revelation 2:12-17, the commendation and the warning. Verse 17 stated:

> *He that hath an ear, let him hear what the Spirit saith unto the churches; To him that overcometh will I give to eat of the hidden manna, and I will give him a white stone, and in the stone a new name written, which no man knoweth saving he that receiveth it.*

Mallory listened attentively. Her purpose for the trip was to understand the Bible better and love the Lord more. The 'diamond girl' from Arkansas wondered if the white stone with a new name might be similar to an engraved diamond in an engagement ring, showing that the wearer was a beloved, betrothed to the Lord. She wondered if His secret name for her would be as tender as *Tater Tot*. She hadn't liked hearing Sam Whitmore call her by her daddy's pet name for her.

She wanted to be an "Overcomer" in her Christian faith! The ruins made the paganism and idolatry real! It was sobering! The ruins were ancient, expansive, and interesting. An ancient medical school called the Asclepieum had been founded there.

Loading up again, they traveled to Izmir where they viewed the ruins of Smyrna, possibly named for myrrh trees indigenous to the area. Most of it had been rebuilt in the second century AD, so the ruins they were viewing were more modern than the warning to the church founded there. The pastor read the passage to the church at Smyrna.

> *Revelation 2:11 He that hath an ear, let him hear what the Spirit saith unto the churches; He that overcometh shall not be hurt of the second death.*

Donovan Cline had tried to get out of earshot of Anderson's words. The whole religious thing on top of his jittery drying-out nerves was nearly too much. He was relieved when everyone boarded for transfer to the Izmir Hilton.

After checking in, the group hurried to check out their accommodations. Several of the small children, having fallen asleep on the coaches, were transferred to comfortable beds to finish their naps. The entire entourage had a dinner reservation for seven thirty at the Windows On the Bay restaurant on the hotel's thirty-first floor.

Callie asked if she could come to Mallory's suite and spend time before the dinner.

Mallory begged off; her head ached and she was hoping to nap before she dressed for dinner. She could tell Callie was disappointed, but she was out of steam!

The hotel was gorgeous! So was the restaurant with the incomparable view across Izmir Bay. Mallie wore her gray tweed linen suit that she had worn to the Adolphus. Diana was wearing the stunning orangy silk! Everyone looked great, drawing attention, even in an atmosphere that was accustomed to well-heeled travelers.

The Anderson family was standing shyly, waiting for someone to direct them to a table. Mallory joined them, even though David was standing with them.

"Well, I don't feel sorry for the Apostle Paul any more," she laughed. "I always imagined him traveling to drab and dismal places. This is all so beautiful!"

Pastor Anderson laughed too. "I never had any idea these places we were reading about were so scenic, either. Some of the early church members probably complained that the leaders were on vacation when they really were doing important missionary work."

"But they still spent their time in jails and dungeons, not hotels like this," Tammi reminded. She looked cute and grown up in a slim black dress that made her look like a porcelain doll.

John had frowned at her, trying to decide if she was wearing make up again.

Mallory sat facing west, wanting to watch the sunset on the bay, maybe get some good shots. The Andersons had found places, except for David, who had walked over to speak with Kerry. They were engaged in conversation when Bransom entered with Shannon. Bransom had gone to the lobby business center to once again check on getting headed to the US with him. A fax had arrived for him from Dawson, changing his priorities.

His eyes sought Faulkner, who rose to join him just inside the restaurant. David picked up on it immediately, surmising something wasn't right; something about Mallory.

Not pulling out the paper, Bransom briefly explained the problem to Daniel. Both Oscar and Otto Malovich had bonded out of their separate facilities! And disappeared!

Bransom figured they had traveled to Eastern Europe~ which he figured was way too close to their present location.

Both of the men's gazes traveled toward where Mallie sat, letting David know he was right. Something was up!

Shannon stood alone, stranded by Bransom. David caught his eye, nodding toward a table and moving toward it himself. Kerry followed him, and Shannon joined them, but he didn't know what was going on. He was just happy still traveling with the group.

Faulkner joined his family and the Sanders; Bransom disappeared, leaving Suzanne sitting alone, staring after him. David, surveying the situation carefully, knew Bransom must be meeting with all of the security guys who weren't in the restaurant, about whatever was going on. He was praying for everyone in security to be better than they had been so far. He thought again of Mallory's chasing after Diana's luggage. It scared him. He caught her looking at him and risked a wink.

Ten minutes later Bransom rejoined the group, only missing appetizers, giving Suzanne a kiss on the cheek as he slid into a chair across from her.

The meal was fabulous, served flawlessly, as the conversational hum carried softly around the sumptuously decorated area.

Delia and Shay asked John Anderson about being baptized, and Erik pulled closer to listen to the answer. John was shocked to learn that Delia's friends in the hierarchy of her former church were trying to hassle her and frighten her about leaving, threatening that she was condemning her soul. She knew they were wrong, but they still managed to trouble her. Shay sat and nodded silently. The pastor instructed the three new converts that the step of obedience is important, explaining the significance of baptism as a testimony of their new life in Christ.

Mallory rose from her place to move discreetly to the ladies' room with Callie. Only David noticed the two girls' exit, unescorted.

"Who's supposed to be watching them, Faulkner?" he demanded, his frustration more than evident! Cline hadn't noticed Callie's departure, either, and neither had his hired security.

David's voice had gotten action. Bransom decided right then that Janice Collins might be worth a shot! At least she should know that ladies run to the ladies' room, and they don't seem to like announcing it to the guys!

The sun slid quietly and ingloriously beyond the sparkling blue horizon. Then the horizon disappeared as the black night sky merged imperceptibly into the inky bay.

"Well, it's a good thing the food was so great! The sunset was kind of a fizzle," Diana observed laughingly. Usually she could see beauty in pretty ordinary stuff, but the lack of color and dazzle had taxed even her perspective.

One member of the serving staff who spoke English tried to console her by letting her know the sunset of the previous day was the most glorious any of them had ever seen.

She just laughed helplessly, not sure how that was supposed to help her. They ordered coffees and desserts in the restaurant rather than going out of the hotel. Erik preferred checking out the surroundings in the daylight, and everyone agreed. The next morning was scheduled for shopping around a little bit, then the afternoon would include visits to Ephesus and one of the other churches, and the rug weaving establishment.

Daniel and Erik withdrew for another cup of coffee. Daniel, trying to remain optimistic, insisted on what the twin brothers would do if they were smart.

"The trouble with you, Faulkner, is that you're too nice and too smart! And too hopeful!" Erik's response to Daniel's argument that the Malovich's weren't on their way to finish Mallory off! "You hope these guys won't be after Mallory again because that wouldn't be nice or smart. When I try to second guess the bad guys, I think, 'What would be a smart move for them?' Then I figure that's what they won't do. You need to accept the fact that they may be here in Izmir, as we speak! Or that they will be soon!"

Daniel's eyes met Bransom's. "You alerted all the security guys? What else can we do?"

"Pack up and get home!"

Daniel laughed uneasily. "That's drastic, don't you agree?"

"I always heard 'drastic times call for drastic measures'. I think she's in danger. We all are. Oscar isn't going to wait for her to wander alone onto some vacant property again so he can strangle her. Look where we are! Turkey! A bomb goes off in this hotel, it's just another radical attack on American interests! I'm pretty sure neither brother would shrink from the loss of lives just because you do. Not if the charges against them go away when Mallory, Shannon, none of us are around to testify.

"But blowing up a hotel!"

Bransom snorted. "You ever watch the news? Happens too often for me to ignore the possibility. Or how about one of the buses? Happens all the time! Who's keeping an eye on them every minute? In the U.S. we could get help from law enforcement. Have people watching for those guys. Here, those brothers can be on top of us without our knowing it."

"But, Mallory hasn't seen Ephesus yet~"

"I know that! And you haven't seen Cappadochia and that weird landscape, or Mt. Ararat! At least, let's not go shopping in the morning. Markets always get blown up. We'll look over the buses the best we can, go to Ephesus, have the jet ready to fly home from here tomorrow afternoon."

"Let me think about it!"

"Yeah, think about it Faulkner! You're still way too nice!"

When Daniel rejoined Diana, his pallor gave him away, and his dilated pupils, and his increased heart rate!

"If you and Bransom were arguing, I'm on his side," she began brightly. "You plan to let me know what's been going on since before dinner?"

He shook his head slowly, then met her gaze. "How do you know you're on his side? What if he wants to end the trip?"

Tears filled her eyes. "He wouldn't want to do that without good reason. What happened?"

"Well, he may be overreacting. I don't want him to panic me into ruining the trip! Melville and his twin both got out on bond, and they seem to have left the U.S. They're from somewhere in Eastern Europe, although they might have come straight here without necessarily going home. I think they'd be crazy to try anything more!"

"Crazy!" she echoed. "Oscar already nearly killed Mallory, and the other one came even closer to killing Shannon. What does Erik think they'll do?"

"He's guessing a bomb."

Her eyes widened in amazement, then her jaw set resolutely.

"Of course! We die! The Malovichs' problems go away; we don't seem pinpointed in the attack. Just the victims of zealots! There are bomb-making instructions all over the internet, in case those guys haven't built bombs before. They can do it, or know someone who will."

"Well, surely it isn't that easy."

"Well, Honey, high school students have tried it"

"Yeah, and thankfully it hasn't worked yet. It's Mallory's trip," he smiled at his wife. "Maybe I'll lay it out for her and let her decide!"

"And she'll decide based on another week of being around David!"

"Come on, Honey, give her more credit than that! She's a sharp girl!"

"Yes, she is," Diana agreed. "But, she's only seventeen, and she's in love! It is her trip, she has paid for it, and you know she'll agree with you."

Mallory slept in! The bed was heavenly, and the surroundings relaxing. At last she brewed some coffee and plumped the pillows behind her so she could read her Bible. She texted Diana that if she saw anything good, to buy it for her, and she'd pay her back; she didn't feel like shopping. Then she texted her back that if she was too tired to shop, too, it was no problem. Mallory still worried about the baby.

Diana and Daniel had been watching for her at breakfast to explain the situation. They hadn't seen Erik or Suzanne, either. Finally, the agent appeared; he had been speaking to Dawson and the American embassy personnel in an attempt to get more intel and warn the local authorities of the possible threat. The FBI was supposed to be domestic in the U.S.; the CIA active clandestinely in other places around the world. Bransom figured no one would be willing to jeopardize their operations to assist this little group. If something happened, the State Department would get involved. He was praying nothing would happen.

After finishing her devotions, Mallory decided to jump into high gear, trying to make the end of the breakfast before it was cleared away.

Dressed in a different combination of the new teal separates, she completed her hair and make-up, thinking of the group photos that were to be taken with the Library of Celsius in the background. Her eyes danced at the prospect! Finally! Ephesus!

Grabbing her bag and key card, she raced for the restaurant.

Seeing Erik conversing earnestly with Diana and Daniel, she thought something was up and figured it was something more serious than the Haynes and their little spat.

She found some Cheerios and toast; the ordinary fare from home, somehow seeming strangely appealing. She grabbed milk for the cereal, and to drink, joining the three with some trepidation.

"There's a problem." She said it more as a statement than a question. "What now?"

Bransom filled her in about the fax, noting they hadn't received any further updates.

Mallory wasn't happy about the two men's being on the loose; she asked worriedly about Martin Thomas. Bransom had checked on him. At least that nut case was still behind bars! But he was proving himself to be a certified nut case. A plea of insanity for him was practically a given! Bransom wasn't real happy about that either!

Mallory studied the three faces as they waited for her response.

"Well, we shouldn't decide for everybody," she spoke thoughtfully, "especially without explaining the situation and the danger. I mean, I know we don't want to create a needless panic and have the hotel management ask us to leave for fear their hotel will get blown up. We can't just expose our group, their kids, and everybody to possible danger without letting them assess it for themselves. Let's pray, and ask the Lord to give us all wisdom."

Each of them prayed a short prayer, then Daniel went to round up the men of the group.

The meeting took place in Mallory's suite, with John's beginning with prayer. Then Erik explained what they knew. A few questions ensued and further discussion before the guys broke up to talk to the ladies. Herb spoke with Linda, Donovan with Callie and Carmine, Shay with Delia.

John was trying to talk to Lana without David's input, but David had been aware that there was a problem from the beginning. He wasn't a kid anymore, to be passed over! Especially where Mallory was concerned!

The final consensus was, that no one wanted to let fear grip them. They wanted to be as wise and safe as possible. There would always be threats of danger. Mallory visited briefly with the hotel manager. A Turkish-American, he had smiled at her, flashing strong white teeth beneath a heavy black moustache. He appreciated her candor. Hilton was aware of their guests and properties being under constant threat; and, consequently, used some of the most sophisticated security measures available! He accepted the mug shots of the twin brothers, forwarding them to the hotel's head of security and to the appropriate people in Turkish law enforcement. The Turkish government didn't want any kind of incident on their soil!

Another prayer meeting, and loading onto the coaches, they headed out of Izmir toward Ephesus!

The late morning was gorgeous! The coaches pulled into a lot crowded with an assortment of tourist vehicles. The tour of Ephesus was arranged so that tourists began at the top of the city and made their way downward through the ruins, where the coaches would retrieve them at the bottom. Everyone listened closely. At its zenith, the city had been populated by a quarter of a million people, the bay on the Aegean, being a major port of the Roman Empire. When the harbor silted up, the city was abandoned. Over the centuries, it had been decimated by earthquakes and erosion. Viewing the detail of the carvings, Daniel laughingly surmised that the earthquakes had caused far more damage than erosion had. As a geologist, he realized that erosion was a real force of nature, but it actually achieved far less than it was given credit for. A Creationist, he believed that catastrophes, such as the world-wide flood of Noah's day, earthquakes, and volcanoes changed the earth's structures far more than the slow, relentless force of erosion.

John Anderson wondered why such sophisticated engineers and builders as the Romans had allowed the harbor to silt up, making their important city inconsequential.

The ancients had built many great, artificial harbors where natural ones like this didn't exist. Surely, they could have kept this one dredged out to guarantee ongoing trade. Maybe the thriving city met its demise because of its dedication to the propagation of worship for their goddess, Diana!

The church founded here had been central to the other six churches of the Revelation, and converts were known of from nearby Lystra and Derbe, and Colossae. John the disciple had moved here and brought Mary, the mother of Jesus. Paul had been here. Timothy had pastored the church. Was he still the pastor when the warning had come from John, who by then was exiled off the coast on the Isle of Patmos? The warning not to let things slip?

Erik Bransom read the passage from Revelation. His voice shook with nervousness in front of the group, and he wasn't a smooth reader.

> *Unto the angel of the church at Ephesus write, These things saith he that holdeth the seven stars in his right hand, who walketh in the midst of the seven golden candlesticks:*
>
> *I know thy works, and thy labor, and thy patience, and how thou canst not bear them which are evil: and thou hast tried them which say they are apostles and are not, and hast found them liars:*
>
> *And hast borne, and hast patience, and for my name's sake hast labored, and hast not fainted.*
>
> *Nevertheless I have somewhat against thee, because thou hast left thy first love. Remember therefore from whence thou art fallen, and repent, and do the first works; or else I will come unto thee quickly, and will remove thy candlestick out of his place, except thou repent.*
>
> *But this thou hast, that thou hatest the deeds of the Nicolaitans, which I also hate. He that hath an ear to hear, let him hear what the Spirit saith unto the churches, To him that overcometh will I give to eat of the tree of life, which is in the midst of the paradise of God.Revelation 2:1~7*

Tears filled the eyes of many of them, as they prayed and asked the Lord to help them not to let anything slip in their Christianity.

The place was more beautiful, by far, than the pictures conveyed. The sunshine was warm, but a playful breeze kept them comfortable. They took in the sites eagerly, huge white marble blocks, paving the agora of the upper city. Little, cranny storefronts and homes tumbled away to their left. Slender, white, elegant columns soared against the blue, or lay in pieces across the area. The ruins of the picturesque Library of Celsius appeared before them. The area was somewhat crowded with other tour groups, but they surveyed the remains of the structure, then posed for a group shot. Then they all continued their touristy snap, snap, buzz, hum, whir, as they tried to recapture the experience for posterity!

Everywhere the vistas of the surrounding mountains were breathtaking. In the sweep downward to the sea, now seven miles distant, a green valley spread where the waters of the bay had once lapped.

At last, they made their way into the ancient theater. Mallory and Callie made their way down to the floor, and Mallory opened her New Testament to the story of the tumult made by the silversmiths: the silversmiths who loved their goddess, but also the fortune they made from pilgrims who traveled here to worship at her temple, and buy the meats and other things necessary for worship. Pilgrims who arrived and bought their own silver idols to carry home with them.

God had intervened by sending the authorities to rescue Paul from the mob. It wasn't really clear what the apostle referenced when he said he had fought with beasts here, except that the persecution of Christians was really a fact. Evidently, God had given him mastery with the beasts, too. Mallory thought about the prophet Daniel and the lions, then about the large shark in Diana's picture. If Mr. Melville wasn't ready to pounce on her again, someone would be. Her eyes swept the tiers of the stadium rising above her. The only person paying any attention to her was David; she waved, and they climbed their way toward where he sat.

From the higher tiers, the sea was within view, even though it had retreated seven miles since the stadium was in its heyday. What a place! Come here to enjoy the ocean view and breezes in the shadow of the mountains, and watch bloody spectacles!

Mallory didn't like the Romans very much. They had tortured Jesus and taken pleasure in the whole mockery and torment. But she had to admit that movies, television, and sporting events in the U.S. seemed to be getting gorier to stimulate the audiences and the ratings. It was sad.

They loaded onto the coaches to make the short drive to the "House of Mary". According to Christian tradition, Saint John had located in Ephesus in approximately 37 AD, not too long after Jesus' ascension into heaven, bringing Mary. The home where she reportedly spent her last years, had, not surprisingly, become a shrine. The group of Baptists believed Mary was very important, but didn't hold her in as high esteem as other religions. Mallory wasn't sure she put a lot of stock in the location, but she felt her grandmother would enjoy viewing the site. The new coaches strained and groaned up the steep, narrow road, the group looking down over the switchbacks as they climbed.

Finally, Diana, laughing, had burst out with: "Wow, if John stuck her up here, he wasn't making it easy on himself to look in on her! They must have all been in really good shape!"

Lana joined in the banter. "John probably gave the job to his wife!"

"Yeah," David entered the fun. "And mom probably sent the oldest son to do it!"

"Hey, it's called delegating," John Anderson defended.

They clambered off the coach to view the site. There was a box for donations, and candles were available. Delia viewed the site reverently, happy to see it, but happy to have the facts in the perspective of the Bible. She hadn't been offended at all by the banter. In fact, they had made a good point. She doubted the aging mother of the Lord had resided on this spot; but it had been somewhere near!

Viewing the shrine, she decided she wanted to follow in baptism.

Chapter 29

TRAVERTINES

FROM EPHESUS, THE group hurried so they could view the ruins of Laodicea, the church accused of being "lukewarm". Nearby Colossae enjoyed natural cold water, and Hierapolis was famous for the hot springs. Water carried by aqueduct into Laodicea, being too far from either source, was only unpleasant; an object lesson for why Christians should stay as close as possible to the Lord, Who is the Source of all they need. With few excavated ruins to view, they hurried to Hierapolis to view the better preserved ruins of that city and to see the world famous Pamukkale.

Pamukkale, translated "Cotton Castle" was an important Turkish tourist destination. The travertine terraces, built up when water from the hot springs loses carbon dioxide, were deposits of limestone. The brilliant white steps, dotted with lovely blue pools, terraced gracefully down the face of the hillside. Everyone began photographing as much of it as they could from as many angles and vantage points as possible. They had rushed up the schedule in order to arrive at this destination to take advantage of the brilliant afternoon sunlight. Mallory, joining the Faulkners, was excited about using the lovely travertine pattern in a fabric print. She and Diana had already discussed utilizing the brilliant colors from the Istanbul Spice Market. Everything seemed to stimulate imaginative and beautiful designs! Diana seemed nimble and sure-footed as she moved to various locations to shoot pictures: Daniel kept his hand on her elbow, protectively, though, just in case.

Mallory left their side to climb around to where she had seen Shay and Delia. To avoid damaging the scenic, protected space, she had to move horizontally quite a distance farther than she had thought, before she was able to descend. She suddenly found herself isolated, not just from her group, but with no tourists around her at all. Glancing around frantically, she finally scrambled, half falling to the base of the site. She was brushing rocks from her hands and tears from her eyes when Erik and Suzanne found her.

"You need to buddy up with someone; this is no time to go off by yourself," Erik was scolding her mildly.

Unable to defend herself, she nodded mutely, following them back to the coach. She knew her imagination was playing tricks on her: for a second up there, she thought she had seen Sheriff Melville coming at her again.

On the coach, she held out her reddened, skinned up palm to David for his binoculars. From the back seat, she scanned across the face of the falls until they disappeared from sight.

She was still shaking when she handed the binoculars back.

No one seemed aware of how shaken she was. Shakes that worsened rather than easing off. She found herself feeling more sorry for Mr. Cline. Trying to talk herself out of the fear that had gripped her, wasn't helping. Tears streamed down her face, making her glad everyone seemed engrossed in conversation, napping, or whatever they were engrossed in. She guessed she was having a flashback, or a panic attack, or something!

Once again, she could feel Melville's hands, tight on her throat! She gasped for air, and a choking sob escaped.

The people around her, joking, laughing, sharing snacks, seemed impervious to her distress, except for David!

Recovering his binoculars from her shaking hands, he had moved to the back of the tour bus, continuing to scan the roadway behind them. Something had scared her! He glanced back over his shoulder. Evidently, she hadn't said anything to Bransom.

No one seemed to be following them, but it had taken a while for the chattering group to load into the coaches. If someone had been up there, watching her, they could easily be ahead of them by now. He texted Bransom, who joined him a few seconds later.

"Something on your mind, Cowboy?" he questioned jovially as he sank down next to the teen.

"Something or somebody up there scared Mallory. She hasn't stopped shaking and crying yet. I've been watching for someone behind us, but if there was somebody, they had time to get out ahead of us while we were loading up. Maybe you should tell the guide to tell the drivers not to stop to help anybody; you know, a wreck, or injury, or breakdown?"

Bransom nodded slowly, starting to rise from the space that was barely adequate for the two of them. He paused. Faulkner was headed down the aisle toward them.

"What's going on back here? Bransom you making trouble?"

"Yeah, you know me; I just can't help it. I'm on my way up to talk to the guide. David can fill you in."

He squeezed out so Faulkner could occupy the spot. David shared pretty much the same information.

"You really think one of the Maloviches was up there?"

"I think it's possible; even probable. She doesn't usually go to pieces over nothing! And she doesn't usually have an overactive imagination! Why don't you talk to her, since I'm not supposed to?"

Faulkner leaned out into the aisle, watching the agent confer with their Turkish guide. He couldn't see Mallory, she seemed to be leaning in toward her window. He headed back toward his seat and whispered something to Diana, who tried to keep from giving him her "I-told-you-so look".

She moved back a couple of rows to join Mallory.

"David rat me out?" Mallory questioned, trying to stop crying and be funny.

"Mallory, why didn't you say something to Erik?"

"Like what? That I thought I saw a pair of binoculars watching me from under a Pike County, Arkansas sheriff's hat? But we're in Turkey? And I isolated myself! I didn't intend to, but it still worked out that way! Then I got scared!"

She was crying harder, her nose was running, and she couldn't find a tissue or any of her linen handkerchiefs. She was determined not to use her sleeve or her hand in front of Diana. She wished David hadn't said anything.

The coach rounded a curve, and the driver slammed on the brakes. A derelict looking car was stopped in their lane. The guide said something in Turkish, and the driver accelerated around the obstacle. The slowing, accelerating, and swerving had knocked Bransom and the guide into the stairwell. They were just regaining their footing when something exploded!

Chapter 30

TRADE

THE EXPLOSIVES CREATED a searing, blinding flash! The coach lurched backwards from the force, lifting the front of the vehicle, and whirling it sideways across the road. The driver of the second coach reacted quickly, almost stopping before impacting the first one. Fire and heavy black smoke rose from the gaping hole where the right front tires had been.

Stunned silence! Then David and Daniel recovered their wits enough to push open the rear emergency-exit! Shouting for everyone to evacuate as calmly as possible, they leapt to the ground and began assisting their fellow passengers. It seemed like the emerging travelers were exiting in slow motion. Tears clouded Daniel's vision when Diana and his three children were all safely clear. He and David were acutely aware of the possibility of more explosives, or marksmen waiting to pick them off as they were forced to move into the open.

Security people, though definitely stunned, were forming a perimeter. Others were charging up the hillsides, weapons drawn, to check the high points for further escalation of the threat.

The other coach was beginning to evacuate, and Roger Sanders sprinted toward Bransom, who was staggering away, assisting the driver and their guide. Bransom, having just regained his feet before the blast, had his back to the flash! The driver and guide seemed blinded, as least partially. Bransom's ears were ringing, but he was pretty sure whatever the device was, it hadn't managed to inflict the devastation intended. It was bad enough, though. He was thanking the Lord as he left the driver and the guide in the care of security and Diana.

David thought Mallory would never appear through the thickening smoke. Terrified for her, he assisted his mom and dad, brother, and sisters, Donovan the drunk, Brad, Janet, and Sarah. He wondered vacantly why the Walters and Sanders had traded places on the coaches.

At last, Mallory was at the exit! Coughing and crying, she handed a limp, pale Sammie Walters to him!

Shocked, he took the child from her, and she jumped free. Daniel gazed once more, or tried to, up the smoky aisle. He was trying to take mental count of everyone.

"Was that everyone?" he asked Mallory, who nodded numbly.

They ran!

Other traffic was beginning to back up in both directions, then funny-sounding, European sirens preceded emergency vehicles. Then a really strange-looking, yet curiously familiar military convoy arrived. Large, armored vehicles sprouting guns, rolled to a stop.

Bransom, weapon in hand, stepped forward as an officer jumped to the ground. The group watched as Bransom conferred with the man. Behind him, men and women dressed in military-looking camouflage were spreading around, some directing traffic around the pile up, others beginning to document the damage with cameras. One of them, wearing latex gloves, had bent to recover a metal fragment. Bransom yelled a warning it would still be hot, just as the Turkish commander was issuing the same warning in Turkish. Both men laughed.

Mallory was vaguely aware of the commotion, on her knees next to Sammie, as Diana examined him gently. Blood oozed from an ugly gash in his scalp. At first, Brad and Janet weren't aware of their child's injury, until Sarah saw her twin and went into hysterics!

"Mallie, ask Jesus! Ask Jesus!" she shrieked. "Jesus has to help my brother!"

Mallory grabbed her. "That's a good idea, Sarah, let's pray." Her voice shaking, she asked Jesus to help Sammie be okay.

He continued to lie pale and motionless. Diana's expression was grim. Mallory was trying to pull Sarah away, but the little girl resisted her gentle tugs. Brad and Janet stood, clasping one another, watching horrified, as their child remained unresponsive.

A medic from the unit knelt momentarily beside Diana, then directed Sammie's evacuation by stretcher to a Turkish version of a care-flight helicopter. Diana shoved a shocky Janet into the chopper with her son; medical personnel would need her permission in order to administer care. Relieved for the quick medical response, she whispered to Mallory to keep praying.

Colonel Ahmir, authoritative and in control, welcomed the dazed and frightened retinue into one of the vehicles. Urged into seats, offered hot coffee or tea with cakes, they were all quickly assessed for injuries. There were quite a few scrapes and bruises and a couple of gashes requiring stitches. Still, pretty miraculous! The colonel affirmed the same opinion. The road side device had, no doubt, been intended to kill!

The convoy was rolling back toward Izmir. Bransom and Faulkner, in Ahmir's crowded office, listened, amazed to the Turkish update. The Turks had a full dossier on Oscar and Otto Malovich, whereas, Bransom and the FBI hadn't gotten to first base assembling information on the two.

Ahmir laughed easily, a rolling, infectious baritone.

"I wish we didn't know about them. They are from a very bad group. Deep pockets! Who would imagine posting such hefty bail, then fleeing? The higher ups in their gang are undoubtedly not happy with their apprehension and what your investigation will reveal. I'm sure the lives of Oscar and Otto depend on how successful they are in making their problems go away! We try to keep these guys out of Turkey, but they try to do business here, as they try anywhere that seems lucrative and easy. They operate out of Macedonia and Romania, mostly. We deal with them more in our area of Thrace; they have traveled east to deal with your group, Agent, Mr. Faulkner."

Bransom nodded agreement.

Diana tapped at the door. Daniel answered and laughed. She was pretty much smoke-blackened, except for white rings where her sunglasses were. Then smeary, black eye makeup created black rings within the white ones. Bransom laughed too. Ahmir, trying to be polite, focused his attention on his computer monitor.

"What's funny?" she demanded, glancing around self-consciously for a mirror. "I'm looking for you to tell you what Mallory was saying before the bus exploded! Or don't you still want to know?"

"I do." He was trying to get serious. "I'm sorry, Honey," he apologized. "You just look like the 'Target' puppy!" He dissolved into laughter and Bransom's cackling wasn't helping him get control of himself.

Diana's hands flew instinctively to cover her face. That was when Daniel noticed she was hurt. Being serious was suddenly not a problem for him! Her always flawless solar nails, jagged, broken, and pulled away, revealed her fingertips, bloody and torn into the quicks.

"Sit down, Honey." At once he was filled with concern. "You're hurt."

She had been in too much shock to be aware of the pain. Once she looked, they started to hurt, and she began to cry.

"Sammie's hurt bad; something must have fallen on him. We should have gone home."

She didn't cry very often! And she wouldn't say it was bad unless it was really bad! Daniel stood surveying her, his face a pallid study in anguish! He should have listened to Bransom! He should have listened to her!

"What was Mallie saying?" Erik's voice.

At Ahmir's order, a member of the medical staff entered, spraying Diana's fingertips with an anesthetic-antiseptic combination that immediately began to ease the pain. He started to bandage both of her hands with gauze, but Diana, laughing through the tears, said just to apply band aids.

Turning to Erik, she told him about Mallory's fleeting impression that Oscar Melville, wearing his sheriff's hat, had been watching her through binoculars when she got separated from the group at Pamukkale.

"What's your take?" he asked her.

The colonel issued another order in Turkish. A lieutenant, an attractive lady with nice wedding rings, appeared carrying the felt hat in question, and expensive binoculars, bagged in clear evidence bags. The items had been retrieved from the area above the falls described by Mallory. In custody was a local who occasionally had brushes with the law. His claim was that some Americans had paid him to stand up there wearing the hat and looking through the binoculars. He didn't know why. It seemed harmless enough, and he needed the money.

It didn't make a whole lot of sense to Bransom, but he was relieved that Melville wasn't up there, when Mallory had been so close, and so alone!

"I don't suppose I can talk you into turning those things over to me to send to the FBI lab," Bransom queried.

"Maybe so, when we have finished." Ahmir's voice was firm. "Since we have American television programs, we know how to treat evidence." He laughed. "That is seriously true. We are getting more trained in forensics now."

Bransom chuckled. They seemed to have a good handle on the investigation. He was relieved.

The convoy returned to Izmir, making its way through areas of the city that seemed highly unsavory. Then, as they approached the area of the bay, affluence and glitz surrounded them, and they were back at the Hilton, albeit, at the back entrance. Ahmir addressed the group. The Turkish government and the department of tourism wanted them to have a chance to clean up before dinner, then there was a special dinner being prepared in a private dining room adjacent to the Windows on the Bay restaurant on the thirty-first floor. The group could begin to assemble up there as quickly as they could get ready. Appetizers, or Mezes, would be available before the dinner

Back within the relative safety and privacy of their suite, Daniel and Diana both burst into tears simultaneously. Their children thought Sammie must be dead, so their wails contributed to the anguish. All five of them huddled together shaking and crying.

Finally, Daniel pulled away, drying his eyes. They needed to get cleaned up for dinner and go find where Sammie had been taken, and check on him.

He showered first, since he could be the fastest. Then, suddenly, he encouraged Diana to get a relaxing soak, put on the big Turkish terry cloth robe, and order room service. Sammie was in good hands; she didn't have to nurse everyone back to health.

She laughed at the offer, genuinely appreciative of Daniel's constant care of her and thoughtfulness. But she was trying to make the thirty-first floor in hopes of a better sunset. She was ready to leave by the time the three kids were showered and dressed. The beautiful family emerged together like they had enjoyed a spa day together, except for the band-aids.

John Anderson had gone with Brad to the hospital, leaving Lana and Tammi with an angry and teary-eyed Sarah. They were trying to coax the little girl to eat some of the appetizers, but she was beside herself.

Mallory was standing at the plate-glass window staring across the bay when the Faulkners entered. She smiled acknowledgment at them, and they joined her. The late afternoon sun was heading toward bed, leaving a dull red sky in its wake. The choppy bay reflected the blood red. It was pretty. It must mean the rain forecast for the next day was coming. That was the reason they had crowded so much into one afternoon. Mallory was glad for the lovely, sunny, pictures of Ephesus and Pamukkale. And she was glad for a nice sunset for Diana. She didn't feel much like taking any more pictures.

Colonel Ahmir arrived with his retinue. Also present with him, were some of the prominent bazaar merchants, politicians, and other well-connected citizens. They were all, not only eager to make sales to this group of Americans, but maybe through their channels, reach more of the American market. It was a pretty good idea, and the Americans traded business cards and discussed possible ways to partner in various endeavors. Finally, it seemed evident that one of the things the Turkish merchants wanted most, was the diamonds! Not too surprising! But they wanted them steeply discounted, trying to purchase around the price control of the cartel. Mallory didn't know! Nor did her attorney! The entire system was so delicate. When they tried to press for a deal, Kerry repeated that they needed to study the offer and its ramifications before they could enter any agreements. He was in over his head, and he knew it! They all were!

International trade in such a valuable commodity! It could be lucrative! It might be just the outlet they needed! He certainly didn't want to alienate their gracious host! But he honestly didn't know the answers.

Chapter 31

TRANQUILLITY

WORD FINALLY CAME to David from his dad that Sammie had regained consciousness. He did have a concussion. The fact that he was little with soft bones had saved him from a skull fracture. His gash had been stapled, and he was starting to bounce around in typical Sammie-fashion. It was miraculous!

Colonel Ahmir, a patient man, was pleased with the progress. He liked the FBI agent, and all of them, really. He was glad the little boy was doing so well. He had thought it looked bad. A little American boy dying in Turkey while vacationing was hardly the picture his country wanted portrayed. He presented a few gifts and was astounded to receive a pair of diamond cuff links and diamond earrings for his wife in return. This group was different from most of the Americans he encountered. Actually, he didn't deal with as many Americans as he wished. But these were all nicer than the stories he usually heard!

The convoy vehicles were back, and he hastened his charges into them. Their luggage was already loaded, and they moved out cautiously into traffic. Shops and hotels sparkled along the water's edge, making a few of them wish they could have checked everything out better. But the gifts they had received were reflective of the best Izmir had to offer, anyway. Ahmir delivered them to the airport tarmac where their jet awaited them. Ahmir's force watched carefully; so did the American security!

Every person, every piece of baggage. Even their things left behind in the hasty evacuation of the coaches had been retrieved, once the colonel had been sure there wouldn't be any further explosions. The Louis Vuitton overnight bag, though smoky beyond salvageability, still contained every piece of Diana's jewelry.

Daniel took it, holding it away so it wouldn't smudge him up.

"You did the right thing just getting yourself and the kids out," he reassured her. He kissed her hand. "Do your fingers hurt? You think everything's still okay?"

"They hurt if I bang them, and I keep banging them on everything. Things seem okay."

An hour and a half later, the jet screamed down, and they were in the Turkish capital, Ankara. A lieutenant colonel greeted them and escorted them to the luxurious Hilton, where they checked in at the private concierge-level check-in. The rain had started, the hour was late, and everyone was pretty well mentally and physically exhausted. Further checks with the Walters were unnecessary. They all arrived within fifteen minutes, accompanied by a trauma nurse who would monitor the now sleepy little boy for the coming twenty-four hours.

Diana could have done it, but she was relieved not to. And relieved his color and response were so unexplainably good! Her family all raced to get ready for bed; the kids nearly asleep before the "amen" of the prayer. She and Daniel sank gratefully into the feather beds, beneath the lavish, duvet-covered comforter. The rain spattered softly against the windows. Diana, exhausted, verged on sleep, then jerked as tense nerves began to relax. Daniel chuckled sleepily next to her, and she smiled in the darkness. She was nearly asleep again! She felt a slight flutter! The baby was moving!

Morning brought more rain, with an unseasonable chill. Gusts of wind swept the rains sideways in sheets, turning umbrellas wrong side out as pedestrians scurried along the sidewalks in front of the hotel. Mallory watched them with sympathy and interest from her warm perch far above. Stretching, she refilled her coffee. Callie had gained freedom from her dad's security oversight to spend the night in Mallory's suite. She was still sleeping in the other king sized bed. They had planned to have an all-night gab-fest, but they were too tired and the stacks of pillows too inviting!

Mallory knew her friend was really curious about her and David, but she had kept changing the subject. She liked her new friend a whole lot, but she couldn't define her feelings about David, even to herself. She didn't want to reveal her heart! David didn't need to know, or his mom and dad, or the Faulkners, or even her mom. Her chapter in Proverbs had cautioned about being prudent and discreet; many chapters repeated the warning. She wrote in her journal. She didn't know why she couldn't talk herself out of the crazy notion that she had nearly stumbled alone into the hands of Oscar Melville again.

In the bathroom, she turned on the strong frame of lighting which circled the mirror above the sink. She couldn't see the bruises at all, any more. But tears came to her eyes as she remembered.

Was he in Turkey? Had he planted a bomb on the bus?

She returned to her coffee and journal, thanking the Lord for safety! And Oh, yes! She had nearly forgotten. For letting her tour the ruins of ancient Ephesus! Christianity had flourished, evidently, in spite of the fact that this particular area had fallen to Islam.

She threw a pillow at Callie, who just tucked it under her, trying to keep sleeping.

Mallory was one of the first of their group to descend hungrily on the breakfast. Daniel and Diana sat at a table in a corner, holding hands, and talking in a special way that husbands and wives who got along did. She suddenly felt lonely and excluded. She wished Callie would have gotten up! She stalled in making her selections, hoping her grandmother, or Aunt Linda, or even her mom and Erik would materialize. She was ready to dash back to her suite with the excuse of taking something to Callie, but Daniel was beside her.

"Get your breakfast and come join us. There are some interesting developments we didn't tell you last night in the confusion. Hope Diana left you something."

She laughed as she finished choosing and followed him to their table.

Diana looked gorgeous and rested. She was wearing a really cute, aqua, soft denim dress that had the cutest sweater-jacket with it. Mallory wondered how she managed to pack so many cute things, ready for hot or cold weather. She was learning the textile terminology gradually; she was pretty sure the jacket was called "boiled wool" It was embroidered with metallic gold oysters, revealing pearls nestled within them. Then gold chains embroidered lavishly over the garment, intertwined with strings of pearls. Looked expensive! The color emphasized her dancing blue eyes. She wore gold and pearl jewelry with gold clamshell charms which also housed pearls Several fingers had band aids where her perfect nails should have been.

"You look great this morning," Diana greeted. "Did you have a hard time getting that sticky smoke out of your hair?"

"Yeah," Mallie responded. " I can still smell it. Wonder if my pillow and throw can be salvaged."

"Probably not. Too bad, because they were really nice!"

"So, what's the latest info that you guys didn't tell me last night?" Mallory forced a cheery smile, but she was dreading any news about Mr. Melville.

"We can't figure out what they're trying to do." Daniel stirred his coffee. "They paid a local small-time thug to stand up there with the hat and binoculars. Colonel Ahmir has that guy in custody and the hat and binoculars in evidence. They have fingerprints that match Oscar's. They know that because they have a thick file on both of the Malovich brothers.

Bransom is trying to get things moving from here, to get your Uncle Ryland's body pulled from the Charles River in Boston. Then, if that develops, he plans to make a murder case against both Oscar and Otto, asking for the death penalty. Then, if he can swing that, none of these European countries will extradite them to the U.S., since they don't agree with the death penalty. If they get arrested in some European country, they'll get stuck with them in their prisons forever. The twins shouldn't want back into the U.S. to face murder charges."

Mallory sighed. "So, if we stay inside the States, we should be safe from those two, but not necessarily from their cronies. And, if we engage in foreign travel~"

Daniel had thought Bransom's plan was pretty brilliant; Mallory was perceptive to see it had some holes in it.

Alexandra entered with her brother and sister, and Mallory rose so they could join their parents.

"Stay and talk to us, Mallie," Jeremiah pled.

She gave him a hug before joining Tammi.

By now, the entire crowd was filtering in, where the plan was to breakfast before heading out late morning to tour the country's most outstanding museum. Mallory and Diana wondered how it could surpass the Treasury in Topkapi Palace. The modern, capital city offered a few tourist sites, but the Museum of Anatolian Civilizations was presented as the premier choice for their short time here. It was an amazing place! The small children stayed pretty interested for awhile, then, as they grew restless, their parents picked up the pace. Carmine, Linda, and Herb acted like they wouldn't mind lingering forever. Some of the ancient artifacts, Linda had viewed with awe in her Art History textbooks. As a quiet student in a small Kansas State College, she had barely allowed herself to dream of such a trip, actually ever being able to view the exquisite articles!

Although Mallory kept an anxious eye on the faces crowding around her, she didn't see anyone who even resembled the former Pike County Sheriff. She knew Erik was extra watchful; so was everyone in their group.

Diana caught up with Shay and Delia to share some information she had just gotten from the guide. Ankara's name was a derivative from angora, because of the original trade in the wool from Angora goats.

"That is so awesome," Shay chortled joyfully. "Something else to seriously look into!"

"I think we're looking into it right away. Colonel Ahmir is still trying to get us more involved with Turkish merchants and merchandise. After our late lunch, those of us who want to are going to a rug place. We get to watch the silk process from the cocoons to finished rugs. It probably sounds dull to most of the group, but I'm dying to go. I've read about the process lots of times, but seeing it!" Diana's laughter rippled softly in the museum vestibule where they waited for the lingering shoppers to emerge from the gift shop. No wonder the colonel wanted to keep them spending; they were all doing their part to stimulate the Turkish economy.

Of course, Shay and Delia almost reached Diana's level of excitement about the silk. Shay wanted to know more about the Angora!

The rug process was more interesting than it had sounded. No one left without purchasing at least one rug and arranging for shipment home. Available in myriads of sizes, patterns, and colors, the hand-loomed treasures were beautiful!

From there, they went to investigate the luxurious leather goods. Soft and supple, the elegant garments worked their magic with the consumers. All the guys claimed at least one leather "bomber" jacket. The ladies found coats, jackets, suits, gloves, and handbags in different styles, colors, and combinations.

Not only did they make purchases; they made friends, exchanging business cards and offers of hospitality should any of the Turkish people visit the States. After enjoying tea and cakes, they were once again on their way.

"Wonder where I can go about linen," Delia was trying to act miffed about her overlooked fiber preference!

Mallory laughed at her grandmother. "For that we have to go to Damascus, Syria!"

"Damascus, Syria!" Bransom had overheard the last of the conversation. Sounded like the worst idea they had come up with yet! Syria was on the State Department list of countries for Americans to avoid.

"Yes, Sir!" Mallory's eyes danced. "The linen Damask Grandmother uses in table linens originated in Damascus! It's one of the oldest cities in the world, too; and it has lots of Bible history!"

Bransom could tell she was baiting him, so he just waved his hands in resignation.

"I'm ready to go home to Arkansas! I don't care where the rest of you crazy people go!"

After a superb dinner at the Hilton, they were transported back to the airport for the flight farther east to Kayseri, from where they would visit the Fairy Chimney landscape of Cappadocia. The hour was growing late, but they checked in at yet another Hilton before heading out as a group in search of coffees and desserts. The Walters rejoined the group. After twenty-four hours of observing Sammie, his oversight by the Turkish nurses was ended. Diana would continue keeping an eye on him.

The area was actually one of Turkey's ski resorts, but the ski season was past, making way for the usual stream of tourists traipsing through the landscape and viewing sites where churches and monasteries had been carved into the soft volcanic substance. It was pretty different. Mallory reaffirmed that her chosen field of Geology was fascinating and unsearchable! The volcanoes and their resulting eroded landscape, the travertine terraces, the meerschaum stuff she was hearing about! Much more of interest in the Earth's crust than just diamonds. She laughed at herself! "Just Diamonds!"

The group once more seem melded together; Mallory hadn't heard anything more about the "spats" and differences of opinions. The fellowship and camaraderie amongst the entire group seemed closer than ever. Callie and Shannon had definitely formed a bond, Donovan seemed to have learned to smile, Carmine was less hostile. Linda and Herb spent every waking minute together, having evidently found lots in common to talk about.

The confections and desserts, rich and gooey, were tantalizing, although most of the Americans had grown tired of Turkish Delight!

Exhausted, they returned to the hotel. Diana helped her kids get settled into bed, then asked Daniel if he would mind if she went to talk to Mallory. Tired himself, in spite of the coffee, he kissed her and sent her on her way. She left with her big portfolio and sketch pads under her arm. He was amazed at how specially the Lord had worked in sending Mallory beneath their protection. She was a real friend to Diana and already an invaluable colleague in her fashion business. Shay and Delia, too. The Fashion Industry could be a lonely place for a Christian. He laughed to himself. So could the field of Geology be.

Mallory opened her door to Diana's tap. She was kind of tired, but Diana's request to come work on some stuff had reenergized her. She had ordered a latte; now she wasn't sure if the espresso in it was keeping her awake, or if the warm milk was putting her to sleep. She brewed some coffee.

In the privacy of the suite, they both began brainstorming about the inspirations that had come to them as they traveled. Diana had been bursting at the seams for days to talk to Mallie about the possibility of talking to Herb about their needs for a jeweler. Diana shared eagerly what she knew about the pawn shop owner. Daniel had done somewhat of a background search. Herb seemed like a good guy. He hadn't gotten saved yet, but the Christians of the group had been praying for salvation of all their fellow travelers.

Mallory gazed across her steaming coffee. "Look at these cute cups and saucers. Wonder what the story is about them and where we can get them."

"Probably China!" Diana giggled. "Probably everything we've seen here is really imported from there!"

Mallory laughed too, then they both got down to business.

"I had an idea when I stayed with you in Tulsa that week end, then I forgot about it, then those beautiful bottles as Topkapi reminded me again," Mallory began. "You know how you have beautiful perfume bottles and atomizers everywhere?"

Diana nodded.

"I was thinking they would be really pretty incorporated into textiles. But then, those bottles with all the gold and precious stones adorning them made the idea seem even better. What do you think?"

Diana was drawing! White background silk with etched and adorned bottles. Cute! She tried them arranged neatly on shelves, then spilling randomly. Both were cute! Working together, each playing off the creativity of the other, they accomplished a great deal. Diana sketched gorgeous complementary jewelry, featuring miniature gem-encrusted, rock-crystal and gold bottles! As scatter-pins on a lapel, as a slide for an Omega, a charm bracelet, earrings! Too cute!

Finally, about one-thirty, with gorgeous things put together, they hurried down to the twenty-four hour business center, scanned in the designs, and e-mailed an order off. They were excited about the garments that would arrive in Tulsa, nearly in time to meet Diana on her return. They were hoping that by adding Herb Carlton to their staff, the accompanying jewelry designs would soon be available, too.

At breakfast, neither woman appeared to have gotten so little sleep. Buoyed up by their accomplishments, and excited about the day's activities, they were more than compensated for the short night.

As the travertine falls of Pamakkule, so, much of the region of Cappadocia, had been proclaimed a World Heritage Site by UNESCO. It was a good thing, for the sake of preserving the spots for posterity. They viewed as much as possible in the short time they had. The rain had ceased, but a chilly, brisk wind remained of the system. Not surprisingly, the hot air balloons were grounded. A few members of their group had hoped to balloon over the landscape. Mallory had just been disappointed not to get to watch the colorful spectacle from the ground.

The coaches had them back at the Hilton by four. Some of them hurried to the business center and some to the electronics in their rooms to check for messages and e-mails. Daniel and Kerry had both been trying to reassure their worried parents that they were completely safe. Of course the news of the explosion and their tour group had been major news in the States.

"Just three more days, and we'll be home," Daniel assured his dad.

Weariness catching up to her, Diana napped before dinner. Mallory met Carmine and Callie for tea in the lobby. It was fun. They all compared pictures and souvenirs. Mallory looked lovely, wearing an orchid sweater with a matching quilted reversible zipper-front vest. The reverse side, dark denim, matched her ankle-length denim skirt. Navy boots met the skirt. Rose de France Amethysts in sterling silver sparkled softly, and she carried the silver slouch bag.

Callie had explained to her mom about Mallie's having so much cute stuff because she was surrounded by designers that "made it happen". Carmine had made a comment that it must be nice to have everything custom-made, and Callie had joined in.

"Hello," Mallory made a funny face at Callie. "This is the sweater I found for you and tried to talk you into buying; remember?"

"It is?" Callie remembered the sweater and their 'argument' about it. "I remember the sweater now; I don't remember the outfit."

"Yeah, I know. After you decided not to get it, I kept thinking about it. When I went back, it was still there. I asked the Lord to help me find something cute to wear with it for this trip. After that, it kind of came together."

Did it ever! Carmine had never heard too much about praying, especially over something like putting an outfit together. But the outfit was pretty cute! She tried not to think about it. She didn't have any money anyway. She wondered vaguely if she would ever really become an attorney, ever have any money. The possibility seemed remote.

Following the recommendation of the concierge, they dined out at a restaurant, the name of which they couldn't begin to pronounce. They took pictures of different groupings of them in front of the sign. The kebabs and dolma were really excellent, but they all agreed that they were getting homesick for America and her cuisine. Then they returned to the hotel. Breakfast would be early, then they would transport to the small local airport to fly the last leg of their journey to the east.

Chapter 32

TROUBLE!

JEREMIAH FAULKNER WAS a cute combination of his mom and dad. Reserved and observant, he didn't say a whole lot; but when he did, he seemed older than his eight years! And he liked Mallory! That was one reason it made such an impression on him that Shannon O'Shaughnessy was still traveling with their group. He had been mad at David and Shay for getting mad at Mallory for "only praying" about the incident with her cousin. Jeremiah had a pretty good idea of how hard his dad and Agent Bransom had worked to get Shannon shipped! And he was still along! He liked Mallory's example of praying about things. He had started his own small prayer journal, and he was starting to write out a sermon he hoped to preach sometime. He didn't know when; he wasn't sure how you got invited.

The pilot announced on the PA that there was a strong tail wind, and sure enough, he came back on about twenty minutes before expected to announce that Mt. Ararat could be viewed from the left side of the craft. Mallory had kind of figured that out ahead, so she was seated by a window and had spotted the famous peak before the announcement came. At nearly seventeen thousand feet, its summit was the highest point in Turkey. The chartered jet, smaller and more crowded than the 747, descended through blue skies to land in Van. Lake Van, the largest body of water in the country had a higher saline concentration than the oceans. After deplaning, the group boarded onto buses for the ride to the mountain.

The guide was speaking in a sing-songy voice about the flora and fauna, temperatures, and average annual precipitation. Mallory tried to remind herself to be hungry for wisdom and knowledge, but she fell sound asleep anyway, not stirring until the brakes ground, announcing the stop at Agri (mountain). Startled, she gazed around, then flopped back against the headrest. She was tired. She waited for everyone to get off and hopped down last.

The air was dry and cool, making her glad she had worn a cute Alpaca sweater set that Shay had ordered her from somewhere. A soft brick red worked in an arrowhead pattern, eased into sage green. The lined cardigan-jacket with patch pockets was trimmed with blanket-stitching in the green. Mallory had discovered about a four inch, soft green agate arrowhead in a jewelry component catalog, fixing it into a necklace on a leather cord. It looked cute, harmonizing with the color and the design of her cute outfit; the problem was that the napped edges were really sharp. Shay had noticed that it was abrading the delicate fibers of the green sweater shell. To his annoyance, she didn't remove it. She just cheerfully told him that her diamond tennis bracelet always roughed up her jacket sleeves and gouged up her watch dial. Textiles were always at risk to jewelry.

The group stood as close to the base of the mountain as they were allowed to get, and gazed up. Snow-capped year round, it created a gorgeous view. They took their normal, excessive number of pictures! Smiling, crying, pouting, making faces, looking thoughtful, making horns on each other. What ever goofy way people could act in front of a camera, they all seemed to be doing. Trying to act amused, Mallory was thinking it must be time to go home. In the morning! She was ready!

Boarding the coaches once more, they headed for Dogubeyazit and their final hotel stay. It was the best in town; comfortable and adequate, although definitely lacking the style and amenities of the others. Erik and Darrell Hopkins, neither one, liked it much from a security standpoint.

Early afternoon, most of them headed out to look for some lunch. Erik didn't like that either. This was probably the loosest law enforcement area they had been in, and they were breaking up more into small groups. He had met with the security guys that weren't currently busy covering their charges, telling them where they would patrol when it was their shift.

Allie, Callie, Mallie, Tammi, and Carmine had opted for the small sidewalk café area of the hotel. It literally was a sidewalk café, nearly spilling into the street. David viewed them and the street from the window of his room. They all looked exceptionally cute. It seemed to him they were drawing quite a bit of attention from the locals, although the girls were just laughing and talking, looking at each others' pictures, and taking more. It wasn't long before a kid on a bike jumped the low wrought iron railing to insist on taking a picture of all of them. Then, a car stopped and three more guys jumped out. David wondered where Donovan Cline was and Callie's shadows. Where was his dad, Daniel Faulkner, Roger Sanders, Shay? He slid his feet back into his sandals and galloped his way down the stair well. Bursting into the enclosure, he seated himself between Tammi and Mallory, telling Alexandra and Callie that Tommy and Shannon were on their way down. Firmly pulling the camera from the bike kid's hand, he nodded a curt thank you and suggested the guys move along. They eyed David somewhat sullenly, but took off.

Gazing around warily, he noticed an old, blue, American-made- in-the-sixties beater. He had noticed it from upstairs, thinking the men in it were either taking pictures of the girls or watching them through binoculars. When he edged up the sidewalk for a closer look, it pulled away, turning at the next corner. With its shot suspension-system and long trailer hitch, it dragged noisily where the street dipped, shooting sparks. David stopped, gazing after it uneasily. He wondered if the girls had managed to capture it in any of their pictures. It seemed odd! He shuddered.

"When's Tommy coming?" Alexandra asked him. "I thought he was going to the old palace with his dad and mom."

"Yeah, David just mentioned the guys so those other guys would leave," Carmine explained. "Thanks, David. Glad you noticed us down here."

As he rejoined them, a server came out, and they ordered. David wasn't sure if kids just cruised here, like some of them did at home, or what the deal was. He nervously felt like the girls, especially Mallory, were generating a great deal of interest. The same cars continued to drive by slowly, guys gawking. The old blue thing had a gray "Bondo" door on the driver's side. It kept crossing the main street at either end of the block, the trailer hitch scraping each time. He took a picture.

By the time the food arrived, they were all ready to move inside. So, to the server's surprise, Mallory signed for the meal and they all carried their food up to her room. They turned on the TV, also not like Istanbul and Ankara. Finding nothing in English, they switched it off. David, positioned by the window, watched the old car stop in front of the hotel. A man, dressed in black, with a thick thatch of dark hair and unkempt beard, darted inside the lobby. David took another picture of the car, then moved from the room to ease his way down toward the front desk. The ratty-looking guy was engaged in conversation with the desk clerk.

"I help you?" the clerk questioned when David approached.

"Change dollars?" he questioned. All he had was a twenty, and the guy looked disgusted.

"Try Banc! Better rate!"

"Yeah, thanks, maybe later," he muttered, turning back toward the elevator.

He thought it was cool to have actually stood at the base of Mt. Ararat! But he suddenly wished they were all on their way home! An inexplicable feeling of dread had engulfed him, giving him goose-bumps. He shrugged, not usually one to get, or pay attention to, "funny feelings"!

Back in Mallory's room where the girls were finishing lunch, he watched from the window as the car eased into traffic. Although he continued to watch, the car didn't materialize again.

Their group seemed to have reassembled at the hotel; everyone accounted for. Erik was glad, but he wished they were on their way back to Van to catch the small jet back to Izmir, where the 747 would be ready to take them back to New York City, and then Dallas.

Some of them were talking about hiring a Dolmus to take them where they could view the border with Iran. Aside from the amazing views of Mt. Ararat, the town didn't offer much, so Daniel didn't blame them for wanting to do something! He wasn't sure the Iranian border was a good choice. Trying to provide entertainment, he opened his laptop and started the Bethlehem Star DVD playing in an empty corner of the lobby. Mallory and Callie loved it, so they sat down to watch; a few others positioned themselves where they could see. Then, some of the locals were drawn. Fewer people seemed to speak English this far east, but, whether they could understand, or not, they watched. For the duration of the film, the crowd grew; when it ended, they clapped politely.

Tea and coffee were being served in the lobby; not a high tea like the one in Istanbul, but something more typically Turkish! And Iranian! Most of the hotel guests were merchants from Iran, either bringing Iranian products into Turkey, or importing Turkish goods into Iran.

In spite of Iran's Supreme Council's continuing to denounce the U.S. as the Great Satan, the Iranian people were extremely friendly to, and curious about the American tourists. The tea time was really fun. Daniel started the concert playing, once more, of his family's Easter evening concert. John Anderson sat down to watch it, amazed at the mileage it had gotten already, and now maybe reaching into the hearts of Iranians. Tears filled his eyes. He and Lana had been so threatened by the Faulkner family, that they almost hadn't wanted to let them participate in the service. Well, they had resented Patrick's asking them to take the oversight of Mallory and her fortune. When the Faulkners showed on the scene, they had struck the whole town of Murfreesboro as interlopers. The pastor was forced to admit that Patrick had made a wise move, and that God does all things well!

David and Shay sat in a conversation area with young Turkish and Iranian men. The foreigners asked them if they saw film and rock stars everywhere in America. They were disappointed that David and Shay didn't know any of the famous Americans they admired. David explained about being from a small town, and his dad's being a pastor of a church. They seemed to have respect for a "holy man", so David gave them the web address for the church.

It was dark when they all left the hotel, walking to a nearby restaurant which featured Iranian food. They had especially made friends with a large family who had driven from Esfahan, Iran to enjoy holiday in Turkey. At the restaurant, they were introduced to shish kabob, various khoresht dishes, Iranian rice with saffron, salads, and bread. It was good, although by now, pizza and burgers were sounding pretty appealing to all of the Americans.

Parvis, the father, confessed to the group that he and his family were Christians. Many of his countrymen were converting. He asked them to tell his story in America and to pray for the spread of the gospel in Iran.

They lingered with the family, sharing stories, inviting them to visit in America. It was late when they headed back to the hotel.

In the fun and excitement, with David's foreboding forgotten, he failed to mention to Bransom, his concern about the big blue land yacht!

Chapter 33

TRAPPED

Mallory, laughing and talking animatedly with her friends, bid everyone good night, giving her mom a quick kiss on the cheek. The entire trip had been awesome. Even this small, backwater area had become lively and fun as they interacted with the other hotel guests. She had Barbara's e-mail address, Parvis' oldest daughter who was fifteen. Mallory was excited about a new friend, but she knew she would have to be extremely careful about her correspondence. She didn't want the family's dangerous situation further imperiled by indiscretion on her part.

Entering her darkened hotel "suite", she sank onto the sagging sofa, the sofa which delineated her room as a "suite", demanding an extra eight dollars per night.

In all of her wildest, most exciting dreams, she had never imagined that she, Mallory O'Shaughnessy, would be sitting in an Iranian restaurant with Iranians, in the farthest eastern province of Turkey! The Lord could certainly infuse life with fun and excitement! She yawned. Grateful for fun and excitement, she was now eager to return to her beautiful home, to relax, settle in, really get going on her course work.

She yawned again as she untied the leather knot to remove her arrowhead. She really needed to get up and get ready for bed~

Something startled her awake! A scraping noise out on her balcony! The heavy, water-stained drapes, still opened, revealed black forms dropping onto her balcony from the roof. There were two of them, visible through the sheer drapery! After conversing briefly, they slid open the glass door~the one which she had carefully locked prior to leaving for dinner! She sat paralyzed with indecision as it slid open, almost noiselessly!

She couldn't fathom what was happening! Surely her security had seen them! She sat frozen. Her cell phone was still turned on in her handbag which rested next to her! No chance for using it!

The two forms paused, confused, as they observed that the bed was still neatly made. They had assumed their quarry would be sleeping soundly by now!

Then they spotted her! She appeared to be asleep, sitting-up on the sofa across the room. Tiptoeing softly, they advanced, planning to chloroform her before she could make any racket! Before she could struggle!

Fighting tears and the trembling her body was trying to do, she waited, the arrowhead clasped desperately beside her! When a hand grasped her, she slashed! Blood spurted, as did some epithets in a language she couldn't understand. In one motion, she had slashed, and stashed the weapon into her jacket pocket.

"Does your mom know you talk like that?" was the last thing she said before a nasty rag covered her face; and she sagged, unconscious!

When she came to, she was in a confined space bumping around roughly. The nauseating odors of gasoline and exhaust burned her eyes; she felt sick. She was trying to remember where she was and what was happening. A huge pothole flung her upwards, then slammed her forcefully against the floor of the car's trunk. She landed on something hard and sharp, and moaned with pain. The car continued to careen crazily, flying across rough terrain at a high rate of speed! She fought to keep her stomach contents in her stomach, knowing vomit wouldn't enhance the cramped space.

The images from the FBI video danced maliciously before her!. Scenes of what happened to victims after they were abducted! Nothing good! Hopelessness and fear tried to engulf her, but Erik hadn't made her watch the film so she would give up. Its purpose was to help her know what to do.

The car continued to hit one bone-jarring bump after another. She tried to brace herself to soften some of the roughness of the ride. She was pretty sure she was in the trunk of the blue car David hadn't liked the looks of. But, why? Still fighting panic and nausea, she tried to quote Scripture and pray. She wished the bruising ride would end; then figured the end of the ride would be worse. Where was she going?

It was so dark! And it was hard to breathe. Was carbon monoxide going to kill her?

Then, calm came. She didn't know how! Miraculous peace!

Raising up on her elbows, she began examining her space with her hands. "That's what you have to do when you can't see," she decided. It felt pretty much, like a car trunk! She almost laughed at her obvious conclusion. But there had to be more!

"Kick out the tail-lights!" a voice from the video. Twisting around slightly, she tried it. It worked! Maybe the police would stop them now; she would holler and pound! That would end this!

The car increased its forward momentum! They were off-road in the low-slung car with no shocks. Mallory could hear the crazy trailer hitch still hitting as the car pounded crazily toward whatever the destination was!

The hard, sharp thing she kept encountering painfully was a tool box! Joy surged! They must not give her much credit! A tool box would be full of weapons she could use whenever they opened the trunk! Maybe, she could pry the trunk lid up and free herself. She felt around her once more. Her hand encountered a belt, or a strap~her handbag! She couldn't believe it! She knew she hadn't had an opportunity to grab it; they must have thrown it in with her!

Fumbling for her iPhone, she pulled it out, elated! They had left her phone? She suddenly thought it must be a trick! Either that, or, she was dealing with dummies! She hoped it was the latter.

The cell indicated that there was still service, but the phones she called were turned off. No one had any idea she wasn't in her room. She sent a text to David's phone; he would see it whenever he turned his phone on. It read, "THE BLUE CAR!"

Using the light from her phone, she gazed around her small area. Old stained-up carpet and the tool box. She pulled out a roll of electrical tape and used it to tape a tissue over a nasty gash on her hand. She couldn't be sure if she had wounded one of her assailants with the double-edge, or just herself.

"Way to go, Mallory," she mumbled.

Using the tape, she wrapped one edge of the weapon. She found a phillips screwdriver and a book of matches. Pulling her jacket lining loose, she secreted the matchbook in the lining of her sleeve; then, she clutched the screwdriver desperately, ready to swing it upwards into the eye of one of her assailants, should she get a chance.

The ride smoothed out; they were back on pavement. The car stopped. Then she knew her kidnappers were pumping gas. Her watch indicated that she had only been riding about forty-five minutes. She thought it strange that her abductors hadn't filled up before grabbing her. She tried to listen and peer out through the broken taillight. Her tormentors were arguing; she couldn't understand the language. She crouched, tense, but the trunk lid didn't open. Then two car door slams, and they were moving again.

The ride was smoother now, with steady thumps like concrete sections, then gravel and dust. Finally after another forty minutes, the car stopped, the engine turned off, car doors opened. Begging for courage, Mallie waited. She could hear conversation, low voices. Finally, she heard the trunk lid release.

Feigning unconsciousness, she waited. One of them poked at her, but she didn't move. Finally, one of them bent forward to lift her from the space. Although the rural night was dark, she lunged upward with the screwdriver, missing his eye, but making a painful gouge at the outside corner of it. He swore, then grabbed her, dragging her roughly from the car toward a wall-encircled abode. He had switched to speaking in accented English, threatening viciously, his grip a vise as he dragged her into the enclosure.

She fought back, in spite of the threats. Finally, yanked through the strangely-constructed house, she was pushed roughly through a sliding glass door onto a small, cluttered patio. The door slid shut behind her, and her keepers dropped an aluminum ball bat noisily into the metal track to lock her out. Sagging, ragged, traverse-rod curtains drew shut, and she was alone.

Gasping in a ragged breath, she surveyed her surroundings. A high wall completely enclosed her small space: there was no gate. The wall blocked the wind a little bit, but the night was cold. She shivered, biting her lip, determined not to cry any more.

She heard two car doors slam again, then the engine turned over, and the car barreled away. Numbly she wondered who had left and who was guarding her. She sank down into the corner most protected from the chill. She was afraid to think about what they wanted her for. She was sure they wanted money: she just didn't know if anyone would pay them any, or if they would release her unharmed, even at that.

She could hear a murmur of voices, then the curtain rod scraped, and she knew someone was coming out. She jumped to her feet as the bat jangled. The door slid open, and a woman, covered from head to foot in black, stared at her. Slamming down a five-gallon plastic bucket, she announced, "Twalot"! Then the door slid shut, the bat dropped in, the drapes closed.

Mallie slid back down into her corner, more shaken than ever! The sinister black covering! She couldn't be in Iran, could she? She was pretty sure they hadn't crossed any border crossings. She would have pounded like everything to get attention from the soldiers. She must still be in Turkey, and Colonel Ahmir and Erik Bransom would find her! And David! Then, she gazed morosely at the bucket. Did the woman mean that was her toilet? Tears slid down her cheeks, in spite of her resolve.

The charter company called Daniel Faulkner early. The room was still black. Sleepily, he fumbled for the phone. The company rep stated that she had tried Mallory first, but had gotten no answer. Heavy weather was forecast for the Van airport; she was calling to see if it were possible for them to make their departure earlier. Otherwise, it might be as much as a twenty-four hour delay.

Daniel didn't like the sound of it. He was past ready to start home. A twenty-four hour hold-up sounded abysmal. He informed her he would do his best to get everyone rounded up and transported for departure from Van by nine-thirty. She thought that should be well ahead of the fog and heavy rain.

Diana mumbled sleepily, asking what was going on. When he told her Mallory hadn't answered her phone, she sat upright in bed, a sense of foreboding sweeping through her, causing her to shudder involuntarily! Mallory would answer! Unless~

"Calm down, Honey," he began. Then paused, meeting her gaze. He didn't even want to consider the possibility. He switched on his cell. A "missed call" from Mallory~at one A.M.

"She tried to call a little after one," he whispered. "I have to go get Erik!" He was pulling his clothes and shoes on.

"Well, don't scare him and Suzanne for nothing! Call her first."

He tried! Her room! Her cell! Her room, again! No answer!

Tears ran down Diana's cheeks as she pulled on her clothes from the previous evening. "Oh, Lord, help us! Oh, Lord, help Mallory. Please help us find her!"

Daniel was out the door, then tapping softly at the door of Eric and Suzanne's room.

The agent was up, wearing jeans and a t-shirt, starting to read his Bible.

"What's up?" He was surprised by the early morning visit.

"You guys haven't heard anything from Mallory, have you?" Daniel tried to make his voice sound casual.

Erik pushed him back out of the room, pulling the door closed behind them. Suzanne was sleeping. If something were going on about Mallory, he hoped she wouldn't find out until after the fact.

"Seen Mallie?" he asked. "Not since we all split up last night. Is she not in her room?"

Daniel explained what he knew, and Bransom checked his cell. He couldn't believe it. Mallory had tried to call him, and his phone was off, too. They both moved to her door, and Erik tapped softly.

"Mallory! Mallory! You in there?"

Diana joined them, already having gone to reception to request an extra key.

Praying fervently to find her just sound asleep, Erik unlocked the door and pushed it open, the Faulkners right at his heels.

He stepped backwards, nearly bowling them over, and closed the door.

His face was ashen! "Crime scene! I'm calling Col. Ahmir!"

Chapter 34

TREETOPS

WHEN MALLORY THOUGHT she couldn't feel any more desolate; large, cold raindrops began splatting down sadistically. Cold and wet, she huddled miserably. The sun didn't really seem to come up, but the dreary sky finally lightened enough for Mallory to look around her prison. The walls seemed to be some plaster-like material, rising straight up; no way to climb out. A tree branch stretched over the wall. She wished the tree were on the inside. Tree-climbing was her specialty! Well, it used to be! She hadn't tried it in a year or two.

She gazed at the bucket in disgust. She was nearly that desperate! Then, she heard movement inside the house, and the drapes parted slightly. A heavier woman than the one she had seen previously, pushed the door open enough to squeeze through, presenting Mallie with rice and tea, and one of the black things of her own. Her smile revealed that dental hygiene must not really be her thing. Her English was very poor, but she was trying to tell Mallory that when the men returned, she would have to cover herself up. Then, evidently feeling sympathetic toward the shivering girl, she chunked some broken pieces of brick, and sticks of firewood into the enclosure, before sealing her off, once more.

The men were gone?

Begging the Lord to help her, she sprang into action. Taking the longest, sturdiest log, she fit it into the outside track of the sliding door. She couldn't get in: they couldn't get out!

Using her arrowhead, she slashed the black thing, ripping strips off, knotting the ends together. It seemed pretty strong. It needed to support her weight so she could pull herself up the wall. Racing against time, and whenever the men would return for her, she continued to work on her makeshift rope. Finally ready, she tied a chunk of brick into one end and sent it sailing toward the overhanging branch. It hit, and caught on the rough bark! She tugged frantically. It needed to sail clear over, and come back down, so she could be supported by a double thickness. This would only tear loose once she put her weight on it. She put her weight on it, and it tore loose. The curtain hadn't moved! Evidently, they weren't paying much attention to her, figuring she couldn't escape. Another prayer and another throw! She could almost reach the other end, but it dangled enticingly just beyond her grasp!

Then, she heard a car approaching! The car with the trailer hitch! Making one more desperate leap, she caught onto both strips. Muscles straining, she hitched her way up the wall. Her hands stinging, her nose running from the cold, she finally grasped the top of the wall and pulled herself free from her prison. She pulled her fabric up and climbed higher into the tree.

From her perch, she viewed nice, mature trees like the one she was in, lining both sides, the entire length of the drive. Beyond that, the countryside seemed devoid of much growth, aside from the sparse ground cover. She could make out enough dull light to determine which direction was east. She hesitated in indecision. Lots of open ground and no cover! No other houses or buildings as far as she could see!

The car stopped in the pitiful yard. Only the driver, no passengers. Mallie watched. The guy was talking on his cell, waving his other hand with a cigarette, impatiently. Finally, he yelled, "Nah, nah, nah!" and broke the connection. The house was quiet. If the women had noticed she was gone, they weren't running out to notify him. He got out, banging the car door, and strode angrily into the house.

Indecision gone, Malllory descended the tree with a speed that would have made monkeys jealous. She was pretty certain the keys were still in the ignition, and she thanked the Lord they were! Then, to her total amazement, her handbag rested in the passenger seat; a passenger seat that looked kind of blood-soaked.

She jammed in the cigarette lighter, turned on the ignition, and spurted gravel and dirt. One swing through the desolate-looking back yard sent a few chickens clucking and flapping . Pulling the red-hot lighter from its socket, she flung it into some dry leaves which had blown against some kind of propane-looking tank. Then, she was barreling down the drive, circling back, still off-road, toward the west, the trailer hitch scraping at each low spot! No one in the rear-view mirror. Then the tank exploded! She kept going!

Colonel Ahmir had colleagues on the crime scene which had been Mallory's suite, within minutes. When he finished his calls, he hurried quickly to his car, continuing calls and giving orders as he sped toward a waiting jet. His mind was whirling! First the small boy injured, now the beautiful corporate CEO kidnapped. How did that happen? They were surrounded with private security, and Agent Bransom, and Ahmir's extra Turkish guard.

Once settled into the jet and airborne, he phoned Bransom back.

A gruff, "Bransom!" responded.

"Has anyone from your group received any communication from the kidnappers demanding ransom or any other terms?" he wanted to know.

Bransom sent Faulkner to notify their entire group of Mallory's disappearance, requesting everyone to assemble in the lobby with their phones and electronics asap. He responded to the Turkish colonel that he wasn't aware of any comms, but Ahmir's techs could look through all their devices to be sure.

David was the first to hit the lobby in response to Daniel's request. His hands shook, and he fought to keep from crying as he showed Bransom and the local counterpart Mallie's text.

David could barely get out his explanation and apology about noticing the car the previous day, then forgetting to confide his concerns to Bransom.The Turkish investigator took over, firing questions. He was relieved to have any lead to follow. Of course, Bransom and the locals were assuming the mystery certainly involved the Malovich twins. The two criminals wanted Mallory dead! That was why there had been no demand for ransom!

David explained about one of the men's coming into this hotel, engaging in conversation with one of the desk agents. After leaving his phone containing the text and the pictures of the car in question, with the policeman, he spoke with his dad a moment: of course, John couldn't believe any of it was happening. As the group in the lobby grew, and the confused chatter escalated, David crept away, and made it to the stairwell without his departure being noticed.

Upstairs, he stood at the threshold of Mallory's room, gazing into the crime scene anxiously. There wasn't any yellow tape, but Turkish investigators were photographing everything, bagging, and tagging. Diana, with her shoes covered to prevent evidence transfer, seemed to have joined herself to the investigation. There was quite a bit of blood spatter.

The room was neat, Mallory's bag was closed, but not latched. Her toiletry articles were arranged neatly in the bathroom, and the bed was made.

Diana thought the blood spatter wasn't Mallory's blood. She asked for a microscope, in order to be certain, but she thought the blood looked diseased, revealing the orange-y color of severe anemia. No way Mallory's blood could have degenerated to this state in the month since her hospitalization in Hope.

No sign of a break-in! The investigator assumed she knew her attacker and opened the sliding glass door. He looked pointedly at David as he said so.

David shrugged, annoyed. It confirmed to him that one of the hotel employees had been involved; had entered the room while Mallory was out for dinner and unlocked the balcony door.

What struggle there was, appeared to have occurred by the sofa. That was where the spatter seemed to have originated, and there was other blood forming a different pattern. Diana suddenly laughed.

"She still had that big arrowhead! Shay was so mad at her for leaving it on, when she knew it was ruining the sweaters he gave her!"

She pulled a leather strip from between the cushions with a latex-gloved hand, and gave it to one of the agents. It had been part of the cute necklace.

"She was sitting here, and she saw her assailants coming. When they grabbed for her, she must have slashed one of their wrists! Of course, in doing so, in the panic, and with all her force, she really cut herself too! Not an artery, but she was bleeding."

The guy in charge had come upstairs, and had heard Diana's reconstruction. Looking around, he nodded agreement. But where had they taken her?

Colonel Ahmir arrived by chopper from Van, surveyed everything pertaining to the case, and was conducting interviews in the hotel lobby, when Daniel Faulkner's phone rang in the stack that had been surrendered in the investigation.

The Colonel grabbed it, studying the screen. A long number from an unknown caller. He recognized the country code! Their hostile neighbor to the east. Grabbing Lana's video camera, he started one of his agents filming and recording the call. He motioned to Faulkner to answer.

"Daniel Faulkner!" Daniel answered, trying to steady his nervous voice.

"Oh, hello, Mr. Faulkner. Have you noticed that a member of your party is missing?"

The taunting voice made his stomach squeeze. Ahmir nodded for him to answer affirmatively.

"Oh, yeah, Mallory O'Shaughnessy. Who are you? How do you know? Where is she?"

"Be silent! I will speak: you listen! Why have you not followed the instructions in the letter? I am not so melodramatic to say, 'I will kill her if you do not comply', because I will not. Why would I kill someone so beautiful and valuable? I know people who will pay lots of money for such nice American wife! Send the money where I said, Mr. Faulkner." The caller swore and disconnected.

Ahmir was furious! "What letter? If you do not tell me everything that is going on, I can not help find the girl."

"We don't know anything about a letter," Bransom stated, perplexed. "We opened the door, I saw the blood, sealed the scene until the authorities arrived. We haven't seen a letter."

Daniel pressed the button on the phone to recall the number, and the same voice answered, "Yes, Agha Faulkner! You wish to say something to me?"

"Yeah, fella. None of us have seen any letter. Who's supposed to get it, and how?"

"It was left when the girl was removed from her room! Follow those instructions! You have already wasted much of your time. Mallory can have a nice husband by twenty-four hours."

"Well, look," Daniel broke in quickly. "Trust me, we don't have your letter. Your clowns that grabbed Mallory must have messed up about leaving any mail for us. What exactly are you wanting?"

Swearing! The connection broke! No answer to their frantic attempts to recontact the caller!

Mallory drove across empty landscape, trying to head west. After an hour of driving, she had been unable to locate the sectioned road she remembered. Hungry and thirsty, with a vicious headache, and her entire body bruised from the bouncing, she fought tears, finally slowing speed, trying to stay calm. But then, when she inadvertently ended up where she had started, the tears broke free. She hadn't meant for the house to blow up: she realized no one had time to get out. She tried not to feel sorry: she hadn't asked to be brought here!

With the sun now high overhead, it was harder for her to discern directions. The car was below half a tank. In her driving, she had spotted one very small village, but had given it wide berth. Now she decided maybe it would be best to head into the mountains. Maybe she could find cover and water before dark. She gazed at her phone forlornly; no service. She switched it off to save the battery.

The mountains, so evident on the horizon, weren't that easy to get to. She had been "off-road", but the ground had been relatively smooth and level. Now, she began to approach gullies and harsher terrain, and she bumped and banged endlessly, trying to circle around. The area was desert; no water at all. Finally, with the car out of gas, she left it behind, making her way along a faint trail leading into foothills.

By now, she figured she was going to die. Snakes had been a fear when she first pulled herself up into the tree. She couldn't remember what species of snakes and wild animals were indigenous, but she was suddenly expecting to run into all of them. She remembered her captor's vicious threat to sell her to be someone's wife. She would rather die, she had decided. She couldn't keep her thoughts off of David. He was the only person she could imagine being married to.

She had on really cute shoes, soft, sage-green, wedge-heeled pumps. Not totally ridiculous, but tennis shoes or hiking boots would be better. She had been on foot for an hour, and she finally sank down to rest in the shade of a ridge. The rock layers were pretty, capturing her attention. She traced the edge of a dyke and a fold in the strata, wishing she were already a Geologist. Rummaging through her bag, she dug out her keys and began scraping into the soft material above the broad streak of brilliant blue. She was pretty sure she had discovered a vein of Lapis Lazuli.

Way out here, away from civilization, God had tucked something beautiful. She thought about Job 28. With her interest in diamonds and gems, the passage was particularly significant for her. She only had her New Testament with her, but she pulled it out! No physical water here, but she could read about the Water of Life. She opened to the Gospel of John, and read a chapter, then bowed her head to pray.

What a prayer. She asked for her guardian angel to protect her and for her somehow to get back home. With the desolation surrounding her, it was a real prayer of faith!

She rose stiffly, continuing through the hostile region. She tried to sing a victory song, but her throat was too dry. Forging ahead on determination alone, she finally topped a ridge to discover greenery. Not much; but compared to the environment she had been in, it appeared to be an oasis.

A rabbit startled her, and she pelted a rock into its path. To her amazement, she hit it!. She had tried to work at target practice in the past month, but everything had been pretty hectic. Lifting the limp carcass, she surveyed it woefully. She considered the possibility of trying to skin and dress it with the arrowhead. She was pretty sure she couldn't do it. She really needed water anyway.

Dropping it, she turned to resume her course! And a huge man blocked the path!

Chapter 35

TRIBULATION

AHMIR'S INVESTIGATORS SPREAD out from the town center of Dogubeyazit. To David's chagrin, the desk clerk that he thought was involved was nowhere to be seen. The hotel manager insisted that neither he, nor anyone on his staff, had anything to do with unlocking a door, or in any way, helping with the abduction.

They had found the rag with Mallie's saliva and traces of chloroform, stashed in a trash receptacle beside the elevator on her floor. Bransom was pretty sure she had been removed in a laundry cart or laundry bag through the back service entrance. Aside from the blood in the room; there was no trail. A hand towel was missing! It must have been used to wrap and apply pressure to the spurting wound. That guy surely had needed medical attention immediately. From the blood's appearance, Diana thought his days were numbered, anyway. Ahmir's staff hadn't found any evidence that anyone with such a wound had received treatment in the area.

A call came from an attendant at a small gas station, that he had found an envelope in the trash that seemed odd. Following the lead without much real hope, they were amazed to discover that it really did seem to be the letter that was to have been left in Mallory's room. Smudged with grease and dirt, the envelope had a single word, cut from newsprint: "AMERICANS".

The letter, composed of newsprint, instructed them to remove the diamonds from the safety deposit box in the New York City bank. When they had done this and brought them into eastern Turkey, they would receive further instructions. There was a narrow window of time to accomplish this, or Mallory would become someone's wife.

Bransom couldn't figure out how any Iranians could be aware of the stash. But thinking back, he was sure their group hadn't been very discreet. They were all excited about them, probably they had all buzzed about it plenty in the NYC airport while Daniel and Kerry were gone on the errand to deposit the stones. He had been involved with Shannon. Maybe this still had something to do with Oscar and Otto. They probably had eyes and ears on the diamond operation. They might have already cleared out the remaining stones from the little unsecured house at the camp property in Arkansas.

He sighed. Why on earth was he worrying about diamonds when Mallory was at stake?

Meanwhile, the questions Ahmir's guys were asking at the border were revealing a problem that Ahmir had suspected for quite some time, but had been unable to prove. The blue car, described by the American boy, and caught on camera, was one that everyone in the province seemed familiar with. He shook his head in wonder. If you are up to no good, why do something stupid to stand out? Thankfully, people did stupid things, or his job would be even harder. The mystery of the big, blue, American-made car was that the Turkish border cameras captured it entering Turkey from Iran every ten to fourteen days! The eastbound, departing border had no records that the same car ever returned to Iran.

"Is this not strange, Agent Bransom?" he questioned smilingly. "This car can reenter Turkey again and again, without ever leaving?"

A grin spread across Bransom's face, then disappeared quickly. "Looks like you got yourself a smuggling route, Colonel. You have ground penetrating radar to help locate it, or you need us to bring some in?"

"You are thinking a tunnel?"

"Yeah, otherwise satellite would pick it up. But I'm not talking about a little tunnel under a wall. I'm thinking it begins quite a way back from the border and runs for quite a distance. He gave an example of a tunnel into the U.S. for illegal smuggling of Mexican people, among other things.

Col. Ahmir sat thinking, regarding his American counterpart thoughtfully. It would explain any number of things that had troubled him. If they could discover and shut down a major smuggling pipeline! It would make his job easier! It wouldn't hurt his career any, either!

Mallory was shocked to see the figure standing on the trail in front of her. He was tall, dressed in black, similar to the garb favored by Iranian men, except that the sleeves were ripped away, revealing powerful arms. He was clean-shaven and neat. Neither fair-skinned nor swarthy, his dark hair curled thickly onto his forehead and around his ears. Expensive-looking sunglasses prevented her from meeting his gaze. She figured she looked like a train wreck. He startled her, but curiously, she felt unafraid.

"Hello, do you speak English?" she asked.

"Yes, a little," came the response. "You are Mallory? Thank you for killing our dinner for us. Nice aim."

As he was speaking, three other men had joined them.

Mallory wasn't surprised they knew her name. She figured the story of her disappearance was all over the place.

Actually, it wasn't. Neither the Turkish nor the Iranian governments wanted the word out. Without such freedom of the press, the government could squelch whatever stories they chose.

One of the others had retrieved the rabbit and begun prepping it. Mallory watched, guessing it wouldn't be too much worse than watching her dad clean fish.

"Come!" It was a command.

She followed a short distance, unresisting! They led the way to a water source, from which she gulped gratefully. The rabbit was being salted and stretched between stakes; no cooking fire and its telltale smoke. They provided her with bread and fruit, and she ate while the men conversed several yards away. Tired and achy, she suddenly just longed for sleep. The leader rejoined her.

"Do you know where you are?" he questioned.

"Not for sure," she confessed. "I got kidnapped from a hotel room near Mt. Ararat. I thought I could find my way back, but I've just been totally lost. You don't really want to help me, do you?"

From behind the mirrored lenses, "If you find yourself back with your friends in Turkey, you must tell nothing."

"Yes, Sir," she responded.

She couldn't understand why she trusted him; maybe because she was short on any other options. Evidently, he decided to trust her, too; and her ability to keep a confidence!

"You must go to sleep!" Even as he spoke, one of the others had pushed her jacket sleeve up to drench her forearm in alcohol. A needle slid in, and sleep overtook her.

Col. Ahmir had been in touch with the U.S. Ambassador and the commander of the U.S. Air Force Base at Incerlick near Adana, Turkey. The eastern provinces were the most lawless area of the country, and Ahmir was eager to be rid of responsibility for the beautiful and wealthy Americans. Local men always tried to hit on American girls and women if they got a chance. If they could persuade the women to marry them, they could get to America and get citizenship. It was a constant scam.

Only after his impassioned plea to Daniel Faulkner had he coaxed them to agree to relocate. Bransom would remain, and Dawson, Bransom's superior who had flown in. Ahmir finally managed to get everyone and their luggage onto a jet at Van, cleared to land at the U.S. air base. He breathed a sigh of relief.

Dawson had flown in with satellite photography, as well as the ground-penetrating radar equipment. The men settled in to study the terrain in question. Then Bransom remembered how much the geological maps had helped find the DiaMo Corp. workers who were hidden underground. He suggested Ahmir request similar information. The maps might show where a tunnel was located, or at least a logical area for the massive excavation they were talking about. Bransom wondered if even organized smugglers could accomplish such a feat; or if the Iranian regime might be a party to it.

Once on the air base, the civilians felt pretty much like intruders. An officer had greeted them, suggesting they return home to the U.S. since there really wasn't much they could accomplish by remaining in Turkey.

David's heart felt like lead, even before that. Ahmir and Bransom, neither one, had thought they could gain Mallory in return for the diamonds. The border guards affirmed the blue car was Iranian. Somehow, Mallory's abductors had smuggled her out of Turkey. She was in danger, even now, of being married off to some rich old geezer that already had a bunch of wives. David had been forcing himself not to think about that. It made him sick to his stomach. He kept trying to pray, but he didn't feel like he had much faith. He numbly followed his group around the base. Ordinarily, he would have thought the fighter jets tearing off, then returning to base, thrilling. They ate with some officers, then Sanders had heard about a Bible Study and prayer group that was meeting, so they found that, and, with heavy hearts, joined in. The various military personnel in the meeting promised to continue to pray for Mallory, but they seemed pessimistic.

After several hours of poring over information, Ahmir, Dawson, and Bransom decided to break for dinner. The colonel and Dawson seemed to hit it off well; Bransom was preoccupied. He called Faulkner to tell him they didn't have too much new info. He agreed with them not to let anyone rush them back to the states.

The three investigators returned to the hotel. Since a different employee was manning the front desk, Bransom photographed him surreptitiously, and forwarded the picture to David. When David confirmed that he was the one, one of Ahmir's officers arrested him. Evidently Turkey didn't require much "probable cause", and soon, Ahmir announced to them that the youth had confessed to everything. Dawson's gaze met Bransom's. Sometimes, they resented some of the legal stuff that hampered their investigations. Now, they were grateful for all of it.

Bransom returned to his room late. Exhausted, he didn't even switch on the light. He didn't figure he'd sleep much, not knowing about Mallory; but it would feel good to stretch out his tired bones. Kicking off his shoes, he sank down on the edge of the bed! Then shot up in panic and confusion. There was a body!

It seemed like he fumbled forever for the light switch! Finally, he flipped the switch, and the darkness fled. There lay Mallory! Coated with dirt and grime, she was sound asleep.

Dazed, he called Ahmir back; he couldn't have gotten far. And Dawson, who was a couple of doors down the hall. At first, they could hardly grasp what Bransom was saying. But when Ahmir vaulted up the stairs and met Dawson at Branom's door, they both burst in to stare in amazement at the sleeping girl.

Once they confirmed that she was really there (Bransom thought he was really losing it there for a couple of minutes) he called David.

"Good news for ya, there, Cowboy!" his rough voice barely comprehendible through the emotion. "Mallory's back. If Shay could see this sweater set now, he'd really be upset. Ahmir is getting us to Van asap, and we'll meet everyone in Izmir. He's arranging for all of you to get there in time to meet us."

"Can I talk to her?" David asked desperately.

"Well, you could, but she's pretty heavily drugged," Bransom responded. "Let me talk to Suzanne, will ya?"

"Erik has Mallory!" he announced dazedly to Suzanne and the group, as he handed over his phone. Everyone would have cheered! Except they hardly believed him!

Suzanne was crying too hard to talk, so Bransom just told her what he needed her to do.

"Love ya, Baby, see ya soon." He broke the connection and dashed to the elevator to keep up with Ahmir and Mallory's gurney.

Mallory was rousing slightly by the time the jet was taxiing for take off. The Turkish Lieutenant and a couple of other ladies had orders to help her get cleaned up.

Limp from exhaustion and the powerful drugs, she submitted helplessly to their scrubbing and massaging. They were going easy on her because of the bruises. It was a good thing. She was too groggy to notice that her ruined outfit had disappeared into evidence bags, that combings from her hair would render pollen, tree-sap, and plenty of other biologicals to trace her episode. They finished by wrapping her in a thick, white, Turkish bathrobe, and twisting her freshly shampooed hair up into a Turkish towel turban. A cabin waiter entered with a tray holding an attractively prepared meal. Mallory drained a small container of water, and it was replaced. Still thirsty, she drank another before falling back asleep.

In Izmir, Suzanne and Diana hurried onto the plane carrying Mallory's change of clothes. She managed to push them out so she could dress herself. Then they walked her zombie-like onto the charter jet that was ready to depart for Istanbul, New York, and Dallas.

Bransom started to shake Ahmir's hand in farewell, but to his chagrin, the man grabbed him, kissing him next to each ear. Red-faced, the agent jogged up the steps, boarding as the engines revved up.

Chapter 36

TREASURE

Proverbs 21:20There is treasure to be desired and oil in the dwelling of the wise; but a foolish man spendeth it up.

ONCE THE CAPTAIN of the charter jet turned off the seatbelt sign, most of the travelers erupted from their seats. Reserve gone, they all jostled for position for manicure services, shaves, shoeshines, the business center.

Roger was trying to show off the latest picture of little Tony, whose wall-eyed lack of focus on the camera, had him and Beth both convinced that the first grandchild was an amazing genius.

"Yeah, yeah, out of the way, Sanders," Daniel was muscling in. "Some of us actually have work to get done!" He had requested copies of some of the contracts they were forging with new Turkish counterparts, be faxed by his personal secretary. Once they arrived, he could get Kerry looking at them. He received a couple of e-mails from his dad about new contracts the senior partner had landed for GeoHy! Really good contracts! That was great, in itself. But the fact that his dad was praising the Lord about the deals~ he pressed the print command, and tears were stinging his eyes as he showed Diana.

All the kids were playing games and watching a video, with Carmine in the middle of them, laughing and cutting up. Then she took Callie on in a game of chess.

Mallory slept on.

Daniel drew Erik aside to ask him if Mallory had said anything to him about her ordeal.

Bransom shook his head slowly. "Nah, she's been knocked out-cold. If she wakes up a little she sings about 'God sending angels to watch over her'. Pretty song. Ahmir was glad we got her back okay. He didn't think the odds were good, at all, of course." His voice had grown emotional. "Of course, he was right about that. He was mad about someone's being able to slip her right back into our midst without any of us seeing or hearing anything. It makes him think there are 'foreign operatives', both in Turkey, and Iran. Course, that's illegal, so he wants a statement from Mallory"

"You tell him he's not getting one?" Daniel demanded.

Bransom frowned. "Told him I'd let him know what I could find out. He's a good guy."

"Yeah," Faulkner acknowledged. "What do you mean by 'foreign operatives'? Who do you think rescued her?"

Bransom's machine-gun laugh echoed through the cabin. "Let's just say I haven't been saved long enough to believe angels flew her into my hotel room! 'Foreign Operatives' are undercover agents. Do you not even watch movies?"

"Oh, you mean like spies?" Fulkner's voice was incredulous. It was hard for him to grasp the 'cloak and dagger' stuff.

Bransom snorted. "Yeah, Faulkner, something like that."

They landed in Istanbul; and not surprisingly, many of them dashed into the terminal for some last-minute shopping. When everyone boarded and the engines whined, they broke into applause! Next stop: USA!

Kerry, with a full glass of iced tea, and a full carafe next to him, settled in to peruse the documents Daniel had handed him. He was amazed! As lavish and extravagant as Mallory had made the trip, it was still more than paying for itself. He closed his eyes, thinking! That was just speaking monetarily. Besides that, they were all enriched by the significance of the Biblical sites, and their times of fellowshipping together. The opportunity afforded to them because of the broken meeting-room door was priceless! Meeting the Iranian family who were all Christians, and being aware of their lack of freedom to worship the Lord openly, was sobering.

He sipped his tea, glancing around for Tammi. She was getting her nails done, so he immersed himself into the legal-speak before him. He wanted to ask Pastor Anderson for permission to speak to Tammi alone for a few minutes before they all parted. Then, he noticed Lana had risen to check on the kids and the chess game. He hadn't really ever talked to her much; she hadn't liked him when she thought he might like Mallory. He was pretty sure he hadn't risen in her ratings by liking Tammi. Rising cautiously so as not to spill tea all over, he moved aft, talking to Jeremiah, then checking on the progress of the chess match. He was able to be in a position to assist Lana in reaching a bag in the overhead bin.

She smiled and thanked him, so he mumbled something inane that he liked her outfit. He would have stumbled back to his seat, totally humiliated, but she was actually blocking the aisle.

"Thanks for having David over that weekend; he really enjoyed everything. Tell your folks thanks for all the apple stuff, too." She was embarrassed, too: he was blocking her getting back into her seat.

By NYC, everyone was pretty fizzled out. Shay and Delia bid everyone a teary good-bye; this was where they connected for Boston. Mallory deplaned, escorted by Bransom, to find a latte and tell Delia and Shay, "Goodbye." Bransom was fairly certain the Malovich men were still in Eastern Europe, but he warned Shay to keep his eyes open.

Back aboard the plane, Mallory was finally waking up, now that everyone else was asleep.

Once again at altitude, Kerry rose resolutely. Best chance! Anderson couldn't throw him out without losing pressure in the cabin. He hesitated, next to Anderson's seats, trying to figure out if the ogre was asleep.

"Hey, Kerry, have a seat," Anderson moved a stack of books and scrunched his long legs over. "Something on your mind?"

"Yes, Sir." Kerry had rehearsed what he wanted to say, wanting to persuade this man as much as he had ever hoped to persuade any judges and juries. In a way, this man was a judge and a jury. "May I talk to Tammi?"

The pastor raised an eyebrow, "About?" He had figured this would come someday! He still wasn't ready. Funny how stuff was tougher to deal with in reality than it was to preach about.

"I want to tell her I love her and ask her to wait for me."

Anderson was silent! Kerry guessed that was better than yelling and waking the whole crowd. He waited.

"You know, Patrick O'Shaughnessy was my best friend, except for the Lord and Lana. We didn't hang out, but he loved me and my family and the ministry. I miss him, and it speaks to me that he trusted you. You seem like a good guy; if you weren't so much older and farther along in life than Tammi~ You're the one who'll be waiting. You can talk to her when we land, while everyone gets loaded up! In the light where I can see you; you can tell her you like her."

The latte, gone, Mallory fixed her make-up and pulled her hair up into a cute pony tail. Then moved aft to find a snack. Returning to her seat with a package of chocolate donuts, she motioned to Daniel to begin distributing a final round of gifts. She was relieved that everyone had allowed her to sleep, and even now were giving her space. She knew they all must wonder what all had happened to her. Remembering her promise for silence in return for freedom, she was trying to decide how much she would be able to relate.

The gifts were beautiful. Each lady was presented with a diamond brooch. Available in either yellow or white gold, they were exquisite open hearts, large and heavy enough to make a statement on jacket lapels. Each had a hidden bail, so they could also be worn as pendants, on up to a five millimeter Omega necklace. The men received heavy-weight ID bracelets in the precious metal, and they looked nice with or without engraving. Herb had promised to do the engraving for anyone who wanted it. Then, there were more gifts for the children. Sammie seemed to be rebounding from his injury, and Mallory had given him an extra hug.

At some point in time, they had finally caught up to the sun in their westward journey. Then they passed it, and it was early evening when they landed in Dallas.

Watching the tractor with the luggage cars racing toward them to unload the cargo bay, Bransom suddenly wondered if Mallory might still be in trouble. She wasn't. The director of airport operations and the owner of the charter company both grabbed at them as they entered the terminal, but it was for the sake of offering profuse apologies for the incident.

With less free press in Turkey, the story of Mallory's abduction had never made it stateside. The story of the bus explosion had made the headlines, but then, it had been played down.

When Mallory asked her aunt Linda when her connecting flight was scheduled to depart, her aunt laughed. "I'm not going back."

Kerry and Tammi had their talk. She looked beautiful, dressed in a soft red, the color of Larson apples.

"Your dad said I could talk to you a minute and tell you how much I like you, but I don't have enough words, or enough time for that. I'm glad God protected you from Adams, and that you didn't get kidnapped. David told me a bunch of guys really tried to move in on y'all. I want you to wait for me, as long as it takes. I have to talk to Mallory; she's my main client. Don't get mad at her and try to stir David up, okay? I can't call you; don't call me. Just know, you are the most beautiful woman I've ever seen, Tammi Anderson. I have to go; see you at the next board meeting."

He threw his suitcases into the Porsche, and she watched until he turned out of sight.

"That looked interesting," Mallory was at her elbow.

"When's the next board meeting?" Tammi was dazed.

Mallory laughed, "When I know, you'll know. The Faulkners, and your family, my mom and Erik, and Herb and Aunt Linda are all going for steaks. Then everyone's spending the night at my house and going home in the morning."

When David heard the plan, he tried to weasel out. He wasn't sure he could handle seeing Mallory in her palatial surroundings. It was intimidating. He wondered if she would ever need him for anything. Besides, he had important business to take care of.

"Yeah, like going to that house all by yourself to collect a fortune in diamonds?" Bransom could be like a mind-reader, but he was right.

No one thought that was a good idea, but David was right! That was certainly a priority.

Over steaks, Mallie continued to avoid questions about her kidnapping, instead talking about the fun and high points of the trip. When the meal was finished, Herb talked to Linda for a few minutes. He needed to get back and see what had happened to his shop during his absence, but he asked Linda's permission to call her.

Mallie's staff was ready for the influx of guests, and she was unbelievably happy to be home. Dinky seemed happy to see her, and she had missed him. Someone unpacked her luggage, and the empty suitcases disappeared. Kind of nice being spoiled. She had no idea when there would be a Red Sox game, or how they had been doing since her departure from Izmir. Lots to catch up on, besides just that.

She yawned, not sure if she was suffering from jet lag, or if some of the powerful drugs were still in her system. Daniel, David, Pastor, and Erik were all playing pool, so Mallory and Tammi slipped out for a swim. It wasn't long before Lana, Linda, and Suzanne joined them. Diana was watching her comedy trio trying to play tennis. The Texas twilight descended silently, warm and fragrant.

Finally, Mallory rose from the deck chair. "Y'all make yourselves at home; if you don't mind, I'm going to bed."

She stepped into the library to find something to read to put her to sleep. To her amazement, many of her purchases had beat her home. There were quite a few boxes and crates awaiting her, which she was too tired to deal with now! Smiling, she was thinking it would be like Christmas tomorrow. She had selected quite a few keepsakes for herself, but she and Callie had also been noticing some of the pieces Carmine had liked. With no shopping money, she had set each thing back down, refusing to allow Callie or Mallory to buy anything for her. Now, they had some surprises for her. Having a better idea than finding a book, she slipped into her suite. Floss, brush, cleanse! Then she was propped up against monogrammed linen throw pillows, scrolling through her camera images! Friends, relatives, hands full of diamonds, the Bosporus trip, Turkish people listening to a gospel concert, Troy, Pergamus, Ephesus, Pamukkale, Mt Ararat!

Her gaze returned once more to the picture of her daddy on the bedside table, the framed letter he had written to her. She scratched Dinky affectionately on the head, and he whimpered softly in response.

She started to say her prayers, enumerating to the Lord the things she was thankful for, the treasure He had filled her life with. She was asleep before she got far.

To continue following Mallory's adventures, watch for WEALTH!